THE REPRIEVE

by Jean-Paul Sartre

TRANSLATED FROM THE FRENCH BY

ERIC SUTTON

VINTAGE BOOKS

A Division of Random House, New York

VINTAGE BOOKS EDITION, January 1973
Copyright 1947 by Eric Sutton
All rights reserved under International and Pan-American
Copyright Conventions. Published in the United States by
Random House, Inc., New York. Originally published by
Alfred A. Knopf in 1947. Originally published in France
as *Les Chemins de La Liberté II: Le Sursis*. Copyright
by Librairie Gallimard 1945.

Library of Congress Cataloging in Publication Data
Sartre, Jean Paul, 1905–
The reprieve.

Translation of Le sursis.
I. Title.
[PZ3.S2494Re8] [PQ2637.A82]   843′.9′14   72–4475
ISBN 0–394–71839–9

Manufactured in the United States of America

THE REPRIEVE

LES CHEMINS DE LA LIBERTÉ

(*The Roads to Freedom*)

I

L'ÂGE DE RAISON (*The Age of Reason*, 1947)

II

LE SURSIS (*The Reprieve*, 1947)

III

LA MORT DANS L'ÂME (*Troubled Sleep*, 1951)

IV

LA DERNIÈRE CHANCE (*in preparation*)

La Mort Dans L'Âme, *copyright by Librairie Gallimard, 1949.*

Friday, September 23

SIXTEEN THIRTY o'clock in Berlin, fifteen thirty o'clock in London. The hotel stood bleakly on its hill, a desolate, solemn edifice with an old gentleman inside it. At Angoulême, Marseille, Ghent, and Dover, people thought: "What can he be doing? It's past three o'clock, why doesn't he come out?" He was sitting in the lounge behind half-closed shutters, his thick-browed eyes staring into vacancy, and his lips slightly parted, as though he were pondering on some ancient memory. He had ceased to read; his hand —an old man's freckled hand—still grasping some typewritten sheets, hung loosely from his knees. He turned to Horace Wilson and said:

"What is the time?"

"About half past four," Horace Wilson replied.

The old gentleman lifted his wide eyes, laughed a short, genial laugh, and said: "It's very hot."

And indeed a crimson, crackling, glistening heat had descended upon Europe; there was heat on men's hands, behind their eyes, and in their bronchial tubes, and they waited, sickened by heat and dust and fear. In the vestibule of the hotel, reporters waited. In the courtyard three chauffeurs waited, motionless at their steering wheels; on the far side of the Rhine, motionless in the vestibule of the Hotel Dreesen, tall black-clad Prussians waited. Milan Hlinka was no longer waiting. He had ceased to wait two days ago, on that awful, black day, lit by a flash of certainty: "They've let us down!" Then time flowed on once more in its usual random fashion, individual days no longer seemed to exist—there were only next days; henceforward all days would be next days.

At fifteen thirty o'clock Mathieu was still waiting, on the threshold of a dreadful future; at the same moment, at sixteen thirty o'clock, Milan no longer possessed a future. The old gentleman rose, crossed the room, stiff-kneed, with dignified, jerky steps, and said: "Gentlemen!" smiling affably; he laid the document on the table, and smoothed out the pages with his closed fist; Milan had assumed position in front of the table; the outspread newspaper covered the whole breadth of the oilcloth. For the seventh time Milan read:

"The President of the Republic, in association with the Government, could not do otherwise than accept the proposals of the two great powers regarding the basis of our future attitude. There was nothing left for us to do, being now alone." Nevile Henderson and Sir Horace Wilson had gone up to the table; the old gentleman turned to them, looking very elderly and inoffensive, and said:

"Gentlemen, this is what we must now do."

And Milan thought: "What else could be done?" A confused murmur drifted through the window, and Milan thought: "We are now alone."

A small squeaky voice ascended from the street: "Long live Hitler!"

Milan ran to the window.

"Wait a moment!" he shouted. "Just wait till I come down."

There was a wild scurry and a clattering of clogs. At the far end of the street, the urchin turned, groped in his apron, and began to wave his arms. Two dull thuds on the wall.

"It's little Liebknecht," said Milan, "he's going his round."

He leaned out; the street was as deserted as on a Sunday. The Schoenhofs had hung out red and white swastika flags from their balconies. All the shutters on the green house were closed. And Milan thought: "We haven't any shutters."

"We must open all the windows," he said.

"Why?" asked Anna.

"When the windows are shut, they aim at the window-panes."

Anna shrugged her shoulders.

"In any case . . ." she said.

Songs and shouts burst in gusts into his room.

"They're still on the square," said Milan.

He had laid his hands on the window-rail and thought: "It's all over." A heavy man appeared at the corner of the street carrying a rucksack and leaning on a stick. He looked exhausted; two women were following him, bowed beneath enormous bundles.

"The Jägerschmitts are coming back," said Milan, without turning round.

They had fled on Monday evening; they must have crossed the frontier Tuesday or Wednesday during the night. And now they were exultantly returning. Jägerschmitt went up to the green house and walked up the front steps. His face was gray with dust and he was smiling strangely. He felt in his jacket pockets and produced a key. The women had put their bundles on the ground and stood watching him.

"You come back when the danger's over," shouted Milan.

"Milan!" said Anna briskly.

Jägerschmitt had raised his head. He saw Milan, and his light eyes flashed.

"You come back when the danger's over."

"Yes, I come back," shouted Jägerschmitt. "And now— it's your turn to go."

He slipped the key into the lock, and opened the door; the two women followed him in. Milan turned round.

"Filthy cowards!" said he.

"Don't provoke them," said Anna.

"Cowards," said Milan, "dirty Germans. They were licking our boots two years ago."

"Never mind. You shouldn't provoke them."

The old gentleman stopped talking; his mouth remained half-open, as though silently continuing to give opinions on the situation. His large round eyes were full of tears; he had raised his eyebrows and was looking questioningly at Nevile and Horace. They said nothing; Horace turned his head abruptly; Nevile walked to the table, picked up the document, considered it for a moment, then pushed it irritably aside. The old gentleman wore an expression of perplexity; he opened his arms helplessly, yet in token of good faith. And he said for the fifth time:

"I found myself faced by a quite unexpected situation; I thought we should quietly discuss the proposals I brought with me. . . ." And Horace thought: "The old fox! Where does he get that grandfatherly voice?" He said: "Very good, sir; in ten minutes we shall be at the Hotel Dreesen."

"Lerchen has come," said Anna. "Her husband is at Prague; she's worried."

"Why doesn't she come here?"

"I suppose you think she'd feel more at ease with a nut like you, standing at the window insulting people in the street," said Anna with a little laugh.

He looked at the serene, fastidious head, the drawn features, narrow shoulders, her huge belly.

"Sit down," he said. "I don't like to see you standing."

She sat down, and clasped her hands in front of her; the

fellow was waving some newspapers, muttering: *"Paris-Soir,* latest edition. Only two left—better buy 'em." He had shouted himself hoarse. Maurice took the paper and read:

"Prime Minister Chamberlain has addressed a letter to Chancellor Hitler, to which, it is intimated in British circles, the latter will reply. The meeting with M. Hitler, which was to have taken place this morning, is consequently postponed to a later hour."

Zézette looked at the paper over Maurice's shoulder.

"Anything new?" she asked.

"No. Same old story."

He turned over the page, and they noticed a blurred photograph of some kind of castle, a medieval business on the summit of a hill, with towers, belfries, and rows of windows.

"It's Godesberg," said Maurice.

"Is that where Chamberlain is?" asked Zézette.

"Police reinforcements have apparently arrived."

"Yes," said Milan. "Two gendarmes. That makes six gendarmes all together. They've barricaded themselves in the police station."

A cartload of shouts was tipped into the room. Anna shivered; but her face remained calm.

She said: "Suppose we telephoned."

"Telephoned?"

"Yes. To Prisecnice."

Milan showed her the newspaper without answering. "According to a dispatch from the D.N.B. dated Thursday, the German population of the Sudeten regions have taken over the maintenance of public order as far as the linguistic frontier."

"Perhaps it isn't true," said Anna. "They told me that had happened only at Eger."

Milan pounded his fist on the table. "God Almighty! Must we ask for help again?"

He stretched out his hands; they were large, gnarled

hands, dotted with brown spots and scars: he had been a woodcutter before his accident. He looked at them, stretched his fingers, and said:

"They may turn up. In twos or threes. There'll be some fun for five minutes or so, I'll bet you."

"There'll be six hundred of them," said Anna.

Milan bent his head; he felt alone.

"Listen," said Anna.

He listened; they could be heard more clearly now, they must be on the march. Anger shook him; he could no longer see clearly, and his skull ached. He went to the chest of drawers, breathing hard.

"What are you doing?" Anna asked.

He was bending over one of the drawers, still breathing hard. He bent down lower and grunted, but did not reply.

"No—not that," she said.

"What?"

"You mustn't. Give it to me."

He turned; Anna had got up and was leaning against the chair, looking quite composed. He thought of what she was carrying in her belly, and he handed her the revolver.

"Right," said he. "I'll telephone to Prisecnice."

He went down to the ground floor and into the school-room, opened the windows, and picked up the telephone.

"Give me the police station at Prisecnice. Hello!"

His right ear caught a dry, zigzag crackle. His left ear heard *them*. Odette laughed nervously. "I have never really known where Czechoslovakia was," she said, plunging her fingers into the sand. After a moment or two he got the click of someone picking up the receiver.

"Well?" said a voice.

Milan thought for a moment. "I am asking for assistance." He gripped the receiver hard.

"This is Pravnitz," he said. "I'm the schoolmaster. We are twenty Czechs here, and three German democrats hiding in a cellar, the rest are Henlein's men; they're officered by fifty fellows of the Free Corps who crossed the frontier last evening and have drawn them up in the square. The mayor has joined them."

A silence followed, then the voice said insolently:

"*Bitte—Deutsch sprechen.*"

"*Schweinkopf!*" shouted Milan.

He replaced the receiver and limped upstairs again. His leg was hurting him. He entered the room and sat down.

"They've got there," he said.

Anna went to him and laid her hands on his shoulders. "Darling," she said.

"The bastards!" said Milan. "They know what's happened, they just jeered at me over the phone."

He drew her pregnant body between his knees. The swollen belly touched his own.

"Now we are quite alone," said he.

"I can't believe it."

He raised his head slowly and looked her up and down; she was steady and dependable when there was something to be done, but she was like all women in that respect—she always had to confide in someone.

"There they are," said Anna.

The voices seemed nearer; they must be marching down the main street. From a distance the exultant shouts of a crowd sound very much like shrieks of terror.

"Is the door barricaded?"

"Yes," said Milan. "But they can always get through the windows, or go round by the garden."

"If they come upstairs . . ." said Anna.

"You don't need to be afraid. They can smash up everything, I won't lift a finger."

He suddenly felt Anna's warm lips against his cheek. "Darling, I know it's for my sake."

"No, not for you. For *you* is really *me*. It's for the child's sake."

They started; someone had rung.

"Don't go to the window!" exclaimed Anna.

He got up and went to the window. The Jägerschmitts had opened all their shutters; the Hitler flag was hanging above the door. As he leaned out he saw a tiny shadow.

"I'm coming down," he cried.

He crossed the room.

"It's Marikka," he said.

He went downstairs and opened the front door. Firecrackers, shouts, and band music floated across the roofs; it was a day of celebration. He eyed the empty street, and his heart turned over.

"Why have you come here?" he asked. "There's no school today."

"Mummy sent me," said Marikka. She was carrying a little basket, filled with apples and slices of bread spread with margarine.

"Your mother must be crazy; you're going straight home."

"She said you wouldn't send me back."

She held out a sheet of paper folded in four. He unfolded it and read: "Father and Georg are terrified. Please keep Marikka until evening."

"Where is your father?" asked Milan.

"He's behind the door, with Georg. They've got axes and rifles." And she added with a touch of importance: "Mummy sent me out by the yard, she said I would be safer here because you're sensible."

"Yes," said Milan. "Yes, I'm sensible. All right, come up."

Seventeen thirty o'clock in Berlin, sixteen thirty o'clock in Paris. Slight low-pressure cell to the north of Scotland. M. von Dörnberg appeared on the staircase of the Grand Hotel, the reporters crowded round him, and Pierryl said: "Is he coming down?" M. von Dörnberg had a paper in his right hand; he raised his left hand, and said: "It is not yet settled whether Mr. Chamberlain will see the Führer this evening."

"This is the place," said Zézette. "I used to sell flowers here, on a little green wagon."

"You always looked so well," said Maurice.

He contemplated the pavement and the street obediently, that being what they had come to see, for she had begun to talk about it lately. But it meant nothing to him. Zézette had let go his arm; she was laughing to herself in silence as she watched the traffic going past.

"Did you have a chair?" Maurice asked.

"Sometimes; a folding chair," said Zézette.

"That mustn't have been much fun."

"It was all right in the spring," said Zézette.

She was talking to him in an undertone, without looking at him, as one talks to a sick person; and for the last couple of minutes she had begun to wriggle her shoulders and back, in an affected sort of way. She didn't seem herself; Maurice was getting bored. Twenty some people were gathered in front of a shop-window; he went up to them and peered over their heads. Zézette remained in ecstasy on the edge of the pavement; after a moment she rejoined him and took his arm again. On a bevelled glass plaque stood two scraps of red leather with a blob of red fluff, rather like a powder-puff. Maurice burst out laughing.

"What's so funny?" whispered Zézette.

"They're shoes," laughed Maurice.

Two or three heads turned round. Zézette said: "Sh!" and drew him away.

"So what! We ain't in church, are we?" said Maurice.

However, he spoke in an undertone. People were padding along the street, looking as if they were all acquainted, but not uttering a word.

"It must be five years and more since I was here," he whispered.

Zézette pointed proudly to Maxim's.

"That's Maxim's," she confided into his ear.

Maurice looked at Maxim's and abruptly turned his head away. He had heard about it, and a filthy joint it was, where the bourgeois swilled champagne in 1914 while the workers fell in battle. And he said between his teeth:

"The bastards!"

But he felt ill at ease, without quite knowing why. He walked with a brisk, springy step; the passers-by looked so fragile to him that he was afraid of bumping into them.

"That may be," said Zézette. "But it's a fine street anyhow, don't you think?"

"Doesn't impress me," said Maurice. "Not enough air."

Zézette shrugged her shoulders, and Maurice found himself thinking of the avenue de Saint-Ouen. When he left his lodging in the morning, guys would pass him, whistling, with satchels on their backs, bent over the handlebars of their bicycles. He used to feel happy; some stopped at Saint-Denis, and others went on farther; everybody was going in the same direction, the workers were on their way. And he said to Zézette:

"This is bourgeois country here."

They walked on a little way enveloped in a smell of incense paper, then Maurice stopped and begged pardon.

"What did you say?" asked Zézette.

"Nothing," said Maurice with embarrassment, "nothing at all."

He had again bumped into somebody; other people, for all they walked with their eyes on the ground, always managed to avoid one another at the last moment; it must be a matter of habit.

"Are you coming?"

But he no longer wanted to walk on, he was afraid of breaking something, and besides, this street didn't lead anywhere; it had no direction; some people were making their way towards the boulevards, others down to the Seine, and others stand with their noses glued to shop-windows—isolated eddies, but no co-ordinated movements; a man felt isolated. He reached out a hand, laid it on Zézette's shoulder, and gripped the yielding flesh beneath the fabric. Zézette smiled at him, she was enjoying herself, she eyed everything with alert avidity without losing her natural sophistication, swaying her small hips neatly as she walked. He tickled her neck and she laughed.

"Don't, Maurice!" she said.

He liked the loud colours she put on her face—the sugary white, and the crimson on her cheekbones. From near by she smelt of honey. He said to her in a low voice:

"Having fun?"

"I remember it all so well," said Zézette with shining eyes.

He let go of her shoulder and they walked on in silence; she had known many bourgeois, they came to buy her flowers, she smiled at them, and indeed there were some who tried to get fresh. He looked at her white neck, and an odd feeling came over him; he wanted at the same time to laugh and get mad.

"*Paris-Soir,*" cried a voice.

"Shall we buy one?" asked Zézette.

"There won't be anything new in it."

People thronged round the paper-boy and silently snatched the papers. A woman emerged from the crowd, in high-heeled shoes and a killing hat perched on the top of her head. She unfolded the paper and read it as she pattered off. Her face dropped and she heaved a deep sigh.

"Get a load of that old gal," said Maurice.

Zézette looked at her. "Perhaps her man's going to be called up."

Maurice shrugged his shoulders; it seemed odd that anyone could be really unhappy in that hat and those whore-shoes.

"So what!" he said; "her husband's probably a brass hat."

"Even if he is," said Zézette, "he can leave his hide behind like our buddies."

Maurice threw her a sidelong glance. "You kill me with your damned officers. I guess you saw in 1914 if they lost their hides or not!"

"That's what I mean," said Zézette. "I thought lots of them were killed."

"It's the mud-arsers that were killed, and the rest of us," said Maurice.

Zézette snuggled up to him. "Oh, Maurice," she said, "do you really think there's going to be a war."

"What do *I* know about it?" said Maurice.

That morning he had been sure of it, and the other fellows were as sure as he was. They were on the bank of the Seine, looking at the line of cranes and the dredger, guys in shirt-sleeves, toughs from Gennevilliers who were digging a trench for an electric cable, and it was evident that war was on the way. After all, it wouldn't make much difference to those guys from Gennevilliers: they would be somewhere in the north, digging trenches in the sunshine, in peril from bullets, shells, and bombs, just as they were now in peril from earth-slides, falls, and all occupational accidents; they would wait for the end of the war just as they waited for the end of the day's work. And Sandre had said: "We guys'll do the job. But when we come back, we'll keep our rifles."

Right now, he was no longer sure of anything; at Saint-Ouen it was war all the time, but not here. Here was peace: shop-windows, displays of luxuries, coloured fabrics, mirrors to look at yourself in, all the comforts of life. The people looked depressed, but that was natural enough. Why should they fight? They were waiting for nothing, they had all they wanted. It must be rather grim to hope for nothing except that life would continue indefinitely the way it started.

"The bourgeoisie doesn't want war," observed Maurice

suddenly. "They are afraid of victory, because it would mean the victory of the proletariat."

The old gentleman got up and escorted Nevile Henderson and Horace Wilson to the door. He looked at them for a moment with an air of deep emotion, he was like all those old gentlemen with rather worn-out faces who gather round the news-venders in the rue Royale and Pall Mall and ask no more than that their life should terminate as it had begun. He thought of these old gentlemen and of their children, and he said:

"You will further ask Herr von Ribbentrop if Chancellor Hitler considers it desirable that we should have a last conversation before my departure, drawing his attention to the point that an acceptance in principle would entail on Herr Hitler the necessity of putting fresh proposals before us. You will lay particular stress on the fact that I am determined to do all that is humanly possible to settle the issue by means of negotiation, as it seems to me incredible that the nations of Europe, who do not want war, should be plunged into a sanguinary conflict over a question on which agreement has to a large extent been reached. Good luck."

Horace and Nevile bowed and went downstairs, the ceremonious, nervous, tired, suave voice still ringing in their ears, and Maurice looked at the flabby, worn, civilized flesh of the old men and women all around him, and he reflected with disgust that they would have to be bled.

They must be bled; it would be a nastier process than squashing snails, but it couldn't be helped. The machine-guns would enfilade the rue Royale, which would lie desolate for several days, windows broken, star-shaped smashes in the shop fronts, the tables outside the cafés overturned in a litter of glass; airplanes would be circling overhead above the corpses. Then the dead would be removed, the tables picked up, the glass replaced, and life would resume its course; sturdy citizens with strong red necks, leather jackets, and helmets would repopulate the street. That indeed was what had happened in Russia, Maurice had seen photographs of Nevski Prospect; the proletariat had taken possession of that resplendent avenue and were walking up and down it, no longer dazzled by the palaces and the great stone bridges.

"I beg pardon," said Maurice with confusion.

He had swung his elbow into the back of an old lady, who was eying him indignantly. He felt tired and depressed; beneath the large billboards under the blackened gold letters hung from the balconies, among the confectioners' and bootmakers' shops, in front of the columns of the Madeleine, it was impossible to imagine any other crowd than this—old ladies trotting on their way, and children in sailor suits. The melancholy, golden light, the smell of incense, the honeyed voices, bemused and anxious faces, the bleak shuffling of footsteps on the asphalt, all this was consistent, all this was *real;* the Revolution was nothing but a dream. "I oughtn't to have come," thought Maurice, with a malicious glance at Zézette. "This is no place for a proletarian."

A hand touched his shoulder; he blushed with pleasure as he recognized Brunet.

"Good morning, young fellow," said Brunet with a smile.

"Morning, comrade," said Maurice.

Brunet's fist was as hard and horny as his own, and it had a powerful grip. Maurice looked at Brunet and burst into a hearty laugh; he was snapping out of it; he could see all the fellows around him, at Saint-Ouen, Ivry, Montreuil, in Paris itself—at Belleville, Montrouge, and La Villette, squaring their shoulders and preparing for the fray.

"What are you up to here?" asked Brunet. "Are you on strike?"

"It's my paid holiday," explained Maurice with some

embarrassment. "Zézette wanted to come because she used to work here once."

"Ah, there's Zézette," said Brunet. "Greeting to you, Comrade Zézette."

"It's Brunet," said Maurice. "You saw his article this morning in the *Huma*."

Zézette looked boldly at Brunet and gave him her hand. She was not afraid of men, whether they were bourgeois or big noises in the party.

"I've known him from a lad," said Brunet, pointing to Maurice. "He was with the Red Falcons, one of the singers, and I never heard such a voice. In the end it was agreed that he should only pretend to sing during the processions."

They laughed.

"Well?" said Zézette. "Is there going to be a war? You ought to know; you're in a position to hear what's going on."

It was a silly question, a woman's question, but Maurice was glad she had asked it. Brunet looked serious.

"I don't know if there's going to be a war," he said. "But anyhow we mustn't be afraid of it; the working classes ought to realize that it can't be avoided by concessions."

He talked well. Zézette gazed at him with trustful eyes and smiled softly as she listened. Maurice was annoyed; Brunet talked like a newspaper, and said no more.

"Do you think Hitler would cave in if we showed him our teeth?" asked Zézette.

Brunet had assumed an official expression; he did not appear to understand that he was being asked his personal opinion.

"Quite possible," he said. "Besides, whatever happens, the U.S.S.R. are with us."

"It's only to be expected," thought Maurice, "that the big shots of the party shouldn't feel inclined to give their

views on demand to a paltry mechanic from Saint-Ouen."
None the less he was disappointed. He looked at Brunet,
and all his satisfaction vanished; Brunet had strong peasant's hands, a powerful jaw, and purposeful eyes, but he
was wearing a collar and tie and a flannel suit, and seemed
at ease in middle-class surroundings.

A dark window mirrored their reflections; Maurice saw
a woman without a hat, and a tall strapping fellow with a
cap on the back of his head, in a gay-coloured jacket, talking to a gentleman. However, he remained standing, with
his hands in his pockets; he couldn't make up his mind to
leave Brunet.

"Are you still at Saint-Mandé?" asked Brunet.

"No," said Maurice, "Saint-Ouen. I'm working at
Flaive's."

"Ah? I thought you were at Saint-Mandé. Fitter?"

"Mechanic."

"Good," said Brunet. "Excellent. Well—so long, comrade."

"So long, comrade," said Maurice. He felt ill at ease and
vaguely disappointed.

"So long, comrade," said Zézette, with a toothy smile.

Brunet watched them depart. The crowd had closed
upon them, but Maurice's huge shoulders emerged above
the hats. He had to hold Zézette about the waist; his cap
was close to her chignon, and, with heads together, they
sped through the throng. "A good guy," thought Brunet.
"But I don't like his babe." He walked on with a serious air,
conscious of a feeling of skin-deep remorse. "What answer
could I give him?" he thought. At Saint-Denis, Saint-Ouen,
Sochaux, Creusot, hundreds of thousands of them were
waiting, with the same anxious, confiding look in their
eyes. Hundreds of thousands of heads like that one, good
round solid heads, rough-hewn, cropped heads, the heads
of true men, had turned towards the east, to Godesberg
and Prague and Moscow. What answer could be given to

them? There was nothing to be done now except to protect them, protect their slow tenacious minds against the machinations of unscrupulous politicians. Today he had to see old Mother Boningue, tomorrow Dottin, secretary of the Teachers' Union, and on the following day the Pivertistes; it was his job. Well, he would go from one to the next and try to soothe them all. Mother Boningue, waving her idealist hands, would look at him with velvety eyes and talk to him about "the horror of shedding blood." She was a large woman of about fifty, with a florid complexion, white down on her cheeks, short hair, and a suave priestlike expression behind her spectacles; she wore a man's jacket, with the ribbon of the Legion of Honor in the lapel. "I shall say: 'Women always get in wrong; in 1914 they bundled their men off to the front, when they ought to have lain down on the rails to prevent the train from starting, and now when there might be some sense in fighting, you're founding peace leagues and doing all you can to break your men's morale.'" Maurice's face came back to him, and Brunet shrugged his shoulders angrily. "One word, just one word, does help them sometimes, and I couldn't think of one." Bitterly he thought: "It was that girl's fault, girls have a knack of asking silly questions." Zézette's floured cheeks, her lewd little eyes, her vulgar scent; they would go about collecting signature after signature, gently persistent—corpulent Radical doves, Trotzkyist Jewesses, Oppositionists of the S.F.I.O.; with their damned nerve they go anywhere—they would descend upon an old peasant woman in process of milking a cow, thrust a fountain pen into her large damp hand, and say: "Sign there if you are against war." *No more war. Negotiations, not war. Peace first.* And what would Zézette do if she were suddenly offered a fountain pen? Had she retained sufficient class reflexes to laugh at these large benevolent ladies? She had dragged her man into the fashionable districts, she was looking excitedly into the shop windows, and she had plastered her cheeks with make-up. . . . Poor guy, it would be a bad job if she hung round his neck to stop his going. That would be too much. . . . *Intellectual. Bourgeois.* "I can't stand her with her plastered face and gnawed fingers. And yet all the comrades can't be bachelors." He felt all of a sudden weary and heavy; he thought: "I'm blaming her for her make-up because I can't stand cheap make-up." *Intellectual. Bourgeois.* To be able to love them—all, every man and woman without distinction! He thought: "I shouldn't *want* to love them; it ought to be one of those things, necessary, like breathing." *Intellectual. Bourgeois. Separated forever.* "No use, we shall never have the same backgrounds." Joseph Mercier, aged thirty-three, congenital syphilitic, Professor of Natural History at the Lycée Buffon and the College Sévigné, was walking up the rue Royale, sniffing, and from time to time sucking his lips with a faint damp smack; he had his usual pain in his left side, he felt wretched, and he was wondering whether the salaries of mobilized officials would be paid. He looked at his feet to avoid all those merciless faces and bumped into a tall red-haired man in a gray flannel suit who jostled him against a shop window. Joseph Mercier looked up and thought: "What a ton of bricks!" He was indeed a veritable human wall, one of those cruel, unfeeling brutes like that hulking boy Chamerlier in the elementary mathematics class who defied him to his face in school, one of those guys who never question anything, least of all themselves, who are never ill, never suffer from nerves, take women and life as they come, and march straight to their goal, shoving you against shop windows. The rue Royale flowed quietly towards the Seine, and Brunet flowed along with it; someone had bumped into him; he noticed an emaciated creature flee by with a bulbous nose, a derby, and a tall celluloid collar; he thought of Zézette and of Maurice, and all the old familiar anguish came back into his mind: his shame at his inexpiable memories, the white house on the banks of the Marne, his father's library, his mother's tapering, perfumed hands, all of which set him apart from them for ever.

It was a lovely, golden evening, of a true September vintage. Stephen Hartley, leaning over the balcony, murmured: "The vast slow eddies of the vesperal crowd." Hats —a sea of felt, with a few bare heads afloat among the billows—"like gulls," he thought; two fair heads, and a gray head, a fine conspicuously red cranium already slightly bald. "A French crowd," thought Stephen, with a touch of emotion. A little crowd of heroic little men. He would write: "The French crowd awaits events with calm and dignity." A heading for the *New York Herald,* in heavy type: "I have contacted the French public." Little men, not too clean, interspersed with large feminine hats, a silent crowd, serene and rather shabby, gilded by that hour— the calm of a Paris evening between the Madeleine and the Concorde. "The face of France," he would write; "the eternal face of France." Shuffling feet, decorous whispers of astonishment—no, astonishment was rather too strong a word: a tall, red-haired, slightly bald Frenchman, serene as a sunset, gleams of sunshine on the windows of the passing cars, bursts of voices; sparkles of voices, said Stephen to himself. And he thought: "My article is written."

"Stephen," said Sylvia, addressing his back.

"I'm busy," said Stephen curtly, without turning round.

"But you must answer me, dear," said Sylvia; "there are only first-class berths left on the *Lafayette.*"

"Take first class, take a luxury cabin," said Stephen. "The *Lafayette* is very likely the last boat that will sail for America for a long while."

Brunet walked quietly on, inhaling the smell of incense, he looked up and noticed some tarnished gilt letters affixed to a balcony; war had come; it was there, in the

depths of that luminous haze, inscribed for all to see on
the walls of that frail city; it was a palpable explosion
that had split the rue Royale. People passed and did not
see it, but Brunet saw it. Brunet had thought: "The sky
will fall on our heads." The city was in the act of falling;
he had seen the houses as they really were—in imminent
collapse. Above that elegant shop were tons of stone, and
each stone, interlocking with the rest, had been falling
steadily for fifty years past; a couple more pounds and the
collapse would start again. The columns would swell and
reel and splinter into slivers; the plate-glass window would
be smashed; cartloads of stone would hurtle into the cellar
and overwhelm the stores of merchandise. They have two-
thousand-pound bombs. Brunet's heart contracted; just
now, upon those symmetrical façades, there had been a human smile shining through the powdered gold of evening.
It had vanished—measureless miles of stone; men astray
among avalanches, poised and stabilized. Soldiers among
the ruins—he would be killed, perhaps. He saw the black-
ish furrows on Zézette's plastered cheeks. Dusty walls,
blank walls with yawning gaps in them, strips of blue and
yellow paper dangling here and there, and leprous patches
everywhere; red tiles among the wreckage, upthrusting
weeds between the flagstones. Then lines of timbered huts
—encampments. In time vast monotonous barracks would
come into being, like the buildings on the outer boulevards. Brunet shuddered; "I love Paris," he thought with
anguish. The vision vanished, and the city encompassed
him once more. Brunet stopped; a craven acquiescence
seemed to soak into his being, and he thought: "If only
there were no such thing as war! If only war need not
exist!" And he gazed avidly at the great arched gateways,
Driscoll's glittering shop window, the royal-blue hangings
of the Brasserie Weber. Then he felt ashamed, walked on,
and thought: "I am too fond of Paris." Like Pilniak, at
Moscow, who had been too fond of ancient churches. The

party rightly distrusts intellectuals. Death is imprinted
upon man, and ruin upon objects; other men will come and
rebuild Paris, and rebuild the world. "I shall say to her:
'So you want peace at any price?' I shall speak gently,
looking straight into her eyes, and I shall say: 'Women
must not be allowed to interfere with us. This is not the
moment to pester men with their follies.'"

"I wish I were a man," said Odette.

Mathieu raised himself on one elbow. He was already
deeply tanned. Smiling, he asked: "So that you might play
soldiers?"

Odette blushed. "Oh no," she retorted. "But I find it
silly to be a woman at this moment."

"It must not be very convenient," he agreed.

She looked, as she often did, like a parakeet; the words
she used always came back against her. And yet she felt
that Mathieu could not have found fault with her justly,
if she had been able to convey her real meaning; the point
was that men always upset her when they talked about
war in her presence. They were not natural, they displayed
too much assurance, as though they wanted to make her
understand that this was a man's affair, and yet they always looked as though they expected something from her
—a sort of arbitration, because she was a woman and
could not fight, and because she remained above the fray.
What could she say to them? Stay? Go? It was not for her
to decide, just because she could not go. Perhaps she ought
to say: "Do what you prefer." But what if they had no
preference? She effaced herself, she pretended not to understand them, she produced coffee and liqueurs for them
and listened to their heated talk. She sighed, picked up a
handful of sand, and let it trickle, warm and white, on to
her tanned leg. The beach was deserted, the sea sparkled
and rustled. On the wooden balcony of the Provençal
three young women in beach slacks were having tea.
Odette closed her eyes. She lay on the sand, enveloped in

a dateless, ageless heat—the heat of her childhood days, when she closed her eyes, lying on that same sand, and played at being a salamander in the depths of a huge red-blue flame. The same heat, the same damply caressing bathing suit, which always seemed to be smoking in the sunshine, the same scorching sand against the back of her neck; in other years she melted into the sea and sky and sand, she no longer distinguished the present from the past. She sat up, wide-eyed; today there was a real present; there was a pain in the pit of her stomach; there was Mathieu, tanned and naked, sitting cross-legged on his white beach robe. Mathieu was silent. She would so have liked to be silent too. But if she did not compel him to speak to her directly, she lost him; he would politely acquiesce, just so far as to make a little speech in his resonant, rather rasping voice, and then he was off, leaving his body in pledge, a very lithe, athletic body. If only he were absorbed in pleasant thoughts! But he looked into vacancy with a distraught expression on his face, while his large hands were busily constructing a sand pie. The pie dissolved, and the hands unweariedly remolded it; Mathieu did not once look at his hands; at last she could bear it no longer.

"You can't make pies with dry sand," said Odette. "Even children know that."

Mathieu burst out laughing.

"What are you thinking about?" asked Odette.

"I've got to write to Ivich," he replied, "and I don't know what to say."

"I'm surprised at that," she answered with a short laugh. "You write her volumes."

"I know I do. But some fools have frightened her. She has taken to reading the newspapers and she doesn't understand what's going on; she wants me to explain. It's going to be an awkward business. She mixes up the Czechs and the Albanians, and she thinks that Prague is by the sea."

"How very Russian!" said Odette dryly.

Mathieu grimaced and did not answer, and Odette began to feel antipathetic. He added with a smile: "What complicates everything is that she's furiously angry with me."

"Why?" she asked.

"Because I'm French. She was living quietly among the French, and here they are suddenly proposing to go to war. She thinks it's abominable."

"Well, really!" said Odette indignantly.

Mathieu assumed a bland expression. "Put yourself in her place," he said quietly. "She disapproves of us because we are risking getting killed or wounded! She regards the wounded as a tactless sort of people who obtrude their bodies on their fellow citizens. That's what she calls physiological, and she hates anything physiological, both in herself and others."

"Little darling," murmured Odette.

"She's quite sincere," said Mathieu. "She fasts for days at a time, because it disgusts her to eat. When she feels sleepy at night, she drinks coffee to wake herself up."

Odette did not answer; she thought: "A good spanking is what she wants." Mathieu was shuffling sand about with a sentimental sort of air. "Never eats, eh? But I'll bet she keeps pots of jam hidden in her room. Men are really so stupid." Mathieu had resumed the construction of sand pies; he was off again, God knew where, nor for how long. "Now, I eat red meat, and sleep when I feel sleepy," she thought bitterly. On the balcony of the Provençal the band was playing the *Sérénade portugaise*. There were three musicians. Italians. The violinist wasn't too bad; he closed his eyes when he was playing. Odette felt quite thrilled; music in the open air always sounded fantastically thin and useless—especially at such a moment. A vast tonnage of heat and war weighed heavily upon sea and sand, and here were these mouselike noises mounting up into high heaven. She turned to Mathieu and was on the point of saying to him: "I like that tune." But she did not; perhaps Ivich detested the *Sérénade portugaise*.

Mathieu's hands stopped moving, and the sand pie collapsed.

"I like that tune," he said. "What is it?"

"It's the *Sérénade portugaise*," said Odette.

Eighteen ten o'clock at Godesberg. The old gentleman waited. At Angoulême, Marseille, Ghent, and Dover they were thinking: "What is he doing? Has he come down? Is he talking to Hitler?" It might be that even then the two of them were in process of arranging a settlement. So they waited. The old gentleman waited likewise, in the drawing-room with the half-closed shutters. He was alone; he belched, and walked towards the window. The hill sloped down to the river, green and white. The Rhine was black, like a tarred road after rain. The old gentleman belched again, there was a sour taste in his mouth. He began to drum on the window, and scared flies darted round him. It was a white and dusty heat, a pompous, skeptical, antiquated heat, a high-collared heat of the time of Frederick II; and in the midst of it an elderly Englishman was waiting wearily, an elderly Englishman of the time of Edward VII, while all the rest of the world belonged to 1938. At Juan-les-Pins, at seventeen ten o'clock on September 23, 1938, a large lady in a white linen frock sat down in a deck-chair, took off her blue spectacles, and began to read the paper. It was the *Petit-Niçois*, Odette Delorme could read the large type headline: "Keep Calm," and, with an effort, she deciphered the subhead: "Mr. Chamberlain addresses a message to Hitler." And she asked herself: "Do I really hate war?" And she thought: "No, not absolutely." For if she had, she would have

leaped out of her chair and rushed to the railway station
crying: "Don't go! Stay at home!" She saw herself for an
instant erect, arms outstretched, and crying out: "Don't
go!" and she felt dizzy. Then she reflected with relief that
she was incapable of so gross an indiscretion. Not absolutely. A woman of character, a Frenchwoman, sensible
and discreet, with a lot of rules of conduct, one being
never to think anything out to its logical end. At Laon, in
an ill-lit room, a frantic girl rejected war with her whole
being, blindly, doggedly. Odette said: "War is a dreadful
thing!" and she added: "I keep on thinking of the poor
fellows who must go." But she really had no thoughts as
yet, she waited placidly; she knew she would soon be told
all that she must think and say and do. When her father
had been killed, in 1917, people had said to her: "He was
a fine fellow, you must be brave"; she had very soon
learned to wear her mourning veils with a sort of jaunty
melancholy and look at people with the ingenuous eyes of
a war orphan. In 1924 her brother had been wounded in
Morocco, he had come back lamed, and people used to say
to Odette: "He's a fine fellow, you must be careful not to
pity him"; and Jacques had said to her, a few years afterwards: "It's very odd, I had thought Étienne had more
strength of mind, he has never got used to his disability,
he has grown embittered." Jacques would go, Mathieu
would go, and all would be well, she was sure of that. For
the moment the newspapers still wavered; Jacques said:
"It would be a silly war," and *Candide* said: "We are not
going to war because the Sudeten Germans want to wear
white stockings." But very soon the country would com-
bine into one vast chorus of approval; the Chambers would
unanimously approve the Government's policy, the *Jour*
would sing the praises of our heroic poilus. Jacques would
say to her: "The workers are splendid"; the passers-by
would smile in sanctimonious complicity—it would be war.
Odette too would approve, and start knitting woollen

helmet-liners. He was there, he appeared to be listening
to the music, he knew what he really ought to think, but
he did not say it. He wrote letters twenty pages long to
Ivich to explain the situation. To Odette he explained
nothing at all.

"What are you thinking about?"

Odette started. "Nothing—nothing at all."

"You don't play fair," said Mathieu. "I answered your
question."

She bent her head and smiled; but she did not want to
talk. He appeared to be quite alert at the moment; he was
looking at her.

"What's the matter?" she asked in a tone of annoyance.

He did not answer. He laughed with an air of surprise.

"Have you just noticed I exist?" said Odette. "I suppose
it gave you quite a shock. Is that it?"

When Mathieu laughed, he screwed up his eyes and
looked like a Chinese child.

"Do you imagine you can escape notice?" he asked.

"I'm not very exciting," said Odette.

"No. Not very communicative either. Added to which
you do what you can to help people to forget you. Well,
you don't succeed; even when you're quite discreet and
decorous, look at the sea, and keep as quiet as a mouse, it
is obvious that you are there. It just happens like that. On
the stage they call it 'presence'; some actors have it and
some haven't. You have."

Odette flushed. "You have been spoilt by your Russian
friends," she said quickly. "Presence must be a very Russian quality. But I don't think it's in my line."

Mathieu eyed her gravely.

"What exactly is in your line?" he asked.

Odette felt her eyes getting a little out of control and
begin to flutter in their sockets. She steadied them and
fixed her gaze on her bare feet with their lacquered nails.
She did not like discussing herself.

"I'm a bourgeois," she said gaily. "A French bourgeois—nothing very interesting."

This was obviously not conclusive enough, so she added forcibly, to clinch the conversation: "A nonentity."

Mathieu did not answer. She looked at him out of the corner of her eye; his hands were again scraping up the sand. Odette wondered what she had said wrong. He might indeed have protested a little, if only from politeness.

In a moment or two she heard his rich, husky voice: "It must be rather trying to feel a nonentity, eh?"

"One gets used to it," said Odette.

"I suppose so. I haven't yet."

"But you aren't a nonentity," she said briskly.

Mathieu stared at his sand pie. This time it was an excellent and solid pie. With a blow of his hand he swept it into ruin.

"We are all nonentities," he said, and laughed.

"How depressing you are!" said Odette.

"Not more so than other people. These threats of war have got on all our nerves a bit."

She raised her eyes and was about to speak, but was met by a calm, affectionate look. And she was silent. Nonentities —a man and a woman looking at each other on a beach. And war was there, all around them; it had entered into them and transformed them into the semblance of everybody else. "He feels he's a nonentity, he looks at me and smiles, but it's not me he's smiling at, it's at a nonentity." He demanded nothing of her except to be silent and anonymous, as usual. Better say nothing. If she had said to him: "You aren't a nonentity, you are a fine romantic fellow, not at all like anybody else"—and if he had believed it, he would then have slipped between her fingers and drifted away into his dreams, he would perhaps have fallen in love with another woman, that Russian girl, for instance, who drank coffee to keep herself awake. A stab of pride stirred her into speech. "It will be dreadful this time," she said rapidly.

"It will be just damned stupid," said Mathieu. "They'll destroy everything within reach. Paris, London, Rome. . . . Just imagine the result!"

Paris, Rome, London. And Jacques's white middle-class villa by the seashore. Odette shuddered; she looked at the sea. The sea was now no more than a glittering expanse of vapor; a water-skier, tanned and naked, sped past, leaning forward, towed by a motor-boat. No human agency could destroy that luminous sheen.

"That at least will be left to us," she said.

"What?"

"That—the sea."

Mathieu shook his head. "No," he said, "not even that."

She looked at him with surprise; she did not always quite understand what he meant. She thought of asking him, but suddenly she felt that she *must* go. She leaped to her feet, put on her sandals, and flung her wrap round her.

"What are you doing?" asked Mathieu.

"I must go," she said.

"Did it suddenly come over you?"

"I've just remembered that I promised Jacques garlic soup this evening. Madeleine won't be able to manage it by herself."

"You never stay long in the same place, anyway," said Mathieu. "Well, I shall have another swim."

She walked up the sandy steps, and when she reached the terrace she turned. Mathieu was running down to the sea. "He's right," she thought. "I'm fidgety. Always on the move, always making a fresh start, always trying to get away from something." As soon as she felt she liked a place a little, she became uneasy; she felt guilty and insecure. She looked at the sea, and thought: "I'm always afraid." Behind her, a hundred yards away, there was Jacques's

villa, the buxom Madeleine, the garlic soup to be made,
reasons for living, meals; she walked on. She would say to
Madeleine: "How is your mother today?" And Madeleine
would answer, with a faint sniff: "Just about the same,"
and Odette would say: "You must make her a little soup,
and take some of the white of the chicken—cut a wing off
before you serve it, she'll like that," and Madeleine would
answer: "Really, she won't touch anything, madame." But
Odette would take the chicken, cut off a wing with her
own hands, and that would be a reason for being alive.
"Not even that!" She threw a final glance at the sea. "He
said: 'Not even that.'" And yet it was so impalpable, so
like the sky inverted, what could they do to damage it?
Oily, viscous, coffee-hued, flat, monotonous, the sea of
every day, smelling of iodine and medicaments, *their* sea,
their sea-breeze, at a charge of a hundred francs a day;
he raised himself on his elbows and looked at the children
playing on the gray sand, little Simone Chassieux laughing
and limping about, her left leg clamped into an orthopedic
boot. Near the stairway there was a small boy he did not
know, a new arrival, no doubt, fearfully emaciated, and
with enormous ears; he had put a finger in his nose and
was gravely eying three little girls who were making sand
pies. He hunched his narrow, pointed shoulders and flexed
his knees; but his bulbous torso remained as rigid as stone.
Corset, of course. Tuberculous scoliosis. "He must be
feeble-minded into the bargain."

"Lie down," said Jeannine. "Flat on your back. You're
so restless today."

He obeyed, and observed the sky. Four little white
clouds. He heard the wheels of a trolley-bed creaking
along the road. "He's coming back early, who can it be?"

"Good afternoon, lame-brain," said a hearty voice.

He flung up both arms and swung the mirror round
above his head. They had already passed, but he recognized the nurse's large behind; it was Darrieux.

"When are you going to get your beard cut off?" he shouted.

"Whenever you get your balls cut off," replied Darrieux's distant voice.

He laughed, in high good humor; Jeannine didn't like such talk.

"When am I to go in?"

He watched Jeannine's hand feel in the pocket of her white blouse and produce a watch.

"In another quarter of an hour. Are you getting bored?"

"No."

He was never bored. Pots of flowers are not bored. They are taken out when the sun shines and brought in when dusk begins to fall. Their opinion is never asked, they have nothing to decide, nothing to expect. It is unimaginably absorbing to soak in air and light through all one's pores. The sky reverberated like a gong, and he saw five little gray specks in triangular formation gleaming between two clouds. He stretched himself and twiddled his toes; the sound descended in great sheets of copper, it was pleasant and caressing, rather like the smell of chloroform on an operating-table. Jeannine sighed, and he looked at her from the corner of his eye; she had lifted her head and seemed uneasy, there must surely be something on her mind. "It's true; there's going to be a war." He smiled.

"So," he said, turning his neck around slightly; "the stand-ups are going to have their war."

"You know what I said," she observed acidly. "If you talk like that I shan't answer."

He was silent, he had all the time there was, the airplane roared in his ears, he felt perfectly at ease—"I don't mind being silent." She couldn't hold out, stand-ups are always agitated, they have to talk or move around; at last she said:

"Yes, I'm afraid it's true; there's going to be war."

She spoke with her operation-day expression, suggesting,

somehow, a poor pathetic child as well as a trained nurse. When she came into his room on the first day and said to him: "You must hoist yourself up, I'm going to take the bedpan," she had worn that same expression. He was sweating, inhaling his own smell, that awful stable smell, while she—erect, expert, unknown—held out manicured hands with just that expression on her face.

He licked his lips slowly; well, he had had his way with her since then.

"You look quite upset."

"Not at all."

"What difference can war make to you? It's no business of ours."

She turned her head away, and he drummed irritably on the arm of his trolley. She oughtn't to be bothering about war. Her job was to look after her patients.

"I don't give a damn for the war," said he.

"Why do you pretend to be so wicked?" she said quietly. "You wouldn't like France to be beaten."

"I shouldn't care."

"Monsieur Charles! You frighten me when you talk like that."

"It isn't my fault I'm a Nazi," he jeered.

"Nazi!" she said despondently. "What will you think of next! Nazi! They beat up the Jews and everybody who doesn't agree with them, they imprison them—and the priests too; they set fire to the Reichstag, they're a pack of gangsters. No one has a right to say such things. A young man like you mustn't say he's a Nazi, even as a joke."

He smiled a knowing little smile, just to provoke her. He felt no antipathy towards the Nazis. They were a violent, dreary sort of people, who apparently wanted to devour everything they could lay hands on; well, how far they would go remained to be seen. A comical idea came into his mind:

"If there was a war, we should all be on a level."

"Ah, you're looking pleased," said Jeannine. "What have you got into your head now?"

"The stand-ups," he said, "are sick of standing up, they'll lie flat down in holes. I on my back, they on their faces; we'll be alike."

Too long had they bent over him, cleaned and scrubbed and rubbed him down with those competent hands of theirs, while he lay motionless, looking at their faces from the chin upwards, scabby nose-holes above protruding lips, and black line of eyebrows on the horizon; it would be their turn to lie down. Jeannine did not respond; she was less vivacious than usual. Gently she laid a hand upon his shoulder.

"You're nasty," she said. "Nasty, nasty, nasty."

It was the moment of reconciliation.

"What's for chow this evening?" he asked.

"Rice soup, mashed potatoes, and—this should make you happy—your favorite fish."

"And what sort of sweet? Plums?"

"I don't know."

"Sure to be plums," he said. "It was stewed apricots yesterday."

Not more than five minutes; he lay full length, filled his lungs the better to enjoy the respite, and viewed his little fraction of a world through his third eye. A dusty, fixed eye, dotted with brown spots; it tended to distort all movements slightly, making them look comically stiff and mechanical like early films. And, at that very moment, a woman in black on a trolley slid into it, across it, and vanished; a small boy was pushing the trolley.

"Who is it?" he asked Jeannine.

"I don't know," said Jeannine. "I think she's at the Villa Mon Repos—you know, the large red house by the sea."

"Where André had his operation?"

"Yes."

He drew a deep breath. The fresh, silky sunshine flooded

into his mouth, his nostrils, and his eyes. That soldier—what was he doing there? Did he want to breathe the air of sickness? The soldier passed into the mirror, stiff as a figure in a magic lantern, he looked worried; Charles raised himself on an elbow and watched him curiously; he walks, he is conscious of his legs and thighs, his feet carry his whole body. The soldier stopped and began to talk to a nurse. "Ah, it's some local man," thought Charles with relief. He talked gravely and nodded, looking rather grim; "he washes and dresses himself without help, he goes where he likes, he's always got to take care of himself, he feels quite strange because he is standing up; I had that experience. Something is going to happen to him. Tomorrow there will be war, and something is going to happen to all these people. But not to me. I am an object."

"Time's up," said Jeannine. She looked at him sadly, her eyes were full of tears. Feeble creature.

"Do we love our little doll?" he said.

"You know I do, yes."

"Don't shake me like you did on the way out."

"No."

The tears welled up and trickled down her pale cheeks. He eyed her mistrustfully. "What's the matter with you?"

She did not answer, she sniffed as she bent over him and smoothed his bedclothes; he could see into her nostrils.

"You're hiding something from me."

Still she did not answer.

"What are you hiding from me? You had an argument with Madame Gouverné, didn't you? Look here, I won't be treated like a child."

She stood up again and eyed him with distraught affection.

"You're going to be evacuated," she said, bursting into tears.

He did not understand, and said: "Me?"

"All the patients at Berck. It's too near the frontier."

He began to tremble. He grabbed Jeannine's hand and squeezed it. "But I want to stay."

"They won't leave anyone here," she said in a despondent tone.

He squeezed the hand with all his strength. "I won't go!" he said. "I won't go!"

She took her hand away without replying, went round to the back of the trolley, and began to push. Charles half rose and began to twist a corner of the coverlet.

"But where are they sending us? When are we to go? Will the nurses go too? Tell me."

She still did not answer, and he heard her sigh above his head. He fell back and said savagely:

"I've had it all the way now."

I won't look into the street. Milan is standing by the window, looking out; he has little hope. They aren't here yet, but their footsteps are shuffling round the houses. I can hear them. I bend over Marikka, and I say:

"Stand over there."

"Where?"

"Against the wall, between the windows."

"Why was I sent here?" she says.

I don't answer, and she goes on: "What are those shouts?"

I don't answer. Shuffling feet. The stealthy sound of them—shoo-shoo-shoo—all round the house. I sit down on the floor beside her. I feel so heavy now. I take her in my arms. Milan is at the window, absent-mindedly biting his nails. I say to him:

"Milan, come here; don't stay by the window."

He grunts, he leans out over the window-rail, he leans out deliberately. Shuffling feet. In five minutes they'll be here. Marikka puckers her little brows.

"What's that sound of footsteps?"

"The Germans."

"Ha?" says she, and her face clears. She listens submissively to the shuffling feet, just as she listens to my voice in class, or the rain, or the wind in the trees—just because it's there. I look at her, and she looks at me with untroubled eyes. Just that look—would that I could be absorbed into that uncomprehending, unforeseeing look. Would that I were deaf, that I might plunge into those eyes and read the sound in them. A sound devoid of sense, like the sound of moving leaves. I know it's the sound of shuffling feet. It's soft, and softly they will come, and they'll beat him to a jelly. There he stands, a tall strong man, looking out of the window; they will hold him in their outstretched hands, a poor limp wretch with a gaping, battered face; they will thrash him, stamp on him, and tomorrow he will shrink from looking at me. Marikka quivers in my arms.

"Are you afraid?" I ask her.

She shakes her head. She's not afraid. She looks solemn, as she does when I write on the blackboard, she watches my moving arm with parted lips. She tries so hard: trees and water, walking animals, people, and the letters of the alphabet. For the moment what has to be understood is the silence of these grown-up people, and the feet shuffling down the street. We are a small country. So they will come; they'll drive their tanks across our fields, they'll shoot our men—just because we are a small country. Pray God the French may come to our aid, pray God they don't desert us!

"There they are," says Milan.

I can't look at his face—only at Marikka's, because she does not understand. They're in our street, their feet are shuffling down our street, they shout our name, I hear them, I am here, sitting on the floor, heavy and rigid, Milan's revolver is in my apron pocket. He looks at Marikka's face: she opens her mouth, her eyes are pure, she doesn't understand.

He was walking along the street-car lines, looking at the

shops and laughing genially. He looked straight ahead of
him at the white street, blinked,· and thought: "So this is
Marseille." The shops were closed, the iron shutters lowered, the street deserted, but this was Marseille. He
stopped, put down his bag, took off his leather jacket and
slung it over his arm, then wiped his forehead and hoisted
the bag on to his back again. He longed for a chat with
someone. He said to himself: "I've got twelve fags, and a
cigar-end in my handkerchief." The car tracks sparkled,
the long white street dazzled him, and he added: "And a
bottle of red wine in my bag." He was thirsty and would
have liked to drink it, but he would have preferred to
drink a glass or two in a bar if only they hadn't all been
shut. "I wouldn't have believed it," said he. He walked
on between the car tracks, the street gleamed like a mirror
between the low dark houses. On the left there were a
number of shops, but what they sold one couldn't tell,
since the iron curtains were lowered; on his right were
houses, open-fronted and deserted, looking like railway
stations, and then from time to time a brick wall. But this
was Marseille.

"Where can they be?" asked Gros-Louis.

"Come in quick," shouted a voice.

At the corner of an alley there was a café still open. A
bruiser of a guy with a couple of stiff babes stood in the
doorway and shouted: "Come in quick"; and people Gros-
Louis had not noticed suddenly appeared from nowhere
and began to run towards the café. Gros-Louis ran too;
the other men jostled their way in, he tried to get in behind them, but the guy with the skirts clapped him on the
chest and said: "Get the hell out."

A boy in overalls had laid hold of a round table rather
larger than himself and was trying to shift it into the café.

"All right, old boy," said Gros-Louis, "I'm going. You
wouldn't be having a drop of liquor, would you?"

"I told you to beat it."

"I'm off," said Gros-Louis. "Ya don't need to be afraid;
I don't stick around where I ain't wanted."

The man turned his back on him, jerked the outside
latch off the door, and went inside, closing it behind him.
Gros-Louis eyed the door; in place of the handle there remained a small round hole with raised edges. He scratched
the back of his neck, and repeated: "I'm going, he needn't
be afraid." He approached the window, however, and tried
to peer into the café, but someone drew the inner curtains
and he could see no more. "I wouldn't have believed it,"
he said to himself. He could see the street to the right and
left of him as far as eye could reach, the shining car tracks,
and on them a derelict black car. "I wish I could get in
somewhere," said Gros-Louis. He wanted to buy a little
nip in some café, and have a little talk with the owner.
And he added, by way of explanation, scratching the top
of his head: "It isn't that I'm not accustomed to being out
of doors." But when he was out of doors, other people were
out of doors too, there were the sheep and the other
shepherds, which made for company anyway, and when
there was nobody, well—there was nobody, and that was
that. Whereas now he was outside, and everybody else
was inside, behind their walls and their locked doors. He
was quite alone outside, he and the little car. He tapped
on the café window and waited. No one answered; if he
had not seen them enter with his own eyes, he could have
sworn the café was empty. He said: "I'm going," and he
went; he began to feel queerly thirsty; he wouldn't have
imagined Marseille could be like this. He walked on. The
street surely smelt very stuffy. "Where am I going to sit
down?" he said to himself, and he heard a noise behind
him, like a flock of sheep on the move. He turned, and saw
in the distance a little crowd carrying flags. "Ah well, I'll
watch them pass," he said. And he recovered his good
humor. Just on the other side of the tracks there was a
sort of square, a fair-ground, with two little green huts

backed against a high wall; and he said to himself: "I'll sit
down there to watch them pass." One of the huts was a
shop, from which came a smell of sausage and fried potatoes. Gros-Louis saw an old fellow in a white apron raking
out a stove inside the shop.

"Hey, Pop! Give me some fried potatoes."

The old man turned. "Go to hell," he said.

"I've got some money," said Gros-Louis.

"Go to hell; I don't give a good God-damn for your
money, I'm shutting up."

He came out and began to turn a crank. An iron curtain
clattered downwards.

"It isn't seven o'clock yet," said Gros-Louis, shouting to
drown the clatter.

The old man did not answer.

"I thought you were shutting because it was seven
o'clock," shouted Gros-Louis.

The iron curtain descended to the ground. The old man
removed the crank, stood up, and spat.

"Look, screwball, you didn't see them coming, did you?
I ain't handin' out my chips free," said he, going back into
his hut. Gros-Louis contemplated the green door for a
moment, then he sat down in the middle of the fair-
ground, propped his back against his bag, and warmed
himself in the sun. He remembered that he had a hunk
of bread, a bottle of red, twelve fags, and a cigar-end, and
he said: "Well, let's have a bite." On the other side of the
tracks the men began to file past, waving their flags and
shouting and singing; Gros-Louis had pulled a knife out
of his pocket and munched as he watched them pass. Some
of them raised their fists, and others shouted: "Come and
join us!" He laughed and hailed them as they tramped
past; he rather liked noise and movement; it cheered him
up a bit.

He heard footsteps and turned round. A tall Negro was
approaching him, bare-armed and wearing a faded pink

shirt; his blue calico trousers flapped and flattened against
his lanky thighs at every stride. He did not seem in a hurry.
He stopped, and wrung out a bathing suit with his pinky-
brown hands. The water dripped on the dust in small
round patches. The Negro rolled the bathing suit into a
towel, and then stood nonchalantly watching the procession and whistled.

"Hi!" exclaimed Gros-Louis.

The Negro looked at him and smiled.

"What are they up to?"

The Negro swung towards him; he didn't seem in a
hurry.

"It's the dockers," he said.

"Are they on strike?"

"The strike's over," said the Negro. "But these guys
want to start it again."

"Ah—so that's it," said Gros-Louis.

The Negro looked at him for a moment in silence, he
seemed to be rallying his ideas. Finally he sat down on the
ground and began to roll a cigarette. He continued to
whistle.

"Where ya come from?" he asked.

"Prades," said Gros-Louis.

"Where's that?" said the Negro.

"Aha! So you don't know where Prades is," said Gros-
Louis with a laugh. They both laughed, and then Gros-
Louis explained: "I didn't like it any more."

"You looking for work?" said the Negro.

"I was a shepherd," explained Gros-Louis. "I kept sheep
on the Canigou. But I got fed up."

The Negro shook his head.

"There are no jobs here," he said severely.

"Oh, I'll find one," said Gros-Louis. He displayed his
hands. "I can do anything."

"There's no more work here," said the Negro.

They fell silent. Gros-Louis looked at the people filing

past and laughing. They shouted: "Hang him! Hang
Sabiani!" There were women with them; they were flushed
and disheveled, their jaws were open wide, but whatever
they were saying was drowned by the men's yells. Gros-
Louis was quite content, he now had company. What a
game! he thought. A fat woman passed among the throng,
her heavy breasts dangling as she walked. Gros-Louis
thought he could have had a pleasant little game with her;
he would have had a handful, too. The Negro burst out
laughing. He laughed so violently that the smoke of his
cigarette choked him. He laughed and coughed; Gros-
Louis clapped him on the back.

"Whatcha laughin' at?" he said, laughing too.

The Negro had recovered his gravity. "Dunno," he said.

"Have a drink," said Gros-Louis.

The Negro took the bottle by the neck and drank her
down. Gros-Louis drank too. The street was again deserted.

"Where did ya sleep?" asked the Negro.

"I don't exactly know," said Gros-Louis. "It was a sort
of square, with trucks under a tarpaulin. It smelt like coal."

"Got any money?"

"Could be."

The door of the café opened and a knot of men came
out. They stopped for a moment in the street, looking in
the direction of the departing strikers, shading their eyes
with their hands. Then some walked slowly away, lighting
cigarettes; others stayed around in little groups. One, a
red-haired, rather corpulent fellow, shook his fist at a
skinny guy beside him:

"We've got war up the butt, and you come and talk
about syndicalism!"

He was sweating, he wore no jacket, his shirt, with two
large damp patches under his armpits, was open at the
collar. Gros-Louis turned to the Negro.

"War?" he asked. "What war?"

"What we want is somewhere to sit down," said Daniel.

A green bench, set against the farm wall, under the open window. Daniel swung the gate open and entered the yard. A dog barked and leaped at them, dragging at his chain; an old woman appeared in the doorway of the house with a saucepan in her hand.

"Now then!" she said, brandishing the saucepan at the dog. "Are you going to shut up?"

The dog growled once or twice and lay down.

"My wife is a little tired," said Daniel, taking off his hat. "Might she sit on that bench?"

The old woman blinked dubiously; perhaps she did not understand French. Daniel repeated in a louder tone:

"My wife is a little tired."

The old woman turned to Marcelle, who was leaning against the gate, and her suspicions vanished.

"Of course the lady can sit down. That's what benches are for. And she won't wear ours out—it's been there long enough. Have you come from Peyrehorade?"

Marcelle also entered and sat down with a smile.

"Yes," she said, "we meant to get to the cliff, but it's rather far for me, at present."

The old woman winked knowingly. "Ah well," she said, "you've got to be careful just now."

Marcelle sank back against the wall, her eyes half-closed, with a little gurgle of contentment. The old lady looked at her with an appreciative eye, then turned to Daniel, nodded and smiled at him with an expression of respect. Daniel clutched the knob of his stick and smiled too. Everybody smiled, and the pregnant belly was safe there. A small boy came tottering out of the farmhouse, stopped dead, and looked dubiously at Marcelle. He wore no knickers; and his little buttocks were red and scabbed.

"I did so want to see the cliff," said Marcelle, peevishly.

"But there's a taxi at Peyrehorade," said the old woman. "It belongs to the Lamblin lad, the last house on the Bidasse road."

"I know," said Marcelle.

The old woman turned to Daniel and shook a finger at him. "Ah, monsieur, you must be very kind to your lady; you must always let her have her way just now."

Marcelle smiled. "He is kind," she said. "It was I who wanted to walk."

She stretched out an arm and stroked the boy's head. She had felt an interest in children for the last few weeks; it had come to her suddenly. She smelt them and touched them when they came within her reach.

"Is he your grandson?"

"He's my niece's boy; nearly four years old."

"A nice child," said Marcelle.

"When he behaves himself." The old woman added in an undertone: "Is it to be a boy?"

"Ah," said Marcelle, "I hope so."

The old woman laughed. "You must pray to St. Marguerite every morning."

A dense silence fell, angelic. All eyes were turned on Daniel. He leaned on his stick and looked down, with a modest, manly air.

"I'm going to trouble you still further, madame," he said politely. "Might I ask for a drink of milk for my wife?" He turned to Marcelle: "You would like a drink of milk, wouldn't you?"

"I'll go and get it," said the old woman. She disappeared into her kitchen.

"Come and sit down beside me," said Marcelle.

He sat down.

"How thoughtful you are!" she said, taking his hand. He smiled. She looked at him with a bewildered air, and he continued to smile, stifling a capacious yawn. And he thought: "Women oughtn't to be allowed to look quite so pregnant." The air was moist and breathless, with clotted smells adrift in it, like strands of seaweed; Daniel stared at the green and red glitter of a bush on the far side of the gate; there was foliage in his nostrils and in his mouth. Another fortnight. Fifteen green and glittering days, fifteen days of the country. He detested the country. A timid finger moved over his hand, as hesitant as a branch swaying in the wind. He looked down at the finger. It was white and rather plump, and it wore a wedding-ring. "She adores me," thought Daniel. Night and day that humble, insistent adoration percolated through his being like the living odors of the fields. He half-closed his eyes, and Marcelle's adoration melted into the rustling foliage, into the smell of manure and clover.

"What are you thinking about?" asked Marcelle.

"The war," replied Daniel.

The old woman returned with a bowl of foaming milk. Marcelle took it and drank deep draughts. Her upper lip protruded over the liquid in the bowl and absorbed it with a faintly clucking sound. The milk gurgled down her throat.

"That does one good," she said with a sigh. A white mustache had appeared above her mouth.

The old woman looked at her benignantly. "Milk fresh from the cow—that's the stuff for baby." They laughed a feminine laugh, and Marcelle got up, leaning against the wall:

"I feel quite rested," she said to Daniel. "We'll go on when you like."

"Good-by, madame," said Daniel slipping a bill into the woman's hand. "Thank you for your kind hospitality."

"I hope to see you again," said the old woman. "Go back slowly."

Daniel opened the gate and stood aside for Marcelle; she tripped over a large stone and nearly fell.

"Careful!" cried the old woman from behind them.

"Take my arm," said Daniel.

"I'm so clumsy," said Marcelle in confusion.

She took his arm; he felt her against him, a warm top-heavy figure. "And Mathieu actually desired the creature," he thought.

Dark hedges. Silence. Fields. A black line of pines on the horizon. With slow and ponderous gait the men were returning to the farms; they would sit at the long table and swallow their soup in silence. A herd of cows crossed the road. One of them took fright and broke into a prancing trot. Marcelle drew close to Daniel.

"Just imagine—I'm afraid of cows!" she said in a low tone.

Daniel squeezed her arm affectionately. "The devil with you," was what he thought. She drew a deep breath and was silent. He threw a sidelong glance at her and noticed her vague eyes, her sleepy smile, and her beatific expression. "That's done it," he thought with satisfaction. "She's off again." She was taken like this from time to time, when the kid stirred within her or an unfamiliar emotion shook her. She must think of herself as a sort of illimitable, pullulating entity, a kind of milky way. However, here were ten good minutes gained. "Here am I," he thought, "walking in the country, cows are passing by, and this large lady is my wife." He wanted to laugh; he had never seen so many cows in his life. "It's your own fault. You wanted a quick, high-powered catastrophe; and you've got it." They were walking slowly, like two lovers, arm in arm, and the flies were buzzing round them. An old man was leaning on a spade, motionless at the edge of his field; he watched them pass and smiled. At that moment Marcelle emerged from her torpor.

"Do you really believe that there's going to be a war?" she asked abruptly.

Her gestures had lost their aggressive angularity, they were now rather clumsy and languid. But she had kept her abrupt, emphatic voice. Daniel looked at the fields. Fields of what? He couldn't tell a cornfield from a field of beets. He heard Marcelle repeat:

"Do you?"

And he thought: "Oh for a war!" She would be a widow. A widow with a child and six hundred thousand francs in cash. Not to mention some memories of an incomparable husband: what more could she ask? He stopped abruptly; the prospect caught him by the throat; he gripped his stick and thought: "Oh God, if only war would come!" A thunderbolt that would shatter this smooth-faced world, plow the countryside into a quagmire, dig shell-holes in the fields, and fashion these flat monotonous lands into the likeness of a storm-tossed sea—war, the hecatomb of righteous men, the massacre of the innocents. "That translucent sky—they will smash it with their own hands. The hatred! And the terror And I—how I shall wallow in that sea of hatred!" Marcelle looked at him with surprise. He wanted to laugh.

"No, I don't believe there's going to be a war."

Children on the road, their shrill innocent voices and their laughter. Peace. The sun flickers in the hedges as it did yesterday, and as it will do tomorrow; the steeple of Peyrehorade appears at the turn of the road. Every object in the world has its smell, its long, pale evening shadow, and its individual future. And the sum of all these futures —is peace: it glows on the worm-eaten wood of that gate there, on that small boy's rosy neck; it can be read in his eager eyes, it rises from those sun-warmed beds of nettles, it is heard in the tolling of those bells. Men are gathered around smoking soup tureens, they break bread, they pour wine into glasses, they wipe their knives, and their daily gestures constitute peace. It is there, enmeshed in all those futures, as slow and obstinate as Nature herself; it is the everlasting return of the sun, the quivering immobility of the countryside, and the purpose of man's toil. Not a ges-

ture that does not evoke and express it, even the sound
of Marcelle's padding footsteps at my side, even the affectionate pressure of my fingers on Marcelle's arm. A hail
of stones through the window—"Get out! Get out!" Milan
only just had time to fling himself backwards. A raucous
voice shouted his name: "Hlinka! Milan Hlinka, get out!"
Someone began to chant: "The Czechs are lice in the German fur." The stones had rattled across the floor. A fragment of paving-stone smashed the mirror over the mantelpiece, another dropped on the table and shattered a bowl
of coffee. The coffee trickled across the oilcloth and began
to drip softly on to the floor. Milan stood with his back
against the wall, looking at the mirror, the table, and the
floor, while they yelled in German under the window. He
thought: "They've upset my coffee," and he picked up a
chair by its back. He was sweating. He swung the chair
above his head.

"What are you doing?" cried Anna.

"I'll smash their heads in if they come."

"Milan! You can't. You're not alone."

He put the chair down and gazed at the walls in bewilderment. It was no longer the room he knew. They had
disembowelled it; a red mist blurred his eyes; he thrust
his hands into his pockets and said to himself: "I'm not
alone. I'm not alone." Daniel thought: "I am alone." Alone
with his ensanguined dreams in a peace that reached beyond his vision. Tanks and guns and airplanes, fields pitted
with muddy holes—all this was no more than a miniature
witches' sabbath inside his head. That sky would never
be cloven; the future lay there, poised upon that countryside; Daniel was within it, like a worm in an apple. One
sole future. The future of all men; they have evolved it
with their own hands, very slowly, as the years rolled on,
and they have not left me the smallest place in it, nor the
meanest chance. Tears of rage welled into Milan's eyes,
and Daniel turned towards Marcelle—*my* wife, *my* future,

the only one remaining to me, since the world has decided for Peace.

Trapped like a rat! He had raised himself on his forearms and watched the shops file past.

"Lie down!" said Jeannine's imploring voice. "And don't toss about like that, you make me dizzy."

"Where are they going to send us?"

"I've told you I don't know."

"You know we are going to be evacuated, and you don't know where? Do you expect me to believe that?"

"I swear I haven't been told. Don't torment me."

"In the first place, who told you? Are you sure it isn't just a story? You would swallow anything."

"It was the superintendent," said Jeannine sorrowfully.

"And he didn't say where we are going?"

The bed was passing the Cusier fish-market; he slid, feet first, into a stale and acrid lavatory smell.

"Faster! This place smells like a messy little girl!"

"I—I can't go any faster. Little doll-baby, I beg you not to get excited, you'll upset yourself again." She sighed and said in an undertone: "I ought never to have told you."

"Of course not. And on the day of the move I should have been chloroformed or told I was being taken out for a picnic, eh?"

He lay down again as they passed the Nattier bookshop. He detested the Nattier bookshop, and its dirty yellow frontage. The old woman was always in the doorway, and clasping her hands as she saw him pass.

"You're shaking me! Be careful!"

Like a rat. Other people could get up, run away, and hide in a cellar or an attic. I'm just a parcel; they come and take me away.

"Will you have to stick the labels on, Jeannine?"

"What labels?"

"The luggage labels—this side up, fragile, please handle with care. One on my stomach, and one on my behind."

"Nasty," said she, "you're mean and nasty."

"O.K., that's enough! They'll send us by train, of course?"

"Certainly. How else?"

"On a hospital train?"

"I don't know," cried Jeannine. "I can't invent things—I tell you I don't know!"

"Don't shout. I'm not deaf."

The bed stopped abruptly, and he heard her blowing her nose.

"What's got hold of you? Are you stopping in the middle of the street? . . ."

The wheels began to roll over the cobbled streets again. "They have often told us we must avoid train journeys," he went on.

Disquieting sniffs above his head reduced him to silence; he was afraid she might begin to cry. The streets swarmed with invalids at that hour: a large man propelled by a weeping nurse would not be a decorous spectacle. But an idea came into his head, and he muttered:

"I loathe new places."

They made decisions, they took everything on themselves, they had health and strength and leisure; they voted and chose their leaders, they had the use of their legs, they ran about the earth with their pompous busy airs, they arranged the destiny of the world, and in particular that of the unfortunate sick persons, whom they treat like grown-up children. And here is the result—war, bloody war. Why should I pay for their imbecilities? They have just remembered my existence, and now they want to push me into their mess. They are going to pick me up by the arms and the legs and say: "Excuse us, we are at war," and they dump me in a corner like a sack of rubbish, so that I shan't have a chance of interfering with their sport of massacre. The question he had suppressed for the last half-hour suddenly rose to his lips. She would be only too happy, but no matter; this time it had to come out:

"You—will the nurses come with us?"

"Yes," said Jeannine. "Some of them."

"Will—you?"

"No," said Jeannine. "I shan't."

He began to tremble, and said hoarsely: "You mean to desert us?"

"My orders read Dunkirk hospital."

"Ah, well," said Charles. "One nurse is as good as another, I guess."

Jeannine did not answer. He sat up and looked about him. His head swung from left to right and right to left, it was all very tiring, and there was a dry tingling at the back of his eyes. A trolley-bed was trundling towards them propelled by a tall, elegant old gentleman. On it lay a young woman with a haggard face and golden hair, and a magnificent fur cloak spread over her legs. She glanced at him, dropped her head, and muttered a few words up into the old gentleman's face.

"Who is she?" asked Charles. "It's a long time since I've seen her."

"I don't know. I think she's a music-hall artiste. She got it in a leg and then an arm."

"Does she know?"

"What?"

"The patients, I mean—do they know?"

"No one knows, the doctor forbade us to tell anyone."

"That's a pity," he grinned. "She might be a little less haughty."

"I think a drop of Fly-tox is needed," said Pierre before getting into the carriage. "There is a strong smell of insects."

The Arab promptly sprayed a little insecticide over the white covers and cushions.

"There," he said.

Pierre frowned. "Hm!" he ejaculated.

Maud put a hand over his mouth. "Hush," she said with

an imploring look. "Hush! That'll be quite all right."

"Very well. But if you catch lice, don't come and complain to me about it."

He helped her up and then sat down beside her. Maud's slim fingers left a dry and living warmth in the hollow of his palm; she was always slightly feverish.

"Drive round the ramparts," he said curtly.

No matter how you look at it, poverty encourages vulgarity. Maud was vulgar; he hated her freemasonry with coachmen, porters, guides, and waiters; she always took their part, and even if they were caught red-handed in some iniquity, she managed to find excuses for them.

The driver whipped up his horse, and the cab clattered forwards.

"What old rattletraps they are," said Pierre with a laugh. "I'm always afraid of a spring breaking."

Maud leaned out and surveyed everything with large, solemn, conscientious eyes.

"It's our last drive."

"So it is," he said. "So it is."

She is feeling poetical because it is the last day, and we are sailing tomorrow. It was annoying; still, he preferred her contemplative to her vivacious mood. She was not pretty, and when she tried to display charm or animation, the result was immediately disastrous. All would be well, he thought. There would be next day, and the three days' crossing; and then, at Marseille, good night; they would each go their own way. He congratulated himself on having reserved a first-class berth; the four women would be traveling third class; he would invite her into his cabin when he wanted her, but she would never venture to come on to the first-class deck unless he fetched her.

"Have you reserved your seats in the autobus?" he asked.

Maud looked a little embarrassed. "As a matter of fact, we aren't taking the autobus. We are being driven in a car to Casa."

"Who is driving you?"

"A friend of Ruby's, a very nice old gentleman, he'll take us round by Fez."

The carriage had left Marrakech and was passing through the European town. In front of them, an expanse of desiccated decay stretched away into the distance, littered with eviscerated gasoline-cans and empty food-tins. The cab rattled on between great white cubes with gleaming windows; Maud put on her dark spectacles, Pierre winced under the strong sunlight. The cubes, decorously located side by side, stood poised upon that desert; a sudden wind would blow them all away. A signboard had been affixed to one of them, bearing the words: "Rue du Maréchal-Lyautey." But there was no street—merely a shaft of tarred desert between buildings. Three natives watched the carriage pass; the youngest had a wall-eye. Pierre sat up straight and fixed them with a steady look. Show your strength, that you may not have to use it—that was good policy, not only in a military sphere, it was a sound rule of conduct for colonists, and even for the mere tourist. No need to make a display of power; the point was never to lose grip—to stand, in fact, upright. His morning gloom had disappeared. Beneath the witless gaze of those Arabs, he felt he represented France.

"What shall we find when we get back?" said Maud suddenly.

He clenched his fists without replying. Fool! In a flash she had revived his gloomy mood. She persisted:

"War, perhaps. You'll have to go; and I shall be out of a job."

He hated to hear her talk about being out of a job, with that grim look, like any working man. After all, she played second violin in Baby's female orchestra, which toured the Mediterranean and the Near East, and could properly be described as an artist. He replied, with a gesture of irritation:

"Look here, Maud, don't let us talk about affairs. Just for once, do you mind. It's our last evening at Marrakech."

She snuggled up to him. "Yes—it's our last evening."

He stroked her hair; but there was still a bitter taste in his mouth. Not fear, not anything like it; he was not to be shaken, he *knew* he would never be afraid. It was a feeling of—disillusion.

The carriage was now driving under the ramparts. Maud pointed to a red door, above which could be seen the green fronds of a palm tree.

"Pierre! Do you remember?"

"What?"

"It's a month, to the very day. That's where we met."

"Ah, yes. . . ."

"Do you love me?"

She had a thin, rather bony little face, with large eyes and a sensitive mouth.

"Yes, I love you."

"You don't say it very nicely!"

He bent over her and kissed her.

The old gentleman looked very angry, he glared at them, contracting his heavy eyebrows. "A memorandum! Are these the only concessions!" Horace Wilson nodded, and thought: "Why does he pretend?" Didn't Chamberlain know there would be a memorandum? Hadn't everything been decided the day before? Hadn't they agreed on the whole performance when the two of them were left alone, except for that shyster of an interpreter, Dr. Schmitt?

"Put your arms round your little Maud. She's got the blues this evening."

He clasped her in his arms, and she began to talk in a sort of girlish whimper:

"You're not afraid of war, are you?"

An unpleasant shiver trickled down his neck. "My poor little girl—no, I'm not. A man is not afraid of war."

"Well, I bet Lucien was!" said she. "In fact, that's what put me off him; he was too yellow."

He leaned over her and kissed her hair, and he wondered why he suddenly wanted to slap her.

"Anyway," she continued, "how could a man look after a woman if he's always got the jitters?"

"He wasn't a man at all," he said quietly. "I am."

She took his face in her hands, sniffed at it, and went on: "Yes, you were a man, monsieur. With your black hair and black beard, I took you for about twenty-eight."

He drew back a little; he was feeling limp and stale, a sense of nausea rose from his stomach into his throat, and he did not know which disgusted him most—the shimmering desert, the red earth walls, or the woman in his arms. "How fed up I am with Morocco!" He longed to be at Tours, in his parents' house, in the early morning, with his mother to come and bring him his breakfast in bed. Well, you will go down to the press room, he said to Nevile Henderson, and you will kindly announce that, in response to Chancellor Hitler's request, I shall arrive at the Hotel Dreesen about twenty-four thirty o'clock.

"Driver!" he said. "Driver! Go back to the town by that gate."

"What's the matter?" asked Maud in astonishment.

"I'm sick of the ramparts," he said to her violently. "I'm sick of the desert, and I'm sick of Morocco."

But he soon controlled himself, and taking her chin between two fingers, he said: "If you are a good girl, we'll buy you a pair of Turkish slippers."

The war *was not* in the merry-go-round music, it *was not* in the swarming cafés of the rue Rochechouart. Not a breath of wind. Maurice was sweating, he felt Nénette's warm thigh against his own (another hand of cards and then O.K.); it *was not* in the fields, in the shimmer of the heated air above the hedge, in the clear white twittering of the birds, in Marcelle's laugh, *it had come forth in the desert,* round the walls of Marrakech. A red, hot wind whirled round the carriage, swept over the waves of the Mediterranean, and struck Mathieu in the face; Mathieu was drying himself on the deserted beach, and he thought: "Not even that"; and he felt the blast of war.

Not even that! It had grown a little cold, but he was not inclined to go in at once. One after another the people had left the beach; it was dinner-time. The sea itself was empty; it lay, like a solar desert, a vast expanse of fallen light, and the black water-ski plank shot through it like a shark's head.

"Not even that," thought Mathieu. She would knit, by the open window, while waiting for Jacques's letters. From time to time she would lift her head, with a feeling of vague hope, and she would look out at *her* sea. *Her* sea: a buoy, a diving-raft, a little water splashing against warm sand. A quiet little garden within the compass of humanity, with a few broad avenues and countless little paths. And each time she would resume her knitting with the same sense of disappointment, for this sea of hers would have altered. The inland country, bristling with bayonets and packed with guns, would have absorbed the seacoast; the water and the sand would have receded, each into its own melancholy existence. Barbed-wire entanglements streaking the white steps with starred shadows; guns on the promenade among the pines; sentries outside the villas; officers groping like blind men through that desolate watering-place. The sea would return to its seclusion. No bathing: the water, guarded by the military, would assume an official aspect by the seashore; the diving-raft and the buoy would no longer seem at any distance from the land; all the highways, traced by Odette upon the waves since childhood days, would have been effaced. But the open sea, the storm-swept, inhuman sea—its naval battles fifty miles off Malta, its clusters of ships sunk near

Palermo, its depths cloven by iron fish—the open sea would be omnipresent, would disclose its glacial menace everywhere, and the high seas would rise up at the horizon like a hopeless bastion. Mathieu sat up: he was now dry; he began to dust the sand off his bathing suit. "War must be a pain in the rear," he thought. And when it was over? Yet another sea. The sea of the vanquished? Or of the victors? In five years', ten years' time he would perhaps be here on a September evening, at this same time, sitting on this same sand, confronting that vast expanse of gelatin, the same red rays skimming the surface of the water. But what would he then see?

He got up and slipped on his robe. The pines on the promenade were black against the sky. He threw a last glance at the sea: war had not yet broken out; people were dining quietly in their villas; no guns, no soldiers, no barbed wire, the fleet at anchor off Bizerte or Toulon; it was still permissible to view the sea in splendor, the sea of the last evenings of peace. But it was inert and non-committal—an expanse of salt water, moving, but indicative of nothing. He shrugged his shoulders and walked up the stone steps; for some days past, his contacts with this world had dwindled. Smells had gone, the multifarious smells of the south; then tastes. And now the sea. "Like rats leaving a sinking ship." When the day of departure came, he would be quite desiccated, with nothing left to regret. He returned slowly to the villa, and Pierre jumped out of the carriage.

"Come along," said he. "You shall have your pair of slippers."

They entered the sooks. It was late; the Arabs were in a hurry to get to the Place Djemaa-el-Fnâ before sunset. Pierre felt in better humor; the bustle of a crowd had an enlivening effect on him. He looked at the veiled women, and when they returned his look, he preened himself in their admiring eyes.

"Look," said he. "There are some slippers."

There were all sorts of objects on the stall—a medley of fabrics, necklaces, and embroidered shoes.

"How pretty!" said Maud. "Do let us stop."

She plunged her hands into the jumble, and Pierre drew back a little; he did not want to provide the Arabs with the spectacle of a European inspecting feminine adornments.

"Choose anything you like," he said nonchalantly.

On the neighboring stall there were some French books for sale; he amused himself by turning them over. Mostly detective stories and film novels. On his right he could hear the click of rings and bracelets in Maud's fingers.

"Have you got what you want?" he asked her over his shoulder.

"I'm having a look," she replied. "I can't decide all at once."

He returned to the books. Under a pile of *Texas Jacks* and *Buffalo Bills,* he discovered a book containing photographs. It was a work by Colonel Picot, on facial wounds; the first pages were missing, the rest were tattered. His impulse was to put it down at once, but he was too late; the book had fallen open by itself. Pierre glimpsed an awful head; from nose to chin there was nothing but a void, no lips nor teeth; the right eye had gone, and the right cheek was seamed by a great scar. The tortured face retained a human intelligence and wore a sort of ghastly grin. Pierre felt an icy tingling all over the skin of his skull and wondered how on earth the book had found its way here.

"That's a grand book," said the shopkeeper. "Very interesting."

Pierre turned over the pages. Men without noses, eyes, or eyelids—their eyeballs bulging as in anatomical illustrations. He was fascinated, he looked at the photographs one by one, and he repeated to himself: "How did it get here?" The most frightful was a head without a lower jaw; the upper jaw had lost its lip and displayed a gum and four teeth. "He can see," he thought. "That fellow is alive." He raised his eyes: a mottled mirror in a gilded frame returned his reflection; he gazed at it horror-struck.

"Pierre," said Maud. "Come and look. I have found the very thing."

He hesitated; the book scorched his hands, but he could not force himself to drop it, to get away from it, to *turn his back* on it.

"I'm coming," he said.

He pointed to the volume and said to the shopman: "How much?"

The boy was pacing up and down the office like a caged animal. Irène was typing an interesting article on the evil effects of militarism. She stopped and raised her head.

"You're making me dizzy."

"I shan't go away," said Philippe. "I shan't go away until he has seen me. . . ."

She burst into a laugh. "What a fuss! So you want to see him? Well, he's there, on the other side of that door; just go on in and you'll see him."

"Right," said Philippe.

He took a step forward and stopped.

"I—no, that would be foolish, it would set him against me. Oh, Irène!—won't you go back and ask him? For the last time—I swear it's for the last time."

"You bother me," she said. "Why don't ya give up? Pitteaux is a dirty bastard; can't you understand that it's lucky for you he won't see you again? It would only do you harm."

"Harm!" he said ironically. "Is it possible to do me harm? It's quite clear you don't know my parents; they have all the virtues, all they left me was Evil."

Irène looked him in the eyes. "Do you suppose I don't know what he wants you for?"

The lad blushed but did not reply.

"And so, so what!" said she, with a shrug of her shoulders.

"Go and ask him again, Irène," said Philippe in an imploring tone. "Do. Tell him I'm just about to make a capital decision."

"He doesn't give a damn!"

"Go and tell him all the same."

She opened the door and entered without knocking. Pitteaux looked up grimly. "What is it?" he boomed.

She was not alarmed. "O.K., relax!" said she. "No need to shout. It's the boy; I'm sick of having him on my hands. Would you mind taking him on for a bit?"

"I have said no," said Pitteaux.

"He says he's going to make a capital decision."

"And what the hell do I care?"

"For God's sake, do something about it," she said impatiently. "I'm your secretary, not his nurse."

"All right," he said, with a glitter in his eyes. "Let him come in. He's going to make a capital decision, is he? A capital decision! Well, he'll find I shall undertake a capital execution."

She laughed derisively and returned to Philippe.

"Go in."

The lad hurried across the room, but on the threshold of the sanctum he stopped, in an impulse of respect, and she had to push him in. She shut the door behind him, came back, and sat down at her table. An angry hum of voices was promptly audible on the other side of the door. She began to type with an air of indifference. She knew the game was lost for Philippe. He pretended to be emancipated, and he had been fascinated by Pitteaux: Pitteaux had wanted to take advantage of that to *have* him—a case of pure vice; he wasn't even a homosexual. But at the last moment the kid got scared. Like all the rest of them, he wanted to get all he could for nothing. At the moment, he was begging Pitteaux to remain his friend, but Pitteaux had told him off properly. She heard him shout: "Get out of this. You're a little coward, a bourgeois, a wretched little rich boy who throws his weight about." She laughed and typed a few lines of the article. "Can one conceive any more sinister ruffians than the high-ranking officers who condemned Dreyfus?" "Oh, what's it all about?" she thought with amusement.

The door opened and then slammed. Philippe stood before her. He had been crying. He leaned over the desk and pointed a forefinger at Irène. "He's driven me frantic," he said, with a frenzied look on his face. "And no man has the right to do that." He flung his head back and burst into a shout of laughter. "You'll hear more of me soon."

"Don't get excited," sighed Irène.

The nurse shut down the lid of the trunk: twenty-two pairs of shoes—he certainly had made work for the boot-makers; when a pair showed signs of wear he had thrown it into the trunk and bought another—more than a hundred pairs of socks, with holes in the heels and at the great toes; six suits much creased from hanging in a wardrobe—the place was filthy, a veritable bachelor's den. She could quite well leave him for five minutes, so she slipped down the corridor into the can and lifted her skirts, leaving the door wide open in case of emergency. She sat with her ears on the alert, listening for the slightest sound. But Armand Viguier remained decorously extended, alone in his room, his yellow hands resting on the sheet, his gaunt head with its bristly gray beard and hollow eyes tipped backwards, and on his face a far-off smile. His skinny legs were outstretched beneath the sheet, his feet lay at an angle of eighty degrees to each other, with his toenails upturned—those horrible great toenails, which he pared with a pen-knife every three months, and which for the past twenty-five years had worn out all his socks. There were sores on his buttocks, despite the indiarubber cushion on which he lay, but they bled no longer: he was dead. On the night-table lay his spectacles, and his false teeth in a glass of water.

Dead. His life was there and everywhere, impalpable, complete, as full and hard as an egg, so compact that all the forces of the world could not have introduced an atom into it, so porous that Paris and the world traversed it; scattered at the four ends of France, and yet condensed at every point of space, a vast, motionless, vociferous country fair: shouts, laughter, the whistle of the locomotives, and the shrapnel-burst on May 6, 1917, the savage buzzing in his head when he fell between two trenches—all those sounds were there, but frozen; and the listening nurse could hear nothing but a trickle underneath her skirts. She got up, not pulling the flush out of respect for the dead, went back and sat by Armand's bed, passing through that fixed glare of sunlight that shone forever on a woman's face, by the Grande Jatte, on July 20, 1900, in the canoe. Armand Viguier was dead; his life was a thing adrift, enclosing agonies now motionless, striating the month of March 1922, and all its intercostal agony, with imperishable little jewels—the rainbow over the Quai de Bercy on a rainy Saturday evening, slippery pavements, two cyclists laughing as they rode past, the patter of rain on a balcony one stifling March afternoon, a tearful gypsy melody, drops of dew gleaming in the grass, and a flight of pigeons on the Piazza San Marco. She unfolded the newspaper, adjusted her spectacles, and began to read: "Latest news: no meeting of M. Chamberlain with Chancellor Hitler this afternoon." She thought of her nephew who would certainly be called up, put the paper down beside her, and sighed. Peace was there, like the rainbow, like the sunlight on the Grande Jatte, like the glimmer of a fair-skinned arm. The peace of 1939 and 1940 and of 1980, the great peace of mankind: the nurse set her lips and thought: "It's war"; she stared fixedly into vacancy, and her gaze pierced through that peace. Chamberlain shook his head and said: "I'll do what I can, of course, but I have no great hopes."

Horace Wilson felt an uneasy shiver down his back and said to himself: "Can he be sincere?" and the nurse thought: "My husband in '14, in '38 my nephew; I shall have lived between two wars." But Armand Viguier knows that peace has just been born; Chantal asks him: "Why did you, with your ideas, join the army?" and he answers: "To ensure that this should be the last war." May 27, 1919. The very last. He listens to Briand talking, a small figure on the platform, under a clear sky; he is engulfed in the crowd of pilgrims, peace has come to them, they touch and see it, and they shout: "Peace!" Peace everlasting. He sits in the Luxembourg garden, on an iron chair; he can now look everlastingly at the chestnut trees in bloom, the war has receded into the past, he stretches out his skinny legs, he watches the children at play, they, he thinks, will never know the horrors of war. The coming years will be a royal thoroughfare, time spreads out like a fan. He looks at his aging hands, now warmed by the sunshine, he smiles and thinks: "It's thanks to us. No more war. Neither in my lifetime nor in time to come." May 22, 1938. Peace everlasting. Armand Viguier was dead, and no one could now declare him right or wrong. No one could change the immutable future of his dead life. One day more, one single day, and all his hopes might well collapse; he would discover that his life had been crushed between two wars, between the hammer and the anvil. But he had died on September 23, 1938, at four o'clock in the morning, after seven days' unconsciousness, and he had taken peace away with him. Peace, the whole peace, the peace of all the world, the peace that passeth all understanding. There was a ring at the front doorbell; she started, that must be the cousin from Angers, his sole relative, who had been

notified by telegram on the previous day. She opened the
door to a little woman in black, with a ratlike profile and
disheveled hair.

"I am Madame Verchoux."

"Ah yes, we were expecting you, madame."

"Can I see him?"

"Certainly. There he is."

Mme Verchoux went up to the bed, looked at the hollow
cheeks and sunken eyes.

"He is greatly changed," she said.

Half past twenty o'clock at Juan-les-Pins, half past
twenty-one at Prague.

"Stay tuned to this station. An important communication will follow immediately. Stand by. An important communication . . ."

"All over," said Milan.

He was standing in the window recess. Anna did not
reply. She bent down and began picking up the broken
glass, putting the largest pieces in her apron, and then
threw it all out of the window. The lamp had been
smashed, the room was plunged in bluish darkness.

"Now," she said, "I'll give the floor a thorough sweep."
She repeated: "A thorough sweep"—and began to
tremble.

"They'll take everything we have," she said, weeping;
"they'll break everything, and they'll throw us out."

"Be quiet," said Milan. "And for God's sake, don't cry."

He went up to the radio, turned the knobs, and the lights
came on.

"It's all right," he said in a tone of satisfaction.

The shrill, mechanical voice suddenly filled the room:

"Stand by, please. An important communication will
follow immediately. Stand by, please. A very important
communication . . ."

"Listen," said Milan in an altered voice. "Listen."

Pierre was striding along. Maud ran beside him clutching her slippers under her arm. She was overjoyed.

"They're just lovely," she said to him. "Ruby will be mad with jealousy; she bought some at Fez that aren't half so nice. And they're so convenient. You slip them on as you jump out of bed, you don't even need to touch them, ordinary shoes are such a bother. You just have to get the knack of keeping them on, by arching the foot, I think; I'll ask the maid at the hotel. She's an Arab."

Pierre still did not answer. She glanced at him uneasily and continued:

"You ought to have bought some too, you're always running about the room in bare feet; they're just as useful for men, you know."

Pierre stopped right in the middle of the street.

"Shut up!" he bellowed.

"What's the matter?"

"They're just as useful for men," said Pierre, mimicking her words. "Look here, you know quite well what I was thinking about all the time. And you were thinking about it too," he added grimly. He passed his tongue over his lips and smiled ironically. Maud was about to speak, but she looked at him, frozen into silence.

"The trouble is that people won't look reality in the face," he continued. "Women especially; when they are thinking of one thing, they promptly talk about another. Isn't that so?"

"But, Pierre," said Maud frantically, "you're crazy. I don't understand. What do you suppose I'm thinking about? What are you thinking about?"

Pierre produced a book from his pocket, opened it, and shoved it under her nose:

"That," he said.

It was a photograph of a mutilated face, noseless, with a bandage over one eye.

"You—you bought that?" she asked in stupefaction.

"Well, yes," said Pierre. "And so what! I'm a man and I'm not afraid; I want to know what I shall look like next year."

He shook the photograph in Maud's face.

"Will you love me when I look like that?"

She did not want to understand, she wished he would say no more.

"Answer. Will you love me?"

"Don't!" she said. "Please don't."

"Those men," said Pierre, "live in an institution on the Val-de-Grâce. They go out at night only, and always masked."

She tried to take the book away from him, but he snatched it from her hands and put it in his pocket. She looked at him with quivering lips, afraid of bursting into sobs.

"Oh, Pierre," she said gently. "So you're afraid!"

He fell abruptly silent and eyed her vacantly. For a moment they stood motionless, then he said dully:

"All men are afraid. All. A man who isn't afraid isn't normal; fear has nothing to do with courage. And you haven't the right to judge me, because you don't have to fight."

They walked on in silence. And she thought: "He's a coward." She looked at his high, tanned forehead, his Florentine nose and handsome mouth, and thought: "He's a coward. Just as Lucien was. I have no luck."

Odette's head and shoulders emerged into the light, the rest of her was still shadowed by the half-lit dining-room, she stood with her elbows on the balcony, looking at the sea; Gros-Louis was thinking: "What a war!" He walked on and on, the red light of the setting sun flickering on his hands and beard; Odette felt, upon her back, the dusky, homely room, the white tablecloth glimmering in the darkness, but she stood in the light—light, knowledge,

and war came in through her eyes, it would soon be time
for him to go; the electric light congealed into egg-yellow
patches against the fluidity of dying day. Jeannine had
turned the switch; Marcelle's hands were moving back
and forward in the yellow lamplight, she asked for the
salt and her hands threw shadows on the tablecloth; Daniel
said: "It's all bluff, if we hold on he'll put his cards on the
table." The light rasps the eyes like sandpaper—it's like
that in the south, up to the last minute. Twelve o'clock and
then night falls, Pierre babbled on, he wanted to make her
believe that he had recovered himself, but she walked
beside him in silence, and the look in her eyes was as inexorable as the light. When they arrived in the square, she
was afraid he might suggest she should spend the night
with him, but he took off his hat and said coldly: "As we
must get up early tomorrow and you will have packing
to do, you had better go back and sleep with your little
girl-friends." She replied: "Yes." And he said: "Till tomorrow, then." "Till tomorrow," she said; "tomorrow on
the boat."

"Stand by, please, a very important communication will
follow." Odette started and said: "You frightened me. Is
Jacques with you?" Charles sighed; Mathieu said no. No,
said Maurice; when ya gotta, ya gotta. He had taken the
key off the board, the place smells like a privy again, it's
too disgusting! It's Mme Salvador's puppy, said Zézette,
she throws him out when she has her guys up and he
drops it all over for amusement.

They went upstairs: "Stand by, please, an important
communication. . . ." Milan and Anna leaned over the
radio, noises of victory came through the windows; "Turn
it down a bit," said Anna, "you mustn't provoke them";
silence, the click of forks, a lingering hiss of tearing fabric
from the radio. Anna started and clutched Milan's arm.

"Citizens!

"The Czechoslovakian Government has decided to proclaim a general mobilization; all men of less than forty years of age and specialists of every kind must come forward at once. All officers, non-commissioned officers, and soldiers of the reserve and the second reserve of all ranks, and all men on leave, must report at their depots without delay. All must wear their oldest civilian clothes and be provided with their military papers and with food for two days. The final date for rejoining their respective units is four thirty a.m.

"All vehicles, automobiles, and airplanes are hereby mobilized. The sale of gasoline is authorized only on permit issued by the military authorities.

"Citizens! The decisive moment has arrived. Success depends on each and all of us. Let everyone put all his strength at the service of our country. Be brave and loyal. Our struggle is a struggle for justice and liberty.

"Long live Czechoslovakia!"

Milan stiffened, he was ablaze, he laid his hands on Anna's shoulders, and he said:

"At last! It's all right, Anna. It's all right."

A woman's voice repeated the decree in Slovak, they understood nothing more except a few words now and then, but it sounded rather like a military band. Anna repeated: "At last! At last!" Tears rolled down her cheeks. Then they once more understood: *"Die Regierung hat entschlossen,"* it was in German, Milan turned the knob all the way around, and the radio began to roar, the voice crushed their loathsome songs and sounds of festival against the walls, the voice would issue from the windows, smash the Jägerschmitts' windowpanes, the voice would penetrate into Munich drawing-rooms, into little family assemblages, and freeze their very bones. The smell of dog and of sour milk had been there awaiting him, he inhaled it into his very being, and with the sweep of a broom it cleansed him from the pretty little perfumes of the rue Royale; this was the smell of penury, the smell that was his own. Maurice stood motionless outside his room, while Zézette slipped the key into the lock; and Odette said gaily: "Come along to dinner, Jacques, there's a surprise for you." He felt firm and strong, he had re-entered the world of anger and revolt; on the second floor the children were yelling because their father had come home drunk; in the next-door room could be heard the pattering footsteps of Maria Pranzini, whose husband, a tiler, had fallen from a roof last month; sounds and colors and smells, all had an air of *reality;* he had re-entered the world of war.

The old gentleman turned to Hitler, he looked at that evil, infantile face, the face of a human fly, and he was stricken to his very soul. Ribbentrop had appeared, he said a few words in German, and Hitler made a sign to Dr. Schmitt. "We are informed," said Dr. Schmitt in English, "That Monsieur Beneš's Government has just ordered a general mobilization." Hitler flung out his arms without a word, like a man lamenting that the event has proved him right. The old gentleman smiled amiably, and a red gleam came into his eyes. A gleam of war. He had only to sulk like the Führer, he had only to fling out his arms with an air of "There you are!" and the pile of plates that he had been balancing for the last seventeen days would crash on the floor. Dr. Schmitt eyed him curiously; it must indeed be tempting to drop a pile of plates after balancing them for seventeen days, and he thought: "Here is the historic moment, the last appeal; the naked will of an elderly London businessman." The Führer and the elderly gentleman looked at each other in silence, and an interpreter was no longer needed. Dr. Schmitt stepped back.

He had sat down on a bench in the Place Gélu and put the banjo beside him. It was dark and blue beneath the plane trees, bands were playing, dusk had fallen, the straight black masts of the fishing-boats seemed to rise out of this earth, and on the far side of the harbor countless windows flashed. A boy was spurting water from the foun-

tain; on the next bench some other Negroes sat down and
hailed him. He was not hungry, he was not thirsty, he had
bathed behind the pier, he had met a large hairy fellow
who seemed to have fallen from the moon and who had
stood him a drink, all of which he had enjoyed. He took
the banjo out of its case, he felt impelled to sing. For one
instant, one sole instant, he coughs, he clears his throat, he
is going to sing; Chamberlain, Hitler, and Schmitt were
awaiting war in silence, and in a moment war would enter;
his foot had swollen, but in an instant he would wrench it
out of the shoe; Maurice, seated on the bed, was tugging
at his foot; in a second or so Jacques would have finished
drinking his soup; Odette would no longer hear that irri-
tating little crackle of fireworks, the sizzle of rockets before they went off; in an instant suns would swirl upwards
to the ceiling, and the voice would rise, richly sentimental,
through the foliage of the plane trees—in that one instant
Mathieu ate, Marcelle ate, Daniel ate, Boris ate, Brunet
ate, their instantaneous souls were brimming with clammy
little joys, in that one instant, war—war that Pierre
dreaded, Boris accepted, and Daniel welcomed—would
enter clad in steel, the great war of the Stand-ups, the
white men's crazy war. In that instant: it had exploded
in Milan's room, it was pouring out of all the windows, it
surged into the Jägerschmitts' abode, it prowled round the
ramparts of Marrakech, it breathed upon the sea, it
crushed the buildings in the rue Royale, it filled Maurice's
nostrils with the smell of dog and sour milk; in the fields
and cowsheds and farmyards it *did not exist,* but it played
heads or tails between two pier glasses in the wainscoted
saloons of the Hotel Dreesen. The old gentleman passed
his hand over his forehead and said in a toneless voice:
"Well then, if you agree, we will discuss the clauses of
your memorandum." And Dr. Schmitt understood that in-
terpreters were once more needed.

Hitler approached the table, and the clear, resonant

voice rose into the translucent air; on the fourth floor of the Massilia Hotel a woman on her balcony heard it, and she said: "Gomez, come and listen to the Negro singing, it's delightful." Milan thought of his leg, and his joy collapsed, he squeezed Anna's shoulder: "They won't want me, I am no good for anything now." The Negro sang on. Armand Viguier was dead, his two pale hands lay outstretched on the sheets, the two women sat beside his bed, discussing events, they had taken to each other at once. Chamberlain said: "As regards the first clause, I have two objections," and the Negro sang: *"Bei mir, bist du schön";* which means: "You're for me the fairest of them all."

Two women stopped, he knew them, Anina and Dolorès, two whores from the rue du Lacydon, Anina said: "Hey! Singing, huh?" but he did not answer, he sang on, and the women smiled at him; Sarah called out impatiently: "Gomez, Pablo, come here, what are you up to? There's a Negro singing so delightfully."

Saturday, September 24

AT CRÉVILLY, on the stroke of six o'clock, Daddy Croulard entered the gendarmerie and knocked on the office door. He thought: "They've waked me up." He thought he would say to them: "Why have I been waked up?" Hitler was asleep, Chamberlain was asleep, snoring shrilly through his nose, Daniel was sitting on his bed streaming with sweat, and he thought: "It was just a nightmare!"

"Come in," said the gendarmerie lieutenant. "Ah, it's you, Daddy Croulard? Well, you'll have to be getting busy."

Ivich moaned faintly and turned on her side.

"The boy woke me up," said Daddy Croulard. He looked at the lieutenant venomously and said: "It must be pretty important. . . ."

"Ah, Daddy Croulard," said the lieutenant, "you must grease your boots."

Daddy Croulard didn't like the lieutenant. He said: "What's all this about boots? I haven't got any boots, I've only got sabots."

"You'll have to grease your boots," repeated the lieutenant. "We're in for it."

Without his mustache he would have looked like a girl. He wore eyeglasses, and his cheeks were as pink as those of the schoolmistress. He was leaning forward with his arms apart, the tips of his fingers resting on the table. Daddy Croulard looked at him and thought: "This is the man that had me waked up."

"Did he tell you to bring the pot of paste?" said the lieutenant.

Daddy Croulard was holding the pot of paste behind his back; he silently displayed it.

"And the brushes?" asked the lieutenant. "You must hurry. You haven't got time to go home."

"The brushes are in my blouse," said Daddy Croulard gravely. "I was waked up all of a sudden, but I'd never forget the brushes."

The lieutenant handed him a roll of paper. "You will put one on the front of the town hall, two on the main square, and one on the notary's house."

"Maître Belhomme's? It's forbidden to put placards on his house."

"Don't make a damn," said the lieutenant. He looked alert, but rather nervous as he added: "I'll take the responsibility for that, and for everything else."

"I suppose it's mobilization at last."

"I should say so," said the lieutenant. "There's going to be a scrap, Daddy Croulard, there's going to be a scrap."

"Is there?" said Daddy Croulard. "Well, I fancy you and I will stay at home."

There was a knock at the door, and the lieutenant opened it smartly. It was the mayor. He was in sabots, but with his scarf across his blouse. He said: "What's this the boy told me?"

"Here are the notices," said the lieutenant.

The mayor put on his spectacles and unrolled the notices. He read in an undertone: "General Mobilization," and slammed the notices on to the table as though he were afraid of scorching his fingers. He said: "I was in the fields; I went home to get my scarf."

Daddy Croulard reached out a hand, rolled up the notices, and put the roll under his blouse. He said to the mayor: "I wondered why they woke me up so early."

"I went home to get my scarf," said the mayor. He looked at the lieutenant uneasily and said: "It says nothing about requisitions."

"There's another notice about that," said the lieutenant.

"Great balls of fire!" said the mayor. "So that's going to start again."

"I've been through one war," said Daddy Croulard. "Fifty-two months and not a scratch." He crinkled his eyes in glee at the recollection.

"That's all right," said the mayor. "You did the other one, you won't do this one. Besides, you don't need to worry about requisitions."

The lieutenant tapped authoritatively on the table. "Well, get on with it."

The mayor wore a bewildered look. He had slipped his hands into his scarf and tried to look important. "The drummer is ill," he explained.

"I can play the drum," said Daddy Croulard. He smiled. For ten years it had been his ambition to play the drum.

"Drum?" said the lieutenant. "You'll have the tocsin rung —that's what you'll do."

Chamberlain was asleep, Mathieu was asleep, the Kabyle put the ladder against the bus, hoisted the trunk to his shoulder, and scrambled up without using the rungs. Ivich was asleep; Daniel swung his legs out of bed, a bell echoed in his head; Pierre looked at the pink and black soles of the Kabyle's feet and thought: "It's Maud's trunk." But Maud wasn't there, she was to leave a little later with Doucette, France, and Ruby in the car of a very rich old gentleman in love with Ruby. At Paris, Nantes, and Mâcon men were pasting white notices on walls; the tocsin was ringing at Crévilly; Hitler was asleep, Hitler was a little four-year-old child, wearing his best suit; a black dog passed, he tried to catch it in his butterfly-net; the tocsin rang, Mme Reboulier awoke with a start and said:

"There's something burning."

Hitler was asleep, he was slitting his father's tousers into narrow strips with a pair of nail scissors. Leni von Riefenstahl came in, picked up the strips of flannel, and said: "I'll make you eat them in a salad."

The tocsin rang and rang and rang. Maublanc said to his wife: "I bet it's the sawmill that's caught fire."

He went out into the street. Mme Reboulier, in a pink nightdress, peered through the shutters, saw him pass and hail the postman, who was running down the street. Maublanc shouted: "Hi! Anselm!"

"It's mobilization," shouted the postman.

"What? What did he say?" Mme Reboulier asked her husband, who had now rejoined her. "It's not a fire, then?"

Maublanc looked at the two notices and read them in an undertone, then turned and went back home. His wife was on the doorstep, and he said to her: "Tell Paul to harness the cart." He heard a noise and turned round; it was Chapin, on his cart; he said to him: "Hullo! Where are you off to?" Chapin looked at him without answering. Maublanc looked at the back of the cart; there were two oxen lumbering behind it, haltered to the back. Said he in an undertone: "Damned fine beasts!" "You can afford to say so," said Chapin wrathfully, "damned fine beasts they are." The tocsin rang, Hitler slept, old Fraigneau said to his son: "If they take the two horses and you, how am I to carry on?" Nanette knocked at the door and Mme Reboulier said to her: "Is that you, Nanette? Go to the square and see why they're ringing the tocsin." And Nanette answered: "But doesn't Madame know? It's general mobilization."

Just another morning. Mathieu thought: "Just another morning." Pierre had elbowed his way to the window and was looking out at the Arabs, sitting on the ground or on multicolored trunks, waiting for the Ouarzazat car; Mathieu had opened his eyes, which felt limp and clammy in their sockets, the eyes of a new-born baby, still sightless, and he thought: "What's the good of it all?" as he did every morning. A morning of terror, an arrow of fire aimed at Casablanca, at Marseille, the autobus vibrated, the engine began to revolve, the driver on the outside seat, a tall fellow wearing a beige cloth cap with a leather visor, composedly finished his cigarette. He thought: "Maud despises me." A morning like all other mornings, stagnant and blank, a pompous, daily ceremony with brass bands and bugles and a public sunrise. In other days there had been other mornings; something had begun; Mathieu leaped out of bed, his eyes steady and his mind alert, as though awakened by a trumpet-call. Nothing now began, there was no task to undertake. And yet he would have to get up, join in the ceremony, find his way through the enveloping heat, and perform all the gestures of the cult, like a priest who has lost his faith. He slid his legs out of bed, stood up, and took off his pajamas. "What's the good of it all?" Then he lay back on the bed, naked, his hands beneath his head, peering through the white haze at the ceiling. "I'm a washout. An utter washout. I once used to carry the days upon my back, I carried them along from one to the next; now they carry me." The autobus throbbed and clattered under his feet, the floor grew hot, he felt as though the soles of his shoes were cracking, Pierre's great cowardly heart throbbed and hammered against the warm cushions, the window was scorching to the touch, and yet he felt frozen; he thought: "This is the beginning." The end would be a hole near Sedan or Verdun, and this was the beginning. She had said to him: "So you are a coward," and eyed him with contempt. Once again he saw the grave, flushed face, the dark eyes and thin lips, his heart turned over, and the autobus shot forward. It was still very chilly; Louisa Corneille, the sister of the grade-crossing guard, who had come from Lisieux to help her sick sister keep house, went out to lift the gates and said: "It's pretty nippy." She was feeling glad because she was engaged. She had been engaged for two years, but every time she thought of it, she felt glad. She began to turn the crank, then suddenly stopped. She was sure there was someone on the road behind her. She had not looked as she came out, but she was sure. She turned and caught her breath; there were more than a hundred barrows, carts, ox-wagons, and ancient carriages waiting, motionless, in single file. The farm boys were sitting stiffly on their drivers' seats, whip in hand and grimly silent. Others were on horseback, others had come on foot, dragging a cow behind them at the end of a rope. It was so comical a sight that she took fright. She hurriedly turned the crank and stepped briskly back to the side of the road. The drivers whipped up their horses, and the vehicles filed past her; the car rolled through a land of long, red steppes, a swarm of Arabs huddled at their backs. Pierre said: "Dirty trash! I'm never comfortable when I feel them behind me, I keep on wondering what they're up to." Pierre flung a glance into the far end of the car; there they lay in silence, their faces mottled green and gray, their eyes closed. A veiled woman had collapsed on her back, between the bags and bundles; her closed eyelids were visible beneath her veil. "How tiresome!" he thought. "They'll start in to be sick in five minutes, these fellows have got no stomachs." Louisa recognized them as they passed, they were lads of Crévilly, all lads of Crévilly, she could have put a name to each of them, but they did not look as usual—that fat, red-faced fellow was young Chapin, she had danced with him at the Saint-Martin, and she cried: "Hi! Marcel, you're very stuck-up today!" He turned and looked at her savagely. She added: "Off to the wedding, eh?" He said: "By God, yes. Off to the wedding!" The cart jolted across the rails, followed by two sleek oxen. Other carts passed; she

watched them, shading her eyes with her hand. She recognized Maublanc, Tournus, Cauchois; they ignored her
and passed on, erect in their seats, carrying their whips like
scepters, looking like angry monarchs. Her heart contracted, and she shouted to them: "Is it war?" But no one
answered. They passed in their jolting, rocking rattletraps,
the oxen following with comic dignity; the vehicles disappeared one after another round the bend in the road,
she stood for a moment with her hand arched over her
eyes, looking into the rising sun; the autobus sped like the
wind, roaring round the corners; she thought of Jean
Matrat, her fiancé, who was doing his service at Angoulême, in a Pioneer regiment; the carts reappeared like flies
on the white road, sticking to the side of the hill; the autobus plunged into a brown, rocky gulley, turned and turned
again, and at every corner the Arabs tumbled over one
another and squealed pathetically. The veiled woman suddenly sat up, and her mouth, invisible under the white
muslin, emitted the most appalling imprecations; she brandished two arms as thick as your thigh, at the end of which
danced two graceful well-formed hands with painted nails;
finally she tore off her veil, leaned over the door groaning,
and began to vomit. "That's the last straw," said Pierre to
himself; "they'll be sick all over us." The carts seemed motionless, looking as if they were glued to the road. Louisa
watched them for a while; they were moving, they were
moving all the same; one by one they reached the summit
of the hill and then became invisible. Louisa dropped her
hand, her dazzled eyes blinked, and she went in to the
children. Pierre thought of Maud, Mathieu thought of
Odette; he had dreamed of her; they were standing with
their arms round each other singing the Barcarolle from
The Tales of Hoffmann on the balcony of the Provençal.
At the moment he was lying naked on his bed, sweating
as he looked up at the ceiling, and Odette kept him company. "If I am not dead of boredom, I owe it to her." A

white haze quivered in his eyes, a faint affection still quivered in his heart. A white affection, the sad little affection
that comes with the awakening hour, a pretext to remain
lying on one's back for a few moments more. In five minutes cold water would flow on to his neck and into his eyes,
frothing soap would crackle in his ears, tooth-paste would
smear his gums, he would feel no more affection for anyone. Colors, lights, smells, sounds. And then words, polite
words, serious words, sincere words, funny words—words
all day until evening. Mathieu—pah! Mathieu was merely
a future. There's no future now. There's no Mathieu now
to think of it, between midnight and five o'clock in the
morning. Chapin thought: "Two such fine animals." Who
cared about the war, anyway? But those beasts, he had
looked after them for five years, he had gelded them himself, it would break his heart to lose them. He lashed at his
horse, and pulled him towards the left; his cart slowly
overtook Simenon's. "What are you up to?" asked Simenon.
"I'm sick of all this," said Chapin: "I want to get there."
"You'll tire your oxen out," said Simenon. "Don't care if
I do," said Chapin. He wanted to get past them all; he
stood up, clicked his tongue, and shouted: "Hue! Hue!"
He slipped past Popaul's cart, past Poulaille's wagon. "Are
you racing us?" asked Poulaille. Chapin did not reply, and
Poulaille shouted after him: "Careful you don't wear out
your oxen!" Chapin thought: "I wish they'd drop dead."
They whipped it up; Chapin was now ahead, pursued by
the others, all whipping up their horses; someone was
knocking, Mathieu had got up, he was rubbing his eyes;
someone was knocking; the autobus swerved to avoid an
Arab on a bicycle carrying a large veiled Mohammedan
woman on the handlebars. SOMEONE WAS KNOCKING;
Chamberlain started up and said: "Hullo! Who is it? Who's
knocking?" and a voice replied: "It's seven o'clock, Your
Excellency." At the entrance to the barracks there was a
wooden barrier. A sentry stood on guard in front of it.

Chapin tugged at the reins and shouted: "Hey, you there!"
"Well?" said the sentry; "well? Where d'ya come from, eh?"
"Just lift that up," said Chapin, pointing to the barrier.
"I've no orders," said the soldier. "Where do you come
from?" "Lift that up, I tell you."

A sergeant emerged from the guard-post. All the carts
had halted; he contemplated them for a moment, then let
out a whistle. "What the hell are you doing here?" he
asked.

"We're mobilized, of course," said Chapin. "What's the
matter—ya don't want us any more, maybe?"

"Have you got your papers?" asked the sergeant. Chapin
fumbled in his pockets; the sergeant eyed all those silent,
grim young fellows, motionless on their seats, holding
their whips as though they were presenting arms, and felt
proud without quite knowing why. He took a step forward
and shouted: "What about you others—have you got your
papers too? Let me see your army book." Chapin had discovered his army book. The sergeant took it and turned
over the pages. "Well," he said, "you've got Form 3, you
silly bastard. You were in too much of a hurry, wait till
next time."

"I tell you I'm mobilized," said Chapin.

"You know better than I do, I suppose," said the sergeant.

"Yes," said Chapin angrily. "I read the notices."

Behind them the others were getting restive; Poulaille
shouted: "Look here, have you finished? We want to come
in."

"The notices?" said the sergeant. "Look, here's your
notice. You've only got to look at it if you can read."
Chapin laid down his whip, jumped to the ground, and
walked up to the wall. There were three notices. Two in
colors: "Join or rejoin the colonial army"; and a third that
was entirely white: "Immediate call-up of certain cate-
gories of reservists." He read slowly, in an undertone, and

said, wagging his head: "That isn't the one that was put up in our village." Maublanc, Poulaille, Fraigneau had got off their carts, they looked at the notice, and they said: "That isn't our notice."

"Where do you come from?" asked the sergeant.

"From Crévilly," said Poulaille.

"Well," said the sergeant, "I've got an idea that there's a prize fathead at the Crévilly gendarmerie. Anyhow, give me your army books and come along to the lieutenant."

On the main square at Crévilly, in front of the church, a throng of women clustered round Mme Reboulier, who was such a friend to all the countryside—Marie and Stéphanie and the tobacconist's wife and Jeanne Fraigneau. Marie was crying quietly, Mme Reboulier had donned her large black hat and said as she brandished her umbrella: "You mustn't cry, Marie, you must bear up bravely. Your husband will come back to you, you'll see, with all sorts of honors and medals. And I dare say he won't be one of the worst off either. Because this time everybody will be mobilized, women as well as men."

She pointed her umbrella towards the east and felt ten years younger. "You'll see," she said. "You'll see. It's the civilians who'll win this war." But Marie had assumed her stolid look, her sobs shook her shoulders, she peered through her tears at the monument to the fallen in the last war, and refused to answer.

"Very good, sir," said the lieutenant. He pressed the receiver to his ear and said: "Very good, sir." And the quiet, angry voice flowed on interminably: "You say they've left? Well, poor guy, you have really put your foot in it. I'm telling you straight, this is enough to bust you."

Daddy Croulard crossed the square with his pot of paste and his brushes, and a white roll of paper under his arm. Marie shouted: "What's up?" and Mme Reboulier was annoyed to notice a gleam of hope in her foolish eyes. Daddy Croulard laughed good-humoredly, waved the white roll of paper, and said: "It's nothing. The lieutenant gave out the wrong notices!" The lieutenant hung up the receiver and sat down, his legs felt very limp. The voice still rang in his ears: "Enough to bust you." He got up and walked to the window; on the opposite wall, quite fresh, still damp, and white as snow, shone the poster: "General Mobilization." Anger took him by the throat; he thought: "I told him to take that one off first, but he'll carefully leave it till the last." He swung himself out of the window, ran to the notice, and began to tear it to shreds. Daddy Croulard dipped his brush into the paste-pot, Mme Reboulier watched him sorrowfully, the lieutenant scratched at the wall until his nails were edged with little blobs of paste; Blomart and Cormier had remained in the barracks; the others had returned to their horses and were watching each other dubiously; they wanted to laugh and lose their tempers, they felt as flat as the day after a fair. Chapin went up to the oxen and stroked them. Their muzzles and chests were covered with foam, and he thought gloomily: "If I had known, I wouldn't have gone so fast."

"What are we going to do now?" asked Poulaille, behind his back.

"We can't go back at once," said Chapin. "We must rest the animals."

Fraigneau looked at the barracks; some memories came back into his mind, he nudged Chapin and said slyly: "What about dropping in you know where, eh?"

"Where do you mean, guy?" asked Chapin.

"Why," said Fraigneau, "the cat-house, of course!"

The fellows from Crévilly gathered round him, clapped him on the shoulders, and said: "Good old Fraigneau! He always has the right idea." Chapin brightened up and said: "I know where it is, men; get back on your carts, I'll lead the way."

Eight thirty o'clock. A skier was already circling round the diving-board, towed by a motor-boat; now and then

Mathieu caught the purr of the motor and then the boat shot off, the skier dwindled to a black spot, and nothing more was heard. The sea, flat and hard and white, looked like a deserted skating-rink. Very soon it would turn blue and sparkle, it would become liquid and deep, the sea of every day, echoing with shouts and dotted with little black heads. Mathieu crossed the terrace and strolled along the promenade. The cafés were still shut, two cars passed by. He had gone out with no definite purpose: to buy a paper, to breathe the thick smell of seaweed and eucalyptus that hung about the harbor, and also to kill time. Odette was still asleep, Jacques always worked until ten o'clock. He turned into a street of shops that led towards the station; two young English girls passed him laughing; four people were gathered round a poster. Mathieu joined them, just to get rid of a moment or two. A small man with a pointed beard looked and wagged his head. Mathieu read:

"By order of the Minister of National Defense and of War and of the Minister for Air, all officers, non-commissioned officers, and men of the reserve in possession of a white mobilization order or form numbered '2' will start immediately, without waiting for an individual notification.

"They will report at the depot designated on their mobilization order or form, under the conditions specified on that document.

"Saturday, September 24, 1938, nine o'clock.

"The Minister of National Defense, of War, and of the Air."

"Tut-tut," said the little man with an air of disapproval. Mathieu smiled at him and reread the notice carefully; it was one of those tiresome but instructive documents which had, for some time past, filled the newspapers under the heading: "Foreign Office Announcement" or "Communication by the Quai d'Orsay." They always had to be read twice to be fully understood. "They will report at the depot designated," and Mathieu thought: "Why, I've got a

Form 2." Suddenly the poster seemed aimed at him personally—as though his name had been chalked upon the
wall, accompanied by insults and threats. Mobilized: there
it was, inscribed on the wall, and perhaps it was already
legible upon his face. He flushed and hurried off. "Form 2.
That's it. I'm about to become interesting." Odette would
look at him with contained emotion. Jacques would assume
his Sunday expression and say: "There's nothing I can say
to you, old boy." But Mathieu felt modest and didn't want
to become an object of interest. He turned to the left,
down the first side-street, and quickened his step; on the
right-hand pavement stood a gloomy little group staring at
a poster and muttering to one another. This was happening
all over France. Two by two, four by four, people stood
and stared at posters. And in each group there would be at
least one man who would feel his bill-fold and his army
folder through the material of his jacket, aware that he
was now an object of interest. Rue de la Poste. Two posters,
two groups; and still talking about it. He plunged into a
long, dark alley, which he felt sure had been passed over by
the bill-posters. He was alone, he could think about himself.
And he thought: "This is it!" This was it—that full and
rounded day, which should have perished decently and in
due order, was now suddenly prolonged; arrowlike, it
hissed into the night, sped into the darkness and the smoke,
into the deserted countryside, across a turmoil of axles and
engines; and he was slipping into it, as if he were on a
toboggan, which would only stop at dead of night, in
Paris, on the platform of the Lyon railway station. Already
artificial lights invaded the broad daylight—the future
nocturnal lights of railway stations. His eye-sockets had
begun to throb with the dry pain of insomnias to come.
He was not upset by this, nor anything else. Nor was he
amused; it belonged to the anecdotal, the picturesque. "I
must inquire the time of the train to Marseille," he thought.
The alley, though he had not realized it, led back to the

Corniche. He suddenly emerged into a blaze of light and sat down outside a café that had just opened. "A cup of coffee and the timetable." A gentleman with a silvery mustache came and sat down near him, accompanied by a middle-aged lady. The gentleman opened the *Éclaireur de Nice,* the lady turned towards the sea. Mathieu eyed her for a moment and felt depressed. He thought: "I must put my affairs in order. Settle Ivich in Paris, in my apartment, and give her a power of attorney so she can draw my salary." The gentleman's head reappeared above his newspaper. "It's war," he said. The lady sighed, but did not reply; Mathieu looked at the gentleman's shining, polished cheeks, his tweed jacket, his violet-striped shirt, and he thought: "This is war."

This is war. Something that now held him by one sole thread dropped away from him, and was left behind. It was his life: and it was dead. Dead. He turned and looked at it. Viguier was dead, his hands lay outstretched on the white sheet, there was a live fly on his forehead, and his future extended as far as eye could reach, infinite, unalterable, as fixed as the fixed gaze beneath those dead eyelids. His future—peace, the future of the world, and the future of Mathieu. Mathieu's future was there, plain to see, fixed, vitreous, unattainable. Mathieu was sitting at a café table, he was drinking, he was ahead of his future, he eyed it, and he thought: "Peace." Mme Verchoux, standing beside the nurse, pointed to Viguier—she had a stiff neck and her eyes were smarting—and said: "He was a fine fellow." She searched for a word, a rather more ceremonious word, with which to designate him; she was his nearest relative, and it was for her to say the concluding word. The word "kindly" came upon her tongue, but it was not sufficiently conclusive. She said: "He was a man of peace," and then was silent. Mathieu thought: "I had a peaceful future." Indeed he had; he had loved and hated and suffered, and the future was here and everywhere,

overhead and all around him, like an ocean, and every
burst of anger, every disaster, every laugh, drew suste-
nance from that invisible and insistent future. A smile, a
mere smile, was a mortgage on tomorrow's peace—on next
year's, next century's peace; otherwise I should never have
dared to smile. Years and years of peace to come had
gathered upon his world of objects, matured them, and
set them aglow; taking out your watch, taking the latch
of a door, taking a woman's hand—all this was taking hold
of peace. The postwar epoch was a beginning. The beginning of peace. It passed unhurried, as a morning passes.
Jazz was a beginning, and the movies, which I enjoy so
much, were also a beginning. Surrealism, too, and Communism. I hesitated, I chose with care. I had time enough.
Time, peace—they were the same. And now that future
lies at my feet, dead. It was a spurious future, an im-
posture. He contemplated those twenty years, like an expanse of sunlit sea, and he now saw them as they had been:
a finite number of days compressed between two high,
hopeless walls, a period duly catalogued, with a prelude
and an end, which would figure in the history manuals
under the heading: Between the two wars. Twenty years:
1918–38. Only twenty years! Yesterday it had seemed both
a shorter and a longer period; and, indeed, no one would
have thought to compute it, since it had not ended. Now it
has ended. A spurious future. All the experiences of the
last twenty years have been spurious. We were energetic
and serious, we tried to understand, and here is the result:
those lovely days led to a dark and secret future, they
deceived us; today's war, the new World War, stole them
surreptitiously away. We were unconscious cuckolds. And
now the war is there; my life is dead; *that* was my life;
everything must be started afresh. He groped for some
random recollection, no matter what—the evening at
Perugia, sitting on the terrace, eating an apricot ice, and
looking at the calm hills of Assisi, far off in the dust. Well,

he ought to have seen war in that reddening sunset. If I had discovered in those red gleams that gilded the table and the balustrade omens of storm and blood, they would have been with me now, and at least that much would have been preserved. But I had no doubts, the ice melted on my tongue, and I merely thought of antique gold, and love, and mystic glory. Now I have lost everything. The waiter made his way between the tables; Mathieu hailed him, paid, and got up, hardly conscious of himself. He was leaving his life behind; I have cast my skin. He crossed the road and stood with his elbows on the balustrade, looking out to sea.

He felt fateful and strangely light—naked, robbed of all that he possessed. I own nothing any more, not even my past. It was indeed a spurious past, and I don't regret it. And he thought: They have rid me of my life. It was a sorry, ineffectual life, Marcelle, Ivich, Daniel—a squalid life, though that doesn't matter now, since it is dead. As of this morning, when they began to plaster those white notices on the walls, all lives are ineffectual, all lives are dead. If I had done what I wanted, if I had once, only once, succeeded in being *free*—well, that would in my case have been a mean delusion, since I should merely have exercised my freedom in this false peace; I should still have been here, looking out to sea, with my elbows on the balustrade, with all those posters at my back—those posters on all the walls of France, announcing that my life is dead and that there never was a peace; there was no sense in all that effort, in those feelings of remorse. The sea, the beach, the tents, the balustrade—all cold, blood-less. They had lost their original future and not yet ac-quired a new one; they were adrift in the present. Mathieu was adrift. A survivor, naked on a beach, among heaps of sea-sodden garments, among shattered crates and random wreckage. A sunburnt youth emerged from a tent, looking calm and blank as he gazed hesitantly at the sea; a survi-

vor—we are all survivors; the German officers smiled and
saluted, the engine revolved, the propeller revolved,
Chamberlain saluted, turned, and set one foot on the
ladder.

The Babylonian exile, the curse on Israel, and the wail-
ing wall, the destinies of the Jewish nation had not altered
since the time when her sons walked in chains between the
red towers of Assyria under the cruel eyes of their curled
and bearded conquerors; Schalom lived his little life among
such men, dark-haired, tight-lipped, and cruel. Nothing
had changed; Schalom thought of Georges Lévy. He
thought: "We have lost our sense of solidarity, and that is
the veritable curse of God!" and he felt rather pathetic,
but not ill-pleased, at seeing those white posters on the
walls. He had asked help from Georges Lévy, but Georges
Lévy was a hard man, an Alsatian Jew, and he had refused.
He had not exactly refused; he had groaned and wrung
his hands, he had talked about his old mother, and the
depression. But everybody knew that he detested his old
mother, and that there was no depression in the fur trade.
Schalom himself had burst into lamentations, he had
waved his arms and talked about the new Exodus and the
poor refugee Jews who had suffered for the rest and in their
flesh. Lévy was a hard man, a rich man of the rich and
nasty type, he propelled Schalom towards the door with
his great paunch, puffing in his face. Schalom groaned as
he stepped backwards, brandishing his arms, smiling in-
voluntarily as he thought of how the clerks in the next room
must be relishing the scene. At the corner of the rue du
Quatre-Septembre there was a prosperous and shining
pork-market; Schalom stopped, quite dazzled; he looked
at the jellied chitterlings, the raised pies, the strings of
sausages like varnished leather, the stocky, wrinkled save-
loys, each with its little pink anus, and he thought of the
pork-butchers of Vienna. So far as was humanly possible
he avoided eating pork, but the poor refugees are obliged

to feed on whatever comes to hand. When he emerged from the shop, he carried, hanging from his finger by a loop of pink string, a small parcel, so white and delicate that it looked like a parcel of cakes; and he was shocked. He thought: "All the French are nasty-rich." The richest nation in Europe. Schalom turned into the rue du Quatre-Septembre, calling down the curse of Heaven on such people, and, as though Heaven had heard his prayer, he saw out of the corner of his eye a group of French people standing motionless and mute before a white poster. He passed quite close to them, with eyes downcast and lips set, because it was not then expedient that a poor Jew should be caught smiling in the streets of Paris. Birnenschatz, Diamond Merchant; this was the place. He hesitated for a moment; then, before entering the archway, he slipped his parcel of sausage into his briefcase. The engines turned and rumbled, the floor-boards quivered, there was a smell of ether and benzol, the autobus plunged into the flames, *Oh, Pierre, so you're a coward;* the airplane swam in the sunlight, Daniel tapped the poster with the ferrule of his cane and said: "I'm not worrying; we're not such fools as to go to war without planes." The airplane slid over the trees, just above them; Dr. Schmitt looked up, the engine rumbled, he could see the airplane between the leaves, a flash of mica in the sky—"*Bon voyage! Bon voyage!*" he said to himself, and smiled; the wretched Arabs, uncomplaining, ghastly pale, lay in a huddle at the back of the car, a Negro boy came out of the hut, waved his hand, looked long at the departing car; you saw the little Yid, he bought a pound of saveloy—and I thought they didn't eat pork! The Negro boy and the interpreter walked slowly back, their heads still humming with the roar of the engines. It was a round iron table painted green, with a hole in the centre for the shaft of the parasol, and covered with brown patches like a pear; the newspaper was on the table, the *Petit Niçois*, still unfolded. Mathieu coughed, she was

sitting near the table, she had had her early breakfast in
the garden; how am I going to tell her? There must be no
fuss, above all no fuss, if only she could keep silent—no,
silence even would be too emphatic—if she could get up
and say: "Well, I'll make you some sandwiches for the
journey." Something like that. She was wearing a dressing-
gown and looking through her letters. "Jacques isn't down
yet," she said; "he was working late last night." Her first
words, every time they met again, were always about
Jacques, after which he was no longer mentioned. Mathieu
smiled and laughed. "Sit down," she said; "there are two
letters for you." He took the letters and asked: "Have you
read the paper?"

"Not yet. Mariette brought it with the letters, and I
haven't yet had the heart to open it. I was never much of a
one for reading newspapers, and at the moment, I just
can't bear them."

Mathieu smiled, and nodded agreement, but his teeth
were still set. All was as before between them. Just a
poster on a wall, and all was as before; she was Jacques's
wife, and he could find nothing to say to her. "Raw
ham," he thought, "that's what I should like for the journey."

"Do read your letters," said Odette briskly. "Don't bother
about me; besides, I must go up and dress."

Mathieu picked up the first letter, which bore the
Biarritz postmark—it was, after all, a moment gained.
When she had got up he would say to her: "By the way,
I'm leaving here—" No, that would sound too casual. "I'm
leaving." That would be better. "I'm leaving. . . ." He
recognized Boris's handwriting, and thought to himself
remorsefully: "It's more than a month since I wrote to
him." The envelope contained a correspondence card. Boris
had written his own address and put a stamp on the left
half of the card. On the right half he had written as follows:

My dear Boris:

I am $\begin{cases} \text{well.} \\ \text{not well.}^1 \end{cases}$

The reason for my silence is: annoyance, pardonable, unpardonable; ill will; sudden conversion; lunacy; illness; laziness; mere perversity.[2]

I will write you a long letter in .... days.

Please accept my profound excuses and the expression of my repentant regard.

Signature:

---

[1] Cross out term that does not apply.   [2] Ditto.

"What are you laughing at?" asked Odette.

"It's from Boris," said Mathieu. "He's at Biarritz with Lola." He handed her the letter and she began to laugh too.

"He's delightful," she said. "Is he— Is he of age to—?"

"Nineteen," said Mathieu. "It will depend on how long the war lasts."

Odette looked at him affectionately. "Your pupils do pull your leg, don't they?" she said.

It became more and more difficult to talk to her. Mathieu opened the other letter. It was from Gomez, Sarah's husband. Mathieu had not seen him since his departure for Spain. He was at present a colonel in the Spanish republican army.

My dear Mathieu,

I am in Marseille on a mission. . . . I am leaving again on Tuesday, but I must see you first. Expect me by the four o'clock train on Sunday, and get me a room anywhere, I shall manage a brief visit to Juan-les-Pins. We have much to talk about.

Yours cordially,

Gomez

Mathieu put the letter in his pocket; he reflected with some annoyance: "Saturday is tomorrow—I shall be gone."

He wanted to see Gomez again; at that moment Gomez was the only friend he did want to see. He must know something of what war meant. "I might perhaps catch him at Marseille, between two trains. . . ." He took the crumpled letter out of his pocket; Gomez had not given his address. Mathieu shrugged his shoulders irritably and threw the letter on the table; Gomez had remained quite unchanged, colonel though he now was, brusque, but rather ineffectual. Odette had made up her mind to unfold the paper and was holding it, with her shapely arms outspread, and reading it intently.

"Oh!" she exclaimed.

She turned to Mathieu and said to him lightly: "Are you a Form 2 man?"

Mathieu blushed, and blinked.

"Yes," he said confusedly.

Odette looked at him severely, as though he were at fault. And he hurriedly added: "But I'm not leaving today, I shall be staying for another forty-eight hours; I have a friend coming to see me."

He felt relieved by this abrupt decision; it would postpone any display of emotion for nearly two days. "It's a good long way from Juan-les-Pins to Nancy, they won't make a fuss over a few hours' delay." But Odette's look did not relax, and he repeated with embarrassment: "I shall be here for another forty-eight hours, I shall be here for another forty-eight hours," while Ella Birnenschatz clasped her thin brown arms round her father's neck.

"Papa, you are a darling," said Ella Birnenschatz.

Odette got up abruptly. "Well, I'll leave you," she said. "I must go and dress anyway. I think Jacques will be down soon to keep you company."

She departed, wrapping her dressing-gown closely round her firm, slim hips, and Mathieu thought: "She did that well—she did that very well," and he felt deeply grateful. What a fine girl, and what a little charmer!—he pushed her away reprovingly; Weiss was standing by the door, dressed apparently in his Sunday best.

"You're making me all wet," said M. Birnenschatz, wiping his cheek. "And you're messing my face up with rouge."

She laughed. "You're afraid of what your typists may think. There!" she said, kissing him on the nose. "There—and there!" And he felt hot lips on the top of his head. He caught her by the shoulders and held her at the length of his long arms. She laughed and struggled, and he thought: "Wonderful girl—wonderful little girl." The mother was fat and flaccid, with a timid and appealing look in her wide eyes, which got on his nerves, but Ella took after him, or rather she did not take after anybody; she had made herself what she was by her life in Paris. I always say: Race? —what do you mean by race? Would you take Ella for a Jewess if you met her in the street? Slim as a Parisienne, with the warm complexion of a southern girl, a sensible, passionate, small face, a sedate and restful face, devoid of defect, race, or destiny, a truly *French* face. He released her, took a jewel-case off the desk, and gave it to her.

"Here you are," he said. And he added, while she was looking at the pearls: "Next year they'll be twice as large, but they will be the last; the necklace will be complete."

She tried to kiss him again, but he said: "Get along, now. Many happy returns. Hurry!—you'll be late for your lecture."

She departed, throwing a smile at Weiss. A girl shut the door, went through the secretaries' office, and disappeared; Schalom, sitting on the edge of his chair, with his hat on his knees, thought: "Pretty little Jewess"; she had the head of a little monkey, bunched rather forwards, small enough to fit in the palm of your hand, with large, shortsighted, lovely eyes—obviously Birnenschatz's daughter. Schalom got up and made her a slight bow, which she did not appear to notice. He sat down again and thought: "She looks *too* intelligent; that's how our people are made, our expressions are branded on our faces; it's as though we endured them like a martyrdom." M. Birnenschatz thought of the pearls and said to himself: "Not a bad investment." They were worth a hundred thousand. Ella had accepted them without excessive rapture and without indifference; she knew the value of things, but she thought it quite natural to have money, to receive handsome presents, and to be happy. Good Lord, if, with my sort of wife, and my Cracow background, if this little spit of a girl—daughter of Polish Jews, who doesn't get excited nor torment herself, who finds it natural to be happy—if she were to be my sole achievement, I should not have lived in vain. He turned to Weiss. "Do you know where she's going?" he asked. "You'll never guess. To a lecture at the Sorbonne! Astounding, isn't it?"

Weiss smiled vaguely, still looking rather sheepish.

"Sir," he said, "I've come to say good-by."

M. Birnenschatz eyed him over the top of his spectacles. "Are you mobilized?"

Weiss nodded, and M. Birnenschatz looked at him sternly. "I was sure of it! You're just fool enough to have a Form 2, aren't you?"

"It's a fact," said Weiss with a smile, "I am."

"Well," said Birnenschatz, folding his arms, "you're going to leave me in a hell of a fix. What can I do without you?"

He repeated absent-mindedly: "What can I do without you? What can I do without you?" He tried to remember how many children Weiss had. Weiss glanced at him uneasily.

"Nonsense! You'll find someone to take my place."

"Not a bit of it! I shall have to pay you a lot of money for not doing a thing. You don't suggest I should take on somebody else into the bargain. Your job will be waiting for you, my boy."

Weiss looked moved, he rubbed his nose and squinted—he was revoltingly ugly.

"Sir—" said he.

M. Birnenschatz stopped him: gratitude was loathsome; besides he hadn't a great deal of sympathy for Weiss, because after all he was a fellow who carried his fate on his face, with those furtive eyes of his and that bulging lower lip which quivered with benevolence and resentment.

"That's all right," he said, "that's all right. You aren't leaving the business, you'll just be representing it among the ground officers. Are you a lieutenant?"

"I'm a captain," said Weiss.

"A washout of a captain," thought M. Birnenschatz. Weiss looked happy, his large ears were crimson. A washout of a captain—and that's war, that's the military hierarchy.

"What God-damned foolishness it all is, huh?" he said.

"Mmm," observed Weiss.

"Well, isn't it?"

"Of course it is," said Weiss. "But I was about to say that *for us* it's not such damned foolishness."

"For us?" asked M. Birnenschatz in astonishment. "For us? Whom are you talking about?"

Weiss lowered his eyes. "For us Jews," he said. "After what they did to the Jews in Germany, we have a reason for fighting."

M. Birnenschatz took a few steps; he was annoyed.

"What's all this—us Jews?" he asked. "Don't know 'em. I'm French myself. Do you feel like a Jew?"

"My cousin from Gratz has been with me since Tuesday," said Weiss. "He showed me his arms. They burnt him with lighted cigars from the elbow to the armpit."

M. Birnenschatz stopped short, he gripped the back of a chair with his great hands, and a dark rage set him ablaze up to the eyes.

"The men who did that," he said, "the men who did that—"

Weiss smiled; M. Birnenschatz cooled down.

"It isn't because your cousin is a Jew, Weiss. It's because he's a man. I can't bear to hear of any man being ill-treated. But what is a Jew? It's a man whom other men take for a Jew. Now, look at Ella. Would you take her for a Jewess if you didn't know who she was?"

Weiss did not look convinced. M. Birnenschatz marched up to him and tapped him on the chest with his outstretched forefinger: "Listen, my little Weiss, I can tell you this: I left Poland in 1910 and came to France. I was well received, I settled down here, and I said to myself: 'Good, France is my country now.' In 1914 the war came. Good. I said to myself: 'I'm going to fight because this is my country.' And I know what war is—I was at the Chemin des Dames. But now, I tell you, I am French. Not a Jew, not a French Jew: French. The Jews of Berlin and Vienna, the Jews of the concentration camps—I'm sorry for them, and it really makes me furious to think of such martyrdom. But mark my words, if there were anything I could do to save a Frenchman, one sole Frenchman, from being slaughtered for their sake, I would do it. I feel more akin to the first fellow I shall soon meet in the street than to my Lenz uncles or my Cracow nephews. The fate of German Jews is not our business."

Weiss looked sullen and obstinate. He said with a sorrowful smile: "Even if it was true, sir, you shouldn't say so. Those who have to fight must find reasons for fighting."

M. Birnenschatz felt a flush of embarrassment mounting to his cheekbones. "Poor fellow," he thought remorsefully.

"You are right," he said abruptly, "I'm nothing but a back number, and it's not for me to talk about this war, since I'm not in it. When do you go?"

"By the four-thirty train," said Weiss.

"Today's train? Then what on earth are you doing here? Run along home to your wife at once. Are you in need of money?"

"Not for the moment, thanks."

"Then get along. Tell your wife to come and see me, I'll settle everything with her. Hurry, now. Good-by."

He opened the door and pushed him out. Weiss bowed and babbled some unintelligible words of thanks. Over Weiss's shoulder M. Birnenschatz noticed a man sitting in the waiting-room, with his hat on his knees. He recognized Schalom and frowned. He did not like any caller to be kept waiting.

"Come in," he said. "Have you been waiting long?"

"Only half an hour," said Schalom, with a smile of resignation. "But what is half an hour? You are such a busy man. And I have all the time there is. What do I do from morning till night? I wait. Life in exile is nothing but a process of waiting, as you know."

"Come in," said M. Birnenschatz briskly. "Come in. They should have told me you were here."

Schalom went in; he smiled and bowed. M. Birnenschatz went in behind him and shut the door. He recognized Schalom perfectly well; he had been something in the Bavarian Syndicalist movement. Schalom appeared now and then, touched him for two or three thousand francs, and disappeared for several weeks.

"Have a cigar."

"I don't smoke," said Schalom, nodding his head forwards slightly. M. Birnenschatz took a cigar, twirled it absent-mindedly between his fingers, and then replaced it in the box.

"Well," he said, "how are you getting on?"

Schalom looked round for a chair.

"Sit down—sit down," said M. Birnenschatz heartily.

No. Schalom did not want to sit down. He went to the

chair and put his briefcase on it, in order to feel more at ease, and then, turning to M. Birnenschatz, emitted a long, melodious groan.

"I'm not getting on at all," said Schalom. "It isn't good for a man to live on other men's territory, it is very hard to bear; he is grudged the bread he eats. And their suspicion —that supremely French suspicion of us! When I get back to Vienna, this is the vision I shall have of France: a long dark staircase, a bell, a door half-opened—'What do you want?'—and then shut again. The apartment-house police, the town hall, the line at the police station. After all, it's quite natural, we are living in their country. But consider: they might set us to work; I ask no more than to make myself useful. But in order to find a job, you need an employment card, and in order to get an employment card, you need to be in some sort of job. With the best will in the world, I can't earn my living. What I find hardest to bear is to be a charge on others. Especially when they make you feel it so cruelly. And the time I waste! I began to write my memoirs—that would have brought in a little money. But there are so many things to be done in a day that I had to give up the idea."

He was a short, brisk little man; he had put his briefcase on a chair, and his hands, now free, fluttered round his crimson ears. "I must say he does look rather Jewish." M. Birnenschatz moved casually to the mirror, and threw a rapid glance at it—just over five feet tall, a broken nose, American boxer's head behind those large spectacles—no, we are not of the same species. But he did not dare look at Schalom, he felt compromised. He wished the man would go at once, but that was unlikely. It was only by the length of his visits, and his cheerful conversation, that Schalom could in his own eyes distinguish himself from a beggar. "I must talk," thought M. Birnenschatz. Schalom had the right to that. He had the right to his three thousand-franc notes and his quarter of an hour's interview. M. Birnenschatz sat on the edge of his desk. His right hand, which he had thrust into his jacket pocket, was fingering his cigar-case.

"The French are hard," said Schalom. His voice rose and then broke down prophetically, but a gleam of amusement quivered in his colorless eyes. "Hard. In their eyes a stranger is suspect on principle, when he isn't actually guilty."

"He talks to me as if I wasn't a Frenchman. It's true, I'm a Jew, a Jew from Poland, who arrived in France on July 19, 1910; no one here remembers that fact, but he hasn't forgotten it. A Jew who has had a little luck." He turned to Schalom and eyed him with annoyance. Schalom had bent his head in a sort of deferential attitude, but he still looked him in the face from beneath his arched eyebrows. He looked at him, and those great pale eyes *saw him as a Jew.* Two Jews, securely sheltered and secluded in an office in the rue du Quatre-Septembre, two Jews, two accomplices; and all around them, in the streets and houses, nothing but French people. Two Jews, the jovial old Yid who had succeeded, and the ill-nourished little kike who hasn't had a chance. Laurel and Hardy.

"Hard!" said Schalom. "Merciless!"

M. Birnenschatz shrugged his shoulders abruptly. "You must put yourself in—in their place," he said curtly—he could not bring himself to say: "in our place"; "do you know how many foreigners there have been in France since 1934?"

"Yes," said Schalom, "I do. And I think it is a great honor for France. But what is she doing to deserve it? You surely know that the young men of Paris comb the Latin Quarter, and if anyone looks like a Jew, they beat him up."

"Blum did us a great deal of harm when he was Premier," observed M. Birnenschatz.

He had said "us"; he had accepted the complicity of this alien. We. We Jews. But it was from compassion that he had done so. Schalom's eyes were fixed on him with respectful insistence. He was small and fragile; they had beaten him up and ejected him from Bavaria, and here he was, lodging in a squalid hotel and spending his days in cafés. And Weiss's cousin, they had burnt him with cigars; M. Birnenschatz looked at Schalom and felt sticky. It wasn't sympathy for the man—by no means. It was—it was—

She looked at him and she thought: "A man of prey. They are marked for what they are, and they are the cause of wars." But she realized that her old love was not dead.

M. Birnenschatz fingered his billfold. "Ah well," he said benignantly, "let us hope it won't last too long."

Schalom compressed his lips and jerked up his round head. "I made my gesture too soon," thought M. Birnenschatz.

A man of prey. He takes women and kills men. He thinks he is a great man. But it isn't true, he is marked for what he is, that's all.

"That depends on the French," said Schalom. "If the French recover the sense of their historic mission . . ."

"What mission?" asked M. Birnenschatz coldly. Schalom's eyes gleamed with hatred.

"The Germans provoke and insult them in every possible way," he said in a hard, high voice. "What do they expect? Do they imagine they can get round Hitler? Each new French concession prolongs the Nazi regime for ten years. And all that time we, the victims, gnaw our nails and wait. Today I saw the white posters on the walls, and I feel faintly hopeful. But even yesterday I thought: 'The French have no blood left in their veins, and I shall die in exile.'"

Two Jews in an office in the rue du Quatre-Septembre. The Jewish standpoint on international events. Tomorrow there will be a statement in *Je suis partout*: "The Jews are pushing France into war." M. Birnenschatz took off his spectacles and wiped them with his handkerchief: he was furious. Quietly he said: "If war comes, will you be in it?"

"Many refugees will join up, I'm sure of that," said Schalom. "But look at me," he added, pointing to his skinny little body; "I should never be accepted by any medical board."

"Well, then, get the hell out and give us some peace!" said M. Birnenschatz in a thunderous voice. "Are you ever going to give us any damned peace? Why the hell do you come here to foul up our place? I'm French, I'm not a German Jew, and I don't give a damn for German Jews. So go and make your war somewhere else."

Schalom eyed him for a moment with stupefaction, then he resumed his deferential smile, reached out a hand, picked up his briefcase, and backed towards the door. M. Birnenschatz took his wallet out of his pocket.

"Wait a moment," he said.

Schalom was already at the door.

"I need nothing," said he. "I sometimes ask for help for the Jews. But you are right: you're not a Jew, and I've come to the wrong address."

He went out, and M. Birnenschatz stood motionless, staring at the door. *He's a hard man, a man of prey, they have a star, and they succeed in everything they do. But they are the cause of wars and of death and pain. They are flame and fire, they do harm, he has done me harm, I carry him like a sliver of wood beneath my fingernails, like a smoldering cinder under my eyelids, like a splinter in the heart.* That's what she thinks of me. He had no need to go and ask her, he knew her, if he could penetrate that dark and tousled head, he would always find in it that set, inexorable thought, she's a hard woman in her way, she never forgets. He leaned in his pajamas out over the Place Gélu; the air was still fresh, the sky was pale blue edged with gray; it was the hour when water streams over the flagstones and the fishmongers' stalls; the city smelt of departure and of morning. Morning, wide-open spaces, and

down yonder a life without remorse, round puffs of bomb-
smoke on the cracked soil of Catalonia. But at his back,
behind the half-open window, in a room filled with slumber and with darkness, there was a dead thought watching
him, judging him; his own remorse. He would set off tomorrow, he would kiss them on the station platform, and
she would go back to the hotel with the boy, she would
trip down the great staircase, she would think: he has gone
off to Spain again. She would never forgive him; it was
another scar on her heart. He leaned out over the Place
Gélu to postpone the imminent hour; he needed shouts,
shrill songs, swift and violent pains; he loathed the soft
atmosphere in which he lived. Water streamed across the
square—water, the damp odors of morning, the rustic cries
of morning. Beneath the plane trees lay the square, glistening, white, and vivid like a fish in the sea. And that night
a Negro had been singing, and the night had seemed sultry
and like a Spanish night. Gomez closed his eyes, he felt a
stabbing nostalgia for Spain and for the war. She did not
understand. Neither night, nor morning, nor the war.

"Bang, bang! Bang, bang, bang, bang, bang!" yelled
Pablo.

Gomez turned and went back into the room. Pablo had
put on his helmet, he was holding his rifle by the barrel
and brandishing it like a club. He staggered up and down
the hotel bedroom dealing violent blows all round him.
Sarah watched him with dead eyes.

"It's a positive massacre," said Gomez.

"I'm going to kill them all," replied Pablo, continuing
his onslaughts.

"All whom?"

Sarah in her dressing-gown sat on the edge of the bed
darning a stocking.

"All the fascists," said Pablo.

Gomez stepped quickly back and burst out laughing.

"Kill them!" he said. "Don't leave one alive. You've forgotten that fellow, over there."

Pablo dashed in the direction of Gomez's outstretched arm and streaked the air with his rifle.

"Bang, bang," he cried. "Bang, bang, bang! No mercy!"

He stopped and turned to Gomez, panting, with a grave, intent look on his face.

"Oh, Gomez," said Sarah, "look—how could you?"

Gomez had just bought Pablo a soldier's outfit.

"He must learn to fight," said Gomez, stroking the boy's head. "Otherwise he'll become a mouse, like the French."

Sarah looked up at him, and he saw that he had deeply wounded her.

"I don't understand," she said, "why people should be called mice because they don't want to fight."

"There are moments when one ought to want to fight," said Gomez.

"Never," said Sarah. "In no circumstances. Fighting means finding myself one day on a road with my house in ruins, and my boy dead in my arms; nothing can justify that."

Gomez did not answer. Indeed, he had no answer. Sarah was right. From her point of view she was right. But Sarah's point of view was one that had to be ignored on principle; otherwise nothing would ever get done. Sarah laughed bitterly. "When I first knew you, you were a pacifist, Gomez."

"Yes, because that was the right time to be a pacifist. The aim has not changed. But the means for attaining it are different."

This baffled Sarah, and she made no comment. She stood with her mouth half-open, and her pendant lip exposed her decayed teeth.

Pablo twirled his rifle, and shouted: "Just wait, you dirty Frenchman, you mousy Frenchman."

"You see?" said Sarah.

"Pablo," said Gomez sharply, "you mustn't abuse the French. The French aren't fascists."

"The French are mice," shouted Pablo. And he dashed the butt of his rifle against the curtains, which bellied backwards into the windows. Sarah said nothing, but Gomez wished he had not seen the look she threw at Pablo. It was not a harsh look—no, it was more of a bewildered look, as though she were seeing her son for the first time. She had laid the stocking on the bed beside her, and was looking at this little stranger, this lively little brat who slashed off heads and smashed skulls, and she was no doubt thinking ruefully: "This is my fault." Gomez was ashamed. "A week," he thought; "one week was enough."

"Gomez," said Sarah brusquely, "do you really think there's going to be a war?"

"I hope so," said Gomez. "I hope Hitler will finally force the French to fight."

"Gomez," said Sarah, "do you know what I am realizing lately?—that men are evil."

Gomez shrugged his shoulders. "They are neither good nor evil. Everyone pursues his own interest."

"No," said Sarah. "They are evil." She kept her eyes on little Pablo, with an air of predicting his destiny. "Evil, and intent on injuring themselves."

"I'm not evil," said Gomez.

"You are," said Sarah without looking at him. "You are evil, my poor Gomez, very evil. And you have no excuses; others are unhappy, but you are evil and happy."

A long silence fell. Gomez looked at her short, thick neck and that unlovely body he had once held in his arms, and thought: "She has no regard for me. No affection. No respect. She merely loves me; which of us is the more evil?"

But suddenly remorse laid hold of him again: he had arrived one evening from Barcelona, happy—indeed, profoundly happy. He had arranged to stay a week. He left on the following day. "I am not a good man," he thought.

"Is the water hot?"

"Tepid," said Sarah. "The faucet on the left."

"Good," said Gomez. "Well then, I shall shave." He went into the dressing-room, leaving the door wide open, turned on the water, and selected a blade. "When I'm gone," he thought, "the soldier's outfit won't last long." When Sarah returned, she would doubtless shut it up in her large medicine-closet; unless she deliberately mislaid it. "She teaches him girls' games," he thought. When would he see Pablo again and what would she have made of him? He certainly looks like a stout little boy! He approached the wash-basin and saw them both in the mirror. Pablo was standing in the middle of the room, panting, flushed, his legs apart, and his hands in his pockets. Sarah was on her knees before him and looking up at him in silence. "She's wondering if he's like me," thought Gomez. He felt uncomfortable and closed the door without a sound.

". . . Has joined me with the boy. Expect me by the four o'clock train on Sunday, and get me a . . ." A hand was laid heavily on his left shoulder, another hand on his right shoulder. A warm and friendly pressure. So that's that: he replaced the letters in his pocket and looked up.

"Hullo!"

"Odette has just told me . . ." said Jacques, looking deep into Mathieu's eyes. "You poor guy!"

He sat down, without taking his eyes off his brother, in the armchair Odette had just vacated; a hand that hardly seemed his own skillfully hitched up his trousers; his legs crossed themselves automatically. He ignored these trifling local incidents; he was simply an embodied look.

"I'm not leaving today, you know," said Mathieu.

"I know. You aren't afraid of any possible unpleasantness?"

"Oh—a few hours one way or the other. . . ."

Jacques drew a deep breath. "What shall I say? In other days, when a chap went off, one could say to him: 'You are going to fight for your children, your liberty, or your property, to fight for France'; indeed, one could provide him with various reasons for risking his skin. But today—"

He shrugged his shoulders. Mathieu had bent his head and was scraping the floor with his heel.

"You don't answer," said Jacques in a penetrating voice. "You prefer not to speak, from fear of saying too much. But I know quite well what's in your mind."

Mathieu was still rubbing his shoe against the floor. He said without looking up:

"As a matter of fact, you don't know."

A brief silence followed, then he heard his brother's hesitant voice: "What do you mean?"

"Well, I'm not thinking about anything at all."

"All right," said Jacques with faint irritation. "You're not thinking about anything, but you're desperate—it's the same thing."

Mathieu forced himself to look up and smile. "Neither am I desperate."

"Look here," said Jacques, "you're not asking me to believe that you are resigned to going off, like a sheep to the slaughterhouse?"

"Well," said Mathieu, "I am rather sheeplike, don't you think? I'm going because I can't do otherwise. That being so, the question whether this war is or is not a just war is, for me, quite secondary."

Jacques tilted his head back and surveyed Mathieu with eyes half-closed.

"Mathieu, you astonish me. You astonish me prodigiously. I no longer recognize you. What? I had a turbulent, cynical, sarcastic brother, who would never consent to be a dupe, who would not lift his little finger without trying to understand why he was lifting his little finger rather than his forefinger, and the little finger of his right hand rather than of his left. Then comes war, he is sent into the front line, and my rebel, my plate-smasher, goes off politely, without any hesitation, merely saying: 'I'm going because I can't do otherwise.'"

"It's not my fault," said Mathieu. "I have never been able to form an opinion on matters of that kind."

"But surely," said Jacques, "the issue is quite clear; we are confronted by a man—I mean Beneš—who is formally pledged to establish Czechoslovakia as a federation on the Swiss model. He is pledged," he repeated with emphasis; "I read it in the report of the proceedings at the Peace Conference, so you see I can quote my sources. And that promise was equivalent to giving the Sudeten Germans a genuine ethnographic autonomy. Good. Whereupon the said person ignores his engagements and places these same Germans under Czech administration, law, and police. The Germans don't like it, and they claim their strict rights. Moreover I know these Czech officials, I have been in Czechoslovakia; I know what petty tyrants they can be. Well then, the proposal is that France—the land, so they say, of liberty—should shed her blood in order that Czech officials should continue to torment the German population, and that is why you, professor of philosophy at the Lycée Pasteur, are going to spend the last years of your youth ten feet underground, between Bitche and Wissembourg. And so you must understand that when you come and tell me that you are departing in a spirit of resignation, and that you don't give a damn whether this war is just or unjust, I get a bit hot under the collar."

Mathieu looked at his brother with perplexity; he thought: "Ethnographic autonomy—I should never have thought of that." "However," he observed, to salve his conscience, "it isn't ethnographic autonomy that the Sudetens now want; it's union with Germany."

Jacques made a pained grimace. "Please, Mathieu, don't

talk like my concierge, don't call them the Sudetens. The Sudetens are mountains; say the Sudeten Germans, if you like, or just Germans. Well, and what then? They want to join Germany? That's because they have been goaded beyond endurance. If they had been granted what they asked at the outset, we shouldn't be in this mess. But Beneš has practiced every sort of trickery and finesse because the bigwigs here have been so misguided as to let him believe that he had France behind him; and this is the result."

He looked gloomily at Mathieu. "I can stand all this, if need be; I know what sort of people politicians are. But that you, a sensible man, a graduate of the university, should have so utterly abandoned your most elementary principles as to assure me that you are going off to the slaughter because you can't do otherwise—that I really cannot stand. If there are many like you, it's all up with France, my poor fellow."

"But what do you want us to do?" asked Mathieu.

"What? We are still a democracy, Thieu! There is still such a thing as public opinion in France, I imagine."

"Well?"

"Well, if millions of Frenchmen, instead of exhausting themselves in vain disputes, had closed their ranks and said to our Government: 'So the Sudeten Germans want to return to the bosom of Germania, do they? Then let them; it's their affair!' Not a single politician would have dared to risk a war over such a trifle."

He laid a hand on Mathieu's knee and continued in a conciliatory tone:

"I know you don't like the Hitler regime. But, after all, it is quite possible not to share your prejudices against it; it is a young and energetic regime, which has proved its effectiveness and exercises an undeniable attraction on the nations of central Europe. Besides, it is in every sense their affair; it's none of our business."

Mathieu stifled a yawn and drew his legs back under his chair: he threw a quizzical look at his brother's rather puffy countenance, and thought that he was beginning to age.

"Perhaps—" he said, meekly, "perhaps you are right."

Odette came downstairs, and sat down with them in silence. She had the grace and tranquillity of a domestic animal; she sat down, went away, came back, and sat down again, certain that she would pass unnoticed. Mathieu turned to her with annoyance; he did not like to see them together. When Jacques was present, Odette's face did not change, it remained smooth and elusive, like that of a statue without pupils to its eyes. What lay behind it had to be divined.

"Jacques thinks I ought to be more upset about being called up," he said with a smile. "He's trying to put death into my soul by explaining that I'm going to get myself killed for nothing."

Odette returned him a smile. It wasn't the conventional smile that he expected, but a special smile directed to him alone; in one instant the sea had reappeared, the lightly heaving sea, the Chinese shadows speeding across the waves, the streak of sunlight quivering on the water, the green aloes and the green pine-needles that carpeted the ground, the stippled shadows of the tall pines, the dense white heat, the smell of resin, all the richness of a September morning at Juan-les-Pins. Dear Odette. Mismarried and misloved; but had she wasted her life when she could, with a smile, resuscitate a garden by the water's edge, and the heat of summer on the sea? He looked at Jacques—a sallow, fleshy figure, whose hands trembled as he angrily tapped his newspaper. "What is he afraid of?" said Mathieu to himself. On Saturday, September 24, at eleven o'clock in the morning, Pascal Montastruc, born at Nîmes on February 6, 1899, and commonly known as One-eyed Pascal (because he had stuck a knife in his left eye on August

6, 1907 while trying to cut the ropes of his little friend
Julot Truffier's swing, to see what would happen), was
selling, as was his custom every Saturday, irises and butter-
cups on the Quai de Passy, just by the entrance to the
metro station. He had his own personal technique; he took
some bunches of flowers out of the wicker basket on a
camp-stool and went out into the street, the cars drove
past him hooting, and he shouted: "A bunch of flowers, a
lovely bunch of flowers for the lady!" brandishing the yellow bouquet. The car dashed at him like a bull in an arena;
he did not move; he merely drew in his stomach, flung his
head back, and let the car bear down upon him as he
shouted through the open window: "A bunch of flowers, a
lovely bunch of flowers." The driver usually stopped, he
climbed on the running-board, and the car drew up against
the pavement, because it was the week-end and they liked
to go back to their fine houses in the rue des Vignes or
the rue du Ranelagh with a bunch of flowers for the lady.
"A lovely bunch of flowers"; he jumped back to avoid the
car, the hundredth that had passed without stopping.
"Blast them! What's the matter with them all this morning?" They were driving fast, bent over their wheels, deaf
and unheeding. They did not turn into the rue Charles-
Dickens or the avenue de Lamballe; they raced along the
quays as though they meant to get as far as Pontoise; One-
eyed Pascal was completely baffled. "Where on earth are
they going to?" He trotted back to his basket of yellow and
pink flowers, much chagrined.

"It's pure lunacy," said he. "The most portentous suicide
in history. Consider. France has been bled white twice in
a hundred years, once in the wars of the Empire, and again
in 1914; added to which, the birth-rate is falling every day.
Is this the moment to start another war, which would cost
us three to four million men? Three or four million men
whom we could never replace," said he, rapping out the
words. "Win or lose, the country would decline into a

second-class power; that is quite certain. And then there
is something else: Czechoslovakia will be knocked out before we can move a finger. Look at a map: it's like a haunch
of meat between the jaws of the German wolf. If the wolf
tightens his jaws a bit . . ."

"But," said Odette, "that would only be temporary, the
Czechoslovak State would be reconstituted after the war."

"Indeed?" said Jacques, with a sarcastic laugh. "You
think so? Is it really likely that the English will allow such
a storm-center to be reconstituted? Fifteen million inhabitants, nine distinct nationalities—it's an insult to common
sense. Let the Czechs make no mistake," he added grimly,
"their vital interest is to avoid war at any cost."

"*What is he afraid of?*" Grasping his futile bunch of
flowers, he watched the cars pass. It was like the Chantilly
road on the evening of a race day; some had trunks, mat-
tresses, perambulators, or sewing-machines piled up on
their roofs, and all were full to bursting with suitcases,
parcels, baskets. "Well, no kidding!" said One-eyed Pascal.
They sped past so heavily loaded that at every bump the
mudguards rasped against the tires. "They're clearing out,"
he thought, "clearing the hell out." He jumped back a step
or two to avoid a Salmson, but he did not get back on the
pavement. They were clearing out, these gentlemen with
their pumiced, massaged faces, their fat children, and their
handsome wives, they were cats with their tails on fire,
they were scuttling from Germans, bombs, and Communism. All his clients gone. But this procession of cars,
this wild flight to Normandy, seemed to him so comic that
it made up for his losses; he stood in the roadway while
the runaway cars brushed past him, and began to enjoy
the spectacle.

"And where, I ask you, are we to come to their assistance? Because, after all, we should have to attack Germany just the same. Well, then, where? In the east there
is the Siegfried Line, we should break our noses on that.

In the north, Belgium. Are we to violate Belgian neutrality? Well then, where? Are we to go round by Turkey? That's just fantastic. All that we can do is to wait, with ordered arms, until Germany has settled Czechoslovakia's account. After which she will come and settle ours."

"Well," said Odette, "that's just the moment for . . ."

Jacques threw her a conjugal look. "For what?" he asked coldly. He leaned towards Mathieu. "I've spoken to you of Laurent, the former big shot at Air-France, who stayed on as adviser to Cot and Guy La-Chambre. Well, I will pass on to you without comment what he told me last July: the French army has, in all and for all purposes, forty bombers and seventy fighters. If that is typical of our condition, the Germans will be in Paris for New Year's Day."

"Jacques!" said Odette furiously.

What is he afraid of? Pascal laughed and laughed; he had dropped his bunch of flowers in order to laugh more at his ease; he jumped backwards, the wheels of a car crushed the flowers. What is he afraid of? She's furious that anyone should even imagine the defeat of France. She is not completely congenial; words frighten her. "They are afraid of Zeppelins and Taubes; I saw them myself in 1916; they were shivering in their boots then, and it's beginning again"; the cars sped over the crushed flowers, and the tears came into Pascal's eyes, he thought it all so funny. Maurice didn't think it was funny at all. He had stood a round for the guys, and his shoulder-blades were still aching from their slaps on the back. At the moment he was alone, and soon he would have to go and tell Zézette. He saw the white notice on the high gray wall of the Penhoët works and went up to it, he wanted to read it over again alone.

"By order of the Minister of National Defense and War and of the Minister for Air." Death wasn't so very terrible, it was an occupational accident; Zézette was tough, and young enough to pick up her life again; it's always so simple when there aren't any kids. For the rest—well, he would have to go, and then, at the end, he would keep his rifle, that was an understood thing. But when would the end come? In two years? In five years? The last war had gone on for fifty-two months. For fifty-two months he would have to kow-tow to sergeants and adjutants—all those bastards he had so particularly hated. Obey them hand and foot, salute them in the street, whereas he now had to keep his hands in his pockets to stop himself from knocking them down. In the line, of course, they have to behave themselves, they're scared of a bullet in the back; but off duty they made you eat it just as in the barracks. Oh, for the first attack! How I shall enjoy knocking out the sergeant ahead of me! He walked on, feeling as depressed and limp as he had felt when, as a boxer, he undressed in the locker-room a quarter of an hour before a fight. War was a long, long road; better not think of it too much; otherwise one lost faith in everything, even in the hour of victory, when they would all come back with their rifles in their hands. A long, long road. And perhaps he would be killed halfway through, as though his sole purpose were to lay down his life in defense of the Schneider factories, or M. de Wendel's money-bags. He was walking in the black dust between the wall of the Penhoët works and that of the Germain construction-yard; he could see, some distance away on the right, the tilted roofs of the repair-shops of the Nord railway, and, still farther off, the tall red chimney of the distillery, and he thought: "A long, long road." One-eyed Pascal laughed among the cars, Maurice stumped through the dust, and Mathieu was sitting by the sea, listening to Jacques and saying to himself: "Maybe he's right." He reflected that he was soon to shed his profession, his clothes, and his identity and go off naked to the most absurd of wars, to a war lost in advance; he felt submerged by anonymity. He was no longer anything at all, neither Boris's old teacher, nor the former lover of what was formely Marcelle, nor Ivich's elderly admirer—just a man without a name, without the mark of age, robbed of his future, with days before him that could not be foreseen. At half past eleven the autobus stopped at Safi, and Pierre got out of it to stretch his legs. Flat, yellow hutments beside the tarred road; behind him Safi, out of sight, sloped downwards to the sea. Some Arabs, on an expanse of ochrous earth, crouched stewing in the heat; the airplane sped over a yellow and gray checkerboard that was France. "They don't need to give a good God-damn about all this," thought Pierre enviously; he was walking among the Arabs, he could touch them, and yet he was not really there; they calmly smoked their kef in the sunshine; he was going to get his face smashed in Alsace. He tripped over a mound of earth; the airplane dropped into an airpocket, and the old gentleman thought: "I don't like flying." Hitler leaned over the table, the general pointed to the map and said: "Five brigades of tanks. A thousand planes will leave Dresden, Tempelhof, and Munich," and Chamberlain pressed his handkerchief to his mouth and thought: "It's my second journey by air. I don't like flying." They can't help me; there they are, squatting in the sunshine, like little saucepans full of steaming water, they are happy, they are alone upon the earth; "God in heaven," he thought in desperation, "if only I were an Arab!"

At a quarter to twelve François Hannequin, certified chemist, of Saint-Flour, about five feet four inches in height, nose straight, medium forehead, slight squint, short beard, evil-smelling breath and pubic hairs, chronic enteritis up to the age of seven, Œdipus complex liquidated about the age of thirteen, *"bachot"* at seventeen, masturbated twice or three times weekly until his military service, subscriber to the *Temps* and the *Matin,* married to Espérance Dieulafoy, no children, practicing Catholic to the tune of two or three Communions a quarter, went up to the first floor, entered the nuptial chamber where his wife was trying on a hat, and said: "It's just as I told you, they're calling up the No. 2's."

His wife put the hat down on the dressing-table, took the pins out of her mouth, and said: "So you'll be off this afternoon?"

And he said: "Yes, by the five o'clock train."

"Oh dear!" said his wife, "and I'm all upside down, I shall never have time to get things ready for you. What will you want to take?—shirts, of course, and long pants, you've got woolen, muslin, and cotton ones—better take the woolens. And flannel belts, you could take five or six, by rolling them into a bundle."

"No belts," said Hannequin, "regular lice nests."

"How disgusting—but you won't have any lice. Do take them, just to please me; once you get there, you'll find some use for them. Fortunately I've still got some canned stuff—I bought it back in '36 at the time of the strikes, though you laughed at me; I've got a tin of cabbage in white wine, but you won't like that."

"No, it doesn't agree with me. But," he said, rubbing his hands, "if you have a small can of bean stew . . ."

"A can of bean stew," said Espérance, "but, poor baby, how will you manage to heat it?"

"Never mind that," said Hannequin.

"What do you mean? You need a double boiler to heat it."

"Well, there's some jellied chicken, isn't there?"

"Yes, that's the stuff, jellied chicken, and a fine Bologna sausage that the Clermont cousins sent us."

He pondered a moment and then said: "I'll take my Swiss knife."

"Yes. And where can I have put the thermos for your coffee?"

"Ah, yes, coffee, I shall need something hot to settle my stomach; it will be the first time since I married that I shall dine without soup," said he, with a dismal smile.

"Put in a few plums while you're about it, and a flask of brandy."

"Will you take the yellow suitcase?"

He gave a start. "The suitcase? Not on your life, it's awkward to carry, and besides I don't want to lose it. Everything gets stolen in the army. I'll take my musette-bag."

"What musette-bag?"

"Why, the one I used to take when I went fishing, before we were married. What have you done with it?"

"What have I done with it? I really don't know, honey, you confuse me so, I think I put it in the attic."

"The attic! Good Lord, among the mice! That'll be a nice mess."

"You'd much better take the suitcase; it isn't very large, you can sort of keep an eye on it. Ah! I know where it is: at Mathilde's. I lent it to her for a picnic."

"You lent my musette-bag to Mathilde?"

"No, not the musette-bag, silly. The thermos, of course."

"Well, I want my musette-bag," said Hannequin firmly.

"Darling, please think a little of all the things I've got to do for you; you might try to help me a little, go and look for the musette-bag yourself; try the attic."

He went upstairs and opened the door of the attic; it smelt musty, he could hardly see a thing, and a mouse darted between his feet. "Damn it all," he thought, "the rats must have eaten it up."

There were several trunks, a wicker dress-form, a world globe, an old oven, a dentist's chair, a harmonium, all of which would have to be moved out of the way. Perhaps she had put it in a trunk, where it would have been safe. He opened the trunks one by one and shut them angrily. It was so handy; it was made of leather with a zipper; it had two compartments and it was unbelievable what you could stuff in it. It was just the sort of article that helped a man to get through a bad time; no one realized how precious such things were. "In any case, I shan't take the suitcase," he thought angrily. "I would rather take nothing at all."

He sat down on a trunk; his hands were black with dust, he felt dust all over his body, like a dry, viscous paste; he held his hands out so as not to dirty his black jacket; how on earth was he to get out of that attic?—he was sick of it all; he dreaded the night, without even a bowl of hot soup to soothe his stomach; it was all so stupid, and he was feeling so alone up there at the top of the house sitting on his trunk and thinking of the noisy, dark railway station that awaited him, two hundred yards below, when a shrill cry from Espérance made him jump; it was a cry of triumph. "I've got it! I've got it!" He opened the door, and dashed to the staircase.

"Where was it?"

"I've got your musette-bag, it was downstairs in the storeroom cupboard."

He came downstairs, took the musette-bag from his wife's hands, opened it, looked at it, brushed it with the flat of his hand, and then, putting it on the bed, he said: "Look here, darling, I've been wondering whether it wouldn't be a good idea to buy myself a good pair of shoes?"

Lunch-time! They had entered the blinding tunnel of midday; outside, the sky, white with heat; outside, the dead, white roads, no man's land, and war; behind the closed shutters they sat stifling in the heat. Daniel put his napkin on his knees, Hannequin tied his napkin round his neck, Brunet took the paper napkin from the table, crumpled it and wiped his lips, Jeannine wheeled Charles into the large and almost empty dining-room with its smudgy windows and spread a napkin on his chest. This was a truce: the war—well, yes, the war, but what about the heat! butter in a bowl of water; the big blob, blurred and oily, at the bottom of the bowl, and over it slimy gray

water and scraps of dead butter floating belly upwards;
Daniel watched the curls of butter melt in the radish-dish,
Brunet wiped his forehead, the cheese sweated on its plate
like an honest man at work, Maurice's beer was tepid, he
pushed his glass away: "Poo! tastes like piss!" A bit of ice
was floating in Mathieu's red wine, he drank—first he felt
a cold liquid in his mouth, and then a little pool of musty
wine still slightly warm, which promptly melted into
water; Charles turned his head and said: "Soup again!
It's crazy to serve soup in midsummer." His plate was laid
on his chest, it warmed his skin through the napkin and
his shirt, he could see the edge of the plate quite clearly
and dipped his spoon into it, then raised it vertically; but
a man on his back can't be sure of what is vertical, so part
of the liquid splashed back into the plate. Charles moved
the spoon to a point above his lips, lowered it, and—Hell!
it always happened, the burning liquid trickled on to his
cheek and soaked his shirt collar. The war—ah yes! the
war. No, said Zézette, not the radio, I don't want it, I won't
think of the war. Well, let's have a bit of music, said
Maurice. Chersau, good-b—b-r-r-r—my star—here is the
news—sombreros and mantillas—*J'attendrai,* at the request of Huguette Arnal, Pierre Ducroc, his wife and two
daughters of La Roche-Canillac, Mlle Eliane of Calvi and
Jean-François Roquette, for his little Marie-Madeleine,
and a group of typists at Tulle for their soldier sweet-
hearts, *J'attendrai,* day and night, have some more bouilla-
baisse, no thanks, said Mathieu, something can surely be
arranged, the radio crackled, sped over the white, dead
squares, smashed the windows, and penetrated into the
dim, vaporous interiors of the houses, and Odette thought:
It's got to work all right, it's so hot. Mademoiselle Eliane,
Zézette, Jean-François Roquette, and the Ducroc family
of La Roche-Canillac, thought: It's got to work out all
right—it's so hot. What should they do? asked Daniel; it
was a false alarm, thought Charles, they'll leave us where

we are; Ella Birnenschatz laid down her fork, tilted her head back, and said: "War? I don't believe in it." *J'attendrai toujours ton retour*. The airplane was flying above a flat expanse of dusty glass; at the extremity of that expanse, very far away, could be seen a patch of resin; Henry leaned towards Chamberlain and shouted in his ear: That's England, England and the crowd at the airport gates, waiting till you come back, darling, waiting till you come back, he felt slightly faint, it was so hot, he wanted to forget the fly-headed conqueror and the Hotel Dreesen and the memorandum, he wanted to believe—he really did —that everything would still come out all right, he closed his eyes, *Ma poupée chérie*, at the request of Mme Duranty and her little niece, of Decazeville, the war, good Lord, yes, the war and the heat, and the sad, acquiescent sleep of afternoon. Casa, here we are at Casa, the autobus stopped on a white, deserted square, Pierre got out first and scorching tears welled up into his eyes; there was still an atmosphere of morning in the autobus, but outside, in the glaring sunshine, the morning was dead. The end of morning, *ma poupée chérie*, the end of youth and hope— the great catastrophe of noon. Jean Servin had pushed his plate away, he was reading the sports page in *Paris-Soir*, he knew nothing of the Decree of Partial Mobilization, he had been to work, he had come back for lunch, and he would return to work about two o'clock; Lucien Rénier was cracking nuts in the palms of his hands, he had read the white notices, and he thought: It's a bluff; François Destutt, laboratory assistant at the Institut Derrien, was wiping his plate with a bit of bread, thinking of nothing, his wife was thinking of nothing, René Malleville, Pierre Charnier thought of nothing. Morning—war was a sharp sliver of ice in their heads, which soon melted into a little tepid pool. *Ma poupée chérie*, the rich dark savor of beef cooked in Burgundy fashion, the smell of fish, the scrap of meat between two molars, the fumes of red wine, and the heat, the heat! Ladies and gentlemen of the radio audience, France, resolute but pacific, firmly confronts her destiny.

He was tired, he was dizzy, he rubbed his hand three times over his eyes, the daylight hurt him, and Dawburn, who was sucking the point of his pencil, said to his *Morning Post* colleague: "He's off his nut." He raised his hand and said in a faltering voice:

"My first duty, now that I am back, is to report to the French and British Governments on the results of my mission, and until I have done so, it would be difficult for me to say anything more."

Noon enveloped him in its white shroud, Dawburn looked at him and thought of long, lonely roads curving between red rocks and rusted by the fire of heaven. The old gentleman added, in an even more faltering tone: "I will say just this: I am confident that all interested parties will continue their efforts to find a peaceful solution of the problem of Czechoslovakia, because thereby hangs the peace of Europe in our time."

She slowly picks up crumbs off the tablecloth. She looks rather off color, as though she had hay-fever, and she said: I've got a touch of gas on the stomach, and she cried a little; it would upset all her habits. But I said "Just at first. Only at first." She thinks she is unhappy, she fancies that the little shiver in her head must be unhappiness. She sits up straight, she tells herself that she must not give way, all the women of France are as unhappy as she is. Grave and stately, her shapely arms resting on the tablecloth, she looks like the dame enthroned in the cashier's cage of a large shop. She does not think, she refuses to think, that she will be much more comfortable when I have gone. What is she thinking about—that fleck of rust on her knife-rest? She frowns, she scratches it off with the tip of a reddened nail. Much more comfortable. Her mother, her friends, the workroom, the great bed all to herself, no meals, she will fry eggs on the side of the stove, the little girl is not difficult to feed, just pap all the time, but give me anything you like, I used to say, don't try to make up dinners, I never notice what I eat, but she was obstinate; it was her duty.

"Georges?"

"Darling?"

"Would you like some tea?"

"No, thank you."

She drinks her tea with a sigh, her eyes are red. She looks, not at me, but at the sideboard, because it is there, directly facing her. To me she has nothing to say, except perhaps: Take care not to catch cold. She will in fact picture me this evening in the train, a small emaciated figure huddled in the corner of a compartment, but that is the limit of what she can imagine; she thinks of her life here —my absence will make a gap. Quite a small gap, Andrée; I make so little noise. I would sit in the armchair with a book. She would be darning stockings; we had nothing to talk about. The armchair will be always there. The important item is the armchair. She will write to me; three times a week, most conscientiously. She will look very serious, she will hunt for ink and pen and yellow spectacles, and then she will settle down sedately at the rather uncomfortable writing-desk she inherited from her Grandmother Vasseur—"The child is cutting her teeth, my mother will be here for Christmas, Mme Ancelin is dead, Emilienne is going to be married in September, a good match, a middle-aged man in the insurance business." If the child gets whooping-cough, she won't tell me, so as not to cause me any anxiety. "Poor Georges, it isn't fair, he does worry so." She will send me parcels—sausage, sugar, coffee, tobacco, woolen socks, sardines, meat tablets, salted butter. One of ten thousand parcels, identical with the other ten thousand; if I were given the next man's by mistake, I shouldn't notice—parcels, letters, Jeannette's pap, the stains on the knife-rest, the dust on the sideboard, that will suffice her; in the evening she will say: "I'm tired, I can't do any more." She won't read the papers. No more than she does now; she detests them, they make such a lot of waste-paper, which can't be used for two days for the kitchen or the toilet. Mme Hébertot will come and tell her the news—We have won a great victory, or Things aren't going well, my dear, not at all well, we aren't making any progress. Henri and Pascal have already agreed with their wives on a code to indicate where they are by underlining certain letters. But that's no good to Andrée. He did suggest it once:

"I can let you know where I am."

"But isn't that forbidden?" she asked with surprise.

"Well, yes, but it can be done, just as in the war of '14, by reading all the capitals together, for instance."

"It's very complicated," she sighed.

"No, you'll see, it's perfectly simple."

"Yes, and then you'll get caught, your letters will be torn up, and I shall be anxious."

"It's worth risking."

"Just as you like, dear, but you know how I am about geography. I shall look at a map, I shall see a circle with a name underneath, and I shall be none the wiser."

That was that. In one sense it's better, it's much better like that; she will draw my salary. . . .

"Have I given you the power of attorney?"

"Yes, darling, I put it away in the desk."

Much better. It must be trying to have to leave someone who really does mind, one must feel so vulnerable. I push my chair back.

"No, darling, it's not worth while folding up your napkin."

"True."

She does not ask me where I am going. She never asks where I am going. I tell her: "I'm going to see the child."

"Don't wake her."

I shan't wake her; even if I wanted to, I couldn't make enough noise to wake her; I'm too light. He went in, one shutter had swung open, a dazzling, chalky afternoon had entered the room, half of which was still in shadow, while the other half sparkled in a dusty light; the child was asleep in her cradle; Georges sat down beside her. Her fair hair, her innocent little mouth, and her rounded drooping cheeks gave her an odd resemblance to an English magistrate. She was beginning to love me. The sun was gaining ground, gently he pushed the cradle back. There! That will do. She won't be pretty, she is too like me. Poor little mite, much better be like her mother. Still quite soft; practically boneless. And yet she already bears within her the strict law that has been my law: the cells will multiply, the cartilages will harden, the cranium will ossify, in accordance with my law. A skinny, insignificant little girl, with dull hair, scoliosis in the right shoulder, and very short-sighted, she will glide noiselessly on her way, barely touching earth, and skirting round people and things, too light and weak to handle them. Heavens! The years will come upon her pitilessly, one by one—how futile it all is, her fate is written in her flesh, and she must live it out minute by minute, the fate she thinks she has herself discovered; but there it is, complete, repellently obvious, I have tainted her myself, and why must she live, drop by drop, through what I have lived? Why must everything be *repeated* indefinitely? A skinny little girl, a clear-eyed, sensitive small soul, born to suffer sorely in this life. I am going away, I have other things to do; she will grow up, and here, so obstinately and recklessly, she stands for what I was. The whooping-cough, long convalescences, luckless passions for her pretty, plump, pink-fleshed school-friends, and the mirrors in which she will eye herself in passing— Am I too ugly to be loved? Day after day the savor of something already seen—Good Lord, is it worth what she must endure? She awoke for a moment, and looked at him with solemn curiosity, for this was a moment that seemed wholly new. He lifted her from the cradle and clasped her in his arms. "My little one! My little baby! My poor little one!" But she took fright and began to scream.

"Georges!" came a reproachful voice from the other room. He laid the child gently back in its cradle. She again gazed at him for a moment with a set and surly look, then her eyes closed, opened, blinked, then closed again. She had just begun to love me. In time, had I been constantly with her, she would have got so used to my presence that she could no longer *see* me. How long will it last? Five years, six years? I shall return to an actual little girl who will look at me with amazement, and think: "That's my papa!" and she'll be ashamed of me in front of her little friends. That also I have known. When my father came home, I was twelve. The afternoon had now invaded nearly the whole room. The afternoon; the war. War must be a sort of interminable afternoon. He rose noiselessly, gently opened the window, and pulled down the Venetian blind.

Cabin 19—there it was. She did not venture in, she remained outside the door, suitcase in hand, struggling to convince herself that she was still hopeful. And if it did prove to be a really *nice* little cabin, with a bedside rug, and possibly flowers in a tooth-glass on the wash-basin shelf? Such things do happen, one often meets people who say: "On such and such a boat, there's no need to take second-class cabins, the thirds are as comfortable as the firsts." Then perhaps France would yield and say: "Ah, that's quite an exceptional cabin. If the thirds were always like that . . ." Maud put herself in France's place—a conciliatory and rather vacillating France, who would say: "Oh well . . . we shall be all right here." But she remained frozen in her inmost self, frozen and resigned. She heard footsteps, she did not like to be caught wandering about the passageways by night; there had once been a theft, and she had had to submit to rather unpleasant questions; the poor must be so careful in small matters, people are so merciless. She suddenly found herself in the middle of the cabin; well, this in fact was what she had expected. Accommodation for six: three bunks on her right, three others on her left. "Well, I never!" No flowers on the wash-basin, no bedside rug; she wouldn't have believed it. No chairs either, no table. Four persons would have felt rather cramped there, but the wash-basin was clean. She wanted to cry, but it wasn't worth while; she had foreseen it all. France *could not* travel third-class, that was the plain fact beyond dispute. Just as Ruby could not travel in a train with her back to the engine. One might indeed wonder why France should persist in taking third-class tickets. But on that point, as on the other, France deserved no blame; she took third-class tickets because she had a taste for economy and because she managed the finances of Baby's orchestra with the utmost care; she was not to be blamed for that. Maud put her suitcase on the floor, she tried for a moment to strike roots in the cabin, to pretend to have been there for two days. In that event, the bunks, the yellow-painted bolt-heads that dotted the cabin partitions, would all have been familiar, friendly objects. She said to herself in an emphatic undertone: "But this is a very nice cabin." Then she felt tired, she picked up her suitcase and remained standing between the bunks not knowing quite what to do; if we stay, I shall have to unpack, but we certainly shan't stay, and if France sees that I have begun to make myself comfortable, she is rather perverse, and that would be one reason more for her to refuse to stay. She felt such a transitory being in that cabin, on that ship, and on the earth. The captain was a tall, heavy man with white hair. She shivered and thought: "We should be quite all right, all four of us, if only there were no one else." But one look round sufficed to dispel that hope; some baggage had been put down on a right-hand bunk—a wicker basket secured by a rusty rod, and a fiber suitcase—no, not fiber, cardboard—with frayed corners. And then—the last straw—she looked up and saw a woman of about thirty, pallid, with pinched nostrils and closed eyes, outstretched on the upper right-hand bunk. Well, that settled it. He had looked at her legs when she passed him on deck; he was smoking a cigar, she knew that type of man, smelling of cigars and eau de Cologne. Well, they would appear tomorrow, rather flamboyant and heavily made-up, on the second-class deck, when the passengers would be already installed, having made their acquaintances and chosen their companions for the voyage, Ruby very erect, with her gay, swaying hips and laughing, peering eyes, and Doucette saying in her heady voice: "No, darling, come along, since the captain wishes it." Respectable gentlemen, sitting on deck with rugs over their knees, would eye them coldly, the ladies would make offensive comments as they passed, and in the evenings, in the corridors, they would meet sundry more amiable gentlemen with roving hands. How she did long to stay here, within those four yellow-painted iron walls, they would be so comfortable, just the four of them.

France opened the door, Ruby came in behind her.

"Hasn't the luggage been brought down?" asked France in her most impressive voice.

Maud signed to her to be silent, pointing to the sick woman. France raised her wide, clear, lashless eyes to the upper bunk; her face remained imperious and expressionless, as it usually was, but Maud understood that the game was lost.

"We might do worse," said Maud briskly, "the cabin is nearly in the middle of the ship; we shall feel the pitching less."

Ruby's reply was a shrug of her shoulders. France asked nonchalantly: "How shall we arrange ourselves?"

"Just as you like. Shall I take the lower bunk?" asked Maud eagerly.

France could not sleep if she knew two people were above her.

"We'll see," she said; "we'll see."

The captain's eyes were clear and frosty, his face was red. The door opened and a lady in black appeared. She mumbled a few words and sat down on the bunk, between the suitcase and the basket. She looked about fifty, very shabbily dressed, with a coarse, dirty furrowed skin and bulging eyes. Maud looked at her and thought: "That does it." She produced a lipstick from her bag and began to make up her lips. France looked at her out of the corner of her eye with such an air of majestic satisfaction that Maud, in irritation, let her lipstick drop into her bag. There was a long silence, which Maud recognized as having occurred in another cabin just like this, on the *Saint-Georges* bound for Tangier, and the previous year on the *Théophile Gautier*, when they were on their way for a season at the Polytheion at Corinth. It was suddenly broken by an odd little sniff; the lady in black had produced a handkerchief, opened it, and stretched it over her face; she was crying, quietly but without restraint, like a person preparing for a lengthy ordeal. After a moment or two, she opened her basket and took out a piece of buttered bread, a slice of cold lamb, and a thermos wrapped in a napkin. She began to eat still crying, she uncorked the bottle and poured some hot coffee into the cup as she munched, and large glittering tears trickled down her cheeks. Maud looked at the cabin with a fresh vision; it was a waiting-room, just a waiting-room in a dismal little country railway station. She only hoped he wasn't vicious. She sniffed and threw her head back. France glanced at her coldly.

"This cabin is too small," observed France impressively.

"We shall be very uncomfortable here. They promised me at Casablanca that we should have a six-berth cabin to ourselves."

The ritual had begun, there was something sinister and solemn in the air; Maud said feebly: "We might pay extra on our tickets."

France did not reply. She had sat down on the left-hand bunk and seemed to be reflecting. In a moment or two her face cleared, and she said cheerfully: "We might suggest to the captain that we should give a free concert in the first-class saloon—then perhaps he would have our luggage moved to a better cabin."

Maud said nothing; it was for Ruby to reply.

"An excellent idea," said Ruby brightly.

Maud suddenly shivered and felt disgusted with herself. She turned to France and said in a pleading voice: "You go, France! You are our foreman, it's your job to go and see the captain."

"Not at all," said France gaily. "What's the sense in an old woman like me going to see the captain? He'll be much nicer to a pretty young lady like you."

A large red-faced man with white hair and gray eyes. He would be meticulously neat, they always were. France reached out an arm and pressed the bell-button.

"It had better be fixed up at once," she said. The lady in black was still crying. She raised her head abruptly and seemed to notice their presence.

"Are you thinking of changing your cabin?" she asked anxiously.

France fixed her with an icy look. Maud answered briskly: "We have a great deal of luggage, madame. We shall be very cramped and should be in your way."

"Oh no you wouldn't," said the lady. "I like company."

There was a knock at the door, and the steward entered. "This is it!" thought Maud. She produced her lipstick and powder-box, went up to the mirror, and began to make up hastily.

"Would you kindly ask the captain," said France, "if he can spare a minute to receive Mademoiselle Maud Dassignies, of Baby's All-Girl Orchestra?"

"He won't," said he; "I bet he won't."

Wicker armchairs in the shade of the plane trees. Daniel was immersed in ancient, tedious recollections; at Vichy, in 1920, he had sat dozing in a wicker armchair, under the great trees in the park, with the same courteous smile on his lips, his mother knitting by his side; now Marcelle was beside him knitting socks for the baby and dreaming of the war with vacant eyes. The great fly buzzed and buzzed, much time had passed since Vichy, that fly was still buzzing, and the garden smelt of mint; behind them, in the hotel drawing-room, someone was playing the piano, and had been doing so for twenty years—a hundred years. The hairs on his finger-joints bristled in the sunshine, and a flicker of sunshine warmed a drain of coffee and a little glittering reef of sugar left in the bottom of his cup. Daniel broke up the sugar, for the sheer pleasure of feeling it rasp beneath the spoon. The garden sloped gently down to the sluggish, tepid river; he breathed the smell of heated foliage and caught sight of a *Revue des Deux Mondes* that M. de Lestrange, a retired colonel, had left on a table beyond the stairway. Death, eternity, not to be escaped—the soft insinuating onset of eternity; green and viscous leaves overhead; the inevitable heap of early dead leaves. Émile, sole living figure in the landscape, was digging beneath the chestnut trees. He was the son of the hotel-keepers; beside him, at the edge of the ditch, lay a gray tarpaulin sack. In the sack was Zizi, the dead dog. Émile was digging her grave; he was wearing a broad-brimmed straw hat, and the sweat glittered on his bare back. A coarse, commonplace lad, with a brutish face, like a rock with two horizontal, moss-grown fissures in place of eyes, seventeen years old, and already laying the girls, he was the local billiards champion and smoked cigars; but he was the undeserving possessor of a lovely body.

"Ah," said Marcelle, "if only I could believe you! . . ."

Of course. Of course she couldn't believe him. And yet what difference could war make to her? She would continue to enlarge in some little country retreat. Why on earth doesn't she go? She is missing her siesta. The boy put his foot on the spade and threw all his weight upon it; Daniel longed to lay his hands on the boy's sides and slide them gently upwards, like a masseur, while he went on digging—oh, to feel the ripple of those dorsal muscles, to slip his fingers into the moist shadow of the armpits; his sweat smelt of thyme. He swallowed a mouthful of marc.

"It would be too lovely," said Marcelle. "But you see—mobilization has begun."

"My dear Marcelle, you mustn't believe all you hear. The Home Fleet will make its usual trip into the North Sea, and two hundred thousand men will be mobilized in France. Hitler will mass four armored divisions on the Czech frontier. After which, these gentlemen having satisfied their consciences, they will have a quiet little talk around a table."

Women's bodies, like indiarubber, and boned meat, are rather flabbily ebullient and obtrusive. But that lovely body demanded the caresses of the sculptor, it ought to be reproduced in clay. Daniel sat up straight in his armchair and fixed a glittering eye upon Marcelle. This won't do—I mustn't drift into that again. I'm too old for it now. I drink a glass of marc, I talk gravely about the forthcoming war, and my eyes linger on a bare, youthful back, a sinewy rump, and anything likely to amuse me on a summer afternoon. Let it come! Let war come at last, let it batter at my eyes and fill them with visions of tainted, wrecked, and bleeding bodies, save me from the eternal round, this incessant, drab desire of every day, from smiles, and foliage, and buzzing flies; a fiery geyser leaps into the sky, a flame that burns the face and eyes, and seems to tear the cheeks away; let it come at last, the nameless moment that revives no memory.

"But surely," said Marcelle, in a tone of affectionate tolerance—she hardly appreciated his political capacities —"Germany can't draw back, can she? And we have reached the limit of concessions. What then?"

"Don't worry," said Daniel bitterly. "We shall make all the needful concessions; we know no limits. So Germany can afford the luxury of a withdrawal—it would, indeed, look like an act of generosity."

Émile was now erect, wiping his forehead with the back of his hand, his armpit glistened in the sun, he looked up at the sky with a smile—a young god. A young god! Daniel clawed at the arm of his chair. How often, oh Lord, how often had he said: "A young god," as he looked at a boy in the sunshine. The stale patter of an old auntie; I *am* a pederast—he uttered the words, and words they remained; they passed him by, and suddenly he thought: "How could the war change anything?" He would find himself sitting on the slope of an embankment during a lull, listlessly watching the bare back of a young soldier digging, or searching for lice, and his practiced lips would murmur automatically: "A young god." A man's self accompanies him everywhere.

"Anyhow," he said abruptly, "man was born to trouble. Suppose war does come? I guess we'd get used to that just like everything else."

"Oh, Daniel!" Marcelle looked really shocked. "How can you say such a thing! War would be—it would be dreadful."

Words. Words.

"What is dreadful," said Daniel with a smile, "is the fact

that nothing is ever very dreadful. There are no extremes."

Marcelle looked at him with a faint air of surprise, her eyes were dull and red. "She's getting sleepy," thought Daniel with satisfaction.

"As regards moral suffering, yes. But, Daniel, there's physical suffering."

"Ah!" said Daniel, wagging a finger at her. "You are already thinking of the pain you'll have to bear. Well, wait and see; I fancy that, too, has been much exaggerated."

Marcelle smiled at him, stifling a yawn.

"Come," said Daniel, getting up, "the main thing is not to worry. You have nearly missed your siesta. You don't sleep enough; in your condition, you need a lot of sleep."

"Don't sleep enough!" said Marcelle, yawning and laughing at the same time. "Indeed, I feel quite ashamed, I never read a book, I spend all day on my bed."

Fortunately, thought Daniel, kissing her fingertips. "I bet," he said, "you haven't written to your mother."

"It's true," she said. "I'm a bad girl." She yawned and added: "I'll do it before I go to sleep."

"No," said Daniel briskly. "You go and rest. I'll drop her a line myself."

"Oh, Daniel!" said Marcelle with confusion and delight; "a line from her son-in-law—she'll be so proud!"

She walked rather unsteadily up the stairway; he returned and sat down in his armchair. He yawned, time passed, and then he became aware that he was listening to the piano. He looked at his watch: twenty-five minutes past three. Marcelle would come down at six for her apéritif walk. Two and a half hours ahead of me, he said to himself, not without disquiet. The trouble was that his solitude, in other days, was like the air he breathed, he made use of it unconsciously. Now that it was vouchsafed to him in spasms, he didn't know what to do with it. Worse still—I'm really less bored in the company of Marcelle.

"Well," he said to himself, "the choice was yours." A little marc was left in the bottom of his glass, he drank it up. On that June evening when he had resolved to marry her, he had been in utter misery of mind, he anticipated every sort of horror. And here was the result: a wicker armchair, the acrid savor of marc in his mouth, and that naked back over there. War would be just the same. Horrors always come next day. Myself married, and a soldier; I come upon nothing but my own self. Scarcely that: a succession of small impulses, darting centrifugally here and there, but no focus. And yet *there is* a focus: that focus is myself, and there the horror lies. He looked up, the fly was buzzing at the level of his eyes, he brushed it away. Another escape. A wave of the hand and it was gone; but why bother about that fly? If I had been an insensible stone figure, incapable of sound and movement, blind and deaf, flies and earwigs and ladybirds would run up and down me, and I should stand, a fantastic, white-eyed statue, devoid of purpose, impervious to pain; I might then have coincided with myself. Not so as to accept myself, heaven forbid! but thus becoming the pure object of my hatred. A slash in his consciousness—four notes of a polonaise, the gleam of that back, an itch in his thumb, and he got a grip on himself again. Why can't I *be* what I am, *be* a pederast, villain, coward, a loathsome object that doesn't even manage to exist? He set his knees together, laid his hands on his thighs, and almost laughed aloud at the thought of how respectable he must look. He shrugged his shoulders: idiot! He was sick of thinking what he looked like, sick of looking at himself—especially as, when I look at myself, I am two people. Just *to be*. In the dark, at random! To be homosexual just as the oak is oak. To extinguish myself. Extinguish the inner eye. "Extinguish." The word rolled like thunder and reverberated through vast empty saloons. Away with words, they produced a swarm of trivial respites, each proffering an encounter at

the far end of himself. . . . Another slash—Daniel found
another self, a bored and somnolent fellow with only two
hours ahead of him and trying to kill time. Why can't I be
what they see, what Mathieu sees—and Ralph, with his
filthy little mind; words should be brushed off like mos-
quitoes; he began to count, one, two—words came to him
—a summer visitor's entertainment. He counted faster, he
narrowed the links of the chain, and the words could no
longer penetrate. Five, six, seven, eight, depths beneath
the sea, an image of something squat and hideous, a denizen of those depths, a spider-crab, it was opening out,
twenty-two, twenty-three, Daniel became aware that he
was holding his breath, he exhaled, twenty-seven, twenty-
eight, the boy was still digging, up above, on the surface;
the image was now a gaping sore, an acrid mouth, and it
was bleeding, it's myself, I *am* those parted lips and the
blood that bubbles through them, thirty-three, the image
was familiar, and yet it had never appeared to him before.
Away with images too; a strange, impalpable fear possessed him. He must let himself slide, as one did when
trying to sleep. But *I'm going to sleep!* He shook himself,
and came forth to the surface. Here was silence; the
crushing, moribund silence that he sought in vain within
himself was there, outside, and he felt afraid. The meager
sunshine scattering shifting circles on the ground, the
river-ripple in the treetops, the boy's bare back—so near,
so far away!—all this seemed so utterly alien that he set
himself adrift once more, he slipped backwards, he could
see the garden from below, like a diver looking upwards
at the sky. Noiseless, voiceless—silence all around him,
above, below: and himself, a little garrulous hiatus in the
center of that silence. One, two, three—away with words,
let the silence of the garden pass, conjoin, and unify
through me, and equalize my breath. Slowly, steadily, let
each column of air smash like a piston each nascent word.
Oh, *to be*, like a tree, like the boy's back, like the moonlets

flickering over the flushed earth. Let me shut my eyes; but eyes reach too far, beyond the moment and the self, they are *there* already, envisaging the leaves, and the boy's back: the hunted, furtive, fleeting gaze, always ahead of itself, peers into the distance. But he dared not lower his eyelids; Émile was no doubt glancing up at him now and then—an elderly gentleman dozing after lunch; he might submit to the spell of an object, let the look linger and browse, absorb it, and then slip into his own depths, freed now from eyes, *in my enveloping night;* he fixed his eyes on the grass border on the left, which lay like a huge embodied motion, green and solidified; a wave poised at the moment of its break; his vagrant look, shifting from leaf to leaf, melted into that vegetal turmoil. One (breathe in), two (breathe out), three (breathe in), four (breathe out). He spun round as he dropped and met, on his downward passage, a teeming desire to laugh. I'm doing a dervish act, mustn't swallow my tongue, why, it was overhead already, down he plunged, passing two disheveled words —Fear, Defiance—reascending to the surface. A challenge hurled at the clear sky, he conceived it without a visual image and without words, it's coming, opening like the mouth of a sewer. Under the blue heaven, a bitter lament, a futile supplication, *Eli, Eli, lama sabactani,* these were the last words he met, they darted up like dancing bubbles. The green abundance of the grass border was there, unseen, unnamed, a plenitude of presence in his vision, it's coming, *it's coming*. It clove him like a scythe, amazing, awful, and delightful. At long last the husk bursts and opens, I am myself for all eternity, homosexual, mean, coward. *They* see me—no, not even that: *it* sees me. He was *the object* of looking. A look that searched him to the depths, pierced him like a knife-thrust, and was not his own look; an impenetrable look, the embodiment of night, awaiting him in his deepest self and condemning him to be himself, coward, hypocrite, pederast, for all eternity.

Himself, quivering beneath that look, and defying it. That look! The night! As if night was the look. I am *seen*. Transparent, transparent, transfixed. But by whom? "*I am not alone*," said Daniel aloud. Émile straightened up.

"What's the matter, M'sieur Sereno?" he asked.

"I was asking if you would soon be finished," said Daniel.

"It's coming along," said Émile.

He stood for a moment looking at Daniel with insolent curiosity. But, after all, this was a human look, a look that can be looked at. Daniel got up, trembling with fear.

"Don't you get tired when you dig in the sun?"

"I'm used to it," said Émile.

He had an attractive chest, rather fleshy, with two pink points on it, and he leaned on his spade with a provocative air; in three strides. . . . But here was this strange, strange joy, more intense than all the pleasures of the flesh; that Look.

"It's too hot," said Daniel. "I shall go in and rest for a while."

He nodded, and walked up the stairway. His mouth was dry, but he had made up his mind: in his room, with curtains drawn and shutters closed, he would begin the experience afresh.

Seventeen fifteen at Saint-Flour. Mme Hannequin accompanied her husband to the station; they had taken the steep short cut. M. Hannequin was wearing his sports suit, with the musette-bag slung over his shoulder; he had his new shoes on, and they pinched him. Halfway up they met Mme Calvé, who had stopped outside the notary's house to get her breath.

"Ah, my poor legs," she said as she caught sight of them. "I'm getting old."

"You're as active as ever," said Mme Hannequin. "I know very few people who can get up this path without stopping for a rest."

"And where are you off to?" asked Mme Calvé.

"My poor Jeanne," said Mme Hannequin. "I'm seeing my husband off. He's been called up."

"Impossible!" said Mme Calvé. "I didn't know! Well, well!" M. Hannequin thought she was looking at him with particular interest. "It must be hard," she said, "to have to go on such a lovely day."

"Can't be helped," said M. Hannequin.

"He's so brave," said Mme Hannequin.

"That's right," said Mme Calvé, smiling at Mme Hannequin. "Just what I was saying yesterday to my husband; our Frenchmen will all go bravely."

M. Hannequin felt young and bold.

"Well," he said, "we must be getting on."

"We'll be seeing you again soon," said Mme Calvé.

"I don't know about that," said Mme Hannequin, shaking her head.

"Certainly you will," said M. Hannequin emphatically.

They proceeded on their way, M. Hannequin walking briskly, until Mme Hannequin said:

"Easy, François, you know my heart is weak."

They met Marie, whose son was doing his military service.

"Any message for your son, Marie? I shall meet him perhaps; I'm a soldier again now."

Marie looked dumbfounded. "Tender Jesus!" she said, clasping her hands together.

M. Hannequin waved to her and they entered the station. It was Charlot who was punching the tickets.

"Ah, Monsieur Hannequin," said he, "so it's the big bang this time, eh?"

"The bim-bam-boom, the love rumba," replied M. Hannequin, handing him his ticket.

M. Pineau, the notary, was on the platform. He shouted from where he stood: "Off for a spree in Paris, eh?"

"Yes," said M. Hannequin, "or another sort of spree up

Nancy way." And he added gravely: "I'm called up."

"So that's how it is, eh?" said the notary. "But you're a Form 2 man, aren't you?"

"Certainly!"

"Oh well," said he, "you'll soon be back; this is all poppy-cock."

"I'm not so sure," replied M. Hannequin dryly. "In diplomacy, you know, there are situations that start by being comic and end in blood."

"And—do you fancy fighting for the Czechs?"

"Czechs or no Czechs, you always fight for nothing," replied M. Hannequin.

They laughed, and waved farewell. The Paris train was just coming into the station, but M. Pineau managed to kiss Mme Hannequin's hand.

M. Hannequin climbed unaided into his compartment. He flung his musette into his reserved corner, came back into the corridor, pulled down the window, and smiled at his wife.

"Peek-a-boo!" said he. "I'm going to be comfortable. There's plenty of room. I'll be able to lie down to sleep, I hope."

"A lot of people will get in at Clermont."

"Yes, I'm afraid so."

"Write to me," said she. "Just a line every day; it needn't be much."

"Of course I will."

"Don't forget to wear your flannel belts, just to please me."

"I promise," he said with smiling gravity.

He stood up, walked along the corridor, and came down on the step.

"Give me a kiss, old girl," he said.

He kissed her plump cheeks. She shed two tears.

"Oh dear!" she said. "How upsetting it all is! And what's the sense of it?"

"You really mustn't talk like that, darling," said he. "Now please—"

They said no more. He smiled at her, she looked at him with a smile, still crying; they had nothing more to say to each other.

Seventeen fifty-two o'clock at Niort. The large clock-hand jerks forward every minute, oscillates, and stops. The train, and the station, are black with coal dust. She insisted on coming, from a sense of duty. I said: "Don't bother to come." She looked at me with a shocked expression: "What do you mean, Georges? You don't know what you're saying." I said: "Don't stay too long, you mustn't leave the child alone." She said: "I'll ask Mother Cornu to look after her. I'll just see you on the train and then go back." And now, there she is, I lean out of the window and look at her. I want to smoke, but I don't like to, it doesn't seem quite decent. She looks towards the end of the platform, shading her eyes against the sunlight. And then from time to time she remembers I am there and smiles; but she can't think of anything to say. In effect, I have already gone.

"Pillows, rugs, oranges, lemonade, sandwiches."

"Georges!"

"Darling?"

"Would you like a few oranges?"

My musette is cram full. But she wants to give me something, just because I'm going away. If I refuse, she'll be upset. I don't like oranges.

"No, thanks."

"Not?"

"No, really. But it's very nice of you."

A pale smile. I have just kissed those cold, round, pretty cheeks and the corner of that smile. And she kissed me, which makes me feel a little ashamed; why this fuss, in Heaven's name? Because I am going away? Others are going away too. True, they also are being kissed. Many pretty women stand, in the light of the setting sun, in all the smoke and soot, looking with a painted smile at a man leaning out of a coach window. And then? We men must look a trifle ridiculous: she is too pretty, and too cold; I am too ugly.

"Write to me," she said; she had said it before, but one must fill up time—"as often as you can. It needn't be much. . . ."

It won't be. I shall have nothing to say. Nothing will happen to me, nothing ever does happen to me. Besides, I have already seen her reading letters: her intent, solemn, bored expression as she tilts her spectacles on to the end of her nose, reads to herself in an undertone, and manages to skip a line here and there.

"Well then, poor darling, I'll say good-by. Try to get a little sleep tonight."

Ah well, something had to be said. But she knows I never sleep in trains. She'll soon be repeating all this to Mother Cornu: "He got off all right, the train was packed. Poor Georges, I hope he'll get some sleep at least."

She looks round her with a despondent air; her large straw hat is a little on one side. A young man and a young woman have stopped near by.

"I must go away now; I can't leave the child any longer." She says this in rather a loud tone, with her eyes on the youthful pair. They are a little awe-inspiring, being both so handsome. But they do not notice her.

"That's right, darling. Good-by. Hurry back. I'll write as soon as possible."

One small tear, however. Why, in Heaven's name, why? She hesitates. What if she suddenly reached out her arms and said to me—"All this is a misunderstanding, I love you —I do love you."

"Don't catch cold."

"No, no. Good-by."

She goes. A wave of the hand, a flash of her eyes, and she departs, slowly, swaying her lithe hips—seventeen

fifty-five o'clock. I don't want to smoke now. The young
man and woman are still on the platform. He is carrying a
musette-bag and they have been talking about Nancy; he
too has been called up. They've stopped talking; they are
looking at each other. And I look at their hands, nice hands
with no wedding-rings. The woman, pale, tall, and slim,
with a mop of black hair; he, tall and fair, with healthy
tanned skin, his bare arms emerging from a short-sleeved,
blue silk shirt. Doors are slammed, they do not hear; they
no longer look at each other, they no longer need to, in
their inmost selves they are together.

"All aboard for Paris!"

She shivers, and says nothing. He does not kiss her, he
clasps her lovely bare arms at the level of the shoulders,
and slowly slides his hands down to the wrists. Thin, frail
wrists. He seems to be gripping them with all his strength.
She stands impassive, her arms inertly at her side, her face
asleep.

"All aboard!"

The train moves off, he jumps on to the step and stays
there clinging to the bars. She has turned towards him, the
sun whitens her face, she blinks, and smiles. A broad,
warm smile, confiding, calm, and tender; a man, however
handsome and strong, oughtn't to carry away such a smile
all to himself. She does not see me, she sees him only, she
peers into the sunshine that she may see him for yet another moment. And now I smile at her, I return her smile.
Eighteen o'clock. The train has left the station, it comes
out into the sunshine, all its windows glittering. She stays,
a diminutive dark figure, on the platform. Handkerchiefs
are waved all round her. She does not move, she waves no
handkerchief, her arms hang down, but she smiles, as
though her whole being were dissolving into that smile.
She is, no doubt, still smiling, but her smile is no longer
visible. She is visible. She is there, for him, for all the rest,
for me. My wife is back in our quiet house, sitting by the

child, enveloped once more in silence and peace. I'm off now, poor Georges, he's gone, I hope he'll get some sleep, I'm going, I'm escaping into the sunshine, smiling steadily at a small dark figure still standing on the station platform.

Eighteen ten o'clock. Pitteaux was pacing up and down rue Cassette; he had an appointment at eighteen o'clock; he looked at his wrist-watch, ten minutes past eighteen. I'll go up in five minutes. Five hundred and twenty-eight kilometers south-west of Paris, Georges, leaning on a window-bar, was gliding through the pastureland, looking at the telegraph poles, sweating and smiling; Pitteaux said to himself: "What folly can he have been up to now, the little bastard?" He was suddenly seized by a desire to go up, ring the bell, and shout: "Well, what's he done now? It's no affair of mine, anyway." But he forced himself to turn. I'll go as far as that gas-lamp over there; he walked on; the main thing was not to seem too eager; he even re-proached himself for having come, he ought to have re-plied, on letter-headed paper: Madame, if you want to see me, I am at my office every day from ten to twelve o'clock. He turned his back on the street-lamp, and quick-ened his step unconsciously. Paris five hundred and eight-een kilometers; Georges wiped his forehead; he was ap-proaching Paris sideways, like a crab. Pitteaux thought: "It's a dirty business"; he nearly ran, turned into the rue de Rennes, entered No. 71, walked up to the third floor, and rang the bell; at six hundred and thirty-eight kilometers from Paris Hannequin was eying the legs of the lady next to him, fleshy, shapely legs in rather coarse rayon stock-ings. Pitteaux had rung the bell, he was waiting on the landing, wiping his forehead; Georges was wiping his fore-head, amid the clatter of the train trucks; what had he been up to now, it's a dirty business, Pitteaux found it diffi-cult to swallow, his empty stomach had begun to rumble, but he stood up straight, his head stiff-set upon his shoul-ders, he dilated his nostrils and assumed his intimidating

air, the door opened; Hannequin's train plunged into a
tunnel; Pitteaux plunged into a cool and musty darkness,
the maid said: "Please come in," a plump, perfumed little
lady, with soft bare arms—the cool delicious softness of
feminine flesh at forty, with a tuft of white in her black
hair, dashed out at him, he could smell the ripe odor of
her.

"Where is he?"

He bowed; she had been crying. Hannequin's neighbor
uncrossed her legs, he glimpsed a patch of thigh above
the garter; he assumed his intimidating air and said: "Who
do you mean, madame?"

"Where is Philippe?" she said.

He felt quite moved, perhaps she was going to cry and
wave her lovely arms—a woman of her station would
surely shave under her arms.

A male voice startled him, coming from the far end of
the outer room.

"My dear girl, we are wasting our time. If Monsieur
Pitteaux will kindly step into the study, we will tell him
what has happened."

Trapped! He went in, trembling with rage, he plunged
into the white heat; the train emerged from the tunnel, a
shaft of white light slipped into the compartment. They
sat down, with *their* backs to the window, of course, and
with me in the full light. Two of them.

"I am General Lacaze," said the big man in uniform. He
pointed to his neighbor, a very tall man of lugubrious aspect, and added:

"This is Monsieur Jardies, a doctor and a mental special-
ist, who has been good enough to examine Philippe and
keep an eye on him during these last few weeks."

Georges came back into his compartment and sat down;
a short dark-haired man leaned forward and began to talk;
he had a rather Spanish look about him. "You've got your
employer behind you, and it's a nice feeling too—you

clerks and officials don't need to worry. But I've no regular job, I'm a waiter, with nothing but my tips. You tell me it won't last long, that it's just a bluff, and I dare say that's true, but supposing it lasts for two months—how is my wife going to live?"

"Philippe, my stepson," said the general, "left home without notice in the early hours of the morning. About ten o'clock his mother found this letter on the dining-room table." He passed it across the writing-table, and said with an imperious air: "Kindly read it."

Pitteaux took the letter with repugnance, how well he knew that scraggly handwriting, full of erasures and blots; he used to come and wait for hours on end; I used to hear him pacing to and fro, and then go off again, leaving, scattered about the room, scraps of crumpled paper covered with that insect scrawl; Pitteaux scanned the writing without reading it, as though it had been a series of tiresome and too familiar comic strips—I wish I'd never met him.

"Darling Mamma, this is the age of murder; I choose martyrdom. I suppose you will suffer: I should like to think so. Philippe."

He put the letter down on the desk.

"The age of murder," he said. "Rimbaud's influence has been very deleterious."

The general looked at him. "We shall return to the question of influences later on," he said. "Do you know where my stepson is?"

"How should I know?"

"When did you see him last?"

"Aha," thought Pitteaux, "they're interrogating me." He turned to Mme Lacaze and said in a friendly tone: "I don't really know. A week ago, perhaps."

The general's voice struck at him from the side: "Did he inform you of his plans?"

"Certainly not," said Pitteaux, smiling at the mother. "You know Philippe, he acts on impulse. I am pretty sure that he didn't know yesterday evening what he was going to do this morning."

"And since then," continued the general, "did he write or telephone?"

Pitteaux hesitated, but the hand had moved, a docile and obsequious hand that found its way into his breast pocket; then came the decision, and the hand produced a scrap of paper. Mme Lacaze snatched the paper; I could no longer control my hands. He still controlled his face, assumed his intimidating air, and raised one eyebrow.

"I received that this morning."

"*Lætus et errabundus*," read Mme Lacaze laboriously. "For peace."

The train rocked, the ship pitched, Pitteaux's stomach rumbled, he rose wearily to his feet. "That means carefree and vagabond," explained Pitteaux politely; "it's the title of a poem by Verlaine."

The psychiatrist flung a glance at him: "A rather special sort of poem."

"Is that all?" asked Mme Lacaze.

She turned the paper over in her fingers.

"Alas, yes, dear madame, that is all."

He heard the general's rasping voice: "What more do you want, my dear? The letter is perfectly clear, and I wonder why Monsieur Pitteaux should pretend to be ignorant of Philippe's intentions."

Pitteaux turned abruptly towards him, looked at the uniform—not the face, the uniform—and the blood surged into his head.

"Sir," said he, "Philippe wrote me notes like this three or four times a week, until finally I decided to ignore them. Excuse my pointing out to you that I have many other matters on my mind."

"Monsieur Pitteaux," said the general, "since 1937 you have been the editor of a review entitled the *Pacifist*, the policy of which is not merely antagonistic to war, but also to the French Army. You became acquainted with my stepson in October '37 in circumstances unknown to me, and you converted him to your ideas. Under your influence he adopted an attitude that I, as an officer, could not accept, nor could his mother, as my wife; he took part in public demonstrations of a definitely anti-miltarist character. And now he has left home, at the height of an international crisis, merely informing us in the note that you have read that he proposes to become a martyr in the cause of peace. You are thirty years old, Monsieur Pitteaux, and Philippe is not yet twenty, so you will not be surprised if I tell you that I hold you personally responsible for all that may happen to my stepson as a result of this escapade."

"Well," said Hannequin to the lady beside him, "the fact is I have just been called up." "Oh dear," said she. Georges glanced at the waiter, who looked like a pleasant fellow, and he wanted to say to him: "I have been called up too," but refrained, from a sort of modesty; the train vibrated terribly. "There must be wheels just underneath me," he thought.

"I decline any sort of responsibility," said Pitteaux in a categorical tone. "I sympathize with your feelings, but I can't for all that consent to figure as a scapegoat. Philippe Grésigne came to the office of the review in October '37 —that I shall not attempt to deny. He offered us a poem that we thought very promising, and we published it in our December issue. Since then he has often come to see us, and we did all we could to discourage him; he is much too high-strung for our work, and—to tell you the truth— we didn't know what to do with him." (Sitting on the end of his cheeks, he leveled a blue and embarrassing look at Pitteaux; he watched him drink and smoke, he watched his lips move; he did not smoke, he did not drink; from time to time he put a finger into his nose or a fingernail between his teeth, still eying him.)

"But where can he be?" exclaimed Mme Lacaze abruptly. "Where can he be? And what is he doing? You talk about him as though he were dead."

A silence followed. She was leaning forward, with a distraught, disdainful look upon her face; Pitteaux could see the beginning of her breast through the openwork blouse; the general, stiff-set in his chair, waited, according a few minutes' silence to a mother's natural distress. The psychiatrist looked at Mme Lacaze with an air of attentive, if slightly professional, sympathy. Then he wagged his large, melancholy head, turned to Pitteaux, and resumed hostilities.

"I will admit, Monsieur Pitteaux, that Philippe did not grasp all your ideas. Still, it is a fact that he was a very impressionable youth, and an ecstatic admirer of yours."

"Is that my fault?"

"Perhaps it isn't. But you abused your influence."

"Really!" said Pitteaux. "However, since you have examined Philippe, you know he wasn't normal."

"I wouldn't go so far as that," smiled the doctor. "His family history was certainly not all that could be desired—on his father's side," he added, with a glance at the general. "But he wasn't altogether a psychopathic case. He was a solitary, maladjusted, lazy, self-absorbed young man. All sorts of tricks and phobias, of course, with a predominance of sexual obsessions. He came to see me fairly often latterly, and in the course of our talks he admitted—how can I put it?—you will excuse a doctor's bluntness," he said to Mme Lacaze. "Briefly—frequent and systematic masturbation. I am aware that many of my colleagues regard that as merely an effect; I consider it a cause, following Esquirol on that point. In a word, he was going through the rather painful stage which Mendousse calls so aptly the crisis of adolescent eccentricity; he needed a guide. You have been a bad shepherd, Monsieur Pitteaux, a bad shepherd."

Mme Lacaze appeared to be looking quite accidentally

at Pitteaux, but that gaze was more than he could bear. Pitteaux turned frankly to the psychiatrist.

"I offer my excuses to Madame Lacaze," he said, "but since you press me, I had better say quite plainly that I have always regarded Philippe as a definite degenerate. If he needed a guide, why didn't you take charge of him? It's your business."

The psychiatrist smiled sadly, licked his lips, and sighed. She smiled, she was leaning against the cabin door, she shivered, and she smiled an alluring smile.

"Well, my dear," said the captain. "Come and see me again at nine and I'll have some news for you and your friends." He had clear, expressionless eyes, he was very red in the face; he stroked her breasts and neck and added: "Don't forget: this evening, nine o'clock sharp."

"General Lacaze was kind enough to send me a few pages of Philippe's diary, and I thought it my duty to go through them. Monsieur Pitteaux, I gathered from what I read that you practiced a sort of blackmail on this unhappy lad. Knowing how much he wanted to gain your esteem, you took advantage of that fact apparently, to ask certain services of him, not specified in his diary. During these latter weeks he had decided to rebel, and you treated him with such crushing contempt that you reduced him to despair."

How much did they know? But anger prevailed, he smiled in response. Maud smiled and bowed; she was backing out into the corridor, as, with head and shoulders still in the warm and scented air of the cabin, she replied: "Certainly, captain. At nine o'clock, then, I'll be here, captain."

"Who reduced him to despair? Who was it that humiliated him every day? Was it I who boxed his ears last Saturday at the dinner-table? Was it I who pretended he was ill, sent him to a psychiatrist, and forced him to answer humiliating questions?"

"Have you been called up too?" asked the waiter.

Georges smiled at him ruefully, but would have had to talk then, would have had to answer the two young women's questions.

"No," said he, "I'm going to Paris on business."

Mme Lacaze's shrill voice made him start. "I won't hear another word. How you must despise him! A lad of twenty —whom you have deliberately corrupted—can't you even respect his mother? He may have drowned himself in the Seine, and you sit there trying to shift your responsibility on to someone else."

"We are all to blame," he said. "You must not goad me in this way, that's what we all did to him."

The general was red in the face; so was Maud:

"It's all right," she said, "they'll fetch our luggage into second class tonight."

"Darling," said France. "Well, there you are, you made a lot of fuss, but it wasn't so difficult as all that."

"Rose!" said he, without raising his voice, and fixing wooden eyes upon her. She shuddered and looked at him with her mouth open:

"It's—it's loathsome," she said, "I feel utterly ashamed."

He reached out a powerful hand and clasped his wife's bare arm; again he said: "Rose," in a toneless voice. Mme Lacaze settled herself in her chair, she set her lips, shook her head, and seemed suddenly to awaken; she looked at the general, and the general smiled; order was restored.

"I do not share my wife's apprehensions," he said. "My stepson left after stealing ten thousand francs from his mother's bureau. I don't think he is likely to make an attempt on his own life."

A silence followed. The steamer was already beginning to roll; Pierre was feeling rather clammy as he stood beside his bunk and opened his suitcase, which diffused an odor of lavender, dental cream, and American tobacco; it made him feel rather sick, and he remembered that the steward had said the crossing would be rough. The general pondered, the general's wife looked like a well-behaved child, Pitteaux was nonplussed, his stomach rumbled, and his head ached; aah! it was coming up again and it burned his nose, the planking quivered underfoot, the air was hot and sticky, he looked at the general and didn't feel equal to hating him any more.

"Monsieur Pitteaux," said the general, "in concluding this interview, I consider that you can and *ought* to help us to find my stepson. Until now I have confined myself to notifying the various police stations. But if, within forty-eight hours, Philippe has not been traced, my intention is to place the matter in the hands of my old friend the Public Prosecutor, and ask him at the same time whether the legal authorities would not do well to make some inquiry into the sources from which the *Pacifist* is financed."

"I—of course I'll help you," he said. "Anyone can investigate the accounts of the *Pacifist*, we have nothing whatever to conceal."

The steamer pitched heavily, with a sort of roller-coaster motion, and he added, getting his words out with some difficulty: "But I—I don't refuse to help you. On the sole ground of humanity, general."

The general bowed slightly. "That is what I meant," he said.

Gently, gently, almost imperceptibly, it rose, then fell, one couldn't help looking at the bunks or the wash-basin in the effort to catch the motion of something as it rose or fell, but nothing could be seen, except, from time to time, a slightly tilted dark-blue band, level with the lower edge of the porthole, which then vanished; it was a vivid, timid little movement, like the beating of a heart, and Pierre's heart beat with it; for hours and hours it would continue thus—up, then down. Pierre's tongue felt like a large and juicy piece of fruit inside his mouth; at every swallow he could hear a faint cartilaginous crackle somewhere in his ears, there was an iron crown about his temples, and he kept on wanting to yawn. But he was not uneasy; no one really need be seasick. He had only to get up and take a turn on deck; he would recover, and this faint sense of nausea would be dispelled. "I'll go and see Maud," he said to himself. He dropped the suitcase, stood up straight beside his bunk, as though awakening from sleep. The steamer indeed rose and fell beneath his feet, but his stomach and his head were steady; Maud's disdainful eyes reappeared, and, with them, fear—and shame. I shall tell her I was ill—a touch of sunstroke, too much to drink. I *must* explain myself; he would talk, she would transfix him with those implacable eyes of hers—how wearisome it all was! He swallowed his saliva with an effort—it slid down his throat like a horrid silky ooze, a stale liquid had gathered in his mouth—so very wearisome, his ideas fled, his consciousness was possessed by a sense of something large and soft and out of reach, a desire to rise and fall rhythmically, to vomit with deliberation, to fall back on to the pillow, ho-hup, ho-hup, without a thought in his head, adrift on this great heaving world; he saved himself in time; no one need be seasick. He recovered his whole self —a rigid, chilly, stiff entity, a coward, a despised lover, a forthcoming war-casualty, he recovered his immitigable frozen fear. He lifted his second suitcase from the upper bunk, put it on the lower one, and began to open it. He stood erect, not bending down or even looking at the suitcase, his numbed fingers fumbling blindly at the lock; is it worth the trouble? Is it worth putting up a fight? He would relapse into something large and soft, unvisited by thought or fear, he had merely to give way. "I must go and see Maud." He raised a hand and moved it through the air with a kind of soft and hesitant solemnity. Soft gestures, soft throbbings in my eyelashes, a soft taste at the back of my mouth, soft smells of lavender and dental paste, softly the steamer rises, softly she descends; he yawned, time slowed down, and melted into a syrupy haze: he need only pull himself together and take a few steps in the fresh air. But *what for?* To feel his fear upon him once again? He swept the suitcase on to the floor and collapsed on the bed. Syrup: viscous, sticky, sugared syrup; he was no longer afraid or ashamed, it was delightful to be seasick.

He sat on the edge of the wharf, his legs dangling above the water, he was tired, and he said: "Marseille wouldn't be so bad if there weren't so many houses." Below him there was a scurry of boats—small boats, some loaded with flowers, or adorned with rich red curtains and naked statues.

He watched the boats, some pranced like goats, others lay motionless, he looked at the deep-blue water and a great iron bridge in the distance; it is pleasant to look at distant objects, they soothe the mind. His eyes were smarting; he had slept under his truck, and men had come with lanterns, shone their lights on him, cursed him, and driven him away, after which he found a heap of sand, but sleep would not return. "Where," he asked himself, "am I going to bed down tonight?" There must be some grassy corners that would serve. But you had to know them; he ought to have asked the Negro. He felt hungry and got up; his knees were stiff and creaked as he moved. "I've got no more food," he said to himself, "I must find a restaurant." He resumed his walk, he had walked all day, going in here and there to ask: "Got a job for me?" and so on again; the Negro had said there were no jobs to be had. It is tiring to walk about in towns, the pavements are so hard. He crossed the dock slantwise, walking very slowly, looking to right and left to avoid the street-cars, their tinkling bells always made him jump. There were a lot of people about —waterfront derelicts hurrying along and looking at their feet as though in search of something; when they bumped into him they apologized without even looking at him; he would have liked to speak to them, but they looked so brittle that he was nervous. He stepped on to the sidewalk and looked at the cafés with their fine terraces, and then some restaurants, but did not go in: there were tablecloths on the tables, and tablecloths have a way of getting stained. He turned down a dark alley, which smelt of wet-dogs, and said to himself: "But where on earth am I going to get something to eat?" and at that very moment he found what he wanted: in front of a small low-built house stood a dozen or so wooden tables, each of them laid for two or four, and each with a small round lamp not intended to give much light, and no tablecloths. At one of these tables a gentleman was at dinner with a pleasant-looking lady. Gros-Louis sat down at the next table and smiled at them. The lady eyed him gravely and shifted her chair back. Gros-Louis saluted the waitress, a pretty, slim young girl, with a plump and distinctly cute behind.

"What can I have to eat, sweetheart?"

She was pretty and smelt nice, but she didn't seem pleased to see him. She looked at him dubiously.

"There's the menu," she said, pointing to a sheet of paper on the table.

"Thank you," said Gros-Louis.

He picked up the paper and pretended to read it, but was afraid of holding it upside down. The waitress had moved off, she was talking to a man in the doorway. The man listened, nodding his head and looking at Gros-Louis. Then he left her and approached Gros-Louis with a gloomy air.

"What do you want, my friend?" he asked.

"I want something to eat," said Gros-Louis with astonishment. "I expect you've got some soup and a bit of bacon."

The gentleman shook his head gloomily: "No," he said, "we have no soup."

"I've got money," said Gros-Louis. "I'm not asking for credit."

"I'm sure of that," said the gentleman. "But I think

you've made a mistake. You won't be comfortable here, and you would be in the way."

Gros-Louis looked at him. "But isn't this a restaurant?" he asked.

"Of course," said the proprietor. "But we have a special sort of clientele. . . . You had much better go to the other side of the Canebière, you will find all sorts of little restaurants that will be just what you want."

Gros-Louis had got up. He looked perplexed and scratched the top of his head. "I've got money," he said. "I can show it to you."

"Don't trouble," said the man briskly: "I take your word for it."

He grasped him amicably by the arm and led him a few steps along the street. "Go in that direction; when you come out on the quay, turn to the right, you can't go wrong."

"You're very kind," said Gros-Louis, touching his hat. He felt himself in the wrong.

He found himself back on the waterfront, among the little black men who ran between his legs; he walked very slowly for fear of overturning them and felt sad; at this hour of day he used to come down from the Canigou towards Villefranche, his cattle trotting along in front of him, which made for company; he often met M. Pardoux on his way up to the Vétil farm, and M. Pardoux never passed without giving him a cigar and a couple of hearty thumps in the ribs, the mountains were crimson now and silent, at the far end of the valley rose the smoke of Villefranche. He was lost, all these people moved too fast, he could only see the tops of their heads or the crowns of their hats, they were a puny race. An urchin darted between his legs, grinned up at him, and said to his small companion: "Look at him—he must be pretty bored up there all by himself."

Gros-Louis watched them run and felt out of place again; he was ashamed of being so tall. "Well," he said to himself, "I suppose they have their little ways," and leaned against the wall. He felt sad and rather subdued—almost as sad as on the day when he had been ill. He thought of the Negro, so polite and cheerful, his only friend, and he said: "I oughtn't to have let him go." Then suddenly a bright idea came into his head: a Negro can be seen from far away and can't be difficult to find; he resumed his walk, feeling less solitary and looking out for the Negro. "I'll stand him a drink," he said to himself.

All the women were out on the square, their faces reddened by the setting sun—Jeanne, Ursule, the Clapot sisters, Marie, and all the rest. They had begun waiting at home, and then as the hours passed they had returned to the square, one by one, and stood waiting. They saw, through the smudged windows, the first lamps lit in the Widow Tremblin's café, three nebulous patches against the upper panes. And they felt depressed; Mother Tremblin had lit the lamps in her deserted café, she had sat down at a marble-topped table, she had put her work-basket on the table and was darning her cotton stockings quite composedly, being a widow. But they—they remained outside waiting for their men; in their empty houses and their kitchens they felt the shadow lengthening, and before them lay a long adventurous road, leading to Caen. Marie looked up at the church clock and said to Ursule:

"It will soon be nine o'clock, perhaps they've been kept back anyhow." The mayor had said that couldn't have happened, but what did he know? He was just as ignorant of what went on in towns as they were. Was it likely that a lot of stout lads come to join up would be sent back home? Perhaps indeed the reply had been: "Well, since you *are* here—" and they had been told to stay.

Little Rose ran up, out of breath, crying: "Here they are! Here they are!" and all the women began to run, too. They ran as far as the Darbois farm, from which a stretch of road was visible; they saw the men on the white road, between the meadows, on their carts in single file, as they had gone, returning slowly, singing. Chapin was at their head, huddled on his seat, barely grasping the reins, asleep; the horse was walking on mechanically. Marie noticed he had a black eye; he had been fighting again. Behind him, standing on his cart, the Renard boy was singing at the top of his voice, but not looking particularly merry; the others behind, black now against the clear sky.

Marie turned to one of the Clapot sisters and said: "They're drunk—that's all we needed." Chapin's cart creaked slowly on, and the women fell back to let it pass. As it came by, Louise Chapin shrieked: "My God, he has only brought one horse back, what has he done with the other?—he must have sold it to buy drink." The Renard boy was singing at the top of his voice, zigzagging his cart from one ditch to the other, and others behind him were standing in their carts and singing, whip in hand. Marie saw her husband, he did not look drunk, but when she saw his surly face close up, she realized that he was drunk and would beat her. "Worse than a beast," she thought despondently. However, she was glad he had come back, the work was heavy on the farm, and it was better that he should beat her now and then on Saturdays and be there to do his job. He had dropped on to a chair outside a small café, asked for some red wine, which they gave him in a small glass; he became conscious of his legs, stretched them out under the table, and began to twitch the great toes inside his shoes. "It's damned funny," he said. He drank, and said: "And yet I've looked for him everywhere." He would have sat him down opposite, just for the pleasure of looking at his genial black head; they had enjoyed some good laughs together—the Negro had a cow's confiding, gentle look. "I'll stand him smokes and wine."

His neighbor looked at him: thinks me odd because I'm

talking to myself; a stunted, sickly-looking lad of about twenty, with a girlish skin, and beside him a dark-haired, rather handsome fellow with a broken nose, hairy ears, and an anchor tattooed on his left forearm. Gros-Louis realized that they were talking about him, in a lingo of their own. He smiled at them and called the waiter.

"Another glass of the same, my boy. And if you've got any bigger glasses, you can bring one."

The waiter did not move, nor did he say anything, but he eyed Gros-Louis with a knowing air. Gros-Louis took out his pocketbook and laid it on the table.

"What's the matter, young fellow? Think I can't pay? Here!"

He produced three thousand-franc notes and held them under the man's nose.

"What about that? Now go and get me another glass of that muck of yours."

He replaced his pocketbook and noticed that the curly-haired lad was smiling at him politely.

"Everything rosy, huh?" said the lad.

"Eh?"

"Everything all right?"

"Quite all right. I'm looking for my Negro."

"You don't come from hereabouts?"

"No," laughed Gros-Louis, "I don't. Have a drink?"

"I don't mind if I do," said curly-hair. "Can I bring my pal?"

He said a few words to his companion, in their own lingo. The man smiled and got up in silence. They came and sat down opposite Gros-Louis. The lad smelt of scent.

"You smell like a tart," said Gros-Louis.

"I've just had my hair cut."

"So that's it. What's your name?"

"Mario," said the lad; "my pal's an Italian. His name's Starace; we're sailors."

Starace laughed and nodded.

"He doesn't know any French, but he's a scream," said Mario. "Do you know Italian?"

"No," said Gros-Louis.

"Never mind, you'll see; he's a scream."

They spoke to each other, in Italian. It was a very pretty language, they sounded as though they were singing. Gros-Louis was glad of their company, but he still felt solitary.

"What will you have?"

"*Pasti*, I think," said Mario.

"Three *pastis*," said Gros-Louis. "What is it—wine?"

"No, much better than wine; you'll see."

The waiter poured some liquid into three glasses, Mario added water, and the liquid was transformed into a white, effervescent froth.

"Here's yours," said Mario.

He drank noisily and wiped his mouth with his sleeve. Gros-Louis drank also; not bad—it smelt of aniseed.

"Watch Starace, he'll make you laugh," said Mario.

Starace squinted, screwed up his nose, thrust out his lips, and waggled his ears like a rabbit. Gros-Louis did laugh, but he felt shocked and uneasy; he did not like Starace. Mario laughed till the tears came into his eyes.

"I warned you," he said, still laughing. "He's a scream, that's what he is. Now he'll do the saucer trick for you."

Starace set his glass on the table, grasped his saucer in his broad palm, and three times in succession slid his left hand over his right hand. At the third time the saucer vanished. Taking advantage of Gros-Louis's surprise, Starace slipped a hand between his knees. Gros-Louis felt something scrape against his legs, and the hand reappeared holding the saucer. Gros-Louis laughed in moderation, while Mario slapped his thighs in an ectasy of delight.

"You old bum," said Mario between two hiccups. "And he'll make you laugh a few times more before he's done."

Gradually he grew calmer; when he had recovered his

composure, a silence descended upon the three men. Gros-Louis found them tiresome, he wanted them to go away, but reflected that it would soon be dark, he would have to resume his wanderings through the long, shadowed streets, searching interminably for a place to eat and another place to sleep; he felt depressed and ordered another round of *pasti*. Mario leaned towards him, Gros-Louis inhaled his smell.

"So you don't come from here?" asked Mario.

"I don't, and I know no one here," said Gros-Louis. "The only chap I know I can't find. Unless you know him," he said after a moment's reflection. "It's the Negro."

Mario shook his head vaguely.

Suddenly he bent across to Gros-Louis, and looked at him with half-closed eyes. "Marseille is a place where you can have some fun," he said. "If you don't know Marseille, you've never had any fun in your life."

Gros-Louis did not answer. He had often had some fun at Villefranche. And in the brothels at Perpignan, during his military service; and he had enjoyed it. But he could not conceive of any fun in Marseille.

"Don't you want a little fun?" asked Mario. "Wouldn't you like a go with some pretty tomatoes?"

"That's not it," said Gros-Louis. "Just now I would sooner eat. If you know a restaurant, I'll stand you a meal."

As night fell, solids tended to evaporate, leaving vague gaseous masses, somber mists; she walked quickly, with head bent and hunched shoulders, afraid of bumping into a coil of rope; she kept close to the wall, she longed to let the night consume her, to dissolve into a drifting patch of vapor in that omnipresent haze and slither overboard. But she knew that her white frock was a beacon-light. She crossed the second-class deck, she heard no sound except the eternal lamentation of the sea; but on every side of her, motionless, silent men stood out against the flat shadow of the sea, and they had eyes; from time to time a shaft of fire

pierced the night, reddened a face; the eyes gleamed,
looked at her, and vanished—she wanted to die.

She had to go down a stairway, cross the third-class
deck, climb another stairway, steep as a ladder and painted
white; if I'm seen, there can't be any doubt, his cabin is
up there, quite isolated; the man has his job to do, he can't
keep me all night. She was afraid he might get a taste for
it and send a steward to fetch her every evening out of
the saloon, as the Greek captain had done, but no, I'm
much too thin for a fat old fellow like that, he'll be disappointed with such a bag of bones. She didn't need to
knock, the door was ajar; he was waiting in the dark and
said:

"Come in, my dear."

She paused, with a choking sensation in her throat; a
hand drew her into the cabin, and the door closed. She was
suddenly crushed against a great paunch, and an elderly
mouth that smelt of cork fastened on to hers. She did not
resist; she thought with proud resignation: "It's my job, it's
part of my job." The captain flicked the switch, and a head
emerged from the shadow; the whites of his eyes were
moist and bluish, there was a red speck in the left eye. She
drew back with a smile; it was all much more difficult since
the lights had been turned on; hitherto she had pictured
him in the mass, but now he existed down to the minutest
details; she was going to make love with a unique individual, as were all individuals, and this night would be
unique, as were all nights, a night of unique and irrepara-
ble love, irreparably lost. Maud smiled and said: "Wait
a bit, captain, you're in such a hurry; we must get to know
each other first."

What's this? He raised himself uneasily on one elbow;
the ship seemed motionless. He had three or four heaves,
one of them extremely violent, all of them through the nose;
he felt limp and exhausted, but clear in the head. "What
can this be?" he thought. And suddenly he found himself

sitting on his bunk, his head encircled with an iron band, and the too familiar anguish eating at his heart. Time, an inexorable, jerky mechanism, had resumed its progress, every second rent him like the tooth of a saw, every second brought him nearer to Marseille and the gray land where he was going to die. Again the world was there, around his cabin, the abominable world of railway stations, smoke, uniforms, devastated countrysides, a world where he could not live and that he could not leave—and a muddy hole awaiting him in Flanders. A coward, son of an officer, and afraid of war: he loathed himself. And yet he clung desperately to life—which was even more repellent; it's not for what I stand that I want to live; it's for nothing—just to be alive. He would do anything to save his skin—run away, plead for mercy, or betray his cause, and yet he didn't attach so much importance to his skin. He got up; what am I to say to her? Tell her I had a touch of sunstroke, an attack of malaria, that I wasn't normal. He walked unsteadily up to the mirror; he was as yellow as a lemon. That settles it; I can't even depend on my face. And I suppose I smell of vomit into the bargain. He dabbed some eau-de-Cologne on his face and gargled with Bottot water. What a business! he thought with irritation. It's certainly the first time I've worried about what a tart might think of me. A semi-prostitute, a dance-hall violinist, and I've slept with married women, mothers most of them. But she's got me, he thought, as he slipped on his jacket; she *knows*.

He opened the door and went out; the captain was stark naked, his skin was waxen and glossy, hairless except for some on his chest—the rest must have dropped out from old age—and when he laughed, he looked like an overgrown, mischievous baby. Maud touched his great polished thighs with the tips of her fingers; he quivered and said: "You're tickling me."

He knew the number of the cabin: 27—down one corridor on the right, another on the left, a sound of heavy

rhythmic knocking against the bulkhead; ah, here was No.
27. A young woman lay prostrate on her back, as pallid as
a corpse; an old lady was sitting on a bunk, her eyes red
and swollen, and eating bread and butter.

"Oh!" said she, "the three ladies? They were so nice.
But they've gone—they moved to second class: I shall
miss them."

He looked at her with surprise, and he laid a hand on
her hip. "You'd make a nice piece with that pretty little
face, but you're so thin!"

She laughed; when anyone touched her hip it made her
laugh. "Don't you like thin women, captain?"

"I wouldn't say I disliked them—not by any means," he
hurriedly replied.

He ran up the companionway; he *must* see Maud. Now
he was in the second-class corridor, a handsome carpeted
corridor, the doors and walls ripolined in blue-gray. He
had a bit of luck; Ruby suddenly appeared, followed by a
steward carrying her suitcases.

"Hello," said Pierre. "Are you traveling second?"

"Yes," said Ruby. "France is afraid of being ill. So we
agreed to move; when it's a matter of health, one must
make sacrifices."

"Where's Maud?"

Maud was lying on her side, the captain was stroking
her backside with absent-minded courtesy; she felt dread-
fully humiliated. "If I'm not his type, he mustn't feel any
obligation." She slid a hand over his side by way of returning his compliment; it was old man's skin.

"Maud?" said Ruby in a shrill tone. "I couldn't say. You
know what she's like. I expect she felt she'd like to go try to
make the trimmers, if not the captain; she adores sea-cross-
ings, she always runs all over the ship."

"Inquisitive little girl," said the captain. He laughed
and gripped her wrist. "I'll take you on a trip round the
owner," said he. And his eyes lit up for the first time. Maud

acquiesced, she was rather upset by the change of cabins, but after all he must get his due; she sorely regretted that she was so thin, she felt she had cheated him; the captain smiled, dropped his eyes, looking quite modest and domestic; he grasped Maud's wrist and gently but firmly guided her hand. Maud didn't mind; she thought: "It would be mean to refuse the one thing he wants after all the trouble we've made, especially as he doesn't like thin women."

"Thank you! Thank you very much!"

He bowed and resumed his journey—he *must* find Maud; she would be on deck. He climbed to the second-class deck; it was dark and almost impossible to recognize people without looking right in their faces. I'm an idiot, I should have waited for her here; wherever she comes from, she must take this stairway. The captain had closed his eyes, with a calm and pious expression on his face that quite appealed to Maud; her wrist was getting tired, but she was glad to be giving him such pleasure; besides she felt quite alone, as she used to do when she was a little girl and Grandpa Théveneur took her on his knees and suddenly nodded off to sleep. Pierre looked at the sea and thought: "I'm a coward." A fresh wind streamed over his cheeks and ruffled his hair, he watched the sea rise and fall; he looked at himself with astonishment and thought: "Coward. I would never have thought it." Coward beyond redemption. One day had sufficed for him to find out his true character; but for these threats of war he would never have known it. If I had been born in 1860, for instance. He would have made his way through life with calm conviction; he would have been extremely severe on cowardice in others, and nothing—nothing would ever have acquainted him with his veritable nature. No luck. One day, just one day. Now he knew, and he was alone. Cars and trains and boats forged ahead through that clear, resonant night, all converging in the direction of Paris, carrying young fellows

like himself, unsleeping, peering out to sea, or flattening
their noses against dark windows. It isn't fair, he thought.
There are thousands, perhaps millions of people who have
lived in happier times and never known their limitations;
they got the benefit of the doubt. Alfred de Vigny may
have been a coward. And what about Musset, Sainte-
Beuve, Baudelaire? They were lucky. Whereas I—he muttered, stamping his foot. She would never have known, she
would have continued to look at me with her adoring air,
she would have lasted no longer than the rest, I should
have got rid of her in three months. But now she knows;
she knows. The bitch—she's got me.

It was dark outside, but the bar was so bright that Gros-
Louis was dazzled. It looked particularly gay, being in-
visibly lit. A long red tube all round the ceiling, and another, a white one, provided the light; there were mirrors
all round the room. In the mirror opposite, Gros-Louis
~ould see his own entire head and the top of Starace's
skull, but he couldn't see either Mario or Daisy; they were
too short. He had paid for the meals and four rounds of
pasti; he ordered brandies. They were sitting at the far end
of the bar, opposite the counter—an excellent seat—enveloped in a loud and rather soothing restaurant din. Gros-
Louis felt expansive, he wanted to get on the table and
sing. Then his eyes closed, he seemed to drop into a hole,
and he felt overwhelmed, as though something awful had
happened to him, opened his eyes again, and tried to remember what it was, the upshot being that nothing had
happened to him at all. He was, in fact, feeling pretty well
all right, a little annoyed, perhaps, but quite at ease; he
had to make an effort to keep his eyes open. He had
stretched his long legs out under the table, one between
Mario's, the other between Starace's; his reflection in the
mirror made him laugh, he tried to imitate Starace's grimace, but he couldn't squint or waggle his ears. Under the
mirror sat a very nice little lady, smoking meditatively,

she must have taken the grimace as meant for her, she put her tongue out at him, gripped her right wrist in her left hand, clenched her right hand, and turned it round and back again, grinning all the while. Gros-Louis felt abashed and looked away, he was afraid he had hurt her feelings.

Daisy, a plump and warm little person, was sitting at his side. But she paid no attention to him. She smelt nice, she was plastered with paint, and her breasts were alluring, but he liked girls who laughed a bit and teased you—blew in your ear, and looked demure while they whispered dirty stories that you didn't quite understand. Daisy was rather intense; she was talking earnestly to Mario about the war.

"Well," she said, "we shall fight. If we must, we shall."

Starace was sitting very straight in his chair, opposite Daisy; he seemed to be listening, but that was mere politeness, as he could not understand her. Gros-Louis rather liked him, because he kept quiet and never lost his temper. Mario eyed Daisy with a knowing air, wagged his head, and said:

"I wouldn't say so." But he didn't look convinced.

"I prefer war to strikes," said Daisy. "Don't you? Remember what the dockers' strike cost—it made a difference to everybody."

"I wonder," said Mario.

Daisy was talking eagerly and looking despondent; she wagged her head as she went on: "There won't be any strikes during the war," she said severely. "Everybody will work. Aha! You ought to have seen the ships in '17, but you were a kid then. I was a kid too, but I can remember them. It was a grand spree, you could see lights as far as the Estaque. And all the faces in the streets—it might have been anywhere in the world, and how proud we all were! And the lines in the rue Boutherille—English, Americans, Italians, Germans, even Hindus, I tell you! My old mother made a pretty pile."

"There weren't any Germans," said Mario; "we were at war with Germany."

"I tell you there were Germans," said Daisy. "And in uniform too, with a badge on their caps."

"We were at war with them," said Mario.

Daisy shrugged her shoulders. "Of course we were, but up in the north. These fellows didn't come from the trenches; they came by sea, to do business."

A tall girl passed, as fat and fair as butter, but she also looked far too serious. Gros-Louis thought: "It's living in a town that makes them look like that." She leaned over Daisy in apparent indignation. "Well, I don't like war, let me tell you. I have my bellyful of it, and my brother who fought in the '14 war, do you want him to fight again? And I guess my uncle's farm wasn't burnt down maybe. What about that, eh?"

Daisy was disconcerted for a moment, but promptly recovered herself.

"So you prefer strikes?" she said. "Then you should say so."

Mario eyed the tall blonde, and she departed in silence, shaking her head as she went. She sat down near by and began to talk eagerly to a gloomy little man who was chewing a straw. She pointed to Daisy and went on talking with astonishing speed. The little man did not reply, he went on chewing and did not even look as if he heard what she said.

"She comes from Sedan," explained Mario.

"Where's that?" asked Daisy.

"Up north."

She shrugged her shoulders. "Well, then, what's she making such a fuss about? They're used to it up there."

Gros-Louis yawned heavily, and tears trickled down his cheeks. He was bored, but quite contended at the moment, he liked yawning. Mario threw a rapid glance at him. Starace yawned too.

"My pal's bored stiff," said Mario, indicating Gros-Louis. "Be nice to him, Daisy."

Daisy turned to Gros-Louis and put an arm round his neck. She no longer looked serious.

"Getting bored, ducky—with a fine piece of girl beside you?"

Gros-Louis was just about to reply when he caught sight of the Negro. He was standing at the counter, drinking a yellow liquid out of a large glass. He was wearing a green suit, and a straw hat with a multicolored ribbon. "Aha," said Gros-Louis. He looked at the Negro and was glad.

"What's the matter," asked Daisy in astonishment.

He turned his head towards her, then towards Starace, and looked at them with amazement. He was ashamed to be in their company. He shook his shoulders to rid himself of Daisy's arm. The Negro was drinking, and Gros-Louis laughed gleefully. Daisy said sharply across his back: "What's up with the old drip? He hurt me." But Gros-Louis didn't care; he was rescued from Mario and Starace. He raised his right hand over the Negro and gave him a great thump between the shoulder-blades. The Negro nearly choked; he coughed and spat and then turned upon Gros-Louis with an air of fury.

"It's me," said Gros-Louis.

"Who the hell do you think you are?" yelled the Negro.

"Don't you see it's me?" repeated Gros-Louis.

"I don't know you," said the Negro.

Gros-Louis looked sadly at the Negro. "Don't you remember? We met yesterday, you'd been bathing."

The Negro was still coughing and spitting. Starace and Mario had got up, and were standing on each side of Gros-Louis. "Aren't they ever going to let me alone?" thought Gros-Louis wrathfully. Mario tugged him gently by the sleeve.

"Come along," said he. "You see he doesn't like you."

"It's my Negro," said Gros-Louis in a threatening tone.

"Take him away," said the Negro, "and put him to bed."

Gros-Louis looked at the Negro and felt unhappy; it was certainly he, looking very festive in his fine straw hat. Why was he so forgetful and so rude?

"I stood you a drink," said he.

"Come on," repeated Mario. "It isn't your Negro; they all look alike."

Gros-Louis clenched his fists and turned to Mario: "Get out of this. It's no business of yours."

Mario stepped back.

"All Negroes look alike," he said uneasily.

Gros-Louis had raised his fist when the door opened and a second Negro appeared, exactly like the first, in a stiff straw hat and a pink suit. He glanced at Gros-Louis, crossed the room with rather a mincing gait, and sat down with his elbows on the counter. Gros-Louis rubbed his eyes, looked at the two Negroes turn by turn, and burst out laughing.

"Looks like the same chap twice," he said.

Mario approached him. "You see—I was right."

Gros-Louis was bewildered. He didn't much like Starace, nor Mario, but felt he had been unfair to them. He took them by the arm. "I thought it was my Negro," he explained.

The Negro turned his back and took another drink. Mario looked at Starace, then they both turned towards Daisy. Daisy was standing up, her hands on her hips and not looking at all amiable.

"Hmm!" said Mario.

"Hmm!" said Starace.

They swung round, each seized Gros-Louis by an arm, and they led him away.

"We'll go and look for your Negro," said Mario.

The street was narrow and deserted and smelt of cabbage. Above the roofs stars were visible. "They're all alike," thought Gros-Louis gloomily. "Are there many of them at Marseille?" he asked.

"Many what, chum?"

"Negroes."

"A good few," said Mario with a nod. "I must be drunk," thought Gros-Louis. I'll help you, said the captain, I'll be your lady's maid. Mario put his arm round Gros-Louis's waist; the captain had picked up the slip by a shoulder-strap. Maud couldn't help laughing: "You're holding it upside down!" Mario leaned forward, he gripped Gros-Louis by the waist, rubbed his head against his stomach, and said: "You're my pal, isn't he, Starace? You're my little old pal, and we love each other very much." Starace laughed silently, his head turned round and round, his teeth gleamed, it was a nightmare, his head echoed with cries and lights, he was on his way to more noise and lights, they would stick by him all night, Starace's laugh, his brown face heaving up and down, Mario's weasel-mask, he felt sick, the sea rose and fell in Pierre's stomach, he knew that he would never find his Negro. Mario pushed him, Starace pulled him, the Negro was an angel, and I'm in hell. He said aloud: "The Negro was an angel," and three great tears rolled down his cheeks, Mario pushed, Starace pulled, they turned the corner of the street, Pierre closed his eyes, and nothing remained but the flicker of the street-lamp on the pavement and the foaming hiss of the water against the ship's bow.

Shutters closed, windows closed, the place reeked of bedbugs and formaldehyde. He bent over the passport, the candlelight shone on his crisp gray hair and the shadow of his skull across the table. "Why doesn't he turn on the electric light? He'll ruin his eyes." Philippe cleared his throat; he felt immersed in silence and oblivion. Back there I exist, I really do exist, I am a solid, self-subsistent entity; she can't swallow a mouthful—she's got a lump in her throat from crying so much; he is stupefied, the menacing hand falls away, he wouldn't have believed me capable of such a thing; back there I have just entered upon life, and yet here I am, confronting this sedate little old gentleman with the gray mustache, so utterly oblivious of me. Here; *here!* Here—a monotonous presence amid the blind and deaf, I melt into the shadows; back there, under the lights of the candelabra, between the armchair and the sofa, I exist, I am a person. He tapped his foot on the floor, and the old gentleman peered at him with hard, bleared, tired eyes.

"Have you ever been in Spain?"

"Yes," said Philippe. "Three years ago."

"This passport is no longer valid. It ought to have been renewed."

"I know," said Philippe impatiently.

"However, it doesn't matter. Can you speak Spanish?"

"Just as well as French."

"If you get taken for a Spaniard you'll be lucky, with that straw-colored hair of yours."

"There are blond Spaniards."

The old gentleman shrugged his shoulders. "I just tell you that, you know. . . ."

He turned the passport over absent-mindedly. *"I am here,* visiting a forger." It didn't look true. Since that morning nothing looked true. The forger looked more like a gendarme.

"You look like a gendarme."

The old gentleman did not reply; Philippe felt ill at ease. Insignificance: it had reappeared *here*—the transparent insignificance of yesterday, when I was passing through their looks, when I was a jolting sheet of glass on a glazier's back, and I was passing through the sunshine. *Back there*—now that I am as impenetrable as a corpse, she will be saying: "Where is he? What has he done? Is he thinking about me?" But this old creature doesn't look as if he knew that there's a place upon the earth where I am a precious possession.

"Well?" said Philippe.

The old gentleman fixed his weary eyes upon him. "I suppose it was Pitteaux who sent you?"

"That's the third time you've asked that question. Yes, it was Pitteaux," said Philippe genially.

"Right," said the old gentleman. "I usually do the job for nothing; for you it will be three thousand francs."

Philippe assumed Pitteaux's expression. "Certainly. I wasn't asking you to do a job for nothing."

The old gentleman grinned. My voice rings false, thought Philippe irritably. I haven't yet acquired a *natural* insolence. Especially towards older people. Between them and myself there is an ancient score of smacks in the face, which I must wipe off before I can speak to them on equal terms. But the last—he thought in high good-humor—the last in date is canceled.

"There," said he.

He produced his pocketbook and laid three bills on the table.

"You young fool!" said the old gentleman. "I shall now take them and refuse to do the job."

Philippe eyed him uneasily and reached out a hand as though to pick them up again. The old gentleman burst out laughing.

"I thought—" said Philippe.

The old gentleman was still laughing, Philippe snatched his hand away and smiled. "I know my fellow men," he said. "I *know* you wouldn't have done such a thing."

The old gentleman stopped laughing. He looked cheerfully malicious.

"You do, do you? Poor little sucker, you come here, having never seen me before, you produce the doings and put them on the table—why you're fairly asking to be murdered! Go away and leave me to get on with it. I'll take a thousand francs off you at once, in case you change your mind. Bring me the rest when you come for the papers."

One more smack in the face, I shall pay them all back. Tears came into his eyes. He had the *right* to lose his temper, but his real feeling was astonishment. Why are they all so tough, they always have their weapons handy, they're always on the alert, at the slightest slip they're on to you. What have I done to this man or to the people away back in the blue drawing-room? I'll learn the rules of the game, I'll be tough too, I'll make them tremble.

"When will it be ready?"

"Tomorrow morning."

"I thought—I didn't think it would take so long."

"Indeed?" said the old man. "What about the stamps— do you think I just invent them? Go away, and come back tomorrow morning, it will take me all night to do your job."

Outside—the night, the loathsome, lukewarm night with all its monsters, footsteps pattering behind you so you dare not turn your head; night, at Saint-Ouen—a dangerous district.

"When may I come back?" said Philippe in a toneless voice.

"Any time after six o'clock."

"Are there—are there any hotels round here?"

"Plenty in the avenue de Saint-Ouen. Now scram."

"I'll be back at six," said Philippe decisively.

He picked up his suitcase, shut the door, and went downstairs. His tears trickled on to the third-floor landing; he had forgotten to bring a handkerchief, so he wiped his eyes with his sleeve, sniffing once or twice; I'm not a coward. The old ruffian upstairs took him for a coward, his contempt pursued him like a look. They're looking at me. Philippe hurried down the last flight. "Door, please." The door opened into a murky gray haze. Philippe plunged into the dish-water. I am not a coward. Only that loathsome old man thinks so. And he doesn't think so now, he said to himself emphatically. He's not thinking about me at all, he has started work. The look vanished. Philippe quickened his step. "And so, Philippe, you're a sissy?"—"I'm not a sissy, I just *can't* . . ." "You can't, Philippe, you can't . . .?" He had recoiled against the wall. Pitteaux stroked his chest and sides, fingered his nipples through his shirt, then slapped him on the mouth with two fingers of his right hand. "Good-by, Philippe, clear out. I don't like sissies." The street was populous with statues of the darkness, men leaning silently against the wall; they do not smoke, they stand motionless and watch you pass with eyes dimmed by the night. He was almost running now, his heart throbbing. "With a face like that? Nonsense, you're a coward." They shall see, they shall all see, he'll come there like the rest, he'll read my name and say: "Well, for a little rich boy, that's not so bad."

A slash of light on his right; a hotel. A waiter standing in the doorway, he had a squint; is he looking at me? Philippe slowed down, but took one step too many and passed the door, the waiter must now be squinting at his back: he *could no longer* decently retrace his steps. The squinting wine-waiter, or the duel of the Cyclops. Or how would this do for a filthy story for the Cyclops? The Cyclops looks at himself in the glass one fine morning, feeling an itch above his cheekbones; another eye is growing beside the first! How appalling! The two eyes won't work simultaneously, of course, his first eye having got used to functioning by itself. On the opposite sidewalk there was another hotel, the Hôtel de Concarneau, a small one-storied building. What about that? Suppose they ask for my papers, he thought. He didn't dare to cross the street, he went straight on. I need assurance for this sort of thing, and this evening the old man has cleaned me out of that; suddenly he caught sight of a hotel sign: "Café: wines, liqueurs." A drink would be a good idea. He pushed open the door.

It was a very small café, with a zinc counter and two tables, and the sawdust stuck to the soles of his shoes. The landlord eyed him dubiously. "I'm too well dressed," thought Philippe with annoyance.

"A brandy, please," he said, walking up to the counter.

The proprietor picked up a bottle with a small tin spout in its cork and poured out the brandy, Philippe put down his suitcase and watched him with amusement; a thread of alcohol trickled from the spout; he looked as though he were watering vegetables. Philippe sipped a little and thought: "It *must* be bad stuff." He never drank liquor, it tasted like burnt wine and scorched his throat; he hurriedly set down the glass. The boss looked at him. Was there irony in those placid eyes? Philippe picked up the glass again and raised it to his lips with a nonchalant air; his gullet was on fire, his eyes were moist, and he emptied the glass at a gulp, after which he felt rather limp, but not uncheerful. "Here," he thought, "is an opportunity for observation." He had discovered, a fortnight before, that he had no powers of observation—I'm a poet, I don't analyze. Thenceforward he tried to make inventories wherever he went—such as reckoning up the objects displayed in a shop-window.

He glanced round him—I'll begin with the top row of bottles behind the counter. Four bottles of Byrrh, one of Goudron, two of Noilly, and a jug of rum.

Someone had just come in. A workman in a cap. "A proletarian," thought Philippe. He had seldom had a chance of meeting one, but he thought about them a great deal. A strong but rather clumsy man of about thirty with long arms and bandy legs—obviously distorted thus by manual labor—with bristly yellow hairs under his nose; he was wearing a tricolor badge in his hat and seemed distressed and agitated.

"A glass of white wine, quick, please."

"We're closing," said the boss.

"You wouldn't refuse a drop of wine to a man just called up?" said the workman.

He spoke with a strained and husky voice, as though he had been shouting all day. And he added, blinking his right eye: "I'm off tomorrow morning."

The proprietor picked up a glass and a bottle. "Where are you going?" he asked, putting the glass down on the counter.

"Soissons," said the man. "I'm in tanks."

He raised the glass with a shaky hand, and some wine trickled to the floor.

"We'll knock them out right," said he.

"Hm!" said the proprietor.

"Like that," said the man. He slammed his left fist twice on to the palm of his right hand.

"Well," said the boss, "they're pretty tough, those pigs."

"Just like that, I tell you."

He drank, clicked his tongue, and began to sing. He was in an excited and exhausted state; now and then his features sagged, his eyes closed, his lips drooped, but an inexorable force seemed to lift his eyelids and raise the corners of his mouth; he looked like the exhausted victim of a too prolonged celebration. He turned towards Philippe. "Have you been called up?"

"I—not yet," said Philippe, drawing back.

"Why not? We must smash 'em, you know."

He was a proletarian; Philippe smiled and forced himself to join him.

"I'll stand you a glass of white," said the proletarian. "Boss—two glasses, one for yourself, and one for him; it's my round."

"I'm not thirsty," said the proprietor severely. "Besides, it's closing-time; I have to get up at four o'clock."

But he pushed a glass towards Philippe.

"Here's to us all!" said the proletarian.

Philippe raised his glass. A few minutes ago in a forger's room, now clinking glasses at a zinc counter with a proletarian. If they could only see me!

"Your health," said he.

"To victory," said the proletarian.

Philippe eyed him with surprise; he was surely joking: workers stand for peace.

"Now then," said the worker, "I want to hear you drink to victory." He looked grave and annoyed.

"I won't," said Philippe.

"Why not?" said the man.

He clenched his fists. A belch cut short his words; he rolled his eyes, his jaw dropped, and his head swayed feebly.

"Go on," said the boss.

The proletarian had recovered himself, he thrust his face into Philippe's, he stank of wine. "I won't drink to victory."

"You won't? And you dare to say that to me—to a soldier of '38?"

The proletarian grabbed him by the necktie and thrust him against the counter. "You refuse!"

What would Pitteaux do in my place?

"Look here," said the proprietor sternly. "Do what he tells you—I don't want a row—and then get out; I have to get up at four o'clock."

Philippe picked up his glass. "To victory," he muttered.

He drank, but his throat had so contracted that he could scarcely swallow. The man had released him and grinned complacently as he wiped his mustache with the back of his hand.

"He wouldn't drink to victory," he explained to the proprietor. "I had to twist his necktie for him—by gosh, a little tyke like that shan't insult a '14 veteran."

Philippe flung a two-franc piece on the counter, picked up his suitcase, and hurried to the door. The man was a drunk, he had to give in, Pitteaux would have given in; I'm not a coward.

"Hi, young fellow!"

The man had followed him out. Philippe heard the proprietor shutting the door and turning the key in the lock. He shivered; he felt as though he were shut in somewhere with this man.

"You aren't going to get away like that," said the man. "We're going to smash 'em, and we'll have another drink on it."

He came up to Philippe and put an arm round his neck, Mario had taken Gros-Louis's arm and was squeezing it affectionately; it was hell; they marched along dark alleys, never stopping anywhere, Gros-Louis was exhausted, he felt sick, and his ears were buzzing.

"The fact is I'm in rather a hurry," said Philippe.

"Where are we going?" said Gros-Louis.

"We're going to look for your Negro."

"And no crazy tomfoolery next time. When I stand drinks, you've got to drink 'em, see?"

Gros-Louis looked at Mario and he was afraid. "Tired, are you, old pal?" said Mario. But his face had changed. Starace had taken his left arm; it was hell. He tried to free his right arm, but he felt a sharp pain in the elbow.

"Look here—you're breaking my arm," he said.

Philippe dashed away and began to run. The man was a drunkard, there was no discredit in escaping from him. Starace suddenly dropped his arm and stepped back. Gros-Louis half-turned to see what he was up to, but Mario clutched his arm; Philippe heard a voice behind him gasp: "Well, I'll be—you dirty little snot—afraid of me, are you? I'll give you something to be afraid of!" "What's the matter, old pal, what's the matter—aren't we friends any more?" "They're going to kill me," thought Gros-Louis, and fear froze him to the marrow, he seized Mario by the throat with his free hand and lifted him off the ground; but at the same moment his head was cloven to the chin, he let go of Mario and fell to his knees, blood pouring over his eyebrows. He tried to steady himself by grabbing Mario's coat, but Mario jumped backwards, and Gros-Louis saw him no more. He saw his Negro skimming over the ground, not looking in the least like other Negroes, approaching him with extended arms, laughing; Gros-Louis reached out his hands, a vast pain rang like a gong inside his head, he shouted: "Help!" A second blow on the skull flung him face-downwards in the gutter; Philippe ran and ran; Hôtel du Canada—he stopped, recovered his breath, and looked behind him; he had shaken the man off. He retied his necktie and walked with measured steps into the hotel.

Pitch and roll, pitch and roll. The oscillations of the ship ascended in spirals into his calves and thighs and died away in deep vibrations in the pit of his stomach. But his head was clear. He belched sourly once or twice and gripped the railing with both hands. Eleven o'clock; the sky swarmed with stars, a red glow flickered over the horizon; perhaps that is the vision that will visit me and remain forever, when I'm lying in a shell-hole with my jaw shot away, under a blinking sky. A dark, unruffled vision, a rustling of palms, and these presences of men, so far beyond that red glow in the darkness. He saw them, all in uniform, packed like herrings behind their beacon-light, gliding silently towards death. They looked at him in silence, the red glow slid over the waters, they slid with it, filed past Pierre, and eyed him as they passed. He hated them, he felt solitary and defiant beneath the contemptuous eyes of night; and he shouted to them: I am right, I am right to be afraid, I am born to live, to *live!* Not to die; there's nothing worth dying for. She did not come; where could she be? He leaned over the empty between-decks. You bitch, I'll make you pay for keeping me waiting. He had slept with artists' models, mannequins, women with the loveliest figures, but this little skinflint, really badly put together, was the first woman he had desired so violently. It was nice to stroke her neck—and she adored it—just where the hair begins to grow, to watch the thrill rising from her belly to her head, to confuse those prim ideas of hers—I'll lay you, I'll enter into your disdain, I'll burst it like a bubble, and when you are full of me, when you cry: "Darling Pierre," and turn your eyes up, you won't look at me in that contemptuous way, nor call me coward.

"Good-by, my dearest, dearest girl, good-by, come back, come back!"

It was a whisper, and the wind dispelled it. Pierre turned his head, and the air whistled into his ear. Yonder on the foredeck a small lamp above the captain's cabin shone on a white dress ballooning in the wind. The white-clad woman walked slowly down the ladder holding the rail to steady herself against the wind and the motion of the ship; her dress, bellowing out, then flattening against her, looked like a striking clock. Then she vanished, she must be crossing the between-deck, the ship dived into a trough, the sea towered above him, a heaving black and white expanse, then the ship labored upwards again and the woman's head reappeared, she was climbing the companionway on to the second-class deck. So that's why their cabin was changed. She was moist with perspiration and her hair was rather disheveled, she passed Pierre without seeing him, with her usual frank and grave expression on her face.

"Bitch!" muttered Pierre. He felt engulfed in an absolute indifference, he no longer wanted her, nor did he want to live. The ship fell and fell to the bottom of the sea, Pierre fell, a limp and flaccid figure, he hesitated for a moment, then his mouth filled with bile, he leaned over the black water and vomited.

"And now the registration form," said the waiter.

Philippe put his suitcase down, picked up the pen, and dipped it in the ink. The waiter watched him, his hands

clasped behind his back. Was he stifling a yawn or a laugh?
"Just because I'm decently dressed," thought Philippe
angrily. Clothes was what caught their eyes, they saw no
farther. He wrote with a firm hand: Isidore Ducasse.
Traveling salesman.

"Show me my room," he said to the waiter, looking him
straight in the eye.

The waiter unhooked a large key from the board and
they went upstairs one behind the other. The staircase was
dark, lit by blue bulbs at infrequent intervals; the waiter's
slippers flapped against the stone stairs. Behind a door a
baby was crying; there was a pervading lavatory smell.
"It's a rooming-house," thought Philippe. Rooming-house
was a melancholy phrase that he often met with in realistic
novels and always filled him with disgust.

"Here we are," said the waiter, slipping the key into a
lock.

It was a vast room with a tiled floor; the walls were
painted brown halfway, thence a faded yellow up to the
ceiling. One chair, one table, marooned in the center of the
room, two windows, a wash-basin that looked like a sink,
a large bed against the wall. "The nuptial bed has been
moved into the kitchen," thought Philippe.

The waiter did not go away. He said with a smile: "That
will be ten francs. I must ask you to pay for the room now."

Philippe gave him twenty francs. "Keep the change,"
said he. "And call me at half past five."

The waiter did not seem impressed.

"Good night, monsieur, sleep well," he said as he went
out. Philippe stood for a moment listening. When the
shuffle of slippers had died away on the stairs, he turned
the key twice in the lock, shot the bolt, and set the table
against the door. Then he put his suitcase on the table and
looked at it listlessly. The candelabra in the drawing-room
was out, out too was the forger's candle; darkness had devoured everything. Darkness without a name. Only the

long, bare room gleamed in the darkness, impersonal as night. Philippe looked at the table with a sort of numbed indifference. He yawned. And yet he did not feel sleepy; he was devitalized—a forgotten fly awakening in winter when all the other flies are dead, and now without the strength to move. He looked at the suitcase and told himself he must open it and get out his pajamas. But his intentions froze inside his head, he could not even raise his arm. He looked at the suitcase and at the wall, and thought: "What's the good? What's the good of preventing myself from dying because that wall exists and faces me with its vile triumphal colors?" He was not even afraid now.

Hop—she rises! Hop—she falls! He was no longer afraid. The wash-basin, brimming with frothy liquid, rose and fell, he rose and fell, prostrate on his back, and he was no longer afraid. The steward will be furious because I've been sick on the floor, but I don't care. Everything around him was so soft—the liquid in his mouth, the smell of vomit, the lump in his throat, and his whole prostrate body; and the wheel that revolved and crushed his forehead, he saw it and was glad to see it—it was a taxi wheel with a gray worn tire. The wheel revolved, familiar thoughts revolved, but he didn't care—after all, he didn't need to care, in a week I shall be under fire in the Argonne, but I don't care, she despises me, she thinks me a coward, I don't care, what difference can that make to me *today*? I don't care, I think of nothing, I'm afraid of nothing, I blame myself for nothing.

Hop—she rises! Hop—she falls! He reached out a hand, opened the suitcase, his right cheek was burning him like a torch; eleven o'clock, the candelabra had been relit, she was sitting in the armchair, a plump little person with lovely bare arms, his cheek was burning, the torture was renewed, the hand lifted, the cheek burned, I'm not a coward—I'm not a coward, he unfolded his pajamas;

eleven o'clock, good night, Mamma, I kissed the general's
hetæra on her perfumed cheeks, I looked at her arms, I
bowed to him; good night, Father; good night, Philippe;
good night, Philippe. Only yesterday, he thought with
amazement; that was yesterday. But what have I done?
What has happened since? I put my pajamas in my suitcase, I went out as on all other days, and everything was
changed; a rock has fallen on the road behind me and cut
off my retreat. But when—*when* did this happen? I took
my suitcase, opened the door quietly, and walked downstairs. . . . That was yesterday. She is sitting in the armchair, he is standing in front of the fireplace, *yesterday*.
The air in the drawing-room is soft and limpid, I am
Philippe Grésigne, General Lacaze's stepson, Bachelor of
Letters, poet-to-be, *yesterday, yesterday,* yesterday and
forever. He had undressed and slipped into his pajamas;
in a rooming-house these were new and nervous gestures
that he had to learn. The Rimbaud was in his suitcase,
and he left it there, he did not want to laugh. Only once—
if she had only once believed me, if she had put her lovely
arms round my neck and said: "I trust you, you are brave
and will be strong," I should not have gone away. She's a
hetæra, she used to bring the general's fossil words into
my room and drop them there, they were too heavy for
her, they rolled under the bed, and there I let them ac-
cumulate for five years; when the bed is shifted, they will
all be found—country, honor, virtue, family, all there in
the dust, I have not exploited one of them. He stood barefooted on the tiled floor and sneezed, I shall catch cold,
the switch was beside the door, he turned off the light and
groped his way into bed, he was afraid of treading on insects like the enormous spider with tentacles as large as
fingers that looked like a severed hand, the trapdoor spider,
if there was one here—was there one? He slipped between
the sheets, and the bed creaked. His cheek burned like a
torch in the night, a crimson flame, he pressed it against

the pillow. They were going to bed, she has put on her pink laced nightdress. This evening Philippe pictured the scene with less distress; this evening he won't dare to touch her, he'll be ashamed, and she, the hetæra, certainly wouldn't allow him to, while her boy was dying of cold and hunger on the streets; she thinks of me, she pretends to sleep, she sees me, pale and resolute, with set lips and dry eyes, she sees me walking through the night beneath the stars. He isn't a coward, my boy isn't a coward, my little darling boy. If only I could be there, visible to her alone, and drink those tears that trickle down her cheeks, and stroke those lovely arms—Mamma, my dear little Mamma. The general is chancellor, said a grotesque voice in his ear. A small green triangle became detached and began to revolve; the general is chancellor.

The triangle revolved, it was Rimbaud, he expanded like a mushroom into a dry and scabby pustule, a boil on the cheek—to victory, *to victory,* TO VICTORY. I'm not a coward, cried Philippe, awakening with a start. He was sitting on the bed, bathed in sweat and vacant-eyed, the sheet smelt of sulphur, what right have they to watch me? Dolts! They judge me by their rules, and I will admit none but mine. I salute my splendid orgies—I salute my pride! I am of the race of noblemen. Alas, he thought savagely, not yet. In time to come they will put a marble tablet on the wall of this hotel—Here Philippe Grésigne spent the night of September 24-5, 1938. But I shall be dead. A confused soft murmur passed beneath the door. The night expired. He looked at it from the far future, through the eyes of the black-coated gentry who would be making speeches beneath the marble tablet. Every minute sped through the darkness, each a precious sacred minute, and already past. A time would come when this night would belong to a glorious past, like the nights of Maldoror, the nights of Rimbaud. My night. "Zézette," said a man's voice. Pride wavered; the past was shattered; behold the present. The key turned in the lock, his heart leaped within him. "No, it's next door," he heard the door of the next room creak. "There are two of them at least," he thought, "a woman and a man."

They talked. Philippe could not hear all they said, but he gathered that the man's name was Maurice, which reassured him a little. He lay down again, stretched out his legs, and drew the sheet away from his chin for fear of catching the itch. A little flutelike chant began: a singular little chant.

"Don't cry," said the man affectionately, "don't cry, my little baby, it's no good."

He had a hot rasping voice, he attacked his words abruptly and in jerks, they emerged from his gullet, sometimes in a rush, sometimes slowly, with a harsh and grating intonation, but all culminating in a rich vibrating cadence. The flutelike chant gurgled into silence. He leans over her, he takes her by the shoulders. Philippe felt two strong hands upon his shoulders and saw a face bent over his. A thin brown, almost black face, blue cheeks, a boxer's nose, a shapely, rather sardonic mouth, a Negro's mouth.

"Don't cry," repeated the voice. "Darling, don't cry, do be calm."

Philippe was now quite calm. He heard them moving to and fro—almost as though they're in my room. They dragged a heavy object across the floor. The bed, perhaps, or a trunk. Then the man removed his shoes.

"Next Sunday," said Zézette.

Hers was a coarser but more attractive voice. He could visualize her less well: blonde, perhaps, with a pallid face, like Sonia in *Crime and Punishment*.

"Ah well. . . ."

"Oh, Maurice, you have forgotten. We were to go to Corbeil, to see Jeanne."

"You must go alone."

"I shouldn't have the heart," she said.

They lowered their voices, Philippe could not understand what they were saying, but he felt happy because they were sad. These were proletarians. *Genuine* proletarians. The other had been just a sot, an oaf.

"Have you ever been to Nancy?" asked Zézette.

"Yes—awhile ago."

"What's it like?"

"Not a bad sort of place."

"You must send me a lot of postcards. I want to be able to picture where you are."

"They won't leave us there long, you know."

A *genuine* proletarian. He didn't want war, and he wasn't thinking of victory; he went, with death in his soul, because he couldn't help it.

"My big sweet," said Zézette.

They fell silent. Philippe thought: "They are miserable," and soft tears moistened his cheeks. Gentle angels in misery. I'll go in, I'll hold out my hands to them and say: "I'm miserable too, for your sake. It's for your sake that I left my parents' house. For your sake, and for the sake of all those who must go and fight." Maurice and I will stand on either side of her, and I shall say: "I am the martyr of peace." He closed his eyes contentedly; he was no longer alone, two sad angels peered over his shoulders. The recumbent martyr, like a stone effigy with two sad angels at his head, bearing palms in their hands. And they murmured: Big sweet, don't go away, I love you; and another word, too, a sweet and precious word, which he had forgotten already, the most loving of all loving words, it revolved and burst into flame like a Catherine wheel, and Philippe carried it off into his slumber.

"Gosh!" said Gros-Louis. "Gosh!" He was sitting on the sidewalk; the pain in his head was a pain beyond belief, every throb of it stirred him to amazement. "Oh!" he exclaimed. "Oh hell!" He lifted his hand to his cheek, it was moist and tingling; that must be blood. "Well," said he,

"I'd better bandage it. What's become of my bag?" He groped around him, and his hand came upon a hard object—a pocketbook. "One of them must have dropped his pocketbook." He picked it up and opened it—empty. He fumbled in his pocket, produced a sulphur match, and struck it on the tarred road; it was his own pocketbook. "Well now," he observed, "ain't that a pretty kettle of fish?" His army book was still in the pocket of his blouse, but his pocketbook was empty. "What's to be done now?" He was still groping round him, and he said: "I shan't go to the police. They're no good." He closed his eyes and began to gasp; his head was hurting him so much that he wondered whether it hadn't been split. He fingered his skull cautiously, it seemed intact, but the hair had matted into sticky tufts, and if he pressed it he felt as though he were being pounded with a mallet. "I won't go to the police," he said. "But what must I do?" His eyes were becoming accustomed to the half-light, he made out a dark mass a few yards away in the road. "It's my bag." He crawled towards it, being unable to stand upright. "What's this?" He had put his hand into a pool of liquid. "They've broken my bottle," he thought, with anguish in his heart. He picked up the bag; the canvas was soaked, the bottle was in fragments. "Oh no, not that," said Gros-Louis, "not that." He dropped the bag, sat down in the puddle of wine, and burst into tears; his sobs passed through his nose and shook him, his skull felt as though it were bursting; he had not cried like this since the old woman died. Charles was quite naked, with his legs in the air, confronting six staff nurses, the greenest of whom flapped her wings and champed her mandibles, which meant: Passed for service; Mathieu dwindled into a kind of globe, Marcelle was waiting for him, legs apart, Marcelle was a throwing-board; when Mathieu had become quite globular, Jacques threw him, he fell into the black rocket-hole, he fell into the war; war was all the rage, a bomb shattered the tiled floor and rolled to the foot of the bed, Ivich got up, the bomb blossomed into a bouquet of roses, from which Offenbach emerged. "Don't go," said Ivich, "don't go and fight, or what will become of me?" Victory, Philippe charged with bayonet fixed, and he shouted: victory, victory, here's to victory, the twelve czars decamped, the Czarina was rescued, he unloosed her bonds, she was naked, small, and plump, and she squinted; shrapnel and hand-grenades scurried full-speed at his colonel, Pierre grabbed them and put them in his knapsack, that was the order, but the fourth tried to fly away, and he caught it by the wing-sheath as it buzzed and struggled, the colonel looked at him, he lay prostrate, the shrapnel had blown his cheeks and gums away, but his eyes remained, his wide, contemptuous eyes, Pierre fled at top speed, he was a deserter, a deserter, he ran through the desert; Maud asked him: "Can I clear the table?" Viguier was dead and stinking; Daniel took off his trousers, and thought: "There are eyes upon me"; he stood up to confront them, coward, pederast, and villain. They see me, they see me as I *am*. Hannequin could not sleep, he thought: "I am called up," which seemed somehow odd—his neighbor's head weighed heavily on his shoulder, she smelt of hair and brilliantine, he dropped his arm and felt her thigh, which was pleasant, if a little tiring. He had fallen on his stomach, he no longer had any legs. "Darling!" she cried. "What are you talking about?" said a sleepy voice. "I was dreaming," said Odette. "Go to sleep, darling, go to sleep." Philippe awoke with a start—no, it wasn't the crow of a cock, it was a soft and feminine moan, ah-h-h-h; he thought at first that she was crying, but no, he was familiar with that sound, he had often listened to it, with his ear glued to the door, pale with rage and cold. But this time it did not disgust him. It seemed quite novel and attractive, an angel's chant.

"Ah-h-h!—how I love you!" said Zézette, in a throaty voice. "Ah-h-h! Oh—oh! Oh!"

A silence followed. The dark-haired angel with the sardonic mouth lay upon her with the full weight of his body, she beneath him, prostrate in fulfillment. Philippe sat up abruptly, a sneer on his lips, and his heart distraught by jealousy. None the less, he rather liked Zézette.

"Ha-a-a-h!"

He drew a deep breath; that was the sharp acknowledgement of consummation; they had finished. He heard some damp splashes; naked feet pattered over the tiled floor, the faucet twittered like a bird on a branch, and the water-pipes began to gurgle. Zézette had returned to Maurice, fresh and clean, if rather chilly about the legs; the bed creaked, she had lain down in the hot damp bed, cuddled up close to him, and was inhaling the russet odor of his sweat.

"If you died, I should just kill myself."

"Don't say that."

"I should, Momo."

"That would be a pity. You've knocked about a bit, and you're a worker; you enjoy your dinner, and you enjoy going to bed; think of all that you would lose."

"Only with *you*. I only want to go to bed with you," said Zézette passionately. "But you don't care, you're going away, you're perfectly happy."

"No, I'm not happy," said Maurice. "I hate to go."

He's going away. He'll take the train to Nancy, I shall never see them again, I shall never see his face, he will never know who I am. His feet clawed at the sheet; I must see them.

"If only you didn't have to go . . ."

"Don't be silly," said Maurice gently.

I must see them. He jumped out of bed. The spider was watching him, crouching beneath the bed, but he ran faster than the spider, pressed the switch, and it vanished in the light. I must see them. He put on his trousers, slipped his bare feet into his shoes, and went out. The passage was lit by two blue bulbs. A sheet of gray paper had been pinned on the door of No. 18, inscribed: "Maurice Gounod." Philippe leaned against the wall, his heart was pounding in his chest, and he was as breathless as if he had been running hard. What can I do? He reached out a hand and lightly touched the door: they were there, on the other side. I don't ask anything, I simply want to see them. He bent down and peered through the keyhole. A breath of cold air on his eyeball made him blink, and he saw nothing: they had put out the light. I must see them, he said to himself, knocking on the door. No answer. His throat contracted and he knocked louder.

"What is it?" said the voice—an abrupt, harsh voice, but it would change. The door would open and the voice would change. Philippe knocked; he could not speak.

"Well?" said the voice impatiently. "Who's there?"

Philippe stopped knocking. He was out of breath. He drew a deep breath and forced his voice through his contracted gullet.

"I want to speak to you," he said.

A long silence. Philippe was about to go away when he heard the sound of footsteps, then of breathing, just behind the door, and a click; the light had been switched on. The steps moved off, he is putting on his trousers. Philippe drew back, and stood with his back against the wall; he was afraid. The key turned in the lock, the door opened, and in the gap appeared a red and hairy head, with broad cheekbones and a rather wrinkled skin. The man's eyes were clear and lashless; he looked at Philippe with comical amazement.

"You've come to the wrong room," he said.

It was his voice, but in passing through that mouth it became unrecognizable.

"No I haven't," said Philippe.

"Well, what do you want?"

Philippe looked at Maurice and thought: "It's no good

now." But it was too late. He said: "I want to speak
to you."

Maurice hesitated; Philippe realized that he was going
to shut the door again, and leaned heavily against it.

"I want to speak to you," he repeated.

"I don't know you," said Maurice. His pale eyes were
hard and sly. He looked rather like a plumber come to re-
pair the bathroom.

"What is it, Maurice? What does he want?" said Zézette's
uneasy voice.

The voice was *real;* real too was the gentle unseen face.
But Maurice's fleshy countenance was a vision in a dream.
A nightmare. The voice was extinguished, and so was the
sweet face; Maurice's head emerged from the shadow,
massive, hard, and real.

"It's a guy I've never seen," said Maurice. "I don't know
what he wants."

"I can be of use to you," stammered Philippe.

Maurice surveyed him doubtfully. He *sees* my flannel
trousers, thought Philippe, he sees my calf-leather shoes,
he sees my black, Russian pajama jacket.

"I—I was in the next room," he said, setting his back
against the door. "And I—I swear I can be of use to you."

"Come back, Maurice," cried Zézette. "Tell him to go
away."

Maurice was still looking at Philippe. He pondered for
a moment, then his surly face cleared a little. "Did Émile
send you?" he asked in a lowered voice.

Philippe averted his eyes. "Yes," he said, "he did."

"Well?"

Philippe shivered. "I can't talk out here."

"How did you get to know Émile?" asked Maurice
dubiously.

"Let me come in," pleaded Philippe. "Why not let me
in? I can't talk in this corridor."

Maurice opened the door. "All right," he said. "But not for more than five minutes. I'm sleepy."

Philippe entered. The room was exactly like his own. But there were clothes on the chairs—stockings, and a pair of knickers, and a woman's shoes on the red-tiled floor near the bed, and on the table a gas plate with a saucepan on it. It smelt of cold grease. Zézette was sitting up in bed, she had thrown a fleecy mauve shawl round her shoulders. She was plain, with small, deep-set, sparkling eyes. She stared at Philippe with hostility. The door closed and he shivered.

"Well? What does Émile want?"

Philippe threw an agonized look at Maurice; he could no longer speak.

"Look here—be quick," said Zézette angrily. "He's going off tomorrow morning, this isn't the time to come and pester people."

Philippe opened his mouth and made a violent effort, but no sound came. He saw himself with their eyes, and he couldn't bear it.

"Do you understand French?" said Zézette. "I tell you he's going off tomorrow."

Philippe turned to Maurice and said in a strangled voice: "You mustn't go."

"Go where?"

"To the war."

Maurice looked dumbfounded.

"He's a dick," said Zézette shrilly.

Philippe stood limply looking at the red tiles, and felt almost pleasantly benumbed. Maurice gripped his shoulder and shook him.

"Look here—do you know Émile?"

Philippe did not answer. Maurice shook him roughly.

"Answer! I asked you if you knew Émile."

Philippe raised despairing eyes to Maurice. "I know an

old guy who manufactures false papers," he said in a low, quick voice.

Maurice released him abruptly. Philippe bent his head and added: "He'll make you some."

There was a long silence, then Philippe heard Zézette's triumphant voice: "What did I tell you?—he's a provocateur."

He managed to raise his eyes, Maurice was looking at him savagely. He raised a large hairy hand, and Philippe leaped backwards.

"It's not true," he said, lifting his elbow, "it's not true. I have nothing to do with the police."

"Then what the hell are you doing here?"

"I'm a pacifist," said Philippe, on the point of tears.

"A pacifist!" repeated Maurice with stupefaction. "That's all we need!" He scratched his head, then burst out laughing. "A pacifist!" said he. "Did you ever hear anything like that, Zézette?"

Philippe shook. "You mustn't laugh," he said hoarsely. He bit his lips to hold back the tears, then added painfully: "Even if you aren't a pacifist, you ought to respect me."

"Respect you?" repeated Maurice. "What on earth for?"

"I'm a deserter," said Philippe with dignity. "I suggest you should get some false papers, as I have done. I shall be in Switzerland the day after tomorrow."

He looked Maurice straight in the face; Maurice was frowning, there was a Y-shaped wrinkle on his forehead, he seemed to be reflecting.

"Come with me," said Philippe. "I've got enough money for two."

Maurice looked at him with disgust. "You little bastard!" said he. "Look at his clothes, Zézette! I'm sure war revolts you, I'm sure you don't want to fight the fascists. Oh no!— they keep your money safe, you rich little brat."

"I'm not a fascist," said Philippe.

"No—I suppose I am, eh?" said Maurice. "Get the hell out of this, you son of a bitch, before I make trouble."

It was Philippe's legs and feet that itched to run away. But he wouldn't run away. He forced his legs forward, he approached Maurice, he lowered the elbow that had risen in boyish self-defense. He eyed Maurice's chin; but he did not venture to look at those pale, lashless eyes. And he said: "I shan't go away."

They stood for a moment confronting each other, and then Philippe burst out: "You're such brutes—the whole lot of you. I happened to hear you talking, and I hoped— But you're just like the rest, you're impenetrable. You damn everybody without even trying to understand; do you know who I am? It's *for your sake* I deserted; I could perfectly well have stayed at home, where I'm well fed and warm and comfortable, with servants to wait on me, but I threw it all away for your sake. And you are being packed off to the slaughter, you don't mind, you don't lift a finger, a rifle is shoved into your hands and you think you're heroes, and if anyone protests, you call him a plutocrat, and a fascist, and a yellow-belly, because he doesn't do as everybody else does. I'm not yellow, that's where you're wrong. I'm not a fascist, and it isn't my fault if I'm rich. After all, it's much easier to be poor."

"I advise you to go away," said Maurice in a toneless voice: "I don't much like little brats like you, and I might get angry."

"I won't go away," said Philippe stamping on the floor. "I'm about sick of the whole thing. I'm sick of all these people who pretend not to see me or look down their noses at me—with what right, I should like to know. I exist, don't I?—I'm as good as you are! I won't go away, I shall stay all night if I like, I'm going to explain what it all means."

"Oh! So you won't go away, won't you?" said Maurice.

He gripped him by the shoulders and pushed him towards the door; Philippe tried to resist, but in vain; Maurice was as strong as an ox.

"Let me go!" cried Philippe. "Let me go! If you put me out, I shall stay outside your door and make a row, I'm not a coward, I insist on your listening to me. Let me go, you beast," he said, and kicked him several times.

He saw Maurice's lifted hand, and his heart stopped: "No!" he cried. "No!"

Maurice struck him twice with his clenched fist.

"Go easy," said Zézette. "He's only a boy."

Maurice released Philippe and looked at him with a kind of surprise.

"You—I hate you," muttered Philippe.

"Look here, kid," said Maurice with a hesitant air.

"You'll see," said Philippe, "you'll all of you see. And you'll be ashamed."

He ran out, went back into his room, and double-locked the door. The train rumbled on, the ship rose and fell, Hitler slept, Ivich slept, Chamberlain slept, Philippe flung himself on his bed and wept, Gros-Louis staggered along, houses and still more houses, his skull was ablaze but he couldn't stop, he had to make his way through the dreadful whispering night, Philippe wept, his strength had left him, he wept, he heard their whispers through the wall, he could not even hate them, he wept, an exile in the cold and squalid night, in the gray night of street-corners, Mathieu had awakened, he got up and stood at the window, he could hear the whisper of the sea, and he smiled at the lovely, milky night.

❁❁❁❁❁❁❁❁❁❁❁❁❁❁❁❁❁❁❁❁❁❁❁

Sunday, September 25

A DAY of shame, a day of rest, a day of fear, the day of God, the sun rose upon a Sunday. The beacon-light, the cross, the cheek, the CHEEK, God carries the cross inside the churches, I carry my cheek through the Sunday streets, dear me!—what a nasty boil you've got—no; the fact is they've smacked me on the cheek, poor little guy with his buttocks on his face, a huge top-heavy head, a split and bandaged head, a head like a pumpkin or a gourd, they struck from behind, one-two, there were footsteps in his head, tramp-tramp inside his head, it's Sunday, where on earth am I going to get a job, the doors were shut, great iron doors, nail-studded rusty doors, enclosing dark voids that smelt of sawdust, oil, and old iron, earthen floors strewn with rusted junk; closed too were the menacing little wooden doors, closed upon rooms filled to bursting with furniture, knick-knacks, children, hatreds, the dense odor of reddened onions, the starched collar shining on the bed, women brooding behind the windows, he walked on between the windows, between the peering eyes, stiffened, petrified by all those eyes. Gros-Louis walked between brick walls and iron doors, he walked on and on—not a penny in his pocket, nothing to eat, his

head throbbing like a heart, and as he walked, his footsteps hammered in his head—tap-tap, they tramped, already sweating, through the streets murdered by Sunday,
his cheek shone up the avenue, and he thought: "War
streets already." He thought: "How am I to get something
to eat?" He thought: "Isn't there anyone to help me?" But
the small brown men, the tall workmen with their rocky
faces were shaving and thinking about the war, thinking
that they would have a whole day in which to think about
the war, a whole empty day on which to trail their anguish
through those murdered streets. War: closed shops, deserted streets, three hundred and sixty-five Sundays in the
year; Philippe was called Pedro Cazarès, he bore his name
on his chest. Pedro Cazarès, Pedro Cazarès, Pedro Cazarès,
Pedro Cazarès was leaving that very evening for Switzerland, he was taking to Switzerland a large, flowering cheek
bearing the marks of five finger-joints; the women peered
down on him from their high windows.

God looked at Daniel.

Shall I call him God? One sole word and everything
changes. He stood with his back to the gray shutters that
enclosed the saddler's shop, the people were hurrying towards the church that stood up black against the pink
street; and those people were eternal. Everything was
eternal. A young woman passed, a blonde lithe figure, her
hair in elaborate disorder, she lived in the hotel, her husband, a manufacturer at Pau, visited her on two days every
fortnight; she had put her face to sleep because the day
was Sunday, her little feet were pattering towards the
church, her soul was a pool of silver. The church was a
dismal hole: a Romanesque façade, and a handsome recumbent stone effigy in the second chapel on the right as
you went in. He smiled at the dry-goods dealer's wife and
at her little boy. Shall I call him God? He wasn't astonished—it was bound to happen. Sooner or later. I felt sure
there was something. Indeed, I've always done everything

for the benefit of a looker-on. Without a looker-on a man evaporates.

"Good morning, Monsieur Sereno," said Nadine Pichou. "Are you going to Mass?"

"Yes, and I must hurry," said Daniel.

He watched her, she was limping more than usual, two little girls ran gaily round her. He looked at them—but stay, the looker was now looked at. My look is but a shell, God's look has pierced it. "Oh, this is literary stuff," he thought with irritation. God was here no longer. Last night, as he lay sweating in his bed, he had been conscious of God's presence, and had felt like Cain: Here am I, as thou hast made me, cowardly, futile, and a pederast. And then? The look was there, and everywhere, dumb, transparent, and mysterious. At last Daniel had gone to sleep, and when he awoke, he was alone. Merely the memory of a look. A throng poured out of all the gaping doors, black gloves, starched collars, rabbit fur, hands clasping family missals. "Ah!" said Daniel to himself, "what I must have is a method. I am tired of incessantly evaporating into an empty sky, I want a roof." The butcher passed, a large and florid man who wore spectacles of a Sunday to dignify the occasion; a missal in his hairy hand; he will be seen, the look will reach him through the stained-glass windows; they will all be seen; half of humanity lives beneath a look. Does he feel that look upon him when a joint splits under his cleaver and discloses a round and bluish bone? An eye sees him—sees his hard heart as I see his hands, sees his avarice as I see his straggling hair, and the patch of pity that gleams through his avarice, as his skull gleams through his hair; all this he knows as he turns the thumbed pages of his missal, and says with a groan: "Lord, Lord, I *am* a miser." Medusa's petrifying gaze will fall upon him from above. Stone virtues, stone vices—how restful! Those people's technique is sound, said Daniel resentfully to himself, watching their black backs steering into the darkness of the church. Three women trotted side by side in the clear, russet air of morning—three sad, sedate women, natives of that place. They had lit fires, swept floors, poured milk into the coffee, being then merely arms at the end of a broom, hands clasping the teapot handles, as insubstantial as that haze which creeps upon visible things, percolates through walls, and broods over fields and woods. Now, in that dim light, they will soon be what they really are. He watched them from a distance—suppose I joined them. Nonsense! here am I, here am I as thou hast made me, a vile coward, irredeemable. Thou lookest at me, and all hope departs; I am weary of my efforts to escape myself. But I know that, beneath thine eye, I *can* no longer escape myself. I shall enter, I shall stand among those kneeling women, like a monument of iniquity. I shall say: "I *am* Cain. Well? Thou hast made me, now sustain me." Marcelle's look, Mathieu's look, Bobby's look, my cats' look: they always stopped short at my skin. Mathieu, I *am* a pederast. I am, I am, I *am* a pederast, my God. The old man with the wrinkled face and a tear in his eye, peevishly chewing a tobacco-stained mustache, entered the church—shabby, broken, senile, and Daniel entered behind him. It was the hour when Ribadeau would appear at the bowling-alley, whistling, and the lads cried: "Hello, Ribadeau—in form today?" Ribadeau thought of that as he rolled a cigarette, his hands felt hollow, he looked gloomily at the trucks and rows of casks and was conscious of a lack of something in his hand, the weight of a nail-studded globe, nicely adjusted in his palm; he looked at the casks and he thought: "Sunday, confound it!" Marius, Claudio, Remy had gone off turn by turn, they were playing soldiers; Jules and Charlot did their best, they rolled the casks along the rails, and hoisted them together into the trucks; they were powerful men but getting on in years, Ribadeau could hear them panting as the sweat poured down their naked backs; it was an interminable job. A tall fellow with a bandage round his head, who had been prowling round the depot for the last quarter of an hour, came up to Jules, and Ribadeau saw his lips move. Jules listened to the man with his usual crabbed air, then he half rose, laid the palms of his hands on his hips, and jerked his head in the direction of Ribadeau.

"What is it?" said Ribadeau.

The man approached rather diffidently; he walked with a ducklike gait, his feet turned outwards; a ghastly-looking ruffian, who touched his bandage by way of salutation.

"Got a job for me?" he asked.

"A job?" repeated Ribadeau. He eyed the man—a ruffian, his head swathed in a dirty bandage; he looked strong, but his face was ghastly pale.

"A job?" said Ribadeau.

They stared at each other, Ribadeau thought the man was going to collapse where he stood.

"You want to work?" he said, scratching his head. "There's no scarcity of that."

The man blinked. From close at hand he didn't look so bad.

"I can work," he said.

"You don't look healthy," said Ribadeau.

"How do you mean?" said the man.

"You look ill."

The man looked at him with astonishment. "I'm not ill," he said.

"You're quite white. And what's that bandage?"

"That's where they hit me on the head," the man explained. "It's nothing."

"Who hit you on the head? The cops?"

"No. Some chaps I met. I can work all the same."

"That's to be seen," said Ribadeau.

The man bent down, grasped a cask, and lifted it with arm outstretched.

"Gosh!" said Ribadeau with admiration. He added: "What's your name?"

"Gros-Louis."

"Have you got your papers?"

"I've got my army book," said Gros-Louis.

"Give it here."

Gros-Louis felt in the inner pocket of his blouse, produced the booklet cautiously, and handed it to Ribadeau. Ribadeau opened it and began to whistle.

"Well!" he said. "Well!"

"It's all in order," said Gros-Louis with an anxious air.

"In order! Can you read?"

Gros-Louis looked at him with a knowing air. "I can shift casks even if I can't read."

Ribadeau handed him his book. "You're a Form 2 man, brother. You're due at Montpellier, at the barracks. I should advise you to get going or you'll be posted as a defaulter."

"Montpellier?" said Gros-Louis in amazement. "Why should I go to Montpellier?"

Ribadeau lost his temper. "I tell you you're called up," he said. "You're a Form 2 man; you're called up."

Gros-Louis put the book back in his pocket. "So you won't take me on?" he said.

"I can't employ a deserter."

Gros-Louis bent down and lifted a cask. "That'll do, that'll do," said Ribadeau briskly. "You're a stout fellow, certainly. But I should look silly if they came and arrested you within forty-eight hours."

Gros-Louis had hoisted the cask on to his shoulder; he looked steadily at Ribadeau, contracting his heavy eyebrows. Ribadeau shrugged his shoulders. "I'm sorry," he said.

There was nothing more to say. As he moved away, he thought: "I don't want a defaulter, anyway." "Hi! Charlot!" he cried.

"Hello!" said Charlot.

"Keep an eye on that guy, he's a defaulter."

"Pity," said Charlot. "He might have given us a hand."

"I can't take on a draft-dodger."

"Of course not," said Charlot.

They both turned round; the tall man had put down the cask and was gloomily turning the pages of his army book.

The crowd enclosed them and carried them along, thickening as it circled round them. René no longer knew if he were stationary or moving with the crowd. He looked at the French flags floating above the entrance to the Est station; yonder was the war, at the far end of the railway lines, but it did not trouble him, he felt threatened by a much more imminent catastrophe; crowds are always in some sort of peril. *Gallieni's funeral, trailing a small white garment between the black roots of the crowd, beneath the horror of the sun, the scaffolding collapses, don't look, they have carried the woman out, a stiff and lifeless figure, with a red lace foot sticking out of a burst boot;* the crowd enveloped him, beneath a clear and empty sky, I hate crowds —eyes upon him everywhere, suns that made flowers blossom on his back and belly, suns that set his long, pale nose alight—a trip into the suburbs on the first Sunday or two in May, and next day, in the papers: "Red Sunday": a few left lying where they fell. Irène protected him with her little plump person, *don't look, she grabs my hand and pulls me away, and the woman passes behind me, gliding over the crowd like a corpse on the Ganges.* She looked disapprovingly at the raised fists in the distance, beneath the tricolor flags, above the caps.

"Idiots!"

René pretended not to hear: but his sister continued in a voice of slow conviction: "Idiots. They're being packed off to the shambles, and they're happy."

She was a scandal. In buses, at the cinema, in the sub-

way, she was shocking, she always said what ought not
to be said, and made the most scandalous remarks in her
full, rich voice. He glanced behind him—that weasel-
headed fellow with the goggling eyes and corroded nose
was looking at them. Irène put a hand on his shoulder with
a thoughtful air. She had just remembered she was his
elder sister—no doubt she was about to give him some
tiresome advice; anyway, she had insisted on accompany-
ing him to the station, and at the moment she was alone
among all these men, just as when he took her to a boxing
match at Puteaux, and he must consider her feelings. She
read and smoked, lying on her divan, and produced her
own opinions, as she did her hats. She said: "Listen to me,
René, you mustn't behave like all these idiots."

"No," said René in a low voice. "No; of course not."

"Listen," she continued. "You mustn't do more than your
duty."

When she had made up her mind, her voice became
resonant. She said: "What's the good of it? You are going
because you must, but don't attract attention when you
get there, by doing more or less than you need: it comes
to the same thing. And for God's sake goof off as much
as you can."

"Yes, of course," said he.

She held him firmly by the shoulders, looked at him
earnestly but without affection. She was pursuing her idea.

"I know you, René, you love to throw your weight
around, and you'll do anything to get talked about. Now,
I warn you that if you come back with a citation, I'll never
speak to you again; it's too silly. If you come back with a
game leg or a hole in your face, don't expect me to be
sorry for you, and don't tell me it happened by accident;
with a little prudence, those are things that can be perfectly well avoided."

"Yes," said he, "yes."

She was right, but it wasn't the kind of thing to say. It

ought to happen naturally, without discussion, by the force of events, so that afterwards there can be no matter for self-reproach. Caps, a sea of caps, the caps of Monday morning and of every day, caps of factory yards, of Saturday meetings, Maurice felt at ease in the thickest of the crowd. The tide swayed the lifted fists and carried them, with a few halts, hesitations, and fresh starts, slowly to the tricolor flags, *Comrades, comrades, the fists of May, the blossoming fists surge towards Garches, towards the red stands on the Garches meadow, my name is Zézette and the Falcons are singing in honor of the lovely month of May, and the world now coming to birth.* There was a smell of corduroy and wine, Maurice was all around and everywhere, he smelt the corduroy and wine, he rubbed his sleeve against the rough tweed of a jacket, a curly-haired lad thrust a haversack into the small of his back, the shuffle of countless feet thrilled up his legs into his stomach, something buzzed in the sky above his head, he looked up at the plane, then down again, and saw beneath him an expanse of upturned faces, reflections of his own, and smiled at them. Two clear pools in a tanned skin, tousled hair, a scarred cheek—and he smiled. He smiled too at the earnest fellow in eyeglasses, at the thin, pallid, bearded man with set lips, who did not smile. A shout echoed in his ears, a shout and a burst of laughter—Well, no fooling, so it's you, Jojo, there had to be a war for us to meet. It was Sunday. When the factories are closed, when men assemble and wait, empty-handed, in railway stations, with packs on their backs, at the behest of an iron destiny, it is then Sunday, no matter whether they are going off to a war or on a trip to Fontainebleau. Daniel standing at a *prie-dieu* breathed a suave cellar-like odor laden with incense, eyed the array of bald skulls beneath the violet light, the sole standing figure among those kneeling men; Maurice, enclosed by standing men, men without women, in a hectic smell of wine, coal, and tobacco, looked at the caps beneath the light of morning, and thought: It's Sunday. Pierre was asleep; Mathieu pressed the tube, a cylinder of pink paste emerged with a faint hiss, broke, and dropped on to the bristles of the brush. A boy jostled Maurice, laughed, and shouted: "Hello, Simon! Simon!" Simon turned, his cheeks were red, he laughed and said: "Well! This is what you might call a black Sunday, eh?" Maurice laughed too, and repeated: "Black Sunday," a handsome youth returned the smile, he had a slim and rather flamboyant woman with him; she clung to his arm and looked up at him plaintively, but he did not look at her; otherwise they would have merged into a single person. Even so, an isolated pair. He was enjoying himself, he looked at Maurice, the woman did not count, Zézette did not count, *she's gasping now, and how she smells, she's quite limp underneath me, darling, darling, come!*— there was still an hour or two of night left, like a veil of sweat between her body and her nightdress, just a little sweat, a little stale and amorous anguish, but he was enjoying the fresh air, women were out of place; here was war—war, revolution, and victory. We shall keep our rifles. All these men—curly-haired, bearded, bespectacled—they will all return, rifles in hand, singing the *Internationale,* and it will be Sunday. Forever Sunday. He raised his fist.

"He's raising his fist. That's the idea."

Maurice turned, his fist in the air. "What do you mean?" he asked.

It was the bearded man. "Do you want to die for the Sudetens?" demanded the bearded man.

"Oh, shove it!" said Maurice.

He of the beard eyed him with a malignant but rather hesitant air, rather as though he were trying to remember something. Suddenly he shouted: "Down with war!"

Maurice recoiled and bumped his haversack into someone's back. "Keep your big mouth shut!"

"Down with war!" shouted the other. "Down with war!"

His hands quivered and his eyes rolled, he went on shouting because he couldn't help it. Maurice looked at him with disgusted astonishment, but without anger, he thought of knocking him out just to keep him quiet, as one thumps a hiccuping child; but he could still feel flesh beneath his finger-joints, and he was ashamed: he had struck a boy; never again! He thrust his hands into his pockets. "Knock it off, stupid!" he said.

The bearded man went on shouting, in a cultured, weary voice—a rich man's voice; and Maurice suddenly had an unpleasant feeling that the whole performance was a put-up job. He looked round him, and his good humor vanished; it was those other people's fault, they didn't know how to react. At meetings, when a chap made himself a nuisance, the crowd surged upon him and submerged him, his arms waved for a moment, then he disappeared. But these fellows had recoiled and left the bearded man isolated; the young woman eyed him curiously, she had dropped her man's arm, the boys were turning round, they looked shifty and pretended not to hear.

"Down with war!"

Maurice was aware of an odd thrill of disquiet in the center of his back; the sunshine, the man shouting, and the crowd all looking at the ground. . . . His disquiet increased into a pain; he shouldered the crowd aside and made his way towards the station entrance, towards the genuine comrades who stood with lifted fists beneath the flags. The boulevard Montparnasse was deserted. Sunday. Outside the Coupole five or six people were sitting over drinks: the scarf-shop lady was standing in her doorway; on the first floor of No. 99, above the Kosmos, a man in shirt-sleeves appeared at the window and laid his elbows on the railing. Maubert and Thérèse uttered a cry of joy— there was one over there, on the wall between the Coupole and the drugstore, a large yellow, red-edged notice: *Frenchmen!*—still quite damp. Maubert charged, his neck

hunched between his shoulders, his head outthrust,
Thérèse after him, in high glee; they had torn down six,
under the astonished gaze of many worthy citizens, it was
grand to have a young and sporting employer, a fine fellow
who knew his mind.

"Filth!" said Maubert.

He looked round him; a small girl, about ten years old,
had stopped, and twisted her plaits as she stood watching
them; Maubert repeated at the top of his voice: "Dirty
filth!"

Thérèse said loudly, addressing Maubert's back: "I can't
think how the Government can allow such crap to be put
up on the walls."

The scarf-lady did not reply; she was a large, somnolent
woman, with a vague professional smile lingering between
her cheeks.

Frenchmen!
The German demands are inadmissible. We have done every-
thing we could to preserve peace, but no one can expect France
to repudiate her engagements and decline into a second-class
power. If we today abandon the Czechs, tomorrow Hitler will
claim Alsace. . . .

Maubert seized the notice by one end and tore off a long
ribbon of yellow paper, like a strip of flesh from a duck's
breast. Thérèse took the notice by the right-hand corner,
pulled, and a large fragment came away:

> *France to*
> *ments and*
> *a second-class power*
> *if we aban*
> *will claim*

A yellow, jagged star-shaped patch of paper remained
upon the wall. Maubert took a step back to inspect his
handiwork: a yellow star, just a yellow star, displaying a
few innocuous, truncated words. Thérèse smiled and

looked at her gloved hands; a fragment of the notice, a thin sliver of paper, was still sticking to her right glove: "Repu . . ." She rubbed her thumb against her forefinger, and the yellow scrap coagulated into a pellet as hard as a pinhead. Thérèse opened her fingers, the pellet dropped, and she thrilled with an intoxicating sense of power.

"A bit of beefsteak, Monsieur Désiré, something about a pound and a half, a really nice piece, please cut it carefully; yesterday your assistant served me and gave me a very stringy piece. By the way, what has been happening across the street. At No. 24, I mean—the black curtains. Is someone dead?"—"I don't know," said the butcher. "I haven't any customers at No. 24, they get their meat from Berthier's. Now, this is a really special cut, pink and tender, sparkles like champagne, it'll melt in your mouth—wouldn't mind eating it raw."

"No. 24," said Mme Lieutier, "I know, it's Monsieur Viguier."—"Monsieur Viguier? Don't know him. He must be a new tenant?"—"No indeed, it's the little old gentleman, you know him quite well, he used to give Thérèse sweets."—"Oh, that old chap? What a pity! I shall miss him; Monsieur Viguier—fancy that!" "Well, he was pretty old, you know."—"Oh," said Mme Lieutier; "and then, as I said to my husband, the little old fellow died just at the right time, he knew what he was about, I dare say in six months we shall all be sorry we aren't where he is. You've heard of what they've invented?" "Yeh? Who?"—"The Germans. Kills people like flies, in awful agony."—"Good God, you don't say so! The bastards! But what is it?"—"A kind of gas, I believe, or ray, if you like—I have had it explained to me."—"Ah, that would be the death-ray," said the butcher, wagging his head.—"Yes, something of that kind. I begin to think it would be much better to be below ground."—"You're quite right, that's what I always say. No more housekeeping, no more troubles; that's how I should like to die: go to sleep at night and not wake up in the morning."—"Well, that's how he did die, apparently."—"Who?"—"The little old guy."—"Some people have all the luck, we women always get the worst of everything, you saw what happened in Spain. No, a bit of rib, and have you got any scraps for my cat? When I just think—another war! My husband served in '14, and now it's my son's turn; I tell you men are crazy. Is it so difficult to come to an understanding?"—"But Hitler doesn't want an understanding, Madame Bonnetain."—"Hitler, you say? He wants his Sudetens, doesn't he? Well, let him have them. I don't even know whether they're men or mountains, and my son is to be killed for a matter of that sort. I would hand them over, so I would. You want them? Here they are. And wouldn't he be fooled! Tell me," she continued more seriously, "is the funeral today? You don't happen to know at what time? I'd like to be at the window to watch it pass." What's all this about a war? He was still clutching his army book, he couldn't make up his mind to put it back in his pocket; it was his sole possession. He opened it as he walked on, saw his photograph, and felt a little reassured; those little black lines that described him—while he looked at them they didn't seem so formidable. But he said to himself: "All the same, it's a nuisance not to be able to read!" A deserter—the thin exhausted youth who made his way up the avenue de Clichy, trailing his reflection from window to window, this emaciated youth with no hatred in his heart, was a rebel, a deserter, a terrible personage with a shaven crown, living at Barcelona in the Barrio Chino, and kept in hiding by an adoring mistress. But how can one *be* a deserter? What is the true vision of a man's own self?

He was standing in the nave, the priest was chanting for him; and he thought: "Rest and peace—rest and peace." *In himself eternity shall transform him at last.* Thou hast created me even as I am, and thy purpose is inscrutable; I am the most shameful of thy thoughts, thou seest me and

I serve thee, I set myself against thee, I insult thee, and in so insulting thee I serve thee. I am thy creature, thou lovest thyself in me, thou maintainest me, thou who hast created monsters. A bell tinkled, the faithful bowed their heads, but Daniel remained erect, looking steadily before him. Thou seest me, Thou lovest me. He felt calm and sanctified.

The hearse stopped at No. 24. "Here they are, here they are," said Mme Bonnetain.—"It's the third floor," said the concierge. She recognized the undertaker's man, and said: "Good morning, Monsieur René, I hope you're well."— "Good morning," said M. René. "It's an odd notion to get buried on a Sunday."—"Ah," said the concierge, "that's because the gentleman was a freethinker." Jacques looked at Mathieu, drummed on the table, and said: "And even if we win this infernal war, do you know who will profit by it? Stalin."—"And if we do nothing, Hitler will," said Mathieu quietly.—"Well, and what then? Hitler—Stalin, it's all the same. Except that an understanding with Hitler will save us two million men and spare us a revolution."— Ah well. Mathieu got up, walked to the window, and looked out. He wasn't even irritated; he thought: "What is the sense of it all?" He was a deserter, and the sky retained the genial air of Sunday, the streets smelt of rich dishes, frangipani, fowls, and domesticity. A couple passed, the man was carrying some pastry done up in fancy paper and hanging by a loop of pink string from his little finger. Like every other Sunday. *It's all bluff, it makes no difference, see how quiet everything is, not a ruffle on the surface, the miniature death called Sunday, death in the domestic circle, try again, the sky exists, the grocer's shop exists, the pie exists; deserters don't.* Sunday, Sunday, the first line-up outside the urinal on the Place Clichy, the first heat of the day. He saw himself entering the elevator that had just come down, inhaling in the dim shaft the perfume of the blonde lady on the third floor, and pressing the white button; a faint tremor, a smooth upward glide, and he would slip his key into the lock as he did every Sunday, hang his hat on the third peg, settle his tie before the mirror in the hall, open the drawing-room door, and say: "Here I am!" What would she do? Would she run to meet him, as she did every Sunday, murmuring: "Darling!" It was so like life, so stiflingly like life. And yet all that had gone forever. If only I could get angry! He struck me, thought he. He stopped, he had a stitch in his side, he leaned against a tree, but he wasn't angry. "Oh," he thought desperately, "why did I have to grow up?" Mathieu returned and sat down opposite Jacques. Jacques was talking, Mathieu looked at him; it was all so tedious, the bureau in the half-light, the snatches of band music from beyond the pines, the curls of butter in the little dish, the empty bowls on the tray—so futile an eternity. He too wanted to speak; not to say anything in particular, but merely to break that eternal silence on which his brother's voice made no impression.

He said: "Don't worry. War or peace—it's all the same."

"All the same?" said Jacques in astonishment. "Go and tell that to the millions of men who are preparing to be killed."

"And what then?" said Mathieu genially. "They have carried their death within them since the day they were born. And even if they are massacred to a man, humanity will still be up to strength; not an empty place, not one person missing."

"Except for a loss of twelve to fifteen millions," said Jacques.

"It isn't a question of numbers," said Mathieu. "Humanity replenishes itself, none is missed and none awaited. Humanity will continue on its futile journey, the usual people will ask themselves the usual questions and wreck their lives in the usual way."

Jacques looked at him with a knowing smile.

"And what does it all come to?"

"Well, just to nothing," said Mathieu.

"There they are—there they are," exclaimed Mme Bonnetain brightly, "they're just going to put the coffin in the hearse." The war doesn't matter, the train moved out, bristling with lifted fists, Maurice had found his old friends once more. Dubech and Laurent flattened him against the window as he yelled the *Internationale*. "You sing like my ass," said Dubech. "I like it," said Maurice. He was hot, his temples throbbed, it was the finest day in his life. He felt chilly, he had a stomach-ache, he rang for the third time; he heard the sound of hurried footsteps in the corridor, doors slammed, but no one came. "What are they doing? They'll let me mess right in my nightgown." Someone pounded past his door.

"Hi!" yelled Charles.

The noise in the corridor continued and then died away; then came a sound of knocking overhead. Curse them—that would be the little Dorliac woman, who slips them five-thousand-franc notes every month, just in tips, they'd fight to get on her floor. He shivered, there must be windows open somewhere, an icy draught came from underneath the door, they must be airing the place, we haven't gone yet, and they're airing the place already; what with the noise, the draught, and the shouting, I might be in a windmill, or on a public square. He hadn't felt so wretched since his first X-ray was taken.

"Hello there! Hi!" he yelled.

Ten minutes to eleven, Jeannine had not come, he had been alone all the morning. When are they going to stop that row overhead? The hammer-blows thudded in his eye-sockets—they might be nailing down my coffin. His eyes were dry and painful, he had awakened with a start at three in the morning, after a bad dream. Indeed, it was scarcely a dream: he was left alone at Berck; beach, hospitals, clinics, all were deserted; no patients nor nurses, darkened windows, empty wards, gray, bare sands as far as eye could reach. But the emptiness was of the kind seen in dreams alone. The dream continued; his eyes were open, and the dream continued; he was on his trolley in the center of his room, and yet his room was empty; no longer any up or down, or any right or left. Only four walls, four walls that met at right angles, just some sea-air caught between four walls. A heavy object was being dragged into the corridor, a rich patient's trunk, no doubt.

"Hi!" he yelled. "Hi!"

The door opened and Mme Louise came in.

"At last," he said.

"Now, please," said Mme Louise. "There are a hundred patients to be dressed; all must wait their turn."

"Where's Jeannine?"

"She hasn't time to attend to you now—she is dressing the Pottier girls."

"Give me the pan, quick," said Charles. "Quick—quick!"

"What's the matter? It isn't your time."

"I'm in pain," said Charles. "That's why."

"Yes, but I must get you ready. Everybody has to be ready by eleven o'clock. So hurry up."

She undid the cord of his pajamas, and pulled down his trousers; then she lifted him by the small of his back and slipped the pan underneath him. The enamel surface felt chilly and harsh. "I've got diarrhea," thought Charles with vexation.

"How am I going to manage if I have diarrhea in the train?"

"Don't you worry. Everything is provided for."

She looked at him, jingling her bunch of keys.

"You'll have a fine day for the journey."

Charles's lips began to quiver. "I hate to be going away."

"Nonsense!" said Mme Louise. "Well—finished?"

Charles made a last effort. "Yes, I've finished."

She felt in her pocket and produced a sheet of paper and a pair of scissors. She cut the paper into eight sections.

"Up with you," she said.

He heard the crackle of the paper and felt it rub against his skin.

"Ouch," said he.

"There," she said. "Now turn over so that I can get the pan away, and I'll finish you off."

He turned over, he heard her walking about the room, then he felt the touch of expert fingers. That was the moment he most enjoyed. A mere object: a forlorn little object. It hardened under him; he caressed it against the cool sheet.

Mme Louise turned him over like a parcel: and what met her eye set her laughing. "A last little joke, eh?" she said. "Well, we shall miss you, Monsieur Charles, you were the life and soul of the party."

She threw back the bedclothes and took off his pajamas. "A little eau-de-Cologne on your face," she said, rubbing it accordingly. "You won't get much of a wash today, I'm afraid. Lift your arms. Good. Now the shirt. Drawers next—don't wriggle like that, I can't get your socks on."

She drew back to contemplate her handiwork and said with satisfaction: "There you are, as neat as a new penny."

"Will it be a long journey?" asked Charles huskily.

"Probably," she said, putting on his jacket.

"And where are we going?"

"I don't know. I believe you'll stop at Dijon first."

She looked round her. "I must just see I haven't forgotten anything. Ah," she said, "of course. Your cup. Your blue cup. You've been so fond of it."

She took it from the shelf and bent over the suitcase. It was a blue china cup decorated with red butterflies. A very handsome cup.

"I'll put it between the shirts so that it won't break."

"Give it to me," said Charles.

She looked at him with surprise and handed him the cup. He took it, raised himself on one elbow, and hurled it against the wall.

"You vandal!" exclaimed Mme Louise indignantly. "You should have let me keep it if you didn't want to take it with you."

"I didn't want to give it away or take it with me," said Charles.

She shrugged her shoulders, walked to the door, and flung it open.

"Are we going now?" he asked.

"Certainly," she said. "You don't want to miss the train?"

"It's so sudden," said Charles.

She came back and began to wheel the trolley out of the room; he stretched out a hand to touch the table as they passed, he caught sight of the window for an instant, and a section of wall reflected in the mirror above his head, and then nothing more, he was in the corridor, behind some forty trolleys ranged in Indian file against the wall; his heart contracted.

The funeral procession moved off. "They're just starting," said Mme Bonnetain. "I say, there aren't many people to see him to his last home." Progress was slow, a turn of the wheels and then a stop, the dark pit waited at the journey's end, the nurses wheeled the trolley towards it, two by two, but there was only one elevator and progress was slow.

"It's a long business," said Charles.

"You won't be left behind," said Mme Louise.

The hearse passed underneath the window; the small lady in mourning—she must be "the family," the concierge had locked up the lodge, was walking behind the hearse, side by side with a buxom woman in a gray dress and a blue felt hat—the nurse. M. Bonnetain stood beside his wife with his elbows on the balcony. "Old Viguier was a

Third-degree Mason," said he. "How do you know?" "Aha!"
said he complacently; and he added after a moment's
pause: "He used to make a triangle with his thumb inside
my hand when he shook hands with me." A surge of anger
rose into Mme Bonnetain's temples at hearing her husband
speak so lightly of a dead man. She watched the little procession and thought: "Poor man." He lay there prostrate,
they were carrying him feet foremost to the pit. Poor man,
it is sad to have no family. She made the sign of the cross.
Prostrate in a lightless pit, he would soon feel the elevator
sink down beneath him.

"Who is going with us?" he asked.

"No one from here," said Mme Louise. "The three nurses
from the Norman chalet and Georgette Fouquet, a tall
brown-haired girl whom you must know, she's at Dr. Robertal's clinic."

"Ah, yes," said Charles, as she pushed him slowly towards the pit. "A dark-haired girl with pretty legs. She
doesn't look very amiable."

He had often noticed her on the beach, in charge of a
throng of rickety children, cuffing them impartially as
might be needed; she had bare legs and wore straw sandals. Fine, sinewy legs they were, veiled in soft down—he
often used to wish she were nursing him. They will lower
him into the pit and no one will lean over him except that
rather dowdy little female—how sad to die like that! Mme
Louise pushed him into the elevator, there was already a
trolley standing in the dim light against the wall.

"Who is that?" asked Charles, blinking.

"Petrus," said a voice.

"Aha, you old cock," said Charles. "So we're off, eh?"

Petrus did not answer, there was a faint jerk, Charles
felt as though he were hovering a few inches above his
trolley, then they plunged, the floor of the third story was
already above his head, he was quitting life downwards,
through a hole in a sink.

"But where is she?" he said with a convulsive sob. "Where is Jeannine?"

Mme Louise did not seem to hear, and Charles swallowed his tears on account of Petrus. Philippe walked on and on, he could not stop; if he did, he would faint; Gros-Louis went on walking, he had hurt his right foot. A man passed along the deserted street, a short fat man with a mustache, wearing a straw hat. Gros-Louis reached out a hand.

"Can you read?" he said to him. "Can you read?"

The man stepped aside and hurried on.

"Don't run away," said Gros-Louis. "I shan't eat you."

The man walked faster, Gros-Louis limped after him, holding out his army book; the man finally took to his heels and fled, with a squeal like a frightened animal. Gros-Louis stopped and watched him go, scratching his head above the bandage; the man, now dwindled into the small round semblance of a ball, rolled to the corner of a street, rebounded, turned, and vanished.

"Oh dear!" said Gros-Louis. "Oh dear!"

"Don't cry," said Mme Louise.

She dabbed his eyes with her handkerchief, I didn't even know I was crying. He felt rather moved; it was rather pleasant to bewail one's own troubles.

"I was so happy here."

"No one would have believed it," said Mme Louise. "You were always grumbling."

She shot back the grated door of the elevator and wheeled him into the vestibule. Charles raised himself on his elbows; he recognized Totor and the Gavalda boy. The Gavalda boy was as pale as a sheet; Totor had huddled himself into his bedclothes and lay with eyes closed. Men in caps received the trolleys as they emerged from the elevator, propelled them through the doorway of the clinic, and disappeared with them into the park. A man came up to Charles.

"Well, good-by, and a good journey," said Mme Louise. "Send us a postcard when you arrive. And don't forget: the little case with the toilet articles is by your feet, under the bedclothes."

The man was already bending over Charles.

"Hi!" cried Charles. "Take care. You may do me a serious injury if you aren't used to this sort of thing."

"That's all right," said the man. "Don't you worry. What with the barrows at Dunkirk station, the trucks at Lens, and the trolleys at Anzin, there's nothing I don't know about this job."

Charles said no more, he was afraid; the lad who was pushing the Gavalda boy's trolley swung it round a corner on two wheels and rasped the wooden ledge against the wall.

"Stop!" said Jeannine. "Stop! I'm taking him to the station."

She ran down the stairs, quite out of breath.

"Monsieur Charles!" she cried.

She looked at him with a sort of sad intensity; her throat heaved violently, and she fumbled with his bedclothes merely that she might touch him; well, there was one thing that was his wherever he might be, and that was a woman's loving, loyal heart, it would beat for him, in a deserted clinic, at Berck.

"Well," he said, "you've let me down."

"Oh, Monsieur Charles, I was so rushed; I just couldn't make it, as Madame Louise must have told you."

She bustled rather sadly round the trolley on her two sturdy legs, and he quivered with hatred; she was a *stand-up*, she had vertical recollections, he would not long remain in the shelter of that heart.

"Well, well," he said dryly. "We must hurry: take me along."

"Come in," said a feeble voice.

Maud opened the door, and a smell of vomit took her

by the throat. Pierre lay stretched full length on the bunk. He was pale, his eyes were unnaturally large, but he seemed composed. She had a moment of repulsion, but forced herself to walk into the cabin. On a chair, beside Pierre's head, stood a pan filled with turbid, frothy liquid.

"I'm only vomiting phlegm now," said Pierre in a level voice. "I have long since brought up everything in my stomach. Take the basin away and sit down."

Maud took away the pan, holding her breath as she did so, and put it down by the wash-basin. She sat down; she had left the door open to air the cabin. A silence followed; Pierre looked at her with embarrassing curiosity.

"I didn't know you were ill," she said, "or I would have come sooner."

Pierre raised himself on one elbow. "I'm feeling a bit better," he said, "but I'm still very weak. I've been sick continuously since yesterday. Perhaps I'd better eat something at lunch-time—what do you think? I was thinking maybe a chicken wing."

"How can I say?" said Maud pettishly. "You must know if you feel hungry."

Pierre stared uneasily at the coverlet.

"Of course," he said, "there's the risk of overloading the stomach, but food may settle it, and, from another standpoint, if I start being sick again, I had better have something to bring up."

Maud eyed him with amazement. "Well," she thought, "it does take time to get to know a man."

"Right—I'll tell the steward to bring you some vegetable soup, and white of chicken." She laughed a little constrainedly and added: "If you are thinking of food, you can't be very ill."

A silence fell. Pierre had raised his eyes and was observing her with a disconcerting blend of attention and indifference.

"Now tell me; you're in second class now."

"Who told you?" said Maud pettishly.

"Ruby. I met her yesterday in a corridor."

"Well, yes," said Maud. "Yes, we're in second class."

"How did you manage that?"

"We suggested giving a concert."

"Ah," said Pierre.

He continued to look at her. He laid his hands on the sheets and said nonchalantly: "And then you slept with the captain?"

"What are you talking about?" said Maud.

"I saw you come out of his cabin," said Pierre: "there couldn't be any doubt about it."

Maud was at a loss. In one sense, she no longer owed him any account of what she did; at the same time it would have been more regular to tell him. She dropped her eyes and coughed; her sense of guilt restored a little of her affection for Pierre.

"Look here," she said, "if I had refused, France wouldn't have understood."

"But what on earth has France got to do with it?" said Pierre's placid voice.

She raised her head abruptly; he smiled, he still wore his expression of nonchalant curiosity. She felt insulted; she would have preferred him to abuse her.

"If you want to know," she said dryly, "when I'm on a ship, I always sleep with the captain, so that Baby's orchestra can travel second-class. That's how it is."

She waited for him to protest, but he did not speak. She bent over him and added forcibly: "I'm not a whore."

"Who said you were? You do what you like, or what you can. I see no harm in that."

He felt as though he were lashing her across the face. She rose abruptly. "Oh, so you see no harm in it!" she said. "You see no harm in it, do you?"

"Certainly not."

"Well, you are wrong," she said hotly. "You are completely wrong."

"So there is harm in it?" asked Pierre with amusement.

"Don't try to confuse me. No, there's no harm in it. Why should there be? Who has the right to tell me I shouldn't do such things? Not the men who are always after me, nor my friends who get the benefit, nor my mother, who can't earn her living now, so I have to send her what I can. But you ought to think there's harm in it, because you are my lover."

Pierre had clasped his hands on the coverlet; on his face was a sick man's malicious, shifty look. "Don't shout," he said quietly; "I've got a headache."

She controlled herself and looked at him coldly. "Don't be afraid," she said in a low tone, "I won't shout. But I might as well tell you now that it's all over between us. I hate myself enough already for letting myself be mauled over by that old soup-pot, and if you had bawled me out or been sorry for me, I would have thought that you cared a bit about me, and I should have felt better. But if I can sleep with anyone I please, and no one—not even you—cares a damn either way, then I'm just a mangy little bitch, a whore, and whores, fellow, run after pimps and don't have to bother themselves about drips like you."

Pierre did not answer; he had closed his eyes. She kicked her chair across the cabin, went out, and slammed the door.

He glided, reclining on one elbow, between villas, clinics, and pensions; all empty, the hundred and twenty-two windows of the Hôtel Brun were open; in the hall of the villa Mon Désir, in the garden of the villa Oasis, patients were waiting, lying in their coffins, with heads uplifted; they looked silently at the procession of trolleys on its way towards the railway station. No one spoke, nothing could be heard but the creaking of springs and the dull thud of wheels dropping from the sidewalk on to the road. Jeannine walked quickly; they overtook a large, elderly, red-faced lady propelled by a little old man in tears; they overtook Zozo, it was his mother who was taking him to the station, the lame attendant of the public lavatory.

"Hi!" yelled Charles.

Zozo gave a start, lifted himself a little, and looked at Charles with his clear, vacant eyes.

"We're out of luck," he sighed.

Charles dropped flat on his back; he was conscious, on his right and on his left, of all those horizontal presences, ten thousand miniature entombments. He reopened his eyes and saw a patch of sky, and then hundreds of people leaning out of the windows of the Grande Rue waving handkerchiefs. Bastards! Bastards! This isn't the 14th of July. A flight of gulls whirled screaming overhead, and Jeannine, behind him, blew her nose. She wept beneath her veils of crepe; the nurse stared fixedly at the solitary wreath dangling from the rear of the hearse, but she heard the woman weep, she couldn't have regretted him much, it was more than ten years since she had seen him—still, somewhere in the depths of ourselves we all harbor an ashamed, unsatisfied melancholy that quietly awaits a funeral, a first communion, or a marriage, to evoke those latent tears; the nurse thought of her paralyzed mother, the war, her nephew recently called up, the hard, hard life of a nurse, and she too began to cry, glad to be crying in the little lady's company; behind her the concierge had begun to sniff, poor old gentleman, so few people to go with him, we must try to look mournful; Jeannine wept as she wheeled the trolley. Philippe walked on and on, I'm going to faint; Gros-Louis walked on and on—war, illness, death, departure, misery—it was Sunday. Maurice sang out of the window of his compartment, Marcelle went into the confectioner's to buy a cake.

"You haven't got much to say," said Jeannine. "I thought you would be sorry to leave me."

They had turned into the station road.

"Haven't I got enough to worry about as it is?" asked Charles. "They pack me up, they send me off I don't know where, whether I like it or not, added to which you want me to be sorry to leave you."

"You've got no heart!"

"All right," he said severely, "I wish you were in my place. You wouldn't have much of a heart either."

She did not reply, he saw a dark ceiling overhead.

"Here we are," said Jeannine.

To whom could he turn? Was there no one to whom he could say: "For God's sake leave me behind, she'll look after me, she'll take me out in the evening, she'll caress me with those soft hands of hers . . ." ?

"Ah well," he said to her, "I believe I shall die on the journey."

"You're crazy," said Jeannine frantically. "You're completely crazy—how can you say such things!"

She came from behind the trolley and bent over him, he could feel her warm breath.

"Now then," he said, laughing in her face, "no scenes, please. You won't need to worry if I die. It will be the pretty dark-haired girl, you know who I mean—Dr. Robertal's nurse—who will have all the bother."

Jeannine stiffened abruptly. "She's an old bag," said she. "You can't imagine the trouble she gave Lucienne. You'll soon see what she's like," she added through her clenched teeth. "It isn't worth while making eyes at her, she isn't such a mutt as I am."

Charles raised himself and looked uneasily around him. There were more than two hundred trolleys lined up in the hall. The porters pushed them on to the platform, one after the other.

"I won't go," he muttered.

Jeannine gave him a distraught look.

"Good-by," she said to him. "Good-by—little doll."

He was about to reply, but the trolley had started. A tremor ran up him from his feet to his neck; he tilted his head back and saw a flushed face bent over his own.

"Write to me," cried Jeannine. "Do write to me."

He was already on the platform, amid a din of whistles and shouts of good-by.

"But that can't be our train?" he asked frantically.

"Why not? What sort of train do you expect? The Orient Express?" said the porter ironically.

"But they're freight cars!"

The porter spat between his feet. "A passenger train wouldn't do for you folks. The seats would need to be taken out, and that would be too much of a job."

The porters grasped the stretchers at each end, lifted them off the trolleys, and carried them to the train. In the compartments there were railway men in caps, who received the stretchers as best they could and transported them into the darkness. The handsome Samuel, the Don Juan of Berck, who owned eighteen suits of clothes, passed quite close to Charles, in the arms of two porters, and vanished, with his legs up-tilted, into the car.

"There are hospital trains, aren't there?" said Charles indignantly.

"Sure. But you don't suppose they're going to send hospital trains to Berck, just before the war starts, to pick up old wrecks."

Charles was about to reply, but his stretcher dipped and he was slung into the car feet upmost.

"Keep level!" he yelled.

The porters laughed, the pit came nearer and expanded, they released the ropes, and the coffin fell with a soft thud on the fresh earth. Leaning over the edge of the excavation the nurse and the concierge were now sobbing wholeheartedly.

"You see," said Boris, "you see. They're all clearing out."

They were sitting in the vestibule of the hotel, not far from an elderly gentleman with a ribbon in his button-hole, reading a newspaper. The porter had just brought down two pigskin suitcases and deposited them near the entrance, beside some others.

"Five departures this morning," he observed dispassion-ately.

"Look at those suitcases," said Boris; "they're pigskin. Those people don't deserve them," he added severely.

"Why, my lovely?"

"They ought to be covered with labels."

"But in that case one couldn't see the pigskin," said Lola.

"That's the point. Luxury should conceal itself, and la-bels would do that. If I had a pigskin suitcase, I wouldn't be here."

"Where would you be?"

"No matter where—in Mexico, or China," and he added: "With you, of course."

A tall woman in a black hat walked excitedly across the hall, crying: "Mariette! Mariette!"

"That's Madame Delarive," said Lola. "She's leaving this afternoon."

"We shall be left alone in the hotel," said Boris. "What a scream! We'll change our room every evening."

"There were only ten in the audience yesterday at the Casino, so I just made them sit together at the center tables, and I whispered my songs at them."

Boris got up to look at the suitcases. He examined them discreetly and came back to Lola.

"Why are they going away?" he asked, sitting down again. "They would be just as comfortable here. Their house may be bombed the day after they get back."

"Yes," said Lola, "but it's *their* house. Don't you under-stand that?"

"No."

"Well that's how it is. After a certain age one likes to meet trouble at home."

Boris began to laugh, and Lola stiffened uneasily; it was a habit of hers from old days: when he laughed, she always thought he was laughing at her.

"Why are you laughing?"

"Because I admire your nerve. There you sit explaining what middle-aged people feel. But you don't understand anything about it, Lola; you've never had a home."

"No," said Lola sadly.

Boris took her hand and kissed the hollow of the palm. Lola blushed.

"How nice you are to me! You aren't the way you used to be at all."

"Are you complaining?"

Lola squeezed his hand. "Indeed I'm not. But I should like to know why you're so nice."

"It's because I'm getting older," he said.

She let her hand rest in his; and she smiled, lying back in her chair. He was glad that she should be happy; he wanted to leave her pleasant memories. He stroked her hand and thought: "A year; we've only a year left together"; he felt quite moved; their affair already possessed the charm of something past. He used to treat her roughly, but that was because their lease was unlimited: that upset him, he liked definite commitments. One year: he would give her all the happiness she deserved, he would make up for all he had done to hurt her feelings, then he would leave her, but decorously, not for another woman, nor because he was tired of her; it would happen naturally, by the force of events, because he would be of age and due to be called up. He glanced at her; she looked young, her lovely bosom was heaving with satisfaction, and he thought despondently: "I shall have been one woman's man." Mobilized in '40, killed in '41—no, in '42, because he would have to count time for his promotion; that made one woman in twenty-two years. Three months ago he was still dreaming of sleeping with women in high society, it's because I was just a kid, he thought, though not in self-excuse. He would die without having known any duchesses, but he regretted nothing. In one sense, he might, during the months to come, make the most of any opportunities that offered, but he didn't really want to; I should waste my energies. When a man has no more than two years to live, he ought to concentrate on serious matters. Jules Renard had said to his son: "Study one woman only, but study her well and you will know the race of women." He must study Lola carefully, in restaurants, in the street, in bed. He slid his finger along Lola's wrist and thought: "I don't know her very well yet." There were corners of her body of which he was ignorant, and he did not always know what was passing in her mind. But he had a year before him. And he was going to begin at once. He turned his head and considered her attentively.

"Why are you looking at me like that?" asked Lola.

"I'm studying you," said Boris.

"I don't like you to look at me too long, I'm always afraid you'll think I'm getting old."

Boris smiled; she was still suspicious, she had not accustomed herself to her new-found happiness.

"Don't you worry," he said.

A widow bowed curtly as she passed them and sank into a chair beside the beribboned gentleman.

"Well, dear lady," said the gentleman. "We are to have a speech from Hitler."

"Indeed—and when?" asked the widow.

"He's speaking tomorrow, at the Sportpalast."

"Br-r," she said with a shiver. "Then I shall go to bed early and put my head under the bedclothes. I shan't listen. I can't conceive that he can have anything pleasant to say to us."

"I'm afraid not," said the gentleman.

There was a silence, then he went on: "Our great mistake, you see, was in '36, at the time of the remilitarization of the Rhineland. We ought to have sent six divisions there. If we had shown our teeth, the German staff had their withdrawal orders in their pockets. But Sarraut had to defer to the Popular Front, and the Popular Front chose to hand our arms over to the Spanish Communists."

"England wouldn't have joined us," observed the widow.

"That wouldn't have mattered!" snapped the gentleman. "I'll ask you one question: do you know what Hitler would have done if Sarraut had mobilized?"

"No," said the lady.

"He would have *committed suicide*, my dear lady; I had it from an unimpeachable source; I have an officer friend in the Intelligence whom I have known for twenty years."

The widow shook her head despondently.

"What lost opportunities!" said she.

"And whose was the fault, madame?"

"Ah," said she.

"Yes," said the gentleman, "yes. That's what comes from voting red. The Frenchman is incorrigible; with war at the door, he clamors for paid holidays."

The widow looked up; she looked genuinely uneasy. "So you think there will be war?"

"War," said the gentleman, rather abashed. "Don't let us go too fast. No, Daladier is no fool; he will certainly make all appropriate concessions. But there's trouble coming."

"Bastards!" said Lola between her teeth.

Boris smiled at her sympathetically. For her the question of Czechoslovakia was very simple: a small country was attacked, France must defend it. She was rather summary in her political views, but they were at least generous.

"Let's have some lunch," she said. "These people are getting on my nerves."

She got up. He looked at her fine strong hips, and he thought of woman as a type. It was woman, as such, that he was to possess that night. His ears throbbed in a sudden flush of passion.

Behind his back the railway station—and Gomez, in the train, with his feet up on the cushions. He had rather skimped on his good-by's. "I don't like embraces on the platform." She went down the great station staircase while the train was still in the station, Gomez was reading and smoking, his feet upon the cushions, he was wearing a pair of fine new calfskin shoes. She saw the shoes against the gray cloth of the seat; he was in a first-class compartment; war was rather a paying game. I hate him, she thought. She felt arid and empty. For one more moment she saw the glittering sea, the harbor and the ships, and then a vista of dismal hotels and roofs and street-cars.

"Pedro, don't walk so fast! You'll fall down."

The boy stopped on a step with one foot in the air. He is going to see Mathieu. He might have stayed one more day with me, but he preferred Mathieu. Her hands were burning. While he was here, I was in torment; now he has gone, I don't know what to do.

Little Pedro eyed her gravely. "Has my papa gone away?" he asked.

A clock across from them indicated twenty-five minutes past one. The train had left seven minutes ago.

"Yes," said Sarah. "He has gone away."

"Is he going to fight?" asked Pedro, with shining eyes.

"No," said Sarah. "He's going to see a friend."

"Yes, but afterwards, is he going to fight?"

"Afterwards," said Sarah, "he is going to make other people fight."

Pedro had stopped on the next to the last step; he bent his knees and jumped with feet together on to the pavement, then turned and looked at his mother with a smile of pride. The little comedian, she thought. She did not smile, she turned and looked up at the great staircase. The trains rumbled, stopped, and started overhead. Gomez's train was rolling eastwards between chalk cliffs or rows of houses. Overhead, the deserted station, a great gray bubble filled with sunlight and with smoke, odors of wine and sweat, and gleaming rails. She bent her head; it wasn't pleasant to think of that desolate station in the white heat of afternoon. In April '33 he had gone off by the same train, he was wearing a gray tweed suit, Mrs. Simpson was awaiting him at Cannes, they had spent a fortnight at San Remo. I liked that even better, she thought. A small groping fist touched her hand, and she clasped it, dropped her eyes, and looked at Pedro. He was wearing a sailor shirt and a straw hat.

"Why are you looking at me like that?" asked Pedro.

Sarah turned her head away and looked at the street. She was rather horrified to find herself so unrelenting. He's only a child, she thought. Only a child. She looked at him again and tried to smile, but could not, her jaws were clenched and her mouth set. The boy's lips began to quiver, and she realized that he was going to cry. She pulled him to her and strode away. The boy, in his surprise, forgot his tears and pattered along beside her.

"Where are we going, Mamma?"

"I don't know," said Sarah.

She turned down the first street on the right. It was quite deserted; all the shops were shut. She quickened her pace again and turned into another street on the left, between tall, dark, squalid houses. Not a soul in sight.

"You're making me run," said Pedro.

Sarah squeezed his hand without replying and dragged him along. They emerged into a broad straight street, with car tracks. Not an auto nor a street-car was in sight— nothing but lowered iron shutters and the car tracks to the harbor. She tugged at Pedro's fist.

"Mamma," whimpered Pedro. "Oh, Mamma!"

He was running now in order to keep up with her. He was not crying, he was very white, with dark rings under his eyes; he looked up at her with a puzzled and mistrustful air. Sarah stopped; tears were trickling down her cheeks.

"Poor kid," she said. "Poor little innocent kid."

She crouched down in front of him; it mattered little what he might turn into later on. For the moment he was there, an innocent, ugly little boy with a diminutive shadow at his feet, alone in the world, and with all those horrors in his eyes, but, after all, he had not asked to be born.

"Why are you crying?" asked Pedro. "Is it because Papa has gone away?"

Sarah's tears dried up, and she felt a desire to laugh. But Pedro eyed her with an anxious air. She rose and said, turning her head away: "Yes. Yes, it's because Papa has gone away."

"Shall we be going home soon?" he asked.

"Are you tired? We're still quite a way from home. Come along," she said. "We'll walk on slowly."

They walked on a few steps and then Pedro stopped; he held out a finger. "Look!" said he in almost agonized entrancement.

It was a poster, on the door of a blue-painted cinema. They went up to it. An odor of formaldehyde emerged from the dark, cool auditorium. The poster depicted some cowboys pursuing a masked horseman and firing their revolvers. More firing, more revolvers. Pedro panted as he looked; he would get his helmet and his rifle when he got home and run about the room pretending to be a masked bandit. She hadn't the courage to take him away. She simply averted her eyes. The cashier was fanning herself in her glass box-office. She was a large, dark-haired woman, with a pallid complexion and a glitter in her eyes. On the cash desk behind the glass stood a vase of flowers; and a

photo of Robert Taylor was affixed to the wall with draw-
ing-pins. A middle-aged man came out of the hall and
walked up to the cashier.

"Well?" he asked through the ticket window.

"Fifty-three admissions," she said.

"Just about what I guessed. Sixty-seven yesterday. And
such a grand film, full of galloping horsemen."

"People are staying at home," said the cashier, with a
shrug of her shoulders.

A man had stopped near Pedro and stood breathing
heavily as he looked at the poster, but did not seem to see
it. He was a tall, pallid fellow, with torn clothes, a blood-
stained bandage round his head, and dried mud on his
cheeks and hands. He must have come from far away.
Sarah took Pedro's hand.

"Come along," she said.

She was walking very slowly, on account of the child,
but she wanted to run, she felt that someone was looking
at her from behind. In front of her the car tracks glittered,
the tar melted gently in the sun, the air quivered round a
street-lamp, it was no longer the same Sunday. "People
are staying at home." Only a little while ago she could see,
behind those blocks of houses, a vision of cheerful crowded
boulevards redolent of rice powder and American cigarettes; she was walking along a quiet suburban street, accompanied by an unseen throng. One word had been
enough to clear the boulevards. Now they led towards the
harbor, white and deserted; the air danced between blind
walls.

"Mamma," said Pedro, "the man is following us."

"No, he isn't," said Sarah. "He's just taking a walk, like
us."

She turned to her left; it was the same street, interminable, unaltered; there was now only one street straying
through Marseille. And Sarah was in it, out of doors, in the
company of a child; all the inhabitants of Marseille were

indoors. Fifty-three admissions. She thought of Gomez,
and of Gomez's laugh: of course all Frenchmen are cowards. And what then? They stay at home, as is quite natural; they are afraid of war, and they are quite right. But
she remained uneasy. She noticed she was walking faster
again and tried to slow down on account of Pedro. But the
boy dragged her on.

"Quick—quick!" he said in a choking voice. "Oh,
Mamma!"

"What's the matter?" she said curtly.

"He's still there, you know."

Sarah turned her head slightly and saw a hobbling figure, clearly following them. Her heart began to throb.

"Let's run!" said Pedro.

She thought of the blood-stained bandage and turned
abruptly round. The man stopped dead and looked at them
with rheumy eyes as they approached. Sarah was afraid.
The boy had clutched her with both hands and was trying
to drag her backward. "People are staying home." It would
be no use to cry out or call for help, no one would
come.

"Do you want anything?" she asked, looking straight at
the limping figure before her.

He smiled pitifully, and Sarah's fears vanished.

"Can you read?" he asked.

He held out a tattered booklet. She took it—it was an
army book. Pedro was now clasping her legs, she could
feel his warm little body.

"Well?" said she.

"I want to know what's written there," said the man,
pointing to a page.

He looked like a decent fellow, despite his purple, half-
closed eye. Sarah looked at him for a moment, then at the
printed page.

"It's awful," the man muttered ruefully. "It's awful not
to be able to read."

"Well, you've got the white page," said Sarah. "You'll have to go to Montpellier."

She handed him the book, but the man did not take it. "Is it true there's going to be war?"

"I don't know," said Sarah.

"He'll go," she thought. Then she thought of Gomez. "Who made that bandage?" she asked.

"I did," said the man.

Sarah felt in her bag and produced some pins and two clean handkerchiefs.

"Sit down on the pavement," said she authoritatively. The man sat down rather painfully. "My legs have gone to sleep," he said with a rueful laugh.

Sarah tore up the handkerchiefs. Gomez was reading the *Humanité* in a first-class carriage, with his feet up on the cushions. He would see Mathieu and then go on to Toulouse, where he could get a plane for Barcelona. She untied the blood-stained bandage and jerked it gradually off his forehead; the man moaned faintly as she did so. A black, sticky scab extended half across his head. Sarah handed a handkerchief to Pedro.

"Go and get some water at a fountain."

The boy ran off, glad to get away. The man looked up at Sarah and said: "I don't want to fight."

Sarah laid a hand gently on his shoulder. She would have liked to beg his pardon.

"I'm a shepherd," he said.

"What are you doing at Marseille?"

He shook his head. "I don't want to fight," he repeated.

Pedro had returned. Sarah washed the wound roughly and bandaged it again.

"Now get up," she said.

He got up and looked at her with vacant eyes. "So I've got to go to Montpellier?"

She felt in her bag and produced two hundred-franc notes.

"For your journey," she said.

The man did not take them at once; he looked at her intently.

"Take them," said Sarah in a low, quick tone. "Take them. And don't fight if you can help it."

He took the notes. Sarah shook his hand vigorously.

"Don't fight," she repeated. "Do anything—go home, go into hiding; but don't you fight."

He looked at her blankly. She seized Pedro's hand, swung round, and they walked on. In an instant or two, she turned; he was looking at the bandage and the wet handkerchief that Sarah had thrown into the roadway. Then he bent down, picked them up rather unsteadily, and put them in his pocket.

Beads of sweat stood out across his forehead and trickled across his cheeks from the nostrils to the ears, he had thought at first that they were insects and clapped a hand to his face, only to find that he had crushed his own warm tears.

"My God, it's hot," said his left-hand neighbor.

He recognized the voice, it was that detestable fellow Blanchard.

"They do it on purpose," said Charles. "They leave the carriages in the sun for hours on end."

There was a silence, then Blanchard said: "Is that you, Charles?"

"It is," said Charles.

He was sorry he had spoken. Blanchard was addicted to practical jokes, he squirted people with a water-pistol, or steered his trolley past them and fastened a cardboard spider on their bedclothes.

"It's odd that we should meet like this."

"Yes."

"It's a small world."

A jet of water hit Charles full in the face. He wiped it off and spat. Blanchard was delighted.

"You damned fool," said Charles.

He produced a handkerchief and wiped his neck, doing his best to laugh.

"It's your water-pistol, I suppose."

"Sure," said Blanchard. "Got you that time, didn't I? Right in the mug! And I've got all sorts of gadgets in my pockets: we'll have some fun on this trip."

"You stupid ass," said Charles with a laugh. "What a damned kid!"

Blanchard alarmed him; their trolleys were touching, if he wants to pinch me, or put insect-powder under my bed-clothes, he's only got to reach out a hand. I have no luck, he thought; I shall have to be on the *qui vive* during the whole journey. He sighed and found himself looking at the ceiling, a large dark expanse studded with rivets. He had tipped his mirror backwards, and its surface was as dark as a plate of smoked glass. Charles raised himself slightly and glanced around him. They had left the sliding door wide open; a yellow light frothed through the car, hovering over the bedclothes and bleaching the patients' faces. But the illuminated space was exactly delimited by the frame of the door; on the left and right the darkness was almost complete. Lucky devils, no doubt they had been careful to tip the porters; they will have all the air and all the light: now and then, if they raise themselves on one elbow, they will see a green tree go past. He fell back, exhausted; his shirt was soaked. If only the train would start. But the train remained at a standstill in that merciless sunlight. A strange smell of rotten straw and Houbigant scent hung about the floor. He found it nauseating and tried to raise his head above it, but the sweat burst out all over him, he sank back, and the smell gathered once more above his nose. Outside—rails and sunshine, empty cars on the sidings, bushes white with dust: desolation. And then, farther off, Sunday. Sunday at Berck; children playing on the beach, families drinking coffee in the restau-

rants. What a scream, he thought, what a scream! A voice
came from the far end of the car: "Denis! Hi, Denis!"

No one answered.

"Maurice, are you there?"

There was a silence, then the voice concluded, mournfully: "The bastards!"

The silence was broken. Someone groaned near Charles:
"How hot it is!"

And a voice answered, the pallid, wavering voice of
someone gravely ill: "It will be better soon, when the train
starts."

They were talking blindly, not knowing to whom they
spoke; and someone said with a short laugh: "That's how
soldiers travel."

The silence fell once more. Heat, silence, misery. Charles
suddenly caught sight of two shapely legs in white cotton
stockings, his eyes traveled up them to a white blouse: the
pretty nurse. She had just got into the car. She was carrying a suitcase in one hand and a camp-stool in the other;
she surveyed the scene with an air of vexation.

"It's crazy," she said. "It's just crazy."

"What—what?" said a harsh voice from outside.

"If you had thought for a moment, you might have realized that the men mustn't be put with the women."

"We put them just as they came in."

"And how do you suppose I'm to attend to men and
women together?"

"You should have been there when they were put on the
train."

"I can't be everywhere at once. I was getting the luggage
registered."

"What a mess!" said the man.

"It certainly is."

There was a silence, then she continued: "Kindly get
some more porters: the men will be transferred into the
rear coaches."

"What, are you crazy! Who's going to pay for the extra work?"

"I shall make a complaint," said the nurse curtly.

"Complain away, sister."

The nurse shrugged her shoulders and turned away. She stepped cautiously between the bodies and sat down on her camp-stool, not far from Charles, on the edge of the rectangle of light.

"Hi, Charles!" said Blanchard.

"Well," quavered Charles.

"There's females around."

Charles did not reply.

"And what am I to do," said Blanchard at the top of his voice, "if I want to shit?"

Charles flushed with rage, but he thought of the insect-powder and emitted a collusive little laugh.

There was a shuffling noise at the level of the floor—no doubt some of the men straining their necks to see if they had feminine neighbors. But a general sense of uneasiness brooded over the car. Some scattered whispers faded into silence. "What shall I do if I want the pan?" Charles felt dirty, he was aware, inside himself, of a mass of damp and sticky innards; how ghastly to have to ask for a pan in the presence of all these young women! He held himself in and thought: "I'll stick it out." Blanchard was breathing hard, his nose emitted an ingenuous little chant —Oh God, if he could only sleep! Charles had a moment of despair, he took a cigarette out of his pocket and lit it.

"What's the matter?" asked the nurse. She put her knitting on her knees. Charles saw her angry face, in a blue shadow, far away above him.

"I'm lighting a cigarette," he said, and his voice sounded oddly intrusive.

"You mustn't smoke here," she said.

Charles blew the match out and groped round him with the tips of his fingers. Between two sets of bedclothes he

came upon a damp rough plank, which he scratched with
a fingernail before he dropped the scrap of half-carbonized
wood; then suddenly the contact revolted him, and he
brought his hands back to his chest: I'm level with the
ground, he thought. Level with the ground. On the floor.
Under the tables and the chairs, under the heels of the
nurses and the porters, prostrate among the mud and
straw, all the insects that swarm in the cracks of floor-
boards could dart on to his stomach. He shook his legs
and arms, he scraped his heels on the toe of the stretcher
—but softly, so as not to wake Blanchard. The sweat
poured over his chest; he drew his knees up beneath the
bedclothes. These uneasy tinglings in his thighs and legs,
these violent, vague revulsions in his whole body had incessantly tormented him since his earliest days at Berck.
And then it had all passed away: he had forgotten his legs,
he had found it quite natural to be pushed and wheeled
and carried, he had developed into an object. "It won't
start again," he thought with anguish, "surely it won't start
again?" He stretched his legs and closed his eyes. He must
say to himself: I'm just a stone. His clenched hands
opened, he felt his body gradually petrifying beneath the
bedclothes. A stone among stones.

He sat up suddenly, with open eyes and stiffened neck;
a jerk, then a grinding sound that promptly merged into a
monotonous rumble, as soothing as the fall of rain: the
train had started. It was passing *alongside something*: outside, solid objects soaked in sunshine slid past the coaches;
fleeting shadows, slowly at first and then with increasing
speed, crossed the luminous wall opposite the open door;
like a screen in a cinema. The light, on the wall, paled a
little and grew gray—then a sudden blaze: "We're coming
out of the station." Charles had a pain in his neck, but he
felt calmer; he lay back, raised his arms, and tilted his mirror at an angle of ninety. Now he could see in the left
corner of the glass a section of the illuminated rectangle.

That was enough: that shining surface was alive, it embodied a whole countryside; sometimes the light flickered and faded, as though it were about to vanish, sometimes it hardened and set into the semblance of a patch of yellow wash; then from time to time it quivered and slanting undulations shot across its surface, as though a wind had stirred it. Charles looked at it for a long while; in a moment or two he felt almost as free as though he were sitting with his legs dangling on the step of the car, watching the trees, the fields, and the sea pass by.

"Blanchard!" he murmured.

No answer. He waited a moment and whispered: "Are you asleep?"

Blanchard did not answer. Charles heaved a little sigh of satisfaction and relaxed, stretching himself out full length, his eyes still on his mirror. He's asleep; he's asleep; when he came in he could hardly stand, he dropped on to the seat, but his eyes were hard and what they said was: "You won't get me." He ordered his coffee with a very truculent air, there are some customers like that, who treat the waiters like enemies; mostly half-baked kids who believe that life is a conflict, they have read that in books, so they stage a conflict in cafés, they order a grenadine.

"One coffee here," said Felix, "and two ports on the terrace."

She pressed the buttons and swung the crank. Felix winked at her and pointed to the short young man who had fallen asleep. It wasn't a conflict; it was a morass, try to move and you get stuck, but they don't realize it at once and get sucked down all the quicker; I've been there, I've been there; now I'm getting old, I keep calm and quiet, I don't move, at my age one is scarcely likely to get stuck again. He was asleep, his mouth was open and his jaw sagging on to his chest, he didn't look at all inviting, his red and swollen eyelids and red nose gave him an oddly sheeplike look. I guessed at once, when I saw him come into the empty café, with that blind look on his face, so hot outside and all those customers on the terrace, I said to myself: He's got a letter to write, or he is waiting for a woman, or something has gone badly wrong. He lifted a long, pale hand, and brushed the flies away without opening his eyes; there wasn't a fly. He is suffering even in his sleep; troubles pursue us everywhere, I was sitting on a bench looking at the tracks and the tunnel, a bird was singing, I was down and out. I was pregnant and had just been sacked, I had no more eyes to cry with, no more money in my bag, just my ticket, and I went to sleep, I dreamed I was being killed, that someone was pulling my hair and calling me a tart, and then the train came and I got into it. Sometimes I think he'll get his allowance—as an old hand in bad health, they can't refuse it to him, sometimes I think they'll wriggle out of it, they're such a grasping lot; here I am, I'm old, I don't budge now, but I get ideas into my head. He's well dressed, I'm sure he has a mamma to look after his clothes, but his shoes are very dusty; what has he been doing? Where has he come from? The blood gets into young folks' heads, if he'd told me to kill my father and mother, I'd have done it, a girl can be so besotted sometimes; perhaps he has murdered an old woman like me; they'll catch him all right, he can't look after himself; I dare say they'll come here to pinch him, and his photograph will appear in the *Matin,* and they'll see a dirty little mouse face, not in the least like him, and people will say as usual: Aha, he looks just the sort of chap to do such a thing; well, I always say that if you wanted to think the worst of a man, better not see him close up, because when you watch him getting stuck a little deeper, you think it's all just hopeless and in the end there's no difference between drinking a cup of café crème outside a café, saving up to buy a house, or murdering your mother. The telephone rang and she gave a start.

"Hello?"

"I want to speak to Madame Cazin."

"Speaking," she said. "Well?"

"They've refused it," said Julot.

"What?" she said. "What—what?"

"They've refused it."

"You don't mean it."

"They've refused it."

"But an old hand like you, and in bad health; what did they say?"

"They said I hadn't any claim."

"Oh!" she said. "Oh!"

"See you this evening," said Julot.

She hung up the receiver. So they've refused it. And him an old man, and in bad health, they've told him he hadn't any claim. Now I'm going to get angry, she thought. The young man was snoring, he looked silly and pompous. Felix went out, carrying the two ports and the coffee on his tray; he pushed the door open and the sunlight came in, the mirror flashed above the sleeper, then the door closed once more, the mirror was extinguished, and the two of them were left alone. What has he done? Where has he come from? What has he got in his suitcase? Well, he'll pay, and go on paying, for twenty, thirty years, unless he's killed in the war, poor kid, he's the right age to fight. There he is, asleep and snoring, and in trouble, while people on the terrace are talking about the war, and my husband can't get his allowance. "Poor, poor wretches that we are," she said.

"Pitteaux!" exclaimed the young man.

He had awakened with a start; for an instant he looked at her, with reddened eyes and open mouth, then he clicked his jaws, bit his lips, and assumed an air of brisk ill-humor.

"Waiter!"

Felix did not hear; she could see him on the terrace as he came and went, taking orders. The young man looked annoyed and tapped on the marble table, peering to right and left with a hunted expression on his face. She took pity on him.

"It's a franc," she said, from the elevation of the cashier's desk.

He glanced venomously at her, flung a five-franc piece on the table, picked up his suitcase, and limped away. The mirror flashed, a blast of talk and heat came into the room; solitude came in too. She looked at the tables, the mirrors, the door, all those too familiar objects that could no longer hold her thought. She said to herself: "I'm going to get all worked up."

A splash of light fell upon him—it was a flashlight pointed at him from the side. He turned his head and grunted. The light flashed across the floor; he blinked. Behind that flash a calm implacable eye observed him, and it was more than he could bear.

"What's the matter?" he said.

"Yes, it's he," said a lilting voice.

A woman. The oblong package beside me is a woman. After a brief moment of satisfaction he reflected angrily that she had flashed a light on him as though he were an object; he might have been a wall. "I don't know you," he snapped.

"We've often met," she said.

The light went out. He was still dazzled, violet circles revolving within his eyes.

"I can't see you."

"I can see you," she said. "Even without the light I can see you."

The voice was young and pretty, but he felt suspicious. He said again: "I can't see you; I was dazzled by your light."

"I can see in the dark," she said complacently.

"Are you an albino?"

She laughed. "Albino? I haven't got red eyes and white hair, if that's what you mean."

She had a marked accent, which lent a questioning intonation to all she said.

"Who are you?"

"Guess!" she said. "It shouldn't be difficult; you saw me yesterday and looked at me as if you hated me."

"Hated you? I don't hate anybody."

"Oh yes you do," she said. "Indeed, I think you hate everybody."

"Wait! Weren't you wearing a fur?"

Again she laughed. "Reach out a hand," she said, "and feel!"

He stretched out an arm and felt a large soft mass—a fur. Underneath the fur there would be blankets, then layers of clothing, then a soft white body, like a snail in its shell. How hot she must be! He stroked the fur, which exhaled a warm, heavy odor. That was what he had noticed a little while ago. He stroked the fur against the nap and felt quite pleased.

"You have fair hair," he said triumphantly, "and you wear gold ear-rings."

She laughed, and switched on the flashlight again; this time she pointed it at her own face; the rocking of the train made the torch quiver in her hand; the light moved from her chest to her forehead, skimmed over the painted lips, gilded a faint, yellow down at their corners, and reddened the nostrils. The curved and darkened eyebrows stood out like two little paws above the swollen eyelids; they looked like two insects on their backs. Her fair hair frothed in a light cloud around her head. His heart turned over. He thought: "She's beautiful"; and abruptly withdrew his hand.

"I recognize you now. There was always an old gentleman wheeling you about, and you never looked at anybody."

"I looked at you carefully, through my eyelashes."

She lifted her head, and he recognized her.

"I couldn't have believed you would notice me," said he. "You looked so rich, so much above us all; I thought you were at the Pension Beaucaire."

"No," she said. "I was at Mon Chalet."

"Well, I didn't expect to meet you again in a cattle-car." The light went out. "I'm very poor," she said.

He stretched out a hand and laid it lightly on the fur. "How about this?"

She laughed. "It's all I've got left."

She had receded into shadow, and lay there, a large, dark, shapeless package. But the vision of her lingered in his eyes. He clasped his hands across his stomach and stared at the ceiling. Blanchard was snoring gently; the patients had begun to talk among themselves, in twos and threes; the train rumbled on. She was poor and ill, she was lying on her back in a cattle-car, she had to be dressed and undressed like a doll. And she was beautiful. As beautiful as a screen star. Beside him lay all that humiliated beauty, that slim, pure, tarnished body. She was beautiful. She sang in music halls, she had looked at him through her eyelashes, and she had wanted to make his acquaintance; he felt as though he had been lifted on to his two feet.

"You are a singer?" he asked abruptly.

"Singer? No indeed. I can play the piano."

"I took you for a singer."

"I'm Austrian," she said. "All my money is there, in German hands. I left Austria after the *Anschluss.*"

"Were you ill then?"

"I was already on my back. My parents took me away by train. It was just like today, except that we weren't in the dark, and I was on a seat in a first-class compartment.

There were German planes overhead, we kept on imagining they were going to bomb us. My mother was crying, I lay with my nose in the air, I could feel the weight of the sky upon me through the ceiling. It was the last train that got through."

"And then?"

"Then I came here. My mother is in England; she has to keep us all."

"And the old gentleman who was with you?"

"Just a silly old admirer," she said harshly.

"So you are quite alone?"

"Quite."

He repeated: "Quite alone in the world," and felt as strong and enduring as an oak.

"When did you realize it was I?"

"When you struck that match."

He would not indulge his delight; it loomed in the background, almost out of view, but it lent an acid quiver to his voice. He would reserve it for the night time, he wanted to savor it in solitude.

"Did you see the light on the partition?"

"Yes," she said. "I've been looking at it for the last hour."

"Look—look. There's a tree passing."

"Or a telegraph pole."

"The train isn't going fast."

"No," said she. "Are you in a hurry?"

"No. We don't know where we're going."

"Indeed we don't," she said gaily. Her voice was trembling too.

"After all," he said, "this train isn't so bad."

"It's not stuffy," she said. "And I love to watch the passing shadows."

"Do you remember the myth of the cave?"

"No. What is it?"

"It's about some slaves imprisoned in a cave, who see shadows on a wall."

"Why were they imprisoned?"

"I don't know. Plato wrote it."

"Ah yes—Plato," she said vaguely.

"I'll explain to her who Plato was," he thought rapturously. He had a slight stomach-ache, but he found himself wishing that the journey might never end.

Georges shook the door-handle. Through the window he could see a tall mustachioed fellow and a young woman with a napkin knotted round her head, washing cups and glasses behind a wooden counter. A soldier sat dozing at a table. Georges tugged violently at the handle, and the window shook. But the door did not open. The woman and the man did not seem to hear.

"They won't open."

He turned; a large, florid man was watching him with a smile. He wore a black jacket over a pair of army trousers, puttees, a soft hat, and a winged collar. Georges pointed to the notice: "The canteen opens at five o'clock."

The other shrugged his shoulders. A capacious haversack hung against his left hip, a gas-mask against his right hip; he flung his arms out, with his elbows in the air.

"They open when they feel inclined."

The barrack yard was filled with men of middle age who looked very bored. Some strolled about alone, staring at the ground. Some wore a military tunic, others khaki trousers, others were still in civilian clothes, with brand-new sabots, which clattered against the tarred surface of the yard. A tall red-haired fellow who had been lucky enough to get hold of a complete outfit was pacing pensively up and down, his hands in the pockets of his tunic; but he had a derby cocked truculently over one ear. A lieutenant shouldered his way through the little groups and made for the canteen.

"Haven't you got your uniform?" asked the short fat man. He tugged at the straps of his haversack in an effort to sling it round to his back.

"There are none left."

The man spat between his feet. "So here's what they've issued me. I'm suffocating in it; with that sun its enough to kill you. What a fouled-up mess!"

Georges indicated the officer. "Do we have to salute him?"

"How? I can't very well take my hat off."

The officer passed but did not look at them. Georges looked at his skinny back and felt utterly despondent. It was hot, the windows of the barrack buildings were painted blue; behind the white walls lay white roads, and airfields, green beneath the sunshine as far as eye could reach; the barrack walls had cut from the turf of the countryside a small, level, dusty section of land, on which weary men walked up and down as they did in a street. It was the time of day when his wife opened the shutters at home: the sun came into the dining-room; the sun was everywhere, in houses and barracks and over the countryside. He said to himself: "It's always the same." But he didn't quite know what was always the same. He thought of the war and realized that he wasn't afraid to die. A train whistled in the distance, and he felt as though someone had smiled at him.

"Listen," he said.

"To what?"

"To the train."

The small fat man looked at him uncomprehendingly, then produced a handkerchief and began to dab his forehead. The train whistled again and moved off with its load of civilians, pretty women, and children; the fields slid innocuously past the windows. The train whistled and slowed down.

"It's going to stop," said Charles.

The train creaked to a standstill; all sense of movement was drained out of Charles, he was left arid and empty as though purged of all his blood; it was a little like dying.

"I don't like it when a train stops," he said.

Georges thought of the trains packed with travelers moving southwards, towards the sea, and the white villas by the seaside; Charles was conscious of the green herbage growing under the floor-boards and between the rails, his vision penetrated the iron walls and he could see the luminous rectangle outlined on the partition, green fields as far as eye could reach; the train was embedded in the countryside like a ship in an ice-floe, the grass was climbing up the wheels, thrusting through the gaping planks, the country was flooding into the motionless train. The trapped train whistled mournfully; the whistle faded into a romantic cadence and then died away; the train rumbled gently on, the head of Maurice's neighbor lolled to and fro in its yellow collar, he had been singing the *Internationale* since the start, and had drunk two quarts of raw wine. At last he collapsed with a gurgle on Maurice's shoulder. Maurice was very hot, but he did not dare to move—what with the heat, the white wine, and the white sunshine pouring through the grimy windows, he felt quite sick, and thought: "I wish we were there." His eyes smarted, swelled, and hardened, he closed his eyelids and heard the blood buzzing in his ears; the sun stabbed through his eyelids; a white, sweaty, blinding slumber came upon him; the man's hair tickled his neck and chin; it was a ghastly afternoon. The tall man produced a photo from his pocketbook:

"That's my wife," said he.

It was the nondescript type of female usually depicted in photographs, and Georges could find nothing to say about her.

"She looks healthy," said Georges.

"She eats enough for four," said the man.

They remained face to face, irresolute; Georges rather disliked this large, florid fellow, who gasped when he talked, but he wanted to show him his daughter's photograph.

"Married?"

"Yes."

"Any children?"

Georges looked at him and grinned. Then he thrust a hand into his pocket, produced his pocketbook, and took out a photograph, which he handed to the other with eyes averted.

"That's my daughter."

"You've got a nice pair of boots," said the man, taking the photograph. "They'll last you a long while."

"I've got corns," said Georges with a deprecating air. "Do you think they'll let me keep those boots?"

"They'll be only too glad. I dare say they haven't got boots enough to go round."

He surveyed Georges's boots for another moment or two, then regretfully raised his eyes to the photo. Georges felt that he was blushing. "What a fine child!" said the man. "How much does she weigh?"

"I don't know," said Georges.

He looked with amazement at the large man as he held the photograph between his fingers and fixed his chilly gaze upon it. He said: "When I come back, she won't recognize me."

"Quite probable," said the man. "Unless—"

"Yes," said Georges. "Unless—"

"Well," asked Sarraut. "Am I to go?"

He turned the paper over in his fingers. Daladier had trimmed a match with a knife and thrust it between two of his teeth. He did not answer, he sat, a creased and huddled figure, in his chair.

"Am I to go?" repeated Sarraut.

"It's war," said Bonnet quietly, "and a lost one."

Daladier started and fixed Bonnet with a heavy look.

Bonnet returned it with a guileless expression in his clear, shallow eyes. He looked like an anteater. Champetier de Ribes and Reynaud stood a little in the background, two silent, disapproving figures. Daladier sank back and blurted out, "Go on," with a limp wave of his hand.

Sarraut rose and went out of the room. He walked downstairs, conscious of an ache in the top of his head. They were all there, they fell silent at the sight of him and assumed their professional expressions. "What a bunch of dopes!" thought Sarraut.

"I will now read the communiqué," he said.

The responding murmur gave him a moment in which to wipe his spectacles; then he read as follows:

"The Cabinet Council has heard the observations of the President of the Council and of Monsieur Georges Bonnet on the memorandum communicated to Monsieur Chamberlain by the Chancellor of the Reich.

"The Council has unanimously approved the statement that Messieurs Édouard Daladier and Georges Bonnet propose to take to London for communication to the British Government."

"I thought so," said Charles to himelf. "I've got to go." It had happened quite suddenly; his belly was full to running over.

"Yes, yes," he said. "I agree with you. Yes."

The voices rose placidly, side by side. He would have liked to merge himself into his voice, to be just a grave voice beside the lilting blond voice of his neighbor. But *first of all*, the heat, the throbbing urgency within him, the mass of moist matter that gurgled in his intestines—all this was himself. A silence fell; she lay dreaming at his side, a cool and snowy presence; he cautiously lifted a hand and passed it over his damp forehead. "H-r-r-m," he moaned suddenly.

"What's the matter?"

"Nothing," he said. "It's my neighbor snoring."

It had caught him in the stomach like a laugh beyond control—a dark and violent desire to open up and rain from below, a frantic butterfly fluttered between his posteriors. He clenched them, the sweat poured down his forehead, oozed into his ears, and tickled his cheeks. "I must!—I must!" he thought in terror.

"You are very silent," said the blond voice.

"I—" he said, "was wondering—why did you want to know me?"

"You have such nice arrogant eyes," said she. "And I wanted to find out why you hated me."

He shifted his back slightly, to help himself to hold out. He said: "I hated everyone because I was poor. I am an unpleasant sort of fellow."

The words escaped him under pressure of his need; he had evacuated from above; upwards or downwards, he had to do it.

"An unpleasant sort of fellow," he gasped. "I'm envious."

He had never talked so frankly to anyone. She touched his hand with the tips of her fingers.

"Don't hate me: I'm poor too."

Silently he clasped the slim, soft hand.

"How hot your hands are!" said the voice.

Someone whimpered in the sunlight—one of the patients near the door. The nurse got up and went to him, stepping across the intervening bodies. Charles raised his right arm and maneuvered his mirror; the glass suddenly caught the nurse bending over a large red-cheeked youth with prominent ears. She looked contemptuous and annoyed. Then she got up and returned to her place. Charles watched her search in her suitcase. She faced them, holding a urinal. And she said in ringing tones: "Does anyone want this? If so, please speak up while the train is not moving—it's more convenient then. Above all, don't restrain yourselves, don't feel ashamed. There are no men nor women here—only sick people."

She surveyed them sternly, but no one responded. The
large lad grabbed the urinal and slipped it under the bedclothes. Charles squeezed his friend's hand. He had only to
raise his voice and say: "Here, please." The nurse bent
down and removed the urinal. It flashed in the sunshine,
now filled with a frothing yellow liquid. The nurse went to
the door and leaned out; Charles saw her shadow on the
partition, her lifted arm outlined in the rectangle of light.
She tipped the urinal, and a liquid shadow spurted out of
it.

"Madame—" said a quavering voice.

"Ah!" said she. "You've decided to be sensible. I'm coming."

They will give way one by one. The women will hold out
longer than the men. The men will inflict their odors on
the women beside them: how can they dare to speak to
them afterwards! "The bastards," he thought. There was
much bustling at floor level: whispered, shamefaced ap-
peals from every corner. Charles recognized some of the
feminine voices.

"You must wait," said the nurse. "One at a time."

Only sick people. They think they can get away with
anything because they are patients. Not men nor women:
sick people. He was suffering, but proud to suffer; I won't
give way; her shoes creaked across the floor-boards, then
came the rustle of paper. A stale, tepid odor pervaded the
car. "I won't give way," he said to himself, writhing in his
agony.

"Madame," said the blond voice.

He thought he had not heard well, but the lilting voice
repeated, in accents now of shame: "Madame! Madame!
Here!"

"I'm coming," said the nurse.

The hot, slim hand slipped out of Charles's grasp. He
heard the creak of shoes; the nurse towered over them,
like a stern archangel.

"Turn round," said the pleading voice. And again she whispered: "Please turn round."

He turned his head, wishing he could plug his ears and nose. The nurse swooped, like a flight of blackbirds, darkening his mirror. He could see nothing more. "She's a sick person," he thought. She must have had to throw off her fur; for an instant the scent of it drowned everything, then gradually a strong and rancid odor filled his nostrils. Well, she was a sick person; that taut and silky skin enclosed liquid vertebræ and purulent intestines. He hesitated, torn between disgust and foul desire. Then, suddenly, his entrails closed up like a fist, and he was no longer conscious of his body. A sick person. All needs and all desires were extinguished, he felt clean and fresh, like a man who has regained his breath. A sick person. "She held out as long as she could," he thought tenderly. There was a rustle of paper, the nurse got up, several voices already beckoned her to the other end of the car. He would not call her; he was hovering a few inches from the floor, above them. He was not an object nor a helpless infant. "She couldn't hold out," he thought, with so warm a feeling that the tears came into his eyes. She didn't dare to speak to him. "She's ashamed. I'll look after her," he thought affectionately. Standing up, and leaning over her, and gazing at her gentle, haggard face. She was panting faintly in the shadows. He reached out a hand and groped over her fur. The young body recoiled, but Charles found a hand and took it. The hand resisted, he drew it close to him and squeezed it. A sick person. And there he was, hard and dry, a free man; he would look after her.

"What is your name?" he asked.

"Well, read it," said Chamberlain impatiently.

Lord Halifax took Masaryk's message and began to read. "He needn't put all that expression into it," thought Chamberlain.

"My Government," read Halifax, "has now studied the

document and the map. It is a *de facto* ultimatum, such as is commonly presented to a conquered nation, and not a proposal to a sovereign State which has shown every possible disposition to make sacrifices for the peace of Europe. Monsieur Hitler's Government has not shown the faintest trace of a similar disposition. My Government is astonished by the contents of the memorandum. The proposals go far beyond what we agreed to in the so-called Anglo-French plan. They deprive us of all safeguards for our national existence. We are to yield large sections of our carefully prepared fortifications, and allow the German armies to penetrate deeply into our territory before having been able to organize it on a new basis, or make the smallest preparations for defense. Our national and economic independence would automatically disappear with the adoption of Monsieur Hitler's plan. The whole procedure of the transfer of population will be reduced to a mere stampede for those who will not accept the German Nazi regime. They will have to leave home without even the right to take their personal possessions with them, not even, in the case of peasants, their cow.

"My Government wishes me to declare with all possible solemnity that Monsieur Hitler's demands under their present form are absolutely and unconditionally unacceptable to my Government. Against these new and cruel demands, my Government feels constrained to offer a supreme resistance, and, with the help of God, will do so. The nation of Saint Wenceslas, of John Huss, and of Thomas Masaryk will not be a nation of slaves.

"We rely on the three great Western democracies, to whose wishes we have deferred against our own judgment, to stand beside us in our hour of need."

"Is that all?" asked Chamberlain.

"That is all."

"More trouble," he replied.

Lord Halifax did not answer; he stood erect like an embodied conscience, respectful and reserved.

"The French ministers will arrive in an hour," said Chamberlain dryly. "I find this document—inopportune, to say the least."

"Do you think it is calculated to influence their decisions?" asked Halifax with a sting of irony.

The old gentleman did not reply; he took the paper and began to read it with muttered comments.

"Cows!" he ejaculated with annoyance. "What's all this about cows? So very uncalled-for."

"I don't find it so. I was rather touched," said Lord Halifax.

"Touched?" said the old gentleman with a curt laugh. "My dear fellow, we are conducting a negotiation. If we allow ourselves to be touched, we shall lose the game."

Red and pink and mauve fabrics, mauve dresses, white dresses, bare throats, lovely bosoms, scarves, flickers of sunshine on tables and hands, sticky golden liquids, more hands, thighs emerging from shorts, gay voices, red-pink-white frocks, gay voices whirling in the air, thighs, the *Merry Widow* waltz, the smell of pines, warm sand, the vanilla fragrance of the open sea, all the islands of the world unseen and present in that sunlight, the Windwards, Easter Island, the Sandwiches, the sparkling shops along the sea front, lady's waterproofs at three thousand francs, jeweled clips, red-pink-white flowers, hands, thighs, "Here's the band," gay voices whirling in the air, Suzanne—what about your diet? Oh, never mind—let's forget it just for once. Sails on the sea, skiers leaping with outstretched arms from wave to wave, pine-scented breezes, peace. Peace at Juan-les-Pins. There it still lurked, forlorn, forgotten, turning sour. People get caught in it; they mask their petty, embarrassed anguish behind thickets of music and colors. Mathieu strolled past the cafés and the shops, the sea on his left; Gomez's train did not arrive until eighteen seventeen o'clock; he looked mechanically at the women, eying their peaceful thighs and peaceful bosoms. But he was a defaulter. Since three twenty-five o'clock he had been a defaulter. At three twenty-five a train had left for Marseille. "I am no longer here. I am at Marseille, in a café on the avenue de la Gare, I am waiting for the Paris train, I am in the Paris train. I am in Paris on a drowsy early morning, I am in a barracks, I am pacing round and round the barrack yard, at Essey-les-Nancy." At Essey-les-Nancy Georges stopped talking because he could not make himself heard; they all looked up, the plane was thundering over the roofs; Georges watched it, over the walls, over the roofs, over Nancy—at Niort, he was at Niort, in his room with that girl of his, with a savor of dust in his mouth. What is he going to say to me? He will dash out of the train, as gay and sunburned as a holiday-maker at Juan-les-Pins; I am as sunburned as he is, but I've got no answers for him. I was at Toledo, at Guadalajara; what were you doing? I was living. . . . I was at Málaga, one of the last to leave the place; what have you done? I have lived. "Well, well," he thought irritably, "it's a friend I'm going to meet, not a judge." Charles laughed, she said nothing, she was still a little ashamed, he held her hand and laughed. "Catherine—that's a lovely name," he said to her affectionately. He has been lucky; after all, he was in the Spanish war, he *was able* to be in it, no weapons, hand-grenades versus tanks, eagles' nests in the sierra, love-making in desolate Madrid hotels, smoke clouds in the plain, hand-to-hand fighting, Spain hasn't lost her savor; mine is going to be a dreary war, a ceremonious and boring war; anti-tank guns versus tanks, a collective, technical war, a sort of epidemic. Yonder was Spain, a vast flat fish afloat on the blue water. Maud stood with her elbows on the railing, looking at Spain. They're fighting over there. The ship glided past the coast; there, the sound of guns;

here, the sound of waves, the splash of flying fish. Mathieu was walking towards Spain, the sea on his left, France on his right. Maud glided past the coast, with Algeria on her left, voyaging towards her right, towards France; that scorching breath, that hovering haze, was Spain. Maud and Mathieu thought of the Spanish war, which kept them both from brooding on the other war, the verdigris war preparing on their right. They must crawl as far as the ruined wall, round it, and back, then their mission will be done. The Moroccan clambered over the blackened rocks, his fingernails and toenails clogged with dirt, he was afraid, he was thinking of Tangier; at the peak of Tangier there was a yellow one-storied house from which could be seen the eternal glitter of the sea, the abode of a white-bearded Negro who swallowed snakes to amuse the English tourists; he must not forget that yellow house. Mathieu thought of Spain, Maud thought of Spain, the Moroccan clambered over the cracked soil of Spain, he thought of Tangier, and he felt alone. Mathieu turned into a dazzling street, Spain swung round, blazed, then dwindled into a smudge of fire on his left. Nice on the right, and beyond Nice a gap—Italy. Before him lay the railway station, France and war, the *real* war; Nancy. He was at Nancy; beyond the station he was making his way to Nancy. He wasn't thirsty, he wasn't hot, nor tired. His body swung beneath him, but seemed no longer his: colors, sounds, sunshine, smells, found harborage in that body—all of which concerned him no more. "It's like the beginning of an illness," he thought. Philippe slipped his suitcase into his left hand; he was exhausted, but he must endure until the evening. Until the evening: I shall sleep on the train. The terrace of the Tour d'Argent hummed like a beehive, red-pink-mauve frocks, rayon stockings, painted cheeks, caramel drinks, a syrupy, sticky crowd; pity stabbed his heart; they would be snatched out of their cafés and their rooms, and with their bodies the war would be waged. He pitied them, and he pitied himself; they sweltered in the light——clammy, satiated, desperate. Philippe was suddenly possessed by an access of weariness and pride: I am these people's conscience.

Another café. Mathieu eyed these handsome, sunburned men, so smooth and perfectly composed, and felt like a denizen of another world. The casino on their right, the post office on their left, and the sun behind them; and that's all: France, Spain, Italy are lamps that never light up for them. Here they are, solid and together, and the war is a phantom. "I am a phantom," he thought. They would be lieutenants and captains, they would sleep in beds, they would shave every day, and many of them would know how to wangle themselves out of active service. Why not? What should prevent them? Loyalty to their fellows in this filthy business? But I'm one of them. And I ask no loyalty from any man. Why am I going to the war? he asked himself abruptly. "Look out!" exclaimed Philippe to a man who bumped into him. He bent down to pick up his suitcase; the tall man in shabby shoes did not even turn. "Brute!" muttered Philippe. He faced the café and glared at the occupants. But nobody had noticed the incident. A little boy was crying, his mother dabbed his eyes with a handkerchief. At the adjoining table three men were sitting huddled in their chairs, with glasses of orangeade in front of them. "Not so innocent as they look," he thought, surveying them all with the insolent air that he assumed at times. Why should they go? They have only to refuse. The car sped onwards. Daladier lying back on the cushions sucked at an extinct cigarette and watched the passers-by. It bored him to go to London, no decent drinks, disgusting food; a hatless woman was laughing with her mouth wide open; he thought: "They don't realize the situation," and shook his head. Philippe thought: "They are being taken to the slaughter-house, and they don't realize it. They regard war as an illness. War is not an illness," he thought emphatically. "It's an abomination, because it's caused by men." Mathieu swung the barrier open; "I'm coming to meet a friend," he said to the ticket-collector. The station looked cheerful, though deserted, and as silent as a cemetery. Why am I going? He sat down on a green bench. Some will refuse to go. But that's not my business. I might refuse and stand pat, or skip to Switzerland. Why don't I? Well, I just *can't*. And the war in Spain wasn't my business either. Nor the Communist Party. But what is my business? he asked himself, almost in desperation. The tracks gleamed in the sunshine; the train would arrive at the platform on the left. To his left, that little shimmering pool in the distance, where the tracks rejoined—that was Toulon. Marseille, Port-Bou, Spain. An absurd and futile war. Jacques says it is already lost. War is an illness, he thought; my business is to bear it like an illness. Merely from a sense of decency. I shall be a brave patient, anyway. Why make war? I can't approve of war. And, equally, why not? My skin isn't even worth saving. Well, he thought, there it is: I'm pulled into it. I'm a civil-service clerk. And his sole resource was the dismal stoicism characteristic of bureaucrats, who endure everything—poverty, illness, and war—from motives of self-respect. He smiled as he reflected that he didn't even respect himself. A martyr—they need a martyr, thought Philippe. He was adrift and utterly exhausted; not a disagreeable sensation, but not to be resisted; in point of fact he couldn't see very much, two shutters to the right and left blocked his view of the street. The crowd engulfed him, people were converging on him from every direction, children ran between his legs; faces blinking in the sunshine slid above his head, below his head, the same face swaying back to forward—Yes-yes-yes. Yes, we accept these starvation salaries, yes, we will fight, yes, our husbands shall fight, yes, we will line up at the bakers' shops with our children in our arms. It was the crowd—the vast, silent acquiescence called a crowd. And if you try to explain anything to them, they hit you in the eye, thought

Philippe, whose cheek still smarted, they trample you underfoot, and they still shout: Yes. As he looked at those dead faces, he measured his own impotence; one can't say a thing to them, a martyr is what they need; a man who stands up on tiptoe and shouts: "NO." They would fall upon him and tear him to pieces. Blood shed for them, and by them, would inject fresh force into their hearts; the spirit of the martyr would enter into them, they would lift their heads and their unblinking eyes, and a thunderous roar of refusal would roll from one end to the other of the crowd. I am that martyr, he thought. The victim's ectasy possessed him and he bowed his head, dropped the suitcase, and fell on his knees, engulfed in that universal consent.

"Hello!" said Mathieu.

Gomez ran towards him, bareheaded, and still handsome. His eyes were blurred, he blinked, and said: "Where am I?" Voices above him muttered: "What's the matter? He has fainted—what's your address?" A head bent over him, the head of an old woman—is she going to bite me? Your address! Mathieu and Gomez grinned at each other— your address, *your address,* YOUR ADDRESS, he made a violent effort and got up. Then he smiled and said: "It's nothing, madame, it's the heat. I live quite near, I'll go straight home."

"Someone must go with him," said a voice behind him, "he can't go home alone." And the voice was lost in a rustle of leaves: "Yes, *yes,* YES, someone must go with him—go with him—go with him."

"Let me alone!" he exclaimed; "let me alone, don't touch me! No! *No!* NO!" He looked them in the face, he looked at their weary, shocked eyes, and he cried: "No." No to the war, No to the general, No to guilty mothers, No to Zézette and Maurice, No—leave me in peace. They fell back, and he began to run with leaden feet. He ran and he ran, some-one laid a hand on his shoulder and he nearly burst into tears. It was a young man with a small mustache, who handed him his suitcase.

"You've forgotten your suitcase," he said with a laugh. The Moroccan stopped; it was a snake that he had taken for a dead branch. A small snake; he needed a stone to crush its head. But the snake wriggled, streaked over the ground like a flash, and vanished into the ditch. A lucky omen. Nothing stirred behind the wall. I'll come back, he thought.

Mathieu laid both hands on Gomez's shoulders.

"Well," he said. "Well, colonel!"

Gomez smiled a high, mysterious smile. "General," said he.

Mathieu dropped his hands. "General? Promotion must be rapid in your part of the world."

"They're short of officers," said Gomez, still smiling. "How sunburned you are, Mathieu."

"It's luxury tan," said Mathieu rather irritably. "You pick it up at these seaside places, by force of doing nothing."

He scanned Gomez's hands and face for any mark of what he had gone through; he was prepared for any amount of self-reproach. But Gomez, a slim and dapper little figure in a flannel suit, was not yet giving himself away; for the moment he looked like a summer visitor.

"Where shall we go?" he asked.

"We'll find some quiet little restaurant," said Mathieu. "I'm staying with my brother and my sister-in-law, but I won't ask you to dine with them; they're not much fun."

"Let's go to a place where there's music and women." He looked quizzically at Mathieu. "I've just spent a week with my family."

"Right," said Mathieu. "We'll go to the Provençal."

The orderly watched them approach with a not unamiable and rather professional air. He stood motionless, and slightly bent, between two automatic ticket machines; his rifle and helmet gleamed in the sunshine. He hailed them as they passed.

"Where for?"

"Essey-les-Nancy," said Maurice.

"When you get outside, take the car on the left and go on to the terminus."

They emerged into the usual dismal railway-station square, with its cafés and hotels. There were puffs of smoke in the sky.

"It does you good to stretch your legs," said Dornier with a sigh.

Maurice looked up, smiled, and winked. "About as much chance of a tram as hell's freezing over," said Bébert.

A woman looked at them sympathetically. "It hasn't arrived yet. Where do you want to go?"

"To Essey-les-Nancy," said Maurice.

"You've got a good quarter of an hour yet; they go every twenty minutes."

"Time for a drink," said Dornier to Maurice.

It was cool, the train rolled on, the air was red; a thrill of joy swept over him and he tugged at his bedclothes. "Catherine!" he said; she did not reply. But something birdlike brushed against his chest and slowly slid up to his neck, then flew up and alighted on his forehead. It was her hand, her soft, perfumed hand, it glided on to Charles's nose, the light fingers fluttered against his lips and tickled him. He seized the hand and pressed it against his mouth. It was warm; he slid his fingers along it to the wrist and felt the pulse throb. He closed his eyes, kissed the slender hand, and the pulse throbbed beneath his fingers like the heart of a bird. She laughed. "It's as though we were blind; we must get to know each other through our fingers." He reached out an arm in his turn, he was afraid of hurting her; he touched the iron mirror-rod and then a strand of hair outspread on the coverlet, fair hair, then a temple, then a cheek, delicately rounded like a woman's body, then a warm mouth breathed against his fingers, teeth nibbled them, and countless needles tingled up his back and neck. "Catherine!" he said; "This," he thought, "is making love." She let go his hand and sighed, Maurice blew the froth off his beer on to the floor. He drank. She said: "What are those boats in which people lie side by side?" Maurice licked his upper lip and said: "It's nice and cool." "I don't know," said Charles; "gondolas, perhaps." "No, not gondolas—anyhow, it doesn't matter; we might be in a boat like that." He took her hand, they glided side by side downstream, she was his mistress, a star with pale-gold hair, he was another man, and he was looking after her. He said: "I wish the train might never get there." Daniel nibbled his fountain pen, there was a knock at the door, and he held his breath, he looked unseeing at the white paper on the blotting-pad. "Daniel!" said Marcelle's voice. "Are you there?" He did not answer. Marcelle's heavy footsteps moved away; she went downstairs; the stairs creaked one by one. He smiled, dipped his pen in the ink, and wrote: "My dear Mathieu." A clasped hand in the darkness, the scratch of a pen, Philippe's face emerges from the darkness and comes to meet him, pale in the shadowed mirror, a pitching ship, the iced beer gurgles in his throat and half chokes him, the car covers thirty-three yards between Paris and Rouen in a human second, the three-thousandth second of the twentieth hour of the twenty-fourth day of September 1938. A second gone, speeding between the rails after Charles and Catherine through the sweltering countryside, left behind by Maurice in the sawdust of a dark, cool café, afloat in the wake of a steamer, immersed in a pool of ink, glistening and drying in the downstrokes of the *M* in Mathieu, while the pen scratches at the paper, and Daladier, recumbent on the cushions of his car, sucks an extinct cigarette and watches the passers-by. He loathed London: he kept his eyes fixed on the door so as not to see

Bonnet's ugly mug and the wooden face of that stupid
Englishman. "They don't realize what's up," he thought.
He noticed a hatless woman, laughing with her mouth wide
open. They all looked vacantly at the car, two or three of
them shouted: "Hurrah!" but they clearly did not realize
what was happening; they did not understand that the car
was carrying war and peace to Downing Street, war or
peace, heads or tails—that black car hooting along the
road to London. Daniel continued to write. The captain
stopped outside the first-class saloon, and read: "This
evening at twenty-one o'clock Baby's All-Girl Orchestra
will give a symphonic concert in the first-class saloon. All
passengers, without distinction of class, are heartily in-
vited." He puffed at his pipe and thought: "She's much
too thin." Just at that moment he smelt a warm perfume
and heard a faint flutter of wings, it was Maud, and he
turned round; in Madrid the setting sun gilded the ruined
façades of the university city; Maud looked at him, he
stepped forward; the Moroccan glided through the debris;
the Belgian aimed, Maud and the captain eyed each other.
The Moroccan raised his head and saw the Belgian; they
eyed each other, and then, abruptly, Maud smiled an acid
smile and turned her head away, the Belgian pressed the
trigger, the Moroccan fell dead, the captain stepped towards Maud, then thought: "She's too thin," and stopped.
"Dirty bastard," said the Belgian. He looked at the dead
Moroccan and repeated: "Dirty bastard!"

"Well," said Gomez, "and Marcelle? Sarah told me it
was over?"

"It is," said Mathieu. "She has married Daniel."

"Daniel Sereno? That's odd," said Gomez. "However,
it's a way out for you."

"Way out?" said Mathieu. "From what?"

"Marcelle didn't suit you," said Gomez.

"Nonsense!" said Mathieu.

The dinner-tables were arranged in a semicircle round a

sanded dance-floor strewn with pine needles. The Provençal was deserted; a solitary guest was eating a chicken wing and drinking Vichy water. The bandsmen climbed wearily on to their stage, sat down with much clattering of chairs, and began to whisper to one another as they tuned their instruments; the sun was still visible, a dark disk between the pines. Mathieu stretched his legs under the table and sipped a glass of port. For the first time in a week he felt at home; he had suddenly collected himself, he was completely at ease in this strange place which combined the atmosphere of a private room with that of a magic grotto. The pines looked like cardboard trees, and in the soft outdoor darkness the lamps shed a sort of boudoir light on the tablecloths; a spotlight flashed through the trees, suddenly whitening the dance-floor into a semblance of cement. But overhead hovered the shadow of what was not there; the stars flickered in the sky like vague assiduous little insects; a smell of resin, and the sea wind, insistent and uneasy like an anguished soul, fluttering the tablecloths and suddenly thrusting its cold muzzle into one's neck.

"Let's talk about yourself," said Mathieu.

Gomez seemed surprised. "Have you had no adventures?" he asked.

"None," said Mathieu.

"Not during the last two years?"

"No. I am exactly as you left me."

"Oh, you damned Frenchmen!" laughed Gomez. "You're all eternal."

The saxophonist laughed as the violinist said something into his ear. Ruby leaned towards Maud, who was tuning her violin. "Get a load of that old guy in the second row," she said.

Maud giggled; the old guy was as bald as an egg. She surveyed the auditorium, there were a good five hundred people present. She noticed Pierre standing near the door and stopped laughing. Gomez looked at the violinist gloomily, then glanced at the empty chairs.

"For a quiet little corner, one couldn't do better," he said in a voice of resignation.

"There's a band," said Mathieu.

"So I see," said Gomez.

He looked at the players with an air of disapproval. Maud read disapproval in all their eyes, her face was rather flushed, as always on these occasions, and she thought: "Oh dear, what's the good of it all?" But France, an erect and sparkling figure in a tricolor sash, displayed every sign of happiness; she smiled, she beat time in advance; she held the bow with her little finger lifted, as though it were a fork.

"You promised me women," said Gomez.

"I know I did," said Mathieu despondently. "I don't know what's the matter; last week at this time all the tables were taken, and there were plenty of skirts, I assure you."

"It's the march of events," said Gomez in his quiet voice.

"No doubt."

Events: indeed it was true; for them also events existed. They fought, with their backs to the Pyrenees and their eyes on Valencia, Madrid, and Tarragona; but they read the papers and they think of the men and weapons swarming at their backs, and they have their views on France, Czechoslovakia, and Germany. He shifted a little on his chair; a fish had approached the window of the aquarium and was goggling at him. He threw a shrewd grin at Gomez and said in a hesitant tone:

"People are beginning to understand."

"They understand nothing," said Gomez. "A Spaniard may understand, a Czech too, and perhaps even a German, because they're in it. The French aren't; they understand nothing; they're just afraid."

Mathieu felt hurt and said curtly: "They are not to be blamed for that. I personally have nothing to lose, and I don't particularly mind joining up; it's a change for me. But anyone who is really keen about anything can't find it easy to change over from peace to war."

"I did it in an hour," said Gomez. "Do you think I wasn't keen on painting?"

"You're different," said Mathieu.

Gomez shrugged. "You talk like Sarah."

They fell silent. Mathieu did not think very highly of Gomez. Less than Brunet, and less than Daniel. But he felt guilty in the company of a Spaniard. He shivered. A fish against the window of the aquarium. And that look made him feel abysmally French. Guilty. Guilty, and French. He wanted to say: "But damn it all! I was an interventionist." But that was not the point. His personal views did not count. He was French, it would have served no useful purpose to disavow his solidarity with other Frenchmen. I decided on non-intervention in Spain, I sent no arms, I closed the frontier to the volunteers. He must defend himself with all the rest or suffer condemnation with them, together with the maître d'hôtel and the dyspeptic gentleman drinking Vichy water.

"It's very silly," he said, "but I had imagined that you would appear in uniform."

Gomez smiled. "In uniform? Would you like to see me in uniform?"

He produced a packet of photographs from his pocketbook and handed them to Mathieu one by one. "There!" A trim, imperious officer on the steps of a church.

"You don't look very amiable."

"That's the intention," said Gomez.

Mathieu looked at him and burst out laughing. "Yes," said Gomez. "It's a farce."

"I wasn't thinking that," said Mathieu. "I was wondering whether I should look as unpleasant as you do in uniform."

"Are you an officer?" asked Gomez with interest.

"No, a private."

"All Frenchmen are privates," said Gomez with a gesture of annoyance.

"Just as all Spaniards are generals," said Mathieu sharply.

Gomez laughed. "Look at that," he said, holding out a photograph.

A girl, dark-haired and rather sad, but very pretty. Gomez had an arm round her waist and was smiling with the self-complacent air he always assumed in photographs.

"Mars and Venus," said he.

"That's more like you," said Mathieu. "You seem to like them rather young."

"She's fifteen; but war matures them. Here's one of me in action."

Mathieu saw a little man squatting under a section of ruined wall.

"Where is that?"

"Madrid. The university quarter. There's fighting still going on there."

He had fought. He had really crouched behind that wall under fire. He was a captain at the time. Perhaps he was short of cartridges and cursing the French. Gomez sat back in his chair, he had finished his glass of port, he took out his box of matches with a suave, deliberate gesture, lit his cigarette, his fine, rather humorous features leaped out of the shadow and were again extinguished. He had fought; no sign of it is visible in his eyes. The falling night enveloped him, his face looked blue above the pink lamp, the band was playing *No te quiero mas*, the wind fluttered the tablecloth, a woman entered, a luxurious, solitary figure, and sat down at the next table, her perfume drifted to their noses. Gomez inhaled it, dilating his nostrils, his face hardened, and he turned his head with an inquisitive air.

"To your right," said Mathieu.

Gomez fixed a wolfish look upon her, he had become serious now. "That's a pretty girl," said he.

"She's an actress," said Mathieu. "She owns a dozen pairs of beach pajamas. Kept by a Lyon manufacturer."

"Hum!" said Gomez.

She returned his look and averted her eyes with a half smile.

"You won't lose your evening," said Mathieu.

He did not reply. He had laid his forearm on the table, Mathieu looked at the hairy, ringed hand, pink beneath the radiance of the lamp. There he is, a blue-chinned male with pink hands, inhaling the fair-haired lady's perfume, and summoning her with a look. He has fought. Behind him lie scorched villages, eddies of red dust, bare hillridges, bursting flames that do not even glimmer in his eyes. He has fought; he is going back to fight, and he is there; he sees the same white tablecloths that I see. He tried to look at the pines, the dance-floor, the woman, with the eyes of Gomez, eyes burned by flames of war; he succeeded for a moment and then the restless, parched splendor of the vision vanished. He has fought, he has— how romantic he is! "I am not romantic," thought Mathieu. "No," said Odette, "two covers only, Monsieur Mathieu won't be back to dinner." She went to the open window, she could hear the band at the Provençal playing a tango. They listened to the music; Mathieu thought: "He is only passing through." The waiter brought the soup. "No," said Gomez, "no soup." They played the *Tango du chat*; France's violin leaped into the light, then suddenly dived into shadow like a flying fish. France smiled, her eyes half-closed, she dived behind her violin, the bow scraped across the strings, the violin squeaked, Maud heard the violin squeaking against her ear, she heard the bald gentleman cough, and Pierre looked at her, Gomez began to laugh, there was a rather unamiable expression on his face.

"A tango," said he, "a tango! If a French band played a tango like that, in a Madrid café—"

"They would be pelted with boiled potatoes, eh?" said Mathieu.

"Stones!" said Gomez.

"We aren't popular in those parts?" asked Mathieu.

"What do you think?" said Gomez.

He pushed the door open; the Bar Basque was deserted. Boris had gone into it one evening on account of its name: "Bar Basque" was reminiscent of *barbaque*, which was a word he could never utter without laughing. Then he realized that the bar was quite well known, and he had come back there every evening while Lola was at work. Through the open windows could be heard the distant band of the Casino; once, even, he had thought he recognized Lola's voice, but not again.

"Good day, Monsieur Boris," said the proprietor.

"Good day, *patron*," said Boris. "I'll have a white rum."

He felt in high good humor. He would drink two white rums while he smoked a pipe; then, about eleven o'clock, he would have a sausage sandwich. About midnight he would call for Lola. The proprietor bent over him and filled his glass.

"The Marseillais isn't here?" asked Boris.

"No," said the proprietor. "He's got a business dinner."

"Ah yes—I forgot."

The Marseillais was a traveling salesman in corsets, and there was another constant visitor called Charlier, a printer. Boris sometimes played cards with them, sometimes they talked politics and sport, or sat in silence at the bar-counter or at a table in the back. Now and then Charlier would break the silence to say: "Yes, yes, yes. Exactly so," nodding his head, and thus the time passed pleasantly.

"Not many people today," said Boris.

The proprietor shrugged his shoulders.

"They're all clearing out. I usually keep open until All Saints'," said he, making his way back to the counter. "But if this goes on, I shall shut down on October 1st and go to my place in the country."

Boris stopped drinking, he felt startled. In any case, Lola's contract expired on October 1, they would have gone. But he did not like to think of the Bar Basque closed behind their backs. The Casino would close too and all the hotels, Biarritz would be deserted. One had just the same feeling about death; if one was certain that other men would still be drinking white rum, bathing in the sea, and listening to jazz bands, one could feel a little comforted; but if everyone had to die at the same time, and humanity closed down, the prospect would indeed be dismal.

"When do you reopen?" he asked, to reassure himself.

"If there's a war," said the proprietor, "I shan't reopen at all."

Boris counted on his fingers: 26, 27, 28, 29, 30, I shall come back five times more, and that will be the end; I shan't see the Bar Basque again. How funny! Five times. He would drink white rum at that table five more times, and then there would be war, the Bar Basque would close, and in October '39 Boris would be mobilized. Oak candelabra shed a mellow reddish light over the tables. And Boris thought: "I shall never see that light again." Not just that light: red against black. He would of course see many others, flares by night above the battlefields—not a bad sight, so people said. But that light would go out on October 1 and Boris would never see it again. He looked with respect at a white reflection on the table; it was his own fault. He had always treated objects like forks and spoons as though they had been indefinitely renewable—a profound mistake; there was a finite number of bars, cinemas, houses, towns, and villages, and one and the same individual could not go to each of them more than a finite number of times.

"Shall I turn on the radio?" asked the proprietor. "It might amuse you."

"No, thanks," said Boris. "I'm quite all right."

At the moment of his death, in '42, he would have lunched 365 x 22 times, 8,030 times in all, counting his meals in infancy. And assuming that he had had an omelet once out of every ten occasions, he would have eaten 803 omelets. "Only 803 omelets?" he said to himself with astonishment. Oh no; there are the dinners too, that makes 16,060 meals, and 1,606 omelets. Anyway, for a man partial to omelets that was not a considerable total. And what about cafés? he continued. The number of times that I shall go to a café after today can be calculated: suppose I go twice a day, and that I am called up in a year, that makes 730 times. 730 times!—that's not very often. It gave him a shock all the same, but he was not particularly surprised; he had always known he would die young. He had often told himself that he would die of consumption, or be murdered by Lola. But in his inmost self he had never doubted that he would be killed in war. He worked, he prepared for his school diploma or his degree, but it was more or less by way of passing the time, just as girls go to lectures at the Sorbonne while waiting to get married. How funny it all is! he said to himself; there were periods when men studied law or philosophy, thinking they would have a good law practice by the time they were forty, or a professor's pension at sixty. One wondered what was really inside their heads. People who could look forward to 10,000, 15,000 evenings at cafés, 4,000 omelets, 2,000 nights of love! And if they left a place they liked, they would say quite definitely to themselves: we will come back here next year, or in ten years. They must do a lot of idiotic things, he said austerely to himself. One can't conduct one's life forty years ahead. For himself, he was much more modest; he had plans for two years, after which all would be over. One *must* restrict oneself. A junk passed slowly down the Blue River, and Boris suddenly felt despondent. He would never go to India, nor China, nor Mexico, nor

even to Berlin, his life was even more restricted than he
could have wished. A few months in England, Laon,
Biarritz, Paris—and there are people who have gone round
the world! One woman only. It was quite a small life; indeed, it had an air of already being concluded, since he
knew in advance all that it would not contain. One *must*
restrict oneself. He sat up straight, drank a little rum, and
thought: "It's much more sensible, then there's no risk of
waste."

"Another rum, *patron*."

He raised his head and gazed intently at the electric
bulbs.

The clock opposite, above the mirror, began to strike; he
could see his face in the mirror. "Nine forty-five," he
thought. "At ten o'clock!" he thought, and called the
waitress.

"The same again."

The waitress went away and returned with the bottle of
brandy and a saucer. She poured the brandy into Philippe's
glass, and laid the saucer on the three others. She was
smiling rather ironically, but Philippe looked her calmly in
the eyes; he picked up the glass with a steady hand and
lifted it without spilling a drop; he drank a little and put
the glass down, still looking at the waitress.

"How much?"

"Do you want to pay now?" she asked.

"Yes."

"Twelve francs."

He gave her fifteen francs and waved her away. "Now,"
he thought, "I don't owe anything to anyone." And he
laughed to himself. Again he thought: "Not to anyone." He
saw himself laughing in the mirror, and that made him
laugh still more. On the last stroke of ten he would get up,
tear his reflection out of the glass, and his martyrdom
would start. For the moment he felt cheerful and considered the situation in a nonchalant sort of way. A café

was a hospitable place—a sort of Capua; his seat was as
soft as a feather mattress, so soft that he sank into it, a
faint sound of music emerged from behind the counter,
and a clatter of crockery that reminded him of the cow-
bells at Seelisberg. He saw himself in the glass, and he
could have sat looking at himself and listening to the music
for an infinitude of time. At ten o'clock he would get up,
take his reflection in his hands, and rip it off the glass like
a dead skin, or like a speck flicked out of an eye. *Mirrors
operated for cataract. . . .*

Cataracts of the day.

In mirrors operated for cataract.

Or, alternatively,

*The day sinks in cataract in the mirror operated for
cataract.*

Or again:

*Niagara of the day in cataract in the mirror operated for
cataract.*

The words fell into powder, and he clung to the cold
marble, the wind is carrying me away, there was a sticky
taste of alcohol in his throat. THE MARTYR. He looked at
himself in the glass, he was looking at a martyr; he smiled
a salutation at himself. "Ten minutes to ten, aha!" he
thought with satisfaction, I find *time so long.* Five minutes
gone—an eternity. Two more motionless eternities, devoid
of thought or pain, passed in contemplating the martyr's
handsome, emaciated face, and then time will plunge with
a roar into a taxi, into the train, on to Geneva.

Ataraxia.

Niagara of time.

Niagara of the day.

In mirrors operated for cataract.

I'm going off in a taxi.

To Gauburge, to Bibracte.

Whence, indeed, an act!

Whence cataract.

He laughed, he stopped laughing, he looked round him, the café smelt of railway station, train, and hospital; he longed to call for help. Seven minutes. Which would be most revolutionary? he asked himself. To go or not to go? If I go, I revolt against others; if I don't go, I revolt against myself, and that is the nobler deed. Make every preparation, steal some money, procure false papers, break all contacts, and then, at the last moment—pfftt!—I'm not going after all—good night! Freedom in the second degree; freedom contesting freedom. At three minutes to ten he decided to toss heads or tails whether he should go or not. He had a clear vision of the entrance hall of the Gare d'Orsay, desolate and ablaze with light, and the stairway plunging underground, the smoke of the locomotives, there was a taste of smoke in his mouth; he picked up the two-franc piece, heads I go; he flung it into the air—heads I go! heads I go. It came down heads. Very well, I go! he said to his reflection. Not because I hate the war, not because I hate my family, not even because I have decided to go; but by pure *chance;* because a coin turned one side up rather than the other. Admirable, thought he; I am at the extremest point of freedom. A martyr without motive; if only she had seen me tossing that coin! One more minute. A throw of dice. Ding—never—ding, ding—will a throw—ding—of dice—ding, ding—abolish—ding, ding—luck—*Ding!* He got up, he walked quite straight, he placed his feet one after the other on a strip of floor-board, he felt the waitress's eyes upon his back, but he would not give her any cause to laugh at him.

"Monsieur!"

He turned, trembling.

"Your suitcase."

God damn it! He ran across the room, picked up his suitcase, and tottered with difficulty back to the door amid a burst of laughter, went out, and hailed a taxi. He held his suitcase in his left hand, in his right hand he was clutch-

ing the two-franc piece. The cab stopped in front of him.
"Where to?"

The driver had a mustache and a wart on his cheek.

"Rue Pigalle," said Philippe. "To the Cabane Cubaine."

"We have lost the war," said Gomez.

Mathieu knew it, but had thought that Gomez didn't
know it yet. The band was playing *I'm looking for Sally,*
the plates gleamed beneath the table-lamp, and the spot-
lights shed a sort of monstrous moonlight on the dance-
floor, a Honolulu poster moonlight. Gomez was seated
there, the moonlight on his right, and on his left a lady
with a half-smile on her face; he was on his way back to
Spain, and he knew that the Republicans had lost the war.

"You can't be sure," said Mathieu. "No one can be sure."

"Yes, they can," said Gomez. "*We* are sure."

He did not seem cast down; he was merely stating a
fact. He looked at Mathieu with the calm expression of a
man whose task is finished. He said: "All my soldiers are
sure the war is lost."

"And they're fighting anyhow?" said Mathieu.

"What do you expect them to do?"

Mathieu shrugged his shoulders. "Obviously."

I pick up my glass, I drink a little Château-Margaux,
and someone says to me: they are fighting to the last,
there's nothing else they can do. I drink a little Château-
Margaux, I shrug my shoulders, and I say: Obviously.
Yellow bastard!

"What's that?" asked Gomez.

"*Tournedos Rossini,*" said the head waiter.

"Ah, yes," said Gomez. "Give me the dish."

He took it and put it on the table.

"Not bad," he said; "not bad."

The *tournedos* are on the table; one for him, one for me.
He has the right to enjoy his steak, to chew it with those
fine white teeth of his, he has the right to look at that
pretty girl and think: That's a nice bit of stuff! But I

haven't. If I eat, a hundred dead Spaniards leap at my throat. I haven't paid.

"You aren't drinking," said Gomez. He took the bottle and filled Mathieu's glass.

"I will, since you invite me to," said Mathieu with a short laugh. He picked up his glass and emptied it. A *tournedos* suddenly appeared on his plate. He picked up his knife and fork. "I eat, since Spain invites me," he muttered.

Gomez did not seem to hear. He had poured out a glass of wine, drank it, and smiled. "*Tournedos* today, dried peas tomorrow. It's my last evening in France," he said. "And it's the only good dinner that I've had here."

"What!" said Mathieu. "Not at Marseille?"

"Sarah is a vegetarian," said Gomez. He looked straight in front of him with a genial expression. He said: "When I went on leave, there had been no tobacco in Barcelona for three weeks. Can you imagine an entire city where no one smokes?" He turned his eyes on Mathieu, and seemed suddenly to see him. His face resumed his rather unpleasantly penetrating look.

"You'll go through all that," said he.

"It isn't certain," said Mathieu. "War may yet be avoided."

"Oh, of course," said Gomez. "War can *always* be avoided." He laughed curtly and added: "You have only to go back on the Czechs."

"No, old boy," thought Mathieu, "no! Spaniards may lecture me about Spain, that's their department. But at lectures on Czechoslovakia I demand the presence of a Czech."

"Frankly, Gomez," he asked, "ought they to be backed up? It isn't so long since the Communists claimed autonomy for the Sudeten Germans."

"Ought they to be backed up?" asked Gomez, mimicking Mathieu's voice. "Ought we to have been backed up? Or

the Austrians? And what about you? Who will back you up
when your time comes?"

"We don't come into the question," said Mathieu.

"But you do," said Gomez. "Of course you do."

"Gomez," said Mathieu, "eat your *tournedos*. I quite
understand that you detest us all. But anyway this is your
last evening of leave, your food is getting cold, there's a
woman smiling at you, and, after all, I was an interventionist."

Gomez had recovered himself. "Yes," he said with a
smile, "I know."

"Besides," said Mathieu, "you must realize that in Spain
the situation was clear-cut. But when you begin to talk to
me about Czechoslovakia I no longer follow you, because
the issue seems to me much less obvious. There is a question of right that I find I cannot determine: after all, suppose the Sudeten Germans don't want to be Czechs?"

"Never mind questions of right," said Gomez shrugging his shoulders. "You want a reason for fighting. There's
only one; if you don't, you're done for. What Hitler wants
isn't Prague, nor Vienna, nor Danzig—it's Europe."

Daladier looked at Chamberlain, he looked at Halifax,
then he averted his eyes and looked at a gilt clock on the
console; the hands indicated thirty-five minutes past ten;
the taxi stopped outside the Cabane Cubaine. Georges
turned over on his back and groaned a little, his neighbor's
snores were keeping him awake.

"Well," said Daladier, "I can only repeat what I have
already stated; the French Government has undertaken
certain engagements towards Czechoslovakia. If the
Prague Government maintains its refusal of the German
proposals, and if in consequence of that refusal it becomes
the victim of an aggression, the French Government will
regard itself as under an obligation to fulfill its engagements."

He coughed, looked at Chamberlain, and waited.

"Yes," said Chamberlain. "Yes, obviously."

He seemed disposed to add a few words; but no words came. Daladier waited, describing circles on the carpet with the toe of his shoe. At last he looked up and said wearily: "What, in that eventuality, would be the position of the British Government?"

France, Maud, Doucette, and Ruby got up and bowed. From the front rows came a little limp applause, then the crowd dispersed with much clattering of chairs. Maud looked round for Pierre, but he had disappeared. France turned towards her, her cheeks were flushed, and she smiled.

"It was a good evening," she said. "A *really* good evening."

The war was there, on the white dance-floor, in the dead glare of the artificial moonlight, in the rasping falsetto of the muted trumpets, on the cool tablecloth, in the smell of wine, and in the old age lurking behind Gomez's features. Halifax looked at Bonnet, Bonnet looked at Daladier; they were silent, and Mathieu looked at the war on his plate, and in the myriad black eyes of the caviar sauce on his *tournedos*.

"And suppose we, too, lost the war?"

"Then Europe would go fascist," said Gomez lightly. "It's not a bad preparation for Communism."

"What will become of you, Gomez?"

"I imagine their cops will knock me on the head in my lodging, or I shall go to America and scrape some sort of living there. What does it matter? I shall have lived."

Mathieu looked at Gomez with curiosity. "And you regret nothing?" he asked.

"Nothing at all."

"Not even painting?"

"Not even painting."

Mathieu shook his head sadly. He liked Gomez's pictures. "You used to paint good pictures," he said.

"I shall never paint again."

"Why?"

"I don't know. It's physical. I've lost patience; I should find it boring."

"But patience is needed in war too."

"Not the same sort of patience."

They were silent. The maître d'hôtel brought the pancakes on a pewter dish, sprinkled them with rum and Calvados, then he held a lighted match over the dish. A spectral flame hovered a moment in the air.

"Gomez," said Mathieu suddenly, "you are a solid sort of fellow; you know what you are fighting for."

"You mean you wouldn't know?"

"Not at all. I think I should know. But I wasn't thinking of myself. There are men who have nothing but their lives, Gomez. And no one does a thing for them. No one. No government, no regime. If the fasces took the place of the Republic here, they wouldn't even notice. Take a shepherd in the Cévennes. Do you think he would know why he was fighting?"

"In my country the shepherds are the biggest daredevils," said Gomez.

"Why are they fighting?"

"That depends. I've known some who are fighting for the opportunity to learn to read."

"In France everyone can read," said Mathieu. "If I came across a shepherd from the Cévennes in my regiment and saw him die beside me in defense of my Republic and my liberties, I assure you I should feel extremely uncomfortable, Gomez, don't you feel ashamed sometimes?—don't you think of all those people who have died for you?"

"It doesn't worry me," said Gomez. "I risk my skin just as they do."

"Generals die in their beds."

"I haven't always been a general."

"In any case it isn't the same," said Mathieu.

"No, I'm not sorry for them," said Gomez. "I don't pity them." He moved a hand across the tablecloth and grasped Mathieu's arm. "Mathieu," he said in a slow undertone, "war is beautiful."

His face blazed. Mathieu tried to disengage himself, but Gomez gripped his arm and went on: "I love war."

There was nothing more to say. Mathieu laughed a short, embarrassed laugh, and Gomez took his hand away.

"You have made a deep impression on the lady next to us."

Gomez flashed a glance to his left.

"Indeed?" he said. "Well, one must strike while the iron is hot. Is that a dance-floor?"

"Of course."

Gomez rose and buttoned his jacket. He approached the actress, and Mathieu saw him bend over her. She looked up at him with a mechanical smile, then they moved away and began to dance. They danced; she had no Negroid smell, she must be a Martiniquaise. Philippe thought: "Martiniquaise," but it was the word Malabaraise that came to his lips. He muttered: "My lovely Malabaraise."

"You dance well," she answered.

There was a fife-like cadence in her voice that was not at all unpleasant.

"You speak French well," he said.

She looked at him indignantly. "I was born in France."

"That doesn't matter," he said. "You speak French very well all the same."—"I'm tight," he thought, and laughed. She said to him, quite without anger: "You're tight."

"Y-e-e-s," said he.

His fatigue had left him; he could have danced till morning, but he had decided to sleep with the Negress, which was a more serious affair. The attraction of intoxication was the power it gave you over objects. No need to touch them; just a look and you possess them; he possessed that forehead and that dark hair; his eyes caressed that polished face. Farther off, the scene was rather blurred; a large man drinking champagne, and beyond him a sprawling throng of people whom he could not clearly distinguish.

"How well you dance!" said she. "A handsome fellow like you must have had lots of women."

"I'm a virgin," said Philippe.

"You little liar."

He lifted a hand. "I swear I'm a virgin. I swear it by my mother's head."

"Ah?" she said disappointedly. "I suppose you aren't interested in women."

"I don't know," he said. "We shall see."

He looked at her, he possessed her with his eyes, grimaced at her, and said: "So I'm relying on you."

She puffed some cigarette smoke into his face. "You'll see what I can do."

He grasped her hair and drew her towards him; from close up she did smell faintly of grease. He kissed her lightly on the lips. She said: "A virgin, eh? So I'm going to win first prize."

"Win?" he said. "You always lose."

He did not desire her in the least. But he was glad she was pretty and didn't make him nervous. He felt quite at ease and thought: "I know how to talk to women." He released her, she sat up straight; Philippe's suitcase fell on to the floor. "Look out," he said. "You're tight."

She picked up the suitcase. "What's inside it?"

"Hush! Don't you touch it; it's a diplomatic bag."

"I want to know what's inside," she said, with a childish pout. "Darling, tell me what's inside."

He tried to snatch the suitcase away from her, but she had already opened it. She saw the pajamas and the toothbrush.

"A book," she said as she picked up the Rimbaud. "What is it?"

"That," he said, "is by a fellow who went away."

"Where to?"

"You wouldn't be interested," he said. "He went away."

He took the volume from her and put it back in the suitcase.

"He was a poet," he said ironically. "Does that help you to understand?"

"Sure," she said. "You ought to have said that at once."

He closed the suitcase and thought: "But I haven't gone away," and his drunkenness fell from him. "Why? Why haven't I gone?" He could now clearly distinguish the large gentleman opposite; he wasn't particularly large, and his eyes were rather sinister. The human clusters fell apart; there were women, black and white; men too. People seemed to be continually looking at him. "Why am I here? How did I get here? Why haven't I gone?" There was a gap in his recollections: he had tossed the coin, he had hailed a taxi, and here he was; at present he was sitting at this table, over a glass of champagne, in the company of a Negress who smelt of fish paste. He envisaged the Philippe who had tossed the coin, and tried to make him out; but he thought: "I'm *someone else*"; he thought: "I don't recognize myself." He turned to the Negress.

"Why are you looking at me?" she asked.

"I don't quite know."

"Do you think I'm pretty?"

"So-so."

She cleared her throat and her eyes glittered. Leaning her hands on the table, she rose a few inches from the seat.

"If you don't fancy me, I can go; we aren't married."

He felt in his pocket and produced three crumpled thousand-franc notes. "Here," he said. "Take those, and stay."

She took the notes, unfolded them, smoothed them out, laughed, and sat down again.

"You're a nasty kid," said she. "A dirty bad little kid."

An abyss of shame had opened right in front of him; he had only to drop into it. He had been knocked about and thrown into the street, and even so he had not gone. He leaned over the pit and felt dizzy. Shame awaited him at the bottom of it; he had but to *choose* that shame. He closed his eyes, and the day's exhaustion surged back upon him. Exhaustion, shame, and death. Shame, self-chosen. Why didn't I go? Why did I *choose* not to go? He felt like a man with the world on his shoulders.

"You're not very chatty," she said.

He laid a finger under her chin. "What's your name?"

"Flossie."

"That's not a Malabar name."

"I tell you I was born in France," she said irritably.

"All right, Flossie. I've given you three thousand-franc notes. You don't want me to make conversation into the bargain, do you?"

She shrugged her shoulders and turned her head away. The black pit was still there, and at the bottom of it shame. He peered down into it, suddenly he understood, and anguish wrung his heart; it's a trap, if I fall into it I could never face myself again. Never. He sat up straight and said firmly to himself: "I didn't go because I was tight!" The abyss closed; he had chosen. He had come too near to shame; he had been too frightened; from now on he had chosen never to feel shame again. Never again.

"I ought to have caught a train, you see. But I got too tight."

"You'll catch it tomorrow," she said good-humoredly.

He started. "Why do you say that?"

"Well," she said in astonishment, "when you miss a train, you take the next one."

"I'm not going after all," he said with a frown. "I've

changed my mind. Do you know the meaning of a sign?"

"A sign?" she repeated.

"The world is full of signs. Everything is a sign. They need to be interpreted. You were due to go, you got tight, and you didn't go; why didn't you go? It was because you oughtn't to have gone. It's a sign; you had something better to do here."

She nodded. "That's true," she said. "What you say is quite true."

Something better to do. Those sticky crowds in the Bastille district—that's where I must testify. On the spot. And be torn to pieces on the spot. Like Orpheus. *Down with the war!* No one can then call me a coward. I'll shed my blood for all of them, for Maurice and Zézette, for Pitteaux, for the general, for the men whose nails will tear my flesh. He turned to the Negress and eyed her with affection. One night, only one night. My first night of love. My last night.

"You're a pretty girl, Flossie."

She smiled. "You could be a nice boy if you liked."

"Come and dance," he said to her. "I'll be nice till cock-crow."

They danced. Mathieu looked at Gomez and thought: "His last night," and he smiled; the Negress liked dancing, and half closed her eyes; Philippe danced and thought: "My last night, and my first night of love." He no longer felt shame; he was tired, and it was hot; tomorrow I shall shed my blood for peace. But dawn was far away. He danced, his mind at rest, his honor vindicated; indeed, he thought himself rather romantic. Lights slid along the wall; the train slowed down, jerked forward twice, then stopped; light splashed into the car; Charles blinked and let go Catherine's hand.

"Laroche-Migenne," cried the nurse. "We've arrived."

"Laroche-Migenne?" said Charles. "But we didn't go through Paris."

"We must have gone round by another route."

"Get your things together," cried the nurse. "You're going to be taken off the train."

Blanchard had awakened with a start. "What—what?" he said. "Where are we?"

No one answered. The nurse explained: "We shall take the train again tomorrow. We are spending the night here."

"My eyes are smarting," said Catherine with a laugh; "it's this light."

He turned his head towards her, she laughed as she laid a hand over her eyes.

"Get your things together," cried the nurse. "Get your things together."

She bent over a bald man's gleaming cranium. "Finished?"

"Just a minute, for God's sake!" said the man.

"Hurry up," said she. "The porters are coming already."

"All right, all right," said he. "You can take it away—you took the urge away."

She rose, carrying the pan in her outstretched arms, stepped over the rows of prostrate forms, and made her way to the door.

"We needn't worry," said Charles. "There are about a dozen men on the job, and twenty coaches to unload. They'll be some time before they get to us. . . ."

"Unless they start with the tail end."

Charles put his forearm over his eyes. "Where are they going to put us? In the waiting-rooms?"

"I suppose so."

"I wish we didn't have to leave this car. I'd begun to feel at home here—hadn't you?"

"Oh well," she said, "as long as I'm with you. . . ."

"Here they are," cried Blanchard.

Some men entered the car, black figures against the light. Their shadows were outlined on the car wall; they

seemed to have come in from both sides at once. Silence
fell; Catherine said in a low tone: "I told you they would
begin with us."

Charles did not reply. He saw two of the men bend over
a patient, and his heart contracted. Jacques was asleep,
his nose betrayed the fact; she would not sleep; she would
not sleep until he got back. In a line with his feet Charles
saw an enormous shadow bending double, they're taking
the fellow in front, it will be my turn next, night and smoke
and cold, the swaying stretcher, the deserted platforms—
how he dreaded it all! There came a shaft of light underneath the door, she heard a noise on the ground floor—
here he was. She recognized his step on the stairs, and
peace descended on her; he is here, beneath our roof, I've
got him. Another night. The last. Mathieu opened the
door, then closed it, opened the window and closed the
shutters; she could hear the sound of running water. He
is going to bed. Beyond the wall, beneath our roof.

"It's my turn," said Charles. "Tell them to take you
next."

He squeezed her hand while the two men bent over him,
and a puff of vinous breath came full in his face.

"Hah!" said the man behind him.

He felt suddenly afraid and swung his mirror as they
lifted him, so that he could see whether she was coming
next, but could see nothing but the porter's shoulders and
his owlish head.

"Catherine!" he cried.

No reply. He was swaying through the doorway, the
man behind him shouted directions, his legs dipped and
he thought he was falling.

"Gently!" he said. "Gently."

But he could see stars in a black sky; it was very cold.

"Will she be next?" he asked.

"Who?" asked the owl-headed porter.

"My neighbor. She's a friend of mine."

"The women will be taken out later," said the man. "You won't be in the same place."

Charles began to tremble: "But I thought—" he said.

"You wouldn't want the ladies to pee in front of you, now, would you?"

"I thought," said Charles, "I thought . . ."

He passed a hand over his forehead and suddenly began to yell: "Catherine! Catherine! Catherine!"

He was swinging from the porters' outstretched arms, he glimpsed the stars, then a lamp splashed a glare into his eyes; the stars again, then another lamp, and he yelled: "Catherine! Catherine!"

"He's nuts," said the rear porter. "Keep your mouth shut, can't you!"

"I don't even know her last name," said Charles in a voice choked by tears. "I shall never see her again."

They put him down, opened a door, lifted him again; he saw a ghastly yellow ceiling, he heard the door close; he was in the trap.

"Bastards!" said he, as they laid him down. "Bastards!"

"Who do you think you are!" said the owl-headed man.

"That's all right," said the other. "Can't you see he's a little off?"

He heard their footsteps die away, the door opened and then closed.

"Well!" said Blanchard's voice, "we meet again." And in that very instant Charles received a jet of water full in the face. But he remained silent and motionless, like a corpse, he stared up at the ceiling, while the water trickled into his ears and down his neck. She could not sleep, she lay motionless in the darkened room; he's going to bed, he'll soon be asleep, while I watch over him. He is a fine, brave fellow, he heard this morning that he was to be called up, and he did not blink an eyelid. But now he is disarmed; he'll soon be asleep, it's his last night. "How romantic he is!" she thought.

A warm and scented room, with gleaming lights, and flowers everywhere.

"Come in," she said.

Gomez went in. He looked round him, caught sight of a doll on a divan, and thought of Teruel. He had slept in just such a room, with lamps and dolls and flowers, but no scent, and no ceiling; and there was a hole in the middle of the floor.

"Why are you smiling?"

"This is a charming place," he said.

She came up to him and said: "If you like it, you can come here as often as you wish."

"I'm off tomorrow," said Gomez.

"Tomorrow?" said she. "Where to?"

She looked at him with lovely, inexpressive eyes.

"To Spain."

"To Spain? But then—"

"Yes," he said. "I'm a soldier, on leave."

"On which side?" she asked.

"On which side would you like me to be?"

"On Franco's side?"

"Now, look here!"

She put her arms round his neck. "My handsome soldier."

Her breath was exquisite; he kissed her.

"Only one night," she said. "It isn't much. Just when I've met a man I could really love."

"I'll come back," he said. "When Franco has won the war. . . ."

She kissed him again, then softly let him go. "Wait for me. There's gin and whisky on the sideboard."

She opened the door into the dressing-room and disappeared. Gomez went to the sideboard and poured himself out a glass of gin. The trucks rumbled past, the windows shook, Sarah, awakened with a start, sat up in bed. "How many can there be?" she asked herself. "There's no end to them." Heavy trucks, already camouflaged, roofed with gray tarpaulins, with green and brown strips on the hood, packed with men and weapons. She thought: "This means war," and began to cry. *Catherine! Catherine!* She had been dry-eyed for two years; and when Gomez had got into the train, she couldn't produce a single tear. Now the tears were pouring down her cheeks. *Catherine!* Shaken by sobs, she sank back on the pillow and bit into it, so as not to awaken the boy. Gomez drank a little gin and found it good. He took a few steps into the room and sat down on the divan. In one hand he held his glass, with the other he picked up the doll by the back of the neck and set it on his knee; he could hear the sound of running water from a faucet in the dressing-room, a familiar sense of well-being thrilled up his sides, like two smooth hands. He was happy, he drank, and he thought: "I'm a strong man." The trucks rumbled past, the windows quivered, water spouted from the faucet, and Gomez thought: "I'm strong, I love my life and risk it, I expect death tomorrow, or some time soon, and I'm not afraid, I love luxury, and I'm going back to squalor and starvation, I know what I want, I know why I am fighting, I give orders and am obeyed, I've sacrificed everything—painting, and success, and I am perfectly content." He thought of Mathieu and said to himself: "I wouldn't be in his skin." She opened the door, naked under her pink wrap. She said: "Here I am."

"Oh, to hell with it!" said he.

She had spent half an hour in the dressing-room, washing and scenting herself, because white people didn't always like her smell, she approached him smiling and with open arms, and there he lay asleep, naked in the bed, his head buried in the pillow. She grasped his shoulder and shook him indignantly.

"Wake up!" she said contemptuously. "You little stinker, wake up!"

He lifted his eyelids and looked at her with wondering eyes. He put the glass on the table, the doll on the divan, got up, and took her in his arms. He was happy.

"Can you read that?" asked Gros-Louis.

The porter pushed him away.

"That's the third time you've asked me. You've got to go to Montpellier."

"And where's the train for Montpellier?"

"It doesn't leave till four in the morning; it isn't made up yet."

Gros-Louis looked at him uneasily. "Then what am I to do?"

"Park yourself in the waiting-room and grab a snooze until four o'clock. Have you got your ticket?"

"No," said Gros-Louis.

"Well, go and get it. No, not there. At the ticket office, you old buzzard!"

Gros-Louis made his way to the office. A spectacled clerk was dozing behind the window.

"Hi!" shouted Gros-Louis.

The clerk gave a start.

"I'm going to Montpellier," said Gros-Louis.

"To Montpellier?" The clerk looked surprised; no doubt he was still half-asleep. A suspicion flickered through Gros-Louis's mind.

"Is that Montpellier written there?" He produced his army book.

"Montpellier," said the clerk. "Quarter fare—fifteen francs."

Gros-Louis handed him the kind lady's hundred francs.

"And now," said he, "what am I to do?"

"Go to the waiting-room."

"When does the train start?"

"Four o'clock. Can't you read?"

"No," said Gros-Louis. He paused before turning away. "Is there going to be war?"

The clerk shrugged his shoulders. "How should I know? You wouldn't expect me to find that in the timetable, would you?"

He got up, retired to the back of his office, pretended to consult some papers, but after a moment or two sat down with his head in his hands and continued his doze. Gros-Louis looked round him. He wished he could find some-one who would tell him about this war, but the hall was deserted. "All right," he said, "I'll go to the waiting-room." And he shuffled across the hall; he was sleepy and his thighs ached.

"Let me sleep," moaned Philippe.

"No you don't," said Flossie. "You told me you were a virgin, so you've got to do it like anyone else; it'll bring me luck."

He opened the door and entered the waiting-room. It was packed with people sleeping on benches, and suitcases and parcels were strewn over the floor. The light was dim; a glazed door at the far end opened on a dark void. He walked across to a bench and sat down between two women. One was sweating as she slept; her mouth was open, the sweat had trickled down her cheeks and left pink streaks on them. The other woman opened her eyes and looked at him.

"I'm called up," explained Gros-Louis. "I've got to go to Montpellier."

The woman drew away from him and looked at him angrily. Gros-Louis supposed she didn't like soldiers, but asked all the same:

"Is there going to be war?"

She did not reply; her head had fallen back, and she

had gone to sleep again. Gros-Louis was afraid of going to sleep. "If I go to sleep," he said to himself, "I shan't wake up." He stretched his legs; he ached for something to eat, such as a bit of bread and sausage; he had some money left, but it was late now and all the shops would be shut. "Who are we going to fight?" he asked himself. The Germans no doubt—possibly over Alsace-Lorraine. There was a newspaper lying on the floor, he picked it up, then he thought of the kind lady who had bandaged his head and said: "I oughtn't to have reported. But what was I to do? I hadn't any money left. Might try the barracks—they would give me a bite of food." But he didn't like barracks. Nor waiting-rooms either. He felt suddenly despondent and exhausted. They had made him drunk and beaten him up, and now they were going to send him to Montpellier. "Judas priest," said he. "What's it all about? I don't get it at all, and all because I can't read." All these sleeping folk knew more than he did; they had read the paper, they knew all about this war. He was alone in the night, so small and solitary, he knew and understood nothing, like a man about to die. Then he became conscious of the newspaper in his hand; everything was written down in it—all about the war, tomorrow's weather, the prices of goods, and the times of trains. He unfolded the paper and inspected it. What he saw were thousands of black specks, like pianola rolls with the perforations that produce the sounds when the crank is turned; he felt quite dizzy if he looked at them for long. There was also a photograph of a spruce and smiling man with plastered hair. He dropped the paper and burst into tears.

Monday, September 26

SIXTEEN THIRTY o'clock. Everybody looks at the sky, and I look at the sky. "They're not late," says Dumur. He has his Kodak ready, he looks up at the sky and blinks in the blazing sunshine. The plane is a black speck that glitters now and then, it grows larger, but the sound of it remains—a fine rich sound, very satisfying to the ear. "Don't push," I say. They are all there, jostling round me. I turn; they tilt their heads back; they too blink. They look green in the sunlight, and they move with a sort of perky indecision rather like decapitated frogs. Dumur said: "Some day we'll be standing like this in a field with our noses in the air, but we'll be in khaki, and the plane will be a Messerschmitt." And I reply: "And pretty soon too, with such fatheads to look after our affairs." The plane circles round, then drops, bumps on the ground, rises, bumps again, tips over on the grass, and comes to a standstill. We run towards it, fifty of us, Sarraut ahead of the rest, bent nearly double; a dozen gentlemen in derby hats scurry across the turf, everybody stiffens into immobility, the plane stands inanimate, we eye it in silence, the cabin door stays shut, the occupants might be dead. A man in a blue tunic brings a ladder and lays it against the plane, the door opens, one man comes down the ladder, then another, then Daladier. My heart throbs inside my head. Daladier lifts his shoulders and lowers his head. Sarraut goes up to him and I hear him say: "Well?"

Daladier takes a hand out of his pocket and waves it vaguely. He hurries forward with head bent, and the crowd throngs round him. I don't move, I know he will say nothing. General Gamelin jumps out of the plane, a brisk little man in elegant field-boots and with a bulldog head. He looks at the scene in a sharp, fresh manner.

"Well?" said Sarraut. "Well, general? Is it war?"

"Eh! mon Dieu," says the general.

My mouth dries up; I can't bear it. I shout to Dumur: "I'm off, you must take your photographs alone." I dash to the exit and out on the road, I hail a taxi: "To the *Humanité* office!" The driver smiles, I smile too, and he says: "Well, comrade?"

"It's come!" I reply. "They got it in the pants; they couldn't dodge it this time."

The taxi rattles along, I look at the houses and the people; they know nothing, they ignore the taxi, and the taxi rattles past them carrying a man who does know. I look out of the window, I want to shout: The day has come! I jump out of the taxi, I pay, I dash upstairs. There they all are—Dupré, Charvel, Renard, and Chabot—in shirt-sleeves, Renard smoking, Charvel writing, Dupré looking out on the street. They look at me with astonishment. I say to them: "Come on, boys, the drinks are on me."

They are still looking at me; Charvel lifts his head and looks at me. "The day has come," I say. "It's war! Let's all go out, and I'll stand you drinks."

"That's a pretty hat of yours," said the landlady.

"Isn't it?" said Flossie. She contemplated herself in the hall mirror and said with satisfaction: "Such lovely feathers."

"Yes, indeed," said the landlady. And she added:

"There's someone in your room; Madeleine couldn't tidy it."

"I know," said Flossie. "It doesn't matter; I'll do it myself."

She went upstairs and opened the door. The shutters were closed, and the room smelt of the previous night. Flossie closed the door gently, went out and knocked at No. 15.

"Who is it?" said Zou's hoarse voice.

"Flossie."

Zou opened the door, she was in her panties.

"Come in quick."

Flossie went in. Zou flung her hair back, planted herself in the middle of the room, and began to tuck her capacious bosom into a brassière. Flossie reflected that she ought to shave her armpits.

"Have you just got up?" she asked.

"I didn't get to bed till six," said Zou. "What's the matter?"

"Come and see my boy-friend," said Flossie.

"What do you mean, nigger-girl?"

"Come and see my gigolo."

Zou slipped on a wrap and followed her into the corridor. Flossie preceded her into her room, laying a finger on her lips.

"I can't see a thing," said Zou.

Flossie pushed her towards the bed, and whispered: "Look."

They leaned over the bed, and Zou laughed silently.

"Christ," she said. "Why, hell, he's just a kid."

"His name's Philippe."

"He's very handsome."

Philippe slept, lying on his back; he looked positively angelic. Flossie looked at him with an expression of mingled admiration and resentment.

"He's fairer than I am," said Zou.

"He's a virgin," said Flossie.

Zou eyed her with a quizzical smile. "*Was*," she said.

"What?"

"You said: he *is* a virgin. I said: he *was*."

"Ah, yes. Well, as a matter of fact, I think he still is."

"Nonsense!"

"He's been asleep like that since two o'clock this morning," said Flossie acidly.

Philippe opened his eyes, he looked at the two women
leaning over him, grunted, and turned over on his face.

"Look," said Flossie.

She pulled down the bedclothes and revealed a white
and naked body. Zou rolled two large eyes.

"Yum-yum!" she exclaimed. "Cover it up or I might do
something silly."

Flossie slid a light hand over the boy's narrow hips, his
youthful, slim posteriors, and then drew up the bedclothes
with a sigh.

"Bring me," said M. Birnenschatz, "a Noilly-cassis."

He sank on to the seat and wiped his brow. Through the
glass of the revolving door he could keep an eye on the
entrance to his office.

"What will you have?" he said to Neu.

"The same," said Neu.

The waiter departed, Neu called him back: "Bring me
the *Information*."

They looked at each other in silence, then Neu suddenly
raised his arms in the air. "Alas, alas! My poor Birnenschatz!"

"Yes," said M. Birnenschatz.

The waiter filled their glasses and handed the paper
to Neu. Neu looked at the day's quotations, made a wry
face, and laid the paper on the table.

"Shocking," he said.

"Of course. What do you expect? They are waiting for
Hitler's speech."

M. Birnenschatz looked morosely round at the walls and

the mirrors. Normally he rather liked this cheerful, cosy little café; today he was annoyed that he felt so ill at ease there.

"We can only wait," he said. "Daladier has done what he could; so has Chamberlain. There's nothing to do now but wait. We shan't enjoy our dinner, and at half past eight we shall switch on the radio to listen to this speech. And wait for what?" he said abruptly, thumping on the table. "One man's good pleasure. One man. Business is at a standstill, the Bourse is collapsing, my clerks can't settle down to work, poor Sée is called up—all on account of one man; war and peace are in his hands. It's a disgrace to humanity."

Brunet got up; Mme Samboulier looked at him. He rather appealed to her; he would make love well, with no needless noise or fuss, and a sort of countrified deliberation.

"Won't you stay and dine?" she said, and pointing to the radio, she added: "By way of a digestive, I can offer you Hitler's speech."

"I've got an appointment at seven o'clock," said Brunet. "Besides, I don't give a damn for Hitler's speech."

Mme Samboulier looked puzzled.

"If capitalist Germany is to live," said Brunet, "she needs all the European markets; she must therefore forcibly eliminate all her industrial competitors. Germany *has to* make war," he added with emphasis; "and she *has to* lose it. If Hitler had been killed in 1914, we should be exactly where we are today."

"So," said Mme Samboulier, speaking with an effort, "this Czech business isn't a bluff?"

"Hitler may think it is," said Brunet, "but what Hitler thinks is of no importance whatever."

"He can still stop it," said M. Birnenschatz. "If he wishes, he can still stop it. All the trumps are in his hand: England doesn't want war, America is too far off, Poland will stand in with him; if he wished, he could be master of the world tomorrow without firing a shot. The Czechs have accepted the Franco-English plan; he has only to accept it too. If he gave that proof of moderation . . ."

"He can't draw back now," said Brunet. "The whole of Germany is behind him and pushing him on."

"But *we* can draw back," said Mme Samboulier.

Brunet looked at her and laughed. "True," he said, "you are a pacifist."

Neu turned the box upside down and the dominoes dropped on to the table.

"Alas," he said, "I fear Hitler's moderation. Do you realize the prestige he would get out of it?"

He leaned towards M. Birnenschatz and whispered in his ear. M. Birnenschatz drew back with annoyance; Neu couldn't say three words without whispering with a conspiratorial air, waving his hands.

"If he accepted the Franco-English plan, in three months Doriot would be in power."

"Doriot . . ." said M. Birnenschatz, shrugging his shoulders.

"Doriot or someone like him."

"And what then?"

"What about ourselves?" asked Neu in a still lower tone.

M. Birnenschatz looked at his friend's large melancholy mouth and felt his ears flush with anger:

"Anything is better than war," he said acidly.

"Give me your letter, the girl will mail it."

He put the envelope on the table, between a saucepan and a pewter plate: Mlle Ivich Serguine, 12 rue de la Mégisserie, Laon. Odette glanced at the address, but made no comment; she was tying up a large parcel.

"Now don't be impatient," she said. "It will soon be finished.

The kitchen was white and clean, like a room in a sanatorium. It smelt of resin and the sea.

"I've put in two chicken wings," said Odette, "and a little jelly, which I know you like, a few slices of brown bread, and some raw ham sandwiches. There's wine in the thermos. You can keep it; you can use it when you get there."

He tried to catch her eye, but she appeared to be intent upon the parcel. She hurried to the buffet, snipped off a long piece of string, and hurried back.

"Well," said Mathieu, "it's an admirable parcel."

The little maid laughed, but Odette did not reply. She put the string between her teeth and deftly turned the parcel over. The smell of resin suddenly filled Mathieu's nostrils, and for the first time since the evening before last he felt immersed in an atmosphere that he might soon regret—the peace of that afternoon in the kitchen, these quiet domestic tasks, the sunlight filtering through the awning and scattering on to the floor, and, beyond all that perhaps, his childhood, and a certain kind of placid, busy life that he had once for all rejected.

"Hold your finger here," said Odette.

He leaned over her bent head and pressed a finger on the string. He would have liked to say a few affectionate words to her, but Odette's voice did not invite affection. She looked up at him. "Would you like a few hard-boiled eggs? You could put them in your pockets."

She looked quite girlish. He wouldn't miss her. Perhaps because she was Jacques's wife. He would soon forget that demure face of hers. But he could have wished her to feel a little upset at his departure.

"No, thank you," he said. "No hard-boiled eggs."

She put the parcel in his arms. "There," she said. "A nice package."

"Will you come with me to the station?" he asked.

She shook her head. "I think not. Jacques will go with you. I imagine he would sooner be alone with you for the last few minutes."

"Then good-by," he said. "Will you write to me?"

"I just couldn't; mine are girls' letters, full of mistakes in spelling. No, I'll be sending you parcels."

"I wish you would write to me," he said.

"Well then, from time to time you may find a little note between a box of sardines and a box of soap."

He held out his hand and she pressed it hurriedly. Her hand was hot and dry. Vaguely he thought: "It's a pity." The long fingers slipped through his like warm sand. He smiled and went out of the kitchen. Jacques was on his knees in the drawing-room in front of his radio set, turning the knobs. Mathieu passed the door and walked slowly upstairs. He was not sorry to be going. As he approached his room, he heard a faint sound behind him and turned; it was Odette. She was standing on the top step, she was pale, and her eyes were on him.

"Odette!" he said.

She did not reply, she was looking at him with a set expression on her face. He felt embarrassed and slipped the parcel under his left arm to keep himself in countenance.

"Odette!" he repeated.

She approached him, her face wore an unguarded and prophetic look that he had never seen on it before.

"Good-by," she said.

She was quite near him. She closed her eyes and suddenly laid her lips on his. He tried to take her in his arms, but she eluded him. She had resumed her demure expression; and she went downstairs without looking round.

He entered his room and put the parcel in his suitcase, which was so full that he had to kneel on the lid to close it.

"What is it?" said Philippe.

He had started up and was looking at Flossie with terror-stricken eyes.

"It's only me, darling," said she.

He fell back again, lifting a hand to his forehead.

"I've got such a headache."

She opened the drawer of the bedside table and produced a glass tube of aspirin; he pulled out the drawer in the sideboard, took out a glass and a bottle of Pernod, put them on the presidential desk, and sank back on his chair. The airplane engine was still hammering in his head. He had a bare quarter of an hour in which to compose his nerves.

He poured some Pernod into the glass, picked up a carafe of water, and tilted it some distance above the glass. The liquid effervesced and eddied into a silvery froth. He unstuck a cigarette end from his lower lip and threw it into the waste-basket. I've done all I could. He felt exhausted. "France," he said to himself, "France . . ." and drank a mouthful of Pernod. "I've done all I could; now it's up to Hitler." He took another sip, clicked his tongue, and thought: "The position of France is clearly defined. And now I can only wait." He was exhausted; he stretched his legs out under the table, and thought with something resembling satisfaction: "I can do nothing but wait." Like everyone else. The die is cast. He had said: "If the Czech frontiers are violated, France will keep her engagements." And Chamberlain had answered: "If, in consequence of those obligations, the French forces become actively engaged in the hostilities against Germany, we shall feel it our duty to support them."

Sir Nevile Henderson came forward, Sir Horace Wilson stood stiffly erect behind him; Sir Nevile Henderson handed the message to the Chancellor of the Reich; the Chancellor took the message and began to read it. When he had finished, the Chancellor said to Sir Nevile Henderson:

"Is this message from Mr. Chamberlain?"

Daladier drank a little more Pernod, sighed, and Sir Nevile Henderson replied concisely: "Yes, from Mr. Chamberlain." Daladier got up and locked the bottle of

Pernod in the sideboard drawer; the Chancellor said in his rasping voice: "You can consider my speech this evening as a reply to Mr. Chamberlain's message."

"What a stupid ass!" thought Daladier. "What is he going to say?" His temples were faintly flushed from what he had drunk, and he thought: "Events are slipping out of my grasp." A sort of deep repose had come upon him. "I have done everything," he thought, "to avoid war; and now, war and peace are out of my hands." There was no further decision to take, nothing to do but wait; like everybody else, like the loafer at a street-corner. He smiled, he *was* that loafer, he had been stripped of his responsibilities; the position of France is clearly defined. . . . Ineffable repose. He stared at the dark flowers on the carpet and felt a little dizzy. Peace—war. I have done all I could to preserve peace. But he now wondered whether he didn't actually want to be swept away like a straw in this vast torrent, whether he didn't long for that tremendous holiday—war.

He looked about him in bewilderment and exclaimed: "I haven't gone." She had opened the shutters and was now back beside the bed, leaning over him. He felt her warm body and inhaled her fishy odor.

"What have you been up to, you little stinker?"

She had laid one of her sinewy black hands upon his chest. The sunlight made an oily patch on her left cheek, Philippe looked at her and felt profoundly humiliated; she had wrinkles at the corners of her eyes and mouth. "She was so pretty in the light," he thought. She breathed in his face, and slipped her pink tongue between his lips. "I haven't gone," he thought. He said to her: "You're not quite so young as all that."

She made an odd grimace, closed her mouth, and said: "Not so young as you are, stinker."

He tried to get out of bed, but she held him firmly; he was naked and defenseless, and he felt miserable.

"Little stinker," she said, "my little stinker."

The black hands slid slowly down his sides. After all, he thought, it isn't given to everybody to lose his virginity with a Negress. He sank back, and a whirl of black and gray skirts approached within a few inches of his face. The man was now less vociferous; the sounds he uttered were more like gasps and gurgles. A shoe appeared above his head, he saw a pointed sole, with a clod of earth still sticking to the heel; the sole descended with a creak beside his stretcher; it belonged to a large black buttoned shoe. He raised his eyes, saw a cassock, and high up in the air two hairy nostrils above the twin neckbands of a cleric. Blanchard whispered in his ear: "Our chum there must be pretty bad or they wouldn't have sent for a priest."

"What's the matter with him?" asked Charles.

"I don't know, but Pierrot says he's a goner."

Why not I? thought Charles. He surveyed his life and thought: Why not I? Two railway men passed close to him, he recognized the fabric of their trousers; he heard behind him the priest's calm, unctuous voice; the sick man had ceased to groan. "Perhaps he's dead," he thought. The nurse passed, holding a basin in her hands. "Madame," he said timidly, "you couldn't go now, could you?"

She looked down at him, and flushed with anger. "It's you again, is it? What do you want?"

"You couldn't send someone to the women's place? Her name is Catherine."

"For God's sake keep quiet," she replied. "That's the third time you've asked me."

"It's only to ask her last name and tell her mine; it wouldn't be much trouble."

"There's a man dying," she said roughly. "Do you suppose I've got time to bother about such nonsense?"

She departed and the man again began to moan. Charles felt quite unnerved; he swung his mirror round and observed an array of bodies stretched out side by side and, beyond them, the vast posterior view of the priest kneeling beside the sick man. Above them, a mantelpiece with a mirror in a frame. The priest got up; the porters leaned over the body and carried it away.

"Is he dead?" asked Blanchard.

Blanchard's stretcher had no rotating mirror.

"I don't know," said Charles.

The procession passed close to them, raising a cloud of dust. Charles began to cough, then he saw the bent backs of the porters making their way towards the door. A skirt swirled up to him and suddenly hung motionless. He heard the nurse's voice:

"We are completely cut off here, we get no news. How are things going, Monsieur le Curé?"

"Badly," said he. "Badly. Hitler is going to speak this evening, I don't know what he'll say, but I believe it will be war."

His voice dropped in layers on Charles's face. Charles burst out laughing.

"What's the joke?" asked Blanchard.

"The joke is that the parson said there's going to be a war."

"I don't think that's a joke," said Blanchard.

"I do."

"They'll get their war—right up the butt." He will still be laughing. About five feet above his head it was war, tempest, outraged honor, patriotic duty; but on the floor there was neither war nor peace—nothing but the misery and shame of the sub-men, stricken and laid upon their backs. Bonnet didn't want it; Champetier de Ribes did; Daladier looked at the carpet, it was a nightmare, he could not shake off that sense of dizziness behind his ears; let it break out at last; let the big bad wolf of Berlin declare for war that very evening. He scraped his shoe against the floor; Charles felt a qualm rise from his stomach to his head; shame, a pleasant and comforting sense of shame, that was all the feeling that remained. The nurse had nearly reached the door, she stepped over a body, and the abbé stood back to let her pass.

"Madame!" cried Charles. "Madame!"

She turned, a tall and buxom female, with a handsome face, a faint mustache, and angry eyes.

"Madame! Madame! Give me the pan—quick."

Here he is! The thrusting crowd surged forward on to the policeman, who stepped back a pace and stretched out his arms. "Hurrah! Here he is!" they shouted. He walked with stiff unhurried steps, arm in arm with his wife. Fred was touched—just like Father and Mother on a Sunday outing in Greenwich; and he too shouted: "Hurrah!" It was nice to see them there, so placid; who could possibly feel afraid after seeing them there, taking a little afternoon walk like an amicable old married couple? He gripped his briefcase, waved it over his head, and shouted: "Hurrah for peace!" They both turned in his direction and Mr. Chamberlain smiled at him; Fred felt a sense of ease and peace moving right down into his heart; he was safe, protected, governed, fortified, and old Chamberlain still found it possible to walk quietly through the streets, just like anybody else, and smile at him personally. Everybody was cheering all around him, Fred watched Mr. Chamberlain's gaunt back, as he walked away with his rather ecclesiastical stride, and thought: "It's England," and the tears came into his eyes. Little Sadie bent down and took a photograph under the policeman's arm.

"Line up, madame, you must line up like everyone else."

"Line up for a *Paris-Soir?*"

"Certainly! And I shall be surprised if you get a copy."

She could not believe her ears. "What do you take me for? I'm not going to stand in line for the *Paris-Soir;* I've never lined up for a newspaper in my life!"

She turned her back on them as the cyclist arrived with

his bundles of papers. He put them down on the table beside the kiosk, and they began to count them.

"Here they are! Here they are!"

The crowds eddied round the counter. "Look here," said the newspaper woman, "are you going to let me count them?"

"Don't push, please," said a rather stately dame; "don't push, I tell you."

"I'm not pushing, madame," said a short, fat man. "I'm being pushed, which is not the same thing."

"I won't have my wife insulted," said a short and skinny individual.

The lady in mourning turned to Emilie. "That's the third row I've seen this morning."

"Yes," said Emilie, "everyone is so nervous lately."

The plane was nearing the mountains; Gomez looked at them, and then he looked down at the rivers and the fields beneath him, there was a little round town on his left; it was all so absurd and diminutive; it was the green and yellow land of France, with its spreading pastures and its quiet rivers. "Good-by. Good-by." They would plunge between the mountains, good-by to *tournedos Rossini*, coronas, lovely women, he would soon be planing down towards the red and naked sun, towards the land of blood. Good-by! Good-by! All the Frenchmen of France were there beneath him, in the little round town, in the fields, by the seashores; eighteen thirty-five o'clock, they were scurrying about like ants, waiting for Hitler's speech. Three thousand feet below me they are waiting for Hitler's speech. I am not waiting for anything. In a quarter of an hour he would no longer see those pleasant meadows; vast rocks would stand between him and that land of fear and avarice. In a quarter of an hour he would alight among a race of lean men with vivid gestures and hard eyes, *his own* men. He was happy, and indeed there was a lump in his throat. The mountains were approaching, they were brown by now. "How am I going to get back to Barcelona?" thought he.

"Come in," said Zézette.

It was a rather stout and very pretty lady in a straw hat, and a tailor-made suit. She looked round her, dilating her nostrils, and smiled a ready, friendly smile. "Madame Suzanne Tailleur?"

"Yes," said Zézette, rather puzzled.

She had got up. She remembered that her eyes must be rather red, so she stood with her back to the window. The lady looked at her and blinked. At a closer view, she appeared older, and she looked exhausted.

"I hope I'm not disturbing you."

"Not at all," said Zézette. "Do sit down."

The lady bent over the chair and looked at it, then sat down. She sat up very straight and did not touch the chairback.

"I must have walked up forty flights of stairs since this morning. And people don't always think of offering you a chair."

Zézette noticed that her thimble was still on her finger. She took it off and threw it into her workbox. At that moment the beefsteak began to sputter in the oven. She dashed to the stove and turned out the gas; but the smell remained.

"I'm afraid you were just going to have your lunch."

"Oh, I'm not in a hurry," said Zézette. She looked at the lady and felt torn between embarrassment and a desire to laugh.

"Is your husband called up?"

"He went yesterday morning."

"They are all going," said the lady. "It's dreadful. You must be in rather a difficulty—financially. . . ."

"I think I shall go back to my old job," said Zézette. "I was a flower-seller."

The lady shook her head. "It's too, too dreadful!" She looked so woebegone that Zézette felt a thrill of sympathy.

"Has your husband gone too?"

"I'm not married." She looked at Zézette and added quickly: "But I have two brothers who may be called up."

"What is it you want?" asked Zézette rather curtly.

"Well," said the lady, "I'll tell you." She smiled. "I don't know what your views are, and what I'm going to ask you is quite outside politics. Do you smoke? Have a cigarette?"

Zézette hesitated. "I don't mind if I do," she said.

She was standing beside the gas oven, and her hands were grasping the edge of the table behind her back. The smell of the beefsteak was now blended with the visitor's perfume. The lady handed her case to Zézette, who took a step forward. The visitor had slim white fingers and manicured nails. Zézette took a cigarette. She looked at her fingers and the lady's fingers and wished she would go away soon. They lit their cigarettes and the lady said:

"Don't you think this war ought to be stopped at any price?"

Zézette stepped back to the stove and looked at her suspiciously. She felt uneasy. She noticed some garters and a pair of pants lying on the table.

"Don't you think," said the lady, "that if we combined forces . . ."

Zézette walked nonchalantly across the room with a negligent air; when she reached the table, she said: "Who do you mean by 'we'?"

"We women!" said the lady with emphasis.

"We women," repeated Zézette. She hurriedly opened a drawer, threw the garters and pants into it, then turned to the lady with an air of relief.

"We women? But what can we do?"

The lady was smoking like a man, exhaling the smoke from her nose; Zézette looked at her tailored suit, her jade necklace, and felt odd at saying "we" to her.

"You can't do anything alone," said the lady amiably. "But you are not alone; at this moment there are four million women afraid for the life of someone dear to them. On the floor below, it is Madame Panier, whose brother and husband have just gone and who has six children. On the other side of the street it's the baker's wife. At Passy it's the Duchesse de Cholet."

"Oh—the Duchesse de Cholet—" murmured Zézette.

"Well?"

"It's not the same thing."

"What isn't the same thing? Because some women go about in cars while others do their marketing themselves? Ah, madame, I'm a strong supporter of a better social organization. But do you imagine that war will give us that? Class questions count so little in the face of the danger that now threatens us. We are women first of all, madame, women attacked in what they hold most dear. Suppose we all joined hands and shouted, all together: 'We won't have war.' Come now—you surely want him to come back?"

Zézette shook her head: it seemed to her absurd that this lady should be addressing her as madame. "War can't be stopped," she said.

The lady flushed. "And why not?" she asked.

Zézette shrugged her shoulders. So this dame wanted to stop war. Others, like Maurice, wanted to abolish poverty. And in the end nobody stopped anything.

"Because," she said, "it can't be stopped."

"Oh, but you mustn't say that," said the visitor reproachfully. "It is people who say that sort of thing who are responsible for wars. Besides, you must think a little of other people. Whatever you do, you must be loyal to your sex."

Zézette did not answer. She was clutching her cigarette, which had now gone out, rather nervously between her fingers and felt as though she had gone back to school.

"You can't refuse to sign it, madame," said the lady; "you really can't."

She had taken a sheet of paper out of her bag, and held it under Zézette's nose.

"What's that?" asked Zézette.

"It's a petition against the war," said the lady. "We are collecting supporters by the thousand."

Zézette read in an undertone:

"The women of France, signatories of the present petition, declare that they rely on the Government of the Republic to safeguard peace by *every possible means*. They affirm their absolute conviction that war, whatever may be the circumstances in which it breaks out, is always a crime. Negotiations, exchanges of views, yes; recourse to violence, no. For universal peace, against war in all its forms, this September 22, 1938. The League of French Mothers and Wives."

She turned the page over; the back of it was covered with signatures, squeezed one below another, horizontal, oblique, sloping up and sloping down, in black ink, violet ink, and blue ink. Some bold and sprawling, in large angular letters, others in a miserly elongated script, squeezed sheepishly into a corner. Beside each signature there was an address: Mme Jeanne Plémeux, 6 rue d'Aubignac; Mme Solange Péres, 142 avenue de Saint-Ouen. Zézette surveyed the names of all these madames. They had all bent over that sheet of paper, some with children yelling in the next room, others had signed in a boudoir with a gold fountain pen. Here were all their names side by side and looking all alike. Mme Suzanne Tailleur: she had only to borrow a pen from the lady, and she too would become a madame, her name would take its place, looking equally forbidding and important, underneath the others.

"What are you going to do with that?" she asked.

"When we have got enough signatures, we shall send a delegation of women to take them to the Prime Minister's office."

Mme Suzanne Tailleur. She *was* Mme Suzanne Tailleur.

Maurice kept on lecturing her on class solidarity. And now it seemed that she had obligations in common with the Duchesse de Cholet. She thought: "I can't refuse to sign."

Flossie laid her elbows on the pillow: "Well, little stinker, how was it?"

"Quite nice," said Philippe. "It must be even nicer when you don't have a headache."

"I must get up," said Flossie. "I'll get a bite somewhere, and then go along to the Cubaine. Are you coming?"

"I'm too tired," said Philippe. "You must go without me."

"You'll wait for me here, won't you? Promise me you'll wait."

"Certainly," said Philippe with a frown. "Hurry along now, I'll wait."

"Well," said the lady, "will you sign?"

"I haven't got a pen," said Zézette.

The lady handed her a fountain pen. Zézette took it and signed at the bottom of the page. She wrote her name in a copybook hand, and her address beside it, then looked up at the lady; she felt as though something was going to happen.

Nothing happened at all. The lady got up. She took the paper and eyed it attentively.

"Admirable," said she. "Well, my day's work is finished."

Zézette opened her mouth; she felt she had a mass of questions to ask. But the questions did not come. She merely said: "So you are going to take that to Daladier?"

"Certainly," said the lady.

She waved the paper for a moment, then folded it up and slipped it into her bag. Zézette's heart turned over when the bag was shut. The lady raised her head and looked her straight in the eyes.

"Thank you," she said. "Thank you for *his* sake. Thank you for us all. You are a noble woman, Madame Tailleur."

She held out her hand. "And now," she said, "I must run along."

Zézette shook her hand, after having wiped her own on her apron. She felt bitterly deceived.

"Is—is that all?" she asked.

The lady laughed. She had teeth like pearls. Zézette repeated to herself: "Class solidarity." But the word had no longer any meaning.

"Yes, for the moment, that's all."

She walked briskly to the door, opened it, threw a farewell smile at Zézette, and disappeared. Her scent still pervaded the room. Zézette listened while the sound of her footsteps died away, and sniffed two or three times. She felt as if she had been robbed of something. She went to the window, opened it, and leaned out. A car stood by the pavement. The lady emerged from the house, opened the door of the car, got in, and the car started. "I've made a damn fool of myself," thought Zézette. The car turned into the avenue de Saint-Ouen and disappeared, carrying off her signature and the lovely perfumed lady, never to be seen again. Zézette sighed, shut the window, and relit the gas. The fat began to sputter, the smell of cooking meat drowned the perfume, and Zézette thought: "If ever Maurice get's to hear of this, I'll be in for something."

"Mummy, I'm hungry."

"What is the time?" the child's mother said to Mathieu. She was a good-looking, buxom Marseillaise with a shadow of a mustache.

Mathieu glanced at his wrist-watch. "Twenty minutes past eight."

The woman produced from between her legs a basket secured by an iron rod. "All right, you little torment, you shall have something to eat."

She turned towards Mathieu. "She would make a saint swear."

Mathieu responded with a vaguely affable smile. "Twenty minutes past eight," he thought. "In ten minutes Hitler is going to speak. They are in the drawing-room,

Jacques will have been fiddling with the knobs on the radio for the last half-hour."

The woman had set the basket on the seat; she opened it, Jacques exclaimed: "I've got it—I've got Stuttgart!"

Odette was standing near him with her hand on his shoulder. She heard a confused hum—as though a blast of air from a long vaulted hall seemed to strike her in the face. Mathieu edged along the seat to make room for the parcel; he had not left Juan-les-Pins. He was near Odette, in contact with Odette, but blind and dead, the train was carrying his ears and eyes to Marseille. He felt no love for her, his feeling was something quite different: she had looked at him as though he was not wholly dead. He wanted to give expression to the formless affection that weighed upon him; he tried to recall Odette's face, but it eluded him. Jacques's face appeared twice instead of hers, Mathieu finally caught a glimpse of a motionless form in an armchair, an inch or two of neck bent forwards, and an expression of attention on a face devoid of mouth and nose.

"Just in time," said Jacques, turning round towards her. "He hasn't started yet."

My eyes are here. He saw the basket: the contents were wrapped in a handsome red and black striped cloth. Mathieu watched the sunburned neck for another moment or two, then let it go: so little for so engrossing an affection. It vanished into the shadows, and the cloth assumed a capacious existence, occupying his eyes and scattering all other ideas and thoughts. *My eyes are here.* A muffled buzz made him start.

She turned to Mathieu with a deprecating laugh. "It's the alarm clock. I always set it at half past eight."

The little girl hurriedly opened a suitcase, thrust her hands into it, and the buzz ceased. Half past eight, he is just entering the Sportpalast. I am at Juan-les-Pins. I am at Berlin, but *my eyes are here.* Somewhere a long, black car had stopped at a door, and brown-shirted men were getting out of it. *Somewhere* to the northeast, on his right and behind him; but *here* a small checked cloth blocked the view. Plump ringed fingers deftly pulled at its corners, and it disappeared, Mathieu observed a thermos lying on its side and a packet of bread and butter; he was hungry. I am at Juan-les-Pins, I am in Berlin, I am in Paris, I have no life left, nor any future. But *here* I am hungry. Here, beside this large, dark-haired lady and this little girl. He got up, lifted his suitcase down from the rack, and felt for Odette's parcel. Then he sat down again, took out his knife, and cut the string; he ate hurriedly, as though he wanted to have finished in time to listen to Hitler's speech. He entered; a tremendous clamor shook the windows and died away, he raised a hand. *Somewhere* there were ten thousand weaponed men, head erect, arm uplifted. *Somewhere,* at his back, Odette was leaning over a radio set. He speaks, he says: "Fellow citizens," and his voice has already ceased to be his own, it has become an international voice; heard at Brest-Litovsk, Prague, Oslo, Tangier, Cannes, Morlaix, and on the great white steamer plying between Casablanca and Marseille.

"Are you sure you've got Stuttgart?" asked Odette. "I can't hear a thing."

"Hush," said Jacques. "Yes, I'm sure."

Lola stopped outside the entrance to the Casino.

"See you soon, then," she said.

"Sing your best," said Boris.

"Sure. Where are you off to, darling?"

"To the Bar Basque," said Boris. "There are some fellows there who don't know any German and have asked me to translate Hitler's speech."

"B-r-r-r," said Lola with a shudder; "that won't be very amusing."

"I rather like translating," said Boris.

He speaks! Mathieu made a violent effort to *hear* him, then he suddenly felt hollow and switched his mind off.

He ate; the little girl opposite was munching a jam sandwich; nothing could be heard but the rhythmic panting of the engines, it was a honeyed evening, softly intimate. Mathieu turned his head and looked at the sea through the car window. The pink arc of dusk was closing down upon it. And yet a voice was piercing that sugar-coated egg. An all-pervading voice; the train thrusts into it, and it is in the train, under the child's feet, in the lady's hair, in my pocket, and if I had a radio set I could make it burst forth from the luggage rack or under the seat. It is there, enormous, it drowns the rumble of the train, it shakes the windows—and I do not hear it. He was tired, he noticed a sail far away over the sea, and he could think now of nothing but that sail.

"Listen!" said Jacques triumphantly. "Listen!"

A vast din suddenly burst forth from the radio. Odette drew back a step, it was almost unendurable. "What a lot of them there are," she thought, "and how they admire him!" Thousands of miles away, tens of thousands of damned souls. Their voices filled the placid, family drawing-room—and it was her own destiny that was there at issue.

"Here he is," said Jacques. "Here he is!"

The uproar gradually died down; a few harsh and nasal voices came through, then silence fell, and Odette realized that he was about to speak. Boris swung open the door of the bar, and the proprietor signed to him to hurry.

"Come along," said he. "It's just going to begin."

There were three of them, with their elbows on the zinc counter: Charlier, from Marseille, a compositor from Rouen, and a tall, powerful, clumsily built traveling salesman in sewing-machines, whose name was Chomis.

"Evening," said Boris in an undertone.

They threw him a cursory greeting as he approached the radio. He respected their cutting short their dinner to listen to what would certainly be an unpleasant performance.

They were stout fellows, who looked things in the face.

He was standing with his two hands on the table, he looked at the expanse of sea, and he could hear the sound of the sea. He raised his right hand, and the sea grew calm. He said:

"Fellow citizens,

"There is a limit beyond which it is not possible to yield, because to do so would be culpable weakness. Ten millions of Germans situated outside the Reich in two great organized territories wanted to re-enter the Reich. I should not have the right to appear at the bar of German history if I had been willing merely to ignore their claims. Nor should I have the moral right to be the Führer of this people. I have made sufficient sacrifices and renunciations. That was the limit that I could not pass. The plebiscite in Austria has shown how well founded was this feeling. That was a testimony not expected by the rest of the world. But we have already seen that, for the democracies, a plebiscite becomes useless and even deleterious when it does not produce the result they had expected. None the less this problem was settled in a way that satisfied the great German people.

"And now we have before us the last problem that has to be settled, and one *that will be settled.*"

The sea surged into a heaving mass of waters, and he remained for a moment without speaking, surveying its enormous waves. Odette pressed a hand against her chest —the roaring of a crowd always made her heart leap. She leaned over Jacques's ear, he was still frowning and listening with extreme attention, although Hitler had ceased speaking for some seconds. She said to him, without much hope:

"What is he saying?"

Jacques pretended to understand German, having spent three months at Hanover, and for the last ten years had assiduously listened to all the Berlin orators; he even sub-

scribed to the *Frankfurter Zeitung* for its financial articles.
But the information he gave about what he had read or
heard always remained extremely vague. He shrugged his
shoulders.

"Always the same thing. He talked about sacrifices and
the happiness of the German people."

"He agrees to make sacrifices?" asked Odette eagerly.
"Does that mean that he would make concessions?"

"Yes—no. It was left very much in the air."

He reached out a hand and Karl stopped shouting: it
was a command. He turned to his right and left, muttering: "Listen! Listen!" He felt as though the Führer's un-
uttered command had transfixed him and was taking shape
in his mouth. "Listen!" he said. "Listen!" He was merely
an instrument, a sounding-board; he was quivering with
ecstasy. Everybody was silent, the entire hall was engulfed
in silence and darkness; Hess, Göring, and Goebbels had
disappeared, there was no longer anyone in the world but
Karl and his Führer. The Führer was speaking in front of
a huge red swastika'd standard, he was speaking to Karl,
and to him alone. One voice, one sole voice in all the
world. He speaks to me, he thinks for me, he decides for
me. My Führer.

"This is the last territorial claim that I have to formulate
in Europe, but it is a claim from which I shall not deviate
and which I shall realize, if God wills."

He paused. Then Karl understood that he had permis-
sion to shout, and he shouted with all his might. Everybody began to shout, Karl's voice swelled, rose to the
vaulted ceiling, and rattled the very windows. He was
ablaze with joy, he had ten thousand mouths, and he felt
himself historic.

"Oh, shut your hole!" shouted Mimile into the radio. He
turned to Robert and said: "What a gang! Those guys are
never happy except when they can yell in company. Apparently they do it to amuse themselves. They have big

businesses in Berlin that hold twenty thousand people, they meet there on a Sunday and sing in chorus and drink beer."

The instrument continued to bellow. "Look," said Robert, "let's cut it off."

They twisted the knob, the voices died away, the room seemed suddenly to emerge from shadow and enclosed them once again, a small and quiet room, the brandy on the table, they had only needed to turn a knob and all those clamors of the damned had gone back into their box, a lovely placid evening had come through the window, a French evening; they were among Frenchmen.

"This Czech state was established on the foundation of a lie. The author of that lie was called Beneš."

Tumult from the radio.

"This Herr Beneš appeared at Versailles and began by affirming the existence of a Czechoslovak nation."

Laughter from the wireless. The rasping voice continued:

"He was obliged to invent that lie in order to confer more weight and importance on the meager total of his fellow citizens. And the Anglo-Saxon statesmen, who have never been sufficiently familiar with ethnical and geographical questions, did not then think it necessary to verify Herr Beneš's affirmations.

"As this State did not appear likely to survive, three and a half million Germans were simply included in it, in contravention of their right to self-determination and of their desire to exercise that right."

The radio shouted: "Shame! Shame!" and M. Birnenschatz exclaimed: "Liar! Those Germans were not taken from Germany!" She looked at her father, now quite red with indignation, smoking a cigar in his armchair, she looked at her mother and her sister Ivy and almost hated them. "How *can* they listen!"

"As though that were not enough, a million Magyars

had also to be included, together with a mass of sub-Carpathian Russians, and finally several hundred thousand Poles.

"Such is the State that was later called Czechoslovakia, in contravention of the national right of self-determination and of the clearly expressed will of the peoples whose rights were thus violated. In speaking to you thus, I naturally sympathize with the fate of all these oppressed peoples; I sympathize with the fate of the Slovaks, the Poles, the Hungarians, and the Ukrainians, but I am of course speaking only of the destiny of my Germans."

A vast clamor flooded the great hall. How can they listen to this stuff? The yells of "*Heil! Heil!*" made him feel positively sick. "After all, we are Jews," she reflected with annoyance, "we don't have to listen to our executioner. It's all right for him, I have always heard him say that the Jews no longer existed. But *she*," she reflected, looking at her mother, "*she*, she knows she is a Jewess, she feels it and she stays and listens." Mme Birnenschatz, who rather enjoyed prophesying, had exclaimed two days before: "It's war, my children, and a *lost* war, the Jewish nation might as well pick up its begging-bag again." At the moment she was dozing through the uproar, her painted eyes closed from time to time, and her great head, crowned with jet-black hair, nodded. The voice continued, dominating the storm.

"And here is this truly cynical outcome. This State, which is governed by a minority, obliges its nationals to pursue a policy that will compel them one day to fire upon their brothers."

She got up. These raucous words, wrenched from a congested throat, were knife-thrusts. This man has tortured Jews; even while he speaks, thousands of them are agonizing in concentration camps, and here we are, allowing that voice to bellow in the very room in which, only

yesterday, we received our cousin Dachauer, whose eyelids had been burned away.

"Beneš says to the Germans: 'If I make war on Germany,
you will have to fire on Germans. And if you refuse, you
will be traitors and I will have you shot.' And he makes
the same demand on the Hungarians and the Poles."

The voice was there, enormous, the voice of hatred personified—this one man versus Ella. The great plain of
Germany, the mountains of France, had dissolved, he confronted her as an absolute enemy, outside space, he was
threshing about in that box of his—he's looking at me, he
sees me. She turned to her mother, to Ivy; but they had
suddenly receded. She could still see them but not touch
them. Paris also had drifted out of reach, the light from
the windows fell dead upon the carpet. Contacts between
people and things were imperceptibly disintegrating, she
was alone in the world with that voice.

"On the 20th of February of this year I declared to the
Reichstag that the conditions in which ten million Germans outside our frontiers now live must be changed. But
Beneš has acted in a contrary sense. He started a regime of
even more complete repression."

He was addressing her as though they two were alone,
his eyes glaring into hers, his temper rising, intent upon
terrifying and injuring her. She stood fascinated, her eyes
fixed on the speaker. She could not hear his words, but his
voice flayed her.

"A still greater terror . . . An era of dissolution. . . ."

She turned abruptly and left the room. The voice pursued her into the hall, now blurred and flat, but still envenomed; Ella darted into her room and locked the door.
In the drawing-room the threats continued; but she could
hear no more than a confused murmur. She sank on to a
chair. Was there no one, the mother of a tortured Jew, the
wife of a murdered Communist, who would pick up a re-

volver and shoot the man? She clenched her fists—had she
been a German, she was sure she would have killed him.

Mathieu got up, took one of Jacques's cigars out of his
weatherproof pocket, and slid back the door of the compartment.

"If that's on my account," said the lady from Marseille,
"don't bother; my husband smokes a pipe and I'm used
to it."

"Thank you," said Mathieu. "But I want to stretch my
legs a bit."

He was, in fact, tired of looking at her, the child, and the
basket. He strolled along the corridor, stopped, and lit his
cigar. The sea was blue and calm, he was gliding alongside
it, and he thought: "What is happening to me? *This man's
reply was more than ever: 'Shoot, arrest, incarcerate!'—
and that for everyone who for any reason whatsoever
doesn't entirely please him.*" Mathieu wanted to try to
understand. Nothing had ever happened to him that he
did not understand; it was his only strength, his sole defense, his ultimate pride. He looked at the sea, and
thought: "I do not understand—*then came my Nuremberg
demand. That demand was absolutely clear: for the fir—*
and here I am, off to the war." Nothing very odd about
that, and yet it baffled him. In regard to what concerned
him personally, everything was plain and simple: he had
played and lost, his life lay behind him, wasted. I am
leaving nothing; I regret nothing, not even Odette, not
even Ivich, I am nobody. Remained the event itself. *I declared that the right of self-determination ought at last,
twenty years after President Wilson's declarations, to be
applied for the benefit of these three and a half millions*
all that had befallen him up to date had been within his
compass as a man, the little setbacks and catastrophes, he
had seen them coming, and he had faced them. When he
took the money from Lola's room he had seen the notes,
he had touched them, he had inhaled the perfume hover-

ing in the room, and when he had thrown Marcelle over, he had looked her in the eyes while he was talking to her; his difficulties had been solely with himself; he could say to himself: there I was right, or there I was wrong; he could judge himself. This had now become impossible *and again Herr Beneš has given his reply: more dead, more imprisonments, more—* He thought: I am going off to war, and it means nothing. Something had happened that puzzled him. And that was the war. Not so much that it puzzles me as that it *isn't there*. Where is it? Everywhere: it turns up everywhere, the train plunges into war, Gomez lands amidst war, those summer visitors in white linen suits are walking up and down in war, there isn't a heartthrob that doesn't lend it vigor, nor a consciousness that isn't transfixed by it. And yet, like Hitler's voice, it fills this train though I can't hear it: I *stated categorically to Herr Chamberlain that what we now consider the sole prospect of a solution;* from time to time it seemed almost within touch, no matter where—in, say, the sauce on a *tournedos,* but try to touch it, and it isn't there; nothing remains but a dish of meat covered with sauce. "Ah well," he thought, "you would have to be everywhere at the same time."

My Führer, my Führer, you talk and I am changed into stone, I have no thought nor will, I am nothing but your voice, I would wait for him on the way out and aim at his heart, but I am primarily the mouthpiece of the Germans, and it is for these Germans that I have spoken, making plain that I am not disposed to remain a calm and inactive spectator while this madman from Prague thinks he can, I shall be that martyr, I did not start for Switzerland, at present I can do nothing now but endure that marytrdom, I swear I'll be that martyr, I swear, I swear, I swear, hush, said Gomez, we are listening to the clown's speech.

"This is Radio-Paris; in a minute or two we shall be transmitting the French translation of the first part of Chancellor Hitler's speech."

"You see," said Germain Chabot, "you see. It wasn't worth while going out and running around for two hours in search of an *Intransigeant*. I told you so; they always do that."

Mme Chabot put her knitting in the workbasket, and drew up her chair.

"So we shall know what he said. I hate listening to this sort of thing," she said; "it gives me a sinking feeling in the stomach. Don't you feel that way?"

"Yes," said Germain Chabot.

The radio burst into a roar, then died away in rumblings, and Chabot grabbed his wife's arm. "Listen," he said to her.

They leaned slightly forward, listening intently, and someone began to sing the *Cucaracha*.

"You're sure that you've got Radio-Paris?" asked Mme Chabot.

"Sure."

"Then we must just be patient."

The voice sang three verses, then the record stopped.

"Here we go," said Chabot.

There followed a faint crackling sound, and a Hawaiian orchestra started to play *Honey Moon*.

You would have to be everywhere. Gloomily he surveyed the end of his cigar: everywhere, otherwise you get fooled. I have been fooled. I *am* a soldier going off to the war. That is what one ought to *see*: the war and the soldier. The stump of a cigar, white villas by the seashore, the monotonous sliding of the coaches along the rails, and the too familiar traveler, Fez, Marrakech, Madrid, Perugia, Siena, Rome, Prague, London, smoking for the thousandth time in the corridor of a third-class car. No war, no soldier; you would have to be everywhere, I would have *to be seen from everywhere,* from Berlin as a three-millionth part of the French Army, and with the eyes of Gomez, as one of those French hounds that have to be kicked into battle. I

would have to be seen *with the eyes of war*. But where are
the eyes of war? I am *here*—large, clear surfaces glide past
my eyes, I am preternaturally clear-sighted, I see—and
yet I grope blindly for my whereabouts, and each of my
movements lights a bulb or sets a bell ringing in a world I
do not see. Zézette had closed the shutters, but the fading
daylight still filtered through the crevices, she felt worn
out, she threw her slip on a chair and slipped into bed
naked, I always sleep so well when I'm worried; but when
she got between the sheets, it was in that bed that Momo
had caressed her two nights ago, as soon as she began to
drop off, he took her and he crushed her, and if she opened
her eyes he was no longer there, he was asleep far away
in his barracks, and then there was that blasted radio blar-
ing away in a foreign language, it was the set belonging
to the Heinemanns, the refugee Germans on the first floor,
a raucous, viperine voice that rasped the nerves, it will not
stop—Oh, will it never stop! Mathieu envied Gomez and
then said to himself: Gomez doesn't *see* more of it than I
do, he is struggling against what he cannot see—and he
ceased to envy him. What does he see? Walls, a telephone
on his desk, his orderly officer's face. He *makes* war, he
does not see it. And, indeed, in making war we all join in
making it; I raise my hand, I draw at my cigar, and I *make*
war; Sarah curses men's folly, she clasps Pablo in her
arms: she *is making* war. Odette is making war when she
wraps ham sandwiches in a piece of paper. The war takes
and embraces everything, war preserves every thought and
every gesture, and no one can see it, not even Hitler. No
one. He repeated: No one—and suddenly he caught a
sight of it. It was a strange entity, and one indeed beyond
the reach of thought.

"This is Radio-Paris; in a few moments we shall be transmitting the French translation of the first part of Chancellor Hitler's speech."

They did not move. They looked at each other out of the

corners of their eyes, and when Rina Ketty began to sing *J'attendrai,* they smiled at each other. But at the end of the first verse Mme Chabot burst into a laugh.

"*J'attendrai!*" she said. "Very appropriate. They're just making fools of us."

A vast entity, a planet, in a space of a hundred million dimensions; three-dimensional beings could not so much as imagine it. And yet each dimension was an autonomous consciousness. Try to look directly at that planet, it would disintegrate into tiny fragments, and nothing but consciousnesses would be left. A hundred million free consciousnesses, each aware of walls, the glowing stump of a cigar, familiar faces, and each constructing its destiny on its own responsibility. And yet each of those consciousnesses, by imperceptible contacts and insensible changes, realizes its existence as a cell in a gigantic and invisible coral. War: everyone is free, and yet the die is cast. It is there, it is everywhere, it is the totality of all my thoughts, of all Hitler's words, of all Gomez's acts; but no one is there to add it up. It exists solely for God. But God does not exist. And yet the war exists.

"And I have made quite plain that henceforward German patience has a limit. I have made plain the fact that it is a characteristic of the German people to be very patient, but that when the moment comes, a decision must be made."

"What is he saying?" asked Chomis.

"He is saying that German patience has its limits," explained Boris.

"So has ours," said Charlier.

Everybody began to bellow at the radio, and Herrera came into the room.

"Hello!" said he, catching sight of Gomez. "Well? Had a good leave?"

"So-so," said Gomez.

"The French are still—cautious, I suppose?"

"I should just think so. But I imagine they're going to get it right up the butt." He pointed to the radio. "The Berlin clown is loose again!"

"Are you serious?" Herrera's eyes sparkled. "Say, ya' know, that would change a lot of things."

"And how," said Gomez.

They smiled at each other for a moment. Tilquin, who was at the window, came towards them. "Turn it lower, I can hear something."

Gomez turned the knob, and the noise diminished.

"Do you hear?"

Gomez listened; he caught a dull humming sound.

"Aha!" said Herrera. "An alarm. The fourth since this morning."

"The fourth!" said Gomez.

"Yes," said Herrera. "Things have changed since you went away."

Hitler was again speaking; they bent over the instrument. Gomez was listening to the speech with one ear, and with the other to the hum of airplanes. Then followed the dull thud of a distant explosion.

"What is he doing? He hasn't ceded any territory, and now he is expelling the Germans. Monsieur Beneš had scarcely spoken when his military measures of repression were resumed with greater intensity. The following terrible figures are authentic: in one day ten thousand persons were ejected, twenty thousand on the following day. . . ."

The hum diminished, then suddenly grew louder: two reverberating detonations.

"The harbor's getting it," whispered Tilquin.

". . . The next day thirty-seven thousand, two days later forty thousand, then sixty-two thousand, then seventy-eight thousand; now this process is continuing at the rate of ninety thousand, a hundred and seven thousand, a hundred and thirty-seven thousand. And today two hundred and fourteen thousand. Entire districts have been depopulated, towns burnt down, and the Germans expelled by the use of gas and artillery. Monsieur Beneš, for his part, is safe in Prague, and saying to himself: 'I run no risk; in the last resort I can depend on the support of England and France.'"

Herrera pinched Gomez's arm.

"Listen," he said, "listen; he's going to let them have it now."

His face had flushed, he was gazing at the radio with something like approval. The thunderous, harsh voice burst forth once more:

"And now, my fellow citizens, I think the hour has come when it is necessary to speak without reserve."

A string of explosions, gradually approaching, drowned the applause. But Gomez paid little attention to them; he stared at the radio, listened to that threatening voice, and felt within him the revival of an emotion long since buried, something that resembled hope.

> *Vous, qui passez sans me voir*
> *Sans même dire bonsoir*
> *Donnez-moi un peu d'espoir*
> *Ce soir*
> *J'ai tant de peine.*

"I understand," said Germain Chabot. "This time I understand."

"Well, what is it?" said his wife.

"It's a deal with the evening press. They won't broadcast the translation before it is published in the papers."

He got up and took his hat. "I'm going out," he said. "I shall find an *Intran* on the boulevard Barbès."

The moment had come. He swung both legs out of bed, and thought: "Now's the time." She would find the bird flown and a thousand-franc note pinned to the coverlet, and if I have time I'll leave a farewell poem with it.

His head was heavy but had ceased to ache. He passed his hands over his face and dropped them with disgust; they smelt of Negress. On the glass shelf above the wash-basin, there was a cake of pink soap beside a spray, and an india-rubber sponge. He picked up the sponge, but an uprush of nausea came into his mouth, and he searched in his suitcase for his own washing-glove and soap. He washed himself from head to foot, splashing the water all over the floor, but that didn't matter. He combed his hair, took a clean shirt out of the suitcase, and put it on. The martyr's shirt. He was grim but composed. There was a clothes-brush on the chest of drawers, and he carefully brushed his jacket. "But where can I have put my trousers?" he asked himself. He looked under the bed and even between the sheets—no trousers. He said to himself: "I must have been very drunk." He opened the glass door of the ward-robe, he was beginning to be uneasy; the trousers were not there. He stood for a moment in the middle of the room, in his shirt, scratching his head and looking round him; then a gust of anger came upon him; it was a perfectly ri-diculous situation for a budding martyr to be marooned like this in his socks in a whore's bedroom, with his shirt-tails flapping round his knees. At that moment he noticed on his right a cupboard set in the wall. He dashed towards it, but the key was not in the lock; he tried to open it with his nails, and then with a pair of scissors that he found on the table, but failed. He flung the scissors down and stamped on the floor, muttering in a voice of fury: "The little bitch! She has locked up my trousers to keep me from going out."

"On this matter I can only say one thing: two men are now confronted: Herr Beneš and myself!"

The whole crowd began to yell. Anna looked uneasily at Milan. He had gone up to the radio and was looking at it with his hands in his pockets. His face had darkened, and there was something moving inside his cheek.

"Milan," said Anna.

"We are two men of a different stamp. While Herr Beneš, during the great struggle of the nations, came and went about the world, keeping out of danger, I, as a faithful German soldier, did my duty. And today here I am, face to face with him—I the soldier of my people."

They cheered again. Anna rose and laid a hand on Milan's arm; his biceps were contracted, his whole body had stiffened into rigidity. "He'll fall down," she thought.

"Bastard," he stammered.

She gripped his arm, but he pushed her away.

"Beneš and I!" he stammered. "Beneš and I! Just because you've got seventy-five million men behind you."

He stepped forward; she thought: "What is he going to do?" and dashed towards him; but he had already spat on the radio twice.

The voice went on:

"I have only a brief statement to make: I am grateful to Herr Chamberlain for all his efforts. I have assured him that the German people want nothing else but peace; but I also made clear to him that the limits of our patience are now set. I furthermore assured him, and I repeat it here, that—once this problem is settled—there is no other territorial problem for Germany in Europe. I also assured him that whenever Czechoslovakia shall have settled these problems—that is, when the Czechs shall have come to terms with their other minorities, not by oppressive measures, but on a pacific basis—that then I shall have no further concern with the Czech State. On that point I give him my pledged word. We do not want any Czechs among us. But at the same time I desire now to declare before the German people that in so far as the problem of the Sudetens is concerned, my patience is at an end. I made Herr Beneš an offer that is nothing more than the realization of the assurances he has himself already made. The decision now rests in his hands—peace or war. Either he will accept these proposals and give the Germans their freedom now or we shall go and take it ourselves."

Herrera raised his head exultantly. "Well, I'm damned!" he said. "Did you hear that? It's war."

"Yes," said Gomez. "Beneš is tough; he won't give way —it's war."

"By God!" said Tilquin, "if only it were, if only it were!"

"What's this?" asked Chamberlain.

"The rest of it," said Woodehouse.

Chamberlain took the papers and began to read. Woodehouse eyed his face uneasily. After a few moments the Prime Minister looked up and smiled amiably.

"Well," he said, "there's nothing new here."

Woodehouse looked at him with surprise. "Chancellor Hitler has expressed himself with a good deal of violence," he observed.

"That doesn't mean anything," said Chamberlain. "He had to."

"Today I march at the head of my people as their first soldier; and behind me, as the world should know, marches a nation, and a nation that is quite different from what it was in 1918. In this hour the entire German people are with me. They feel my will to be their will, just as I regard their future and their destiny as the motive power behind my action. We must strengthen this joint will—the will of those great days when I, an unknown private soldier, set forth to conquer an empire, never doubting of success or final victory. Around me is arrayed a band of brave men and women, who then marched with me. And now, my German people, I ask this of you all: March behind me, men and women of Germany. At this hour we must have but one will. A will must be stronger than any difficulty or danger; and if it is so, it will master all difficulties and dangers. We are resolved. It is now for Herr Beneš to decide."

Boris turned towards the others and said: "It's all over."

They did not react at once; they went on smoking with an air of concentration. After a few moments the proprietor said: "Well—so we're going to smash him?"

"Let's see you do it!"

The proprietor leaned over the bottles, and turned the knob; for a moment Boris felt uncomfortable; it was as though a void had been created. Night and a faint breeze came in through the open door.

"What did he say?" said the Marseillais.

"Well, at the end he said: all my people are behind me, I am ready for war. It is for Monsieur Beneš to choose."

"My God!" said the Marseillais. "So it's war?"

Boris shrugged his shoulders.

"Well," said the Marseillais, "it's six months since I've seen my wife and my two daughters, and I shall have to go back to Marseille just to say good-night, then wave a hand and off to barracks."

"I very likely shan't even have the time to see my mother," said Chomis. "I come from the north," he said by way of explanation.

"Well, well," said the Marseillais, wagging his head.

They fell silent. Charlier knocked out his pipe against his heel. The proprietor said: "What about another? Since it's going to be war, I'll stand this round."

"Right—the same again, thanks."

The air from out of doors was cool and dark, they could hear the distant band from the Casino; possibly Lola was singing.

"I've been to Czechoslovakia," said the man from the north. "And I'm glad I have; it's a good thing to know what one is fighting for."

"Did you stay there long?" asked Boris.

"Six months. On a timber deal. I got on well with the Czechs. They're workers."

"As to that," said the bartender, "the Germans are workers too."

"Yes, but they shove you around. The Czechs are quiet folk."

"Good health," said Charlier.

"Good health."

They clinked glasses, and the Marseillais said: "It's getting chilly."

Mathieu awoke with a start. "Where are we?" he asked, rubbing his eyes.

"Marseille, Gare Saint-Charles; all change."

"Right," said Mathieu.

He took his raincoat off the peg, and his suitcase from the luggage-rack. He felt adrift. "Hitler must have finished his speech," he thought with relief.

"I saw the boys go off in '14," said the man from the north. "I was ten years old. It was quite different then."

"They wanted to go?"

"Did they want to?—such yelling and singing and waving!"

"I expect they didn't realize what it meant," said the Marseillais.

"Prob'ly not."

"Well, we do," said Boris.

A silence followed. The man from the north was looking straight in front of him. He said: "I saw the Fritzes at close quarters. Our place was occupied for four years. They pretty well stripped us bare. The village was destroyed, for weeks and weeks we used to hide in the quarries. So you can understand that when I think it's all going to start again—" He added: "That doesn't mean that I won't do my duty like the rest."

"My trouble is," said the proprietor smiling, "that I've a horror of death. Ever since I was a small boy. I've got over it a bit lately by saying to myself: "The rotten thing is just death—whether you die of influenza or an exploding shell . . .""

Boris smiled a beatific smile; he liked these fellows, and

he thought: "I prefer men to women." One good thing about war was that it was solely a male concern. For three years, five years, he would see only men. "And I'll transfer my leave to fathers of families."

"What counts," said Chomis, "is to be able to tell yourself that you have lived. I'm thirty-six, and I haven't always had a gay time. There have been ups and downs. But I have lived. They can cut me into little pieces, but they can't deprive me of that." He turned to Boris. "For a young chap like you it must be even harder."

"Oh," said Boris briskly, "I wonder how long people have been telling me that there's going to be a war." He flushed, and added: "It must be worse for married men."

"Yes," said the Marseillais, with a sigh. "My wife has plenty of courage, and besides she has a profession; she's a hairdresser. I worry about my little girls, but it's better to have been a father, isn't it? Anyway, just 'cause you go, you don't *have* to get knocked off."

"Of course not," said Boris.

The music stopped. A couple came into the bar. The woman was red-haired and wore a long, green, low-cut frock. They sat down at a back table.

"None the less," said Charlier, "war is just God-damn silly. I don't know anything sillier."

"Me neither," said the proprietor.

"Me neither," said Chomis.

"Well," said the Marseillais, "what do I owe you? There's one round on me."

"And one on me," said Boris.

They paid. Chomis and the Marseillais went out arm-in-arm. Charlier hesitated a moment, turned on his heel, and sat down, taking his glass of brandy with him. Boris was still standing at the bar, thinking: "They're good fellows," and he was glad. There would be others like them in the trenches, thousands of them, just as good fellows as these. And Boris would live with them, he would not leave them day or night; and he would have plenty to do. He was in luck compared with the poor young men of his own age who had been run over in the street, or had died of cholera, he was indeed obliged to admit that he had been lucky. He had not been taken unawares; this was not one of those wars that wreck a man's life without warning, like a street accident; this war had proclaimed its advent six or seven years ahead, and people had had time to see it coming. Personally Boris had never doubted that it would break out in the end; he had awaited it like a crown prince who knows from childhood that he is born to reign. They had begotten him for the purpose of this war, they had educated him for it, they had sent him to the lycée, to the Sorbonne, they had trained his mind accordingly, the proclaimed intention being that he should become a professor, but that story had always seemed to him extremely thin; he now knew that they had meant him to become an officer in the reserve, and no expense had been spared to ensure that he should become a fine, fresh, healthy casualty. "The ludicrous thing is," he thought, "that I wasn't born in France, I'm merely a naturalized Frenchman." But, after all, that was not a point of much importance; if he had remained in Russia, or if his parents had fled to Berlin or Budapest, it would have been just the same: it isn't a question of nationality, it's a question of age; young Germans, Hungarians, Englishmen, and Greeks had been dedicated to the same war, the same destiny. In Russia there had first been the generation of the Revolution, then that of the Five-Year Plan, and now that of the world conflict: to every man his portion. Ultimately a man is born for war or peace, just as a man is born a worker or a bourgeois, there's nothing to be done about it, everybody hasn't the luck to be born a citizen of Switzerland. "A fellow who would have the right to complain," he thought, "is Mathieu; now, there is a man definitely born for peace; he has always been been convinced that he would die of old age and has

already acquired his little habits; at his age a man does
not change. Whereas, as far as I'm concerned, it's *my* war.
The war made me, and I shall make the war; we are inseparable; I can't even imagine what I should be like if
it hadn't broken out." He thought of his life, and it no
longer seemed to him too short. Lives are neither short nor
long. It was a life, that's all—with war at the end of it.
He felt as though he had been suddenly invested with a
new dignity, because he had a function in society, and also
because he was going to die a violent death, and his modesty was hurt. It must be time to go and get Lola. He
smiled at the proprietor and hurried out.

The sky was cloudy; here and there some stars were
visible; the wind was blowing in from the sea. For a moment Boris's mind was clouded; then he thought: *"My
war,"* and was surprised because he wasn't used to thinking about the same things for any length of time. "How
frightened I shall be!" he said to himself. "God, how scared
I'll be; how scared stiff I'll be!" And he burst into shocked
but rather complacent laughter at the notion of such panic.
But he stopped laughing after a step or two, under the
access of a sudden anxiety: after all, he must not be *too*
afraid. He wouldn't die of old age, certainly, but that was
not a reason for spoiling his life, and allowing himself too
much latitude. He had been pledged from birth, but he
hadn't been robbed of any luck, his war was a *vocation*
rather than a destiny. Obviously he could have wished for
a different one: that of a great philosopher, for instance, or
of a Don Juan or a great financier. But one does not choose
one's vocation: one succeeds or fails in it, that's all; and
the unpleasant aspect of his own was that he wasn't allowed a second try. There were lives that resembled the
examination for the bachelor's degree: the candidate sent
in several papers, and if he failed in physics, he could
make it up in Nat. Sci. or Philo. But his own life rather
suggested the diploma of general philosophy, in which a

candidate is judged on one test alone, which was a terrible ordeal. However, it was in those conditions that he must succeed, not in any others—and it wouldn't be an easy job. He must behave decently, of course, but that wasn't enough. He must acclimatize himself to the war, find his due place in it, and try to take full advantage of all his experiences. He must bear in mind that, from a certain point of view, all experiences have their value: an attack in the Argonne is as good as a trip in a gondola, the dishwater drunk in the trenches in the early morning is as good as the coffee in Spanish railway stations at dawn. And then there are the other fellows, life in the open air, parcels, and, above all, the spectacle of war; a bombardment must be a good show, anyway. If I am afraid, I rob myself of life, I remain a tadpole. I won't be afraid, said he to himself.

The lights of the Casino brought him out of his dream, from the open windows came gusts of music, a black car drew up silently at the entrance. Another year to go, he thought with vexation.

It was past midnight, the Sportpalast was dark and deserted, full of piled chairs and cigar stubs, Mr. Chamberlain was talking on the radio, Mathieu strolled along the quays of the Vieux-Port, thinking: "It's a disease, simply a disease; it has come upon me by chance, it does not concern me, it must be faced like gout or toothache." Mr. Chamberlain said: "I hope the Chancellor will not reject this proposal, which is made in the same spirit of friendship with which I was greeted in Germany, and which, if accepted, will satisfy the German desire to unite the Sudetens with the Reich, without bloodshed in any part of Europe."

He waved a hand to indicate that he had finished, and moved away from the microphone. Zézette, who could not get to sleep, was standing at the window, looking at the stars above the roofs, Germain Chabot was taking off his trousers in the dressing-room. Boris was waiting for Lola in the hall of the Casino; everywhere, on every wave-length, unheard or nearly so, a dark flower struggling into blossom: *If the moon turns green,* played by the jazz orchestra at the Hotel Astoria, and relayed by Daventry.

Tuesday, September 27

TWENTY-TWO THIRTY o'clock. "Monsieur Delarue!" said the concierge. "What a surprise! I didn't expect you for a week."

Mathieu smiled at her. He would have preferred to slip through unobserved; but he had to ask for his keys.

"At least, you are not called up?"

"Me? no," said Mathieu.

"So much the better," said she. "It will come soon enough. Oh dear! Just think of all that has happened since you went away. Do you think there's going to be a war?"

"I don't know, Madame Garinet," said Mathieu. And he added briskly: "Any letters?"

"I forwarded them all to you," said Mme Garinet. "Only yesterday I sent on a circular to Juan-les-Pins; you should have let me know you were coming back—but here's something that came this morning."

She handed him a long gray envelope; Mathieu recognized Daniel's handwriting. He took the letter and put it into his pocket unopened.

"Do you want the keys?" said the concierge. "What a pity you couldn't let me know; I would have had time to clean up a bit. As it is—the shutters aren't even open."

"That doesn't matter," said Mathieu, taking the keys. "Good night, Madame Garinet."

The house was still deserted. From outside, Mathieu had noticed that the shutters were closed. The stair carpet had been taken up for the summer. He walked slowly past the first-floor apartment. There had been some vociferous children in it, and Mathieu had often tossed about at night, deafened by the yells of the last-born. Now the rooms were dark and desolate behind their closed shutters. Vacation. But he thought in his inmost self: War. This was war—blank, bewildered holidays, curtailed for some, prolonged for others. The second floor was occupied by a kept woman; her scent often percolated under the door on to the landing. She was no doubt at Biarritz, in a huge hotel prostrated by the heat and the stagnation of business. He reached the third floor and turned the key in the lock. Below him and above him, stones and night and silence. He made his way into the darkness and put down his bag and raincoat in the darkness; the hall smelt musty. He remained motionless, his arms at his sides, enveloped in shadow, then brusquely turned the switch and walked into all the rooms in his apartment, one after the other, leaving the doors open; he turned on the lights in the sitting-room, the kitchen, the bathroom and lavatory, and his bedroom, one by one, and a current of continuous light circulated from room to room. He stopped beside his bed.

Someone had slept there. The bedclothes were in a huddle, the pillowcase was soiled and crumpled, and there were bread crumbs on the sheets. Someone—myself. "It was I," thought he, "who slept there. I myself, on July 15, for the last time." But he looked at the bed with disgust: that bygone sleep of his had grown cold within the sheets, it was now someone else's sleep. I shan't stay here.

He turned into his study: his disgust remained. A dirty glass on the mantelpiece; on the table, near the bronze crab, a cigarette stub, with strands of dried tobacco oozing out of it. When did I put out that cigarette? He squeezed it and felt the crackle of dead tobacco leaves. Books. A volume of Arbelet, another of Martineau, Lamiel, Lucien Leuwen, the *Memoirs of an Egoist.* Someone had planned out an article on Stendhal. The books remained, and the intention, now petrified, had become an object. May '38: it was not yet absurd to write about Stendhal. An object— like the gray covers of the books, like the dust that had gathered on their backs. An opaque and passive object, an impenetrable presence. *My* project!

His project to drink—now visible as a dim deposit in the transparent glass—to smoke, to write. Here was the green leather armchair in which the man sat of an evening. It was evening now: Mathieu looked at the armchair and sat down on the edge of a straight one. *"Your armchairs are insidious,"* a voice had said, in this very place; your armchairs are insidious. On the divan a fair-haired girl had angrily shaken her curls. In that moment the man barely saw those curls, barely heard those voices: he saw, he heard, his future through them. And now the man had gone, carrying off his old, mendacious future; the presences had grown cold, they remained like a film of grease on the surface of the furniture, and voices hovered at the level of the eyes: they had floated up to the ceiling, dropped down again, and were now hovering in the room. Mathieu felt like an intruder, he went to the window and swung the shutters back. A faint daylight lingered in the sky, a radiance that came from nowhere; he drew a deep breath.

Daniel's letter. He reached out a hand to take it, then dropped his hand on to the window-bar. Daniel had departed down that street one evening in June, he had passed beneath that street-lamp: the man had stood by the window and watched him go. It was to that man that Daniel had written. Mathieu didn't want to read his letter. He turned abruptly and surveyed his room with a sort of

arid satisfaction. They were all there, immured and dead,
Marcelle, Ivich, Brunet, Boris, Daniel. Thither they had
come, there they had been entrapped, and there they
would remain. Ivich's explosions of anger, Brunet's remon-
strances—Mathieu remembered them already as an event,
like the death of Louis XVI, and in the same dispassionate
way. They belonged to the world's past, not to his: he no
longer had a past.

He closed the shutters, walked across the room, paused,
and, on reflection, left the table lamp alight. Tomorrow
morning I'll come back for my suitcases. He shut the outer
door upon all these presences and went downstairs. He felt
devoid of weight or content. Up above and behind him
the lights would shine all night like tapers on his dead life.

"What are you thinking about?" asked Lola.

"Nothing," said Boris.

They were sitting on a bench. Lola was not singing that
evening, there was a gala at the Casino. A couple had just
passed them, followed by a soldier. Boris pondered.

"Aw, come on, be nice to me," said Lola in a pleading
voice; "tell me what you're thinking about."

Boris shrugged his shoulders. "I was thinking about that
soldier."

"Really?" said Lola, surprised. "And what was in your
mind?"

"What does one think about a soldier?"

"Boris," wailed Lola, "what's the matter with you?
You've been so nice to me lately, so affectionate. And now
you're just as bad as ever. You've hardly spoken to me all
day."

Boris did not answer, he was thinking of the soldier; and
what he thought was: "He's lucky; I've got another year
to go." A year: he would go back to Paris, he would walk
down the boulevard Montparnasse and the boulevard
Saint-Michel, both of which he knew by heart, he would
go to the Dôme, to the Coupole, and he would sleep every

night at Lola's place. If only I could see Mathieu, I might be able to take it, but Mathieu will be in the army. And my diploma, he suddenly reflected. For added to all this, there would be an untimely jest known as the higher diploma. His father would certainly insist on his taking the examination, and Boris would be obliged to submit a thesis on Imagination according to Renouvier, or Habit according to Maine de Biran. Why do they keep up this farce? he thought irritably. They had bred him for war, as was their right, but now they wanted to make him get his diploma, as though he had a whole life of peace before him. A sorry prospect: for a whole year he would sit in libraries, pretend to read the complete works of Maine de Biran in the Tisserand edition, pretend to take notes, pretend to prepare for his examination, and all the while he would be thinking about the veritable ordeal that awaited him, wondering whether he would be afraid or whether he would be able to hold out. "If it wasn't for her," he thought, throwing a malevolent look at Lola, "I would join up at once, and the joke would be on them."

"Boris!" cried Lola, suddenly terrified. "You mustn't look at me like that! Don't you love me any more?"

"On the contrary," said Boris through clenched teeth. "You don't know how much I love you. You haven't the faintest notion."

Ivich had lit her bedside lamp and lay outstretched on her bed, naked. She had left the door open, and could see out into the passage; there was a circle of light on the ceiling, and all the rest of the room was blue. A faint haze hovered above the table, the room smelt of lemon, tea, and cigarettes.

She heard a rustle in the passage, and an enormous shape silently passed her door.

"Hey!" she exclaimed.

Her father turned, and eyed her with disapproval.

"Ivich, I have spoken to you about this more than once:

you must either shut the door or put some clothes on."

He had flushed slightly, and spoke with an almost melodious intonation. "I'm thinking of the maid."

"The maid has gone to bed," said Ivich composedly. She added: "I was watching out for you. You pass so quietly, I was afraid of missing you. Come back."

M. Serguine came back; she got up and put on her dressing-gown. Her father was standing stiffly in the doorway, with his back towards her. She looked at his neck, his stalwart shoulders, and began to laugh noiselessly.

"You can look now."

He was now facing her. He sniffed two or three times and said: "You smoke too much."

"It's because I'm so nervous," she said.

He did not reply. The lamp lit up his large, rough-hewn face. Ivich rather admired him in the way she might admire a mountain or Niagara Falls. After a pause he said: "I'm going to bed."

"No," pleaded Ivich. "No, Papa: I should like to listen to the radio."

"What!" cried M. Serguine. "At this hour?"

Ivich ignored his tone: she knew he left his room every evening about eleven o'clock on his way to his study to listen to the news on the sly. He was as elusive as an elf, despite his hundred and ninety pounds.

"You go alone," he said. "I have to get up early tomorrow."

"But, Papa," pleaded Ivich, "you know I can't work the radio."

M. Serguine burst out laughing. "Ha-ha-ha! You surely don't want to listen to music?" he asked, resuming his solemn air. "Remember your poor mother is asleep."

"Of course I don't, Papa," said Ivich furiously. "I want to know how they're making out with their war."

"Come on then."

She followed him barefooted to the office, and he leaned

over the radio. His long, powerful hands manipulated the knobs so gently that Ivich was quite touched and lamented their vanished intimacy. When she was fifteen, they had been inseparable, and Mme Serguine became jealous; when M. Serguine took Ivich to a restaurant, he sat her opposite him and she ordered her own dinner; the waiters called her Madame, which gave her great delight, and he looked proud, like a man lucky with the girls. They heard the closing bars of a military march, and then a German began to speak in rasping tones.

"Papa," she said reproachfully, "I don't know German."

He eyed her quizzically. "He did it on purpose," she thought.

"The best news comes on at this time."

Ivich listened attentively to see if she could catch the word *Krieg*, of which she did know the meaning. The German stopped talking, and the orchestra launched into another march; Ivich was quite stunned, but M. Serguine listened to the end: he did not dislike military music.

"Well?" asked Ivich in an anguished voice.

"Things are going badly," said M. Serguine. But he did not look much concerned.

"Ah," she said hoarsely; "the Czechs are still the trouble, I suppose?"

"Yes."

"How I loathe them," she said passionately. She added after a pause: "But if a country refused to go to war, it couldn't be forced to do so, could it?"

"Ivich," said M. Serguine severely, "you are such a child."

"Yes," said Ivich. "I guess so."

She suspected that her father was as much mystified as she was.

"Is that all the news?"

M. Serguine hesitated.

"Papa!"

He is furious with me for coming, I've spoiled his little ceremony. M. Serguine was secretively inclined, had six padlocked suitcases, and two bolted trunks, which he inspected sometimes when alone. Ivich looked at him with affection, he was so sympathetic that she very nearly told him what her trouble was.

"In a moment or two," he said regretfully, "we shall hear the French news."

His pale eyes looked down at her, and she realized that he was no use to her at all. She merely said: "What would happen if there was a war?"

"The French would be beaten."

"Pfui! Would the Germans invade France?"

"Of course."

"They would get to Laon?"

"I imagine so. I imagine they would head for Paris."

"He doesn't know a thing about it," thought Ivich. "What a clown!" But her heart was throbbing wildly.

She was sorry she had asked the question. Since the Bolsheviks had burned his country houses, her father rather enjoyed catastrophes. He half-closed his eyes and wagged his head.

"Aha!" said he. "Aha!"

Twenty-three thirty o'clock. A dead street, immersed in shadow; at rare intervals a street-light. A nondescript street, edged with tall, nameless mausoleums. All the shutters closed, not a single glint of light. It was once the rue Delambre. Mathieu had crossed the rue Cels, the rue Froidevaux, walked along the avenue du Maine and even the rue de la Gaîté; they were all alike: still warm, already unrecognizable, already streets of war. Something had perished. Paris was no more than a vast street-cemetery.

Mathieu went into the Dôme because the Dôme happened to be there. A waiter hovered round with an ingratiating smile: a puny youth in spectacles, very deferential. He was a new waiter; the old one used to keep the customers waiting for an hour, then strolled up nonchalantly and took the orders without even a smile.

"Where's Henri?"

"Henri?" asked the boy.

"A tall dark fellow, rather goggled-eyed."

"Oh yes. He's been called up."

"And Jean?"

"The blond one? He's been called up too. I'm taking his place."

"Bring me a brandy," said Mathieu.

The boy ran off. Mathieu blinked for a moment or two and then surveyed the room with astonishment. In July the Dôme had no precise confines, it overflowed through the windows and the revolving door into the street, and spread over the road, the passers-by were flooded in the milky haze that lit up the hands and left cheeks of the taxi-drivers parked in the center of the boulevard Montparnasse. One step more, and the haze reddened, the taxi-drivers' right profiles were red too: the Rotonde. But now the outer darkness surged against the windows, and the Dôme was reduced to what it was: a collection of tables, benches, glasses, dry and unresponsive, denuded of that diffused glow which shadowed them by night. Gone were the German émigrés, the Hungarian pianist, the alcholic old American woman. Gone were all those charming couples who held hands under the table and talked of love until the small hours of the morning, their eyes red with sleep. On his left a major was having supper with his wife. Opposite, a little Annamite whore sat dreaming over a café-crème, and at the next table a captain was eating a dish of sauerkraut. On the right a lad in uniform had his arm round a woman's waist. Mathieu knew him by sight, he was a student at the Beaux-Arts, tall, pale, and diffident; but he looked quite truculent in uniform. The captain raised his head, and his look pierced through the wall; Mathieu followed it—what it envisaged was a railway station, flares, gleaming railroad tracks, men with ashen faces and sleep-swollen eyes sitting stiffly in the coaches with their hands on their knees. In July we sat together underneath the lights, our eyes fixed on each other, and none of our looks was lost. Now they are lost, they speed towards Wissembourg, towards Montmédy; people are now divided by abysses, space, and darkness. The Dôme has been mobilized and transformed into one of the essentials of war: a lunch-room. "Ah well," he thought with satisfaction, "there's nothing I regard with any affection or regret, I leave nothing behind."

The little Indo-Chinese smiled at him. She was a pretty little thing, with tiny hands; two years ago Mathieu had decided to spend a night with her. This would be the moment. I should slide my lips over her chilly skin and inhale a musty, insect smell; I should be just a naked entity beneath her professional fingers; I have in me certain antiquated notions that would die of such a contact. He would just return her smile.

"Waiter."

The waiter ran up. "Ten francs, please."

Mathieu paid and departed. I already know her too well as it is.

It was dark. The first night of war. No, not quite. Some lights were still on in alleys and entries. In a month, or a fortnight, the first alarm would extinguish them; for the moment it was no more than a dress rehearsal. But Paris had in fact lost her pink cotton ceiling. For the first time Mathieu could see a dark vaporous pall of sky overhanging the city. The sky of Juan-les-Pins, Toulouse, Dijon, Amiens, the same for the country and the town, and for the whole of France. Mathieu stopped and gazed up at it. A quite ordinary and unprivileged sky. And myself a nondescript entity beneath that vast indifferent arc: that's war. A patch of light caught his eye, and he said to himself, listening to his own voice: "Paris, boulevard Raspail." But all those lovely and familiar names had also been mobilized—all those delicious names, they looked as though they were printed on a staff map or in a war communiqué. Nothing was left of the boulevard Raspail. Roads they were, just roads, speeding south to north, west to east, just numbered roads; paved for a mile or two here and there, set between sidewalks and houses, and named rue, avenue, and boulevard. But they were still segments of the same road. Mathieu, facing towards the Belgian frontier, was walking along a section of the Route Departmentale which ran out of Route Nationale No. 14. He turned into the long, straight highway that formed a continuation of the Ouest railway, once the rue de Rennes. A flame enveloped him, a street-lamp flashed out of the shadows and vanished; a taxi passed, speeding towards the railway stations on the right bank, followed by a black car filled with officers, then silence fell once more. Along that road, under that indifferent sky, the houses had been reduced to their crudest function: they were now just blocks of buildings. Dormitory-refectories for those about to be mobilized and for the families of those already mobilized. Their ultimate purpose could already be surmised: they would become "strategic points" and, in the end, targets. And that would be the end of Paris; the city was indeed already dead. A new world was coming into being: the austere and practical world of functional objects.

A ray of light gleamed through the curtains of the Café des Deux-Magots. Mathieu sat down on the terrace. Behind him the last belated customers were whispering in the darkness. The night was chilly.

"A beer, please," said Mathieu.

"It's nearly midnight," said the waiter. "We aren't serving any more drinks outside."

"Just one beer."

"All right, but you must hurry."

Behind his back a woman burst into a laugh—the first he

had heard since his return, and it almost shocked him. Not that he felt at all depressed, but he did not want to laugh. "It's the war," thought Mathieu.

"Would you pay now, please? Then I needn't bother you again."

Mathieu paid, the waiter went back into the café. A pair of shadows rose, glided between the tables, and departed. Mathieu was alone on the terrace. He looked up and saw, on the other side of the square, a handsome new church, white against the black sky. A village church. Yesterday a very Parisian edifice rose from its site there: the Church of Saint-Germain-des-Prés, a historical monument, Mathieu had met Ivich outside its portal. Tomorrow, perhaps, there would remain in front of the Deux-Magots just a ruined edifice, on which a hundred guns would fire and fire again. But today . . . today Ivich was at Laon, Paris was dead, Peace had just been buried, war had not yet been declared. The church was just a large white bulk standing under a white integument of night. A village church. A new and handsome church, which served no purpose. A light wind rose; a car passed with lights extinguished, then a cyclist, then two trucks that shook the ground. The stone image quivered faintly, then the wind dropped, silence fell, and once more it stood, white, purposeless, inhuman, and in it stood, amid all those vertical implements beside the highway to the east, the impassive, naked destiny of rock. It was eternal, a tiny black speck in the sky could blow it to powder, and yet it was eternal. A man alone, forgotten, devoured by darkness, confronted that precarious eternity. He shivered and thought: "I also am eternal."

It had all happened painlessly. There had once been a kindly, rather diffident man who was fond of Paris and enjoyed walking in its streets. That man was dead. As dead as Waldeck-Rousseau, or Thureau-Dangin; he had become engulfed in the world's past, together with the Peace, his life had been put away in the archives of the Third Republic; his daily budget would provide material for statistics of the middle-class subsistence level subsequent to 1918, his letters would serve as documents for the history of the bourgeoisie between the two wars, his anxieties and his hesitations, his feelings of shame and remorse, would be of the highest value for the study of French social life after the fall of the Second Empire. This man had shaped a future to his measure, a decorous, arid, uncomplaining future, rather overburdened with human contacts and schemes. A historic and mortal little future: the war had thundered down upon it and crushed it to powder. And yet, up to that minute, there was still something that could call itself Mathieu, something to which he clung with all his strength. Something, indeed, beyond analysis. Perhaps some ancient habit, perhaps a way of choosing his thoughts in his own likeness, of choosing *himself* from day to day in the likeness of his thoughts, of choosing his food and clothes, the trees and the houses that he looked at. He relaxed his grip and let it go; all this happened deep in his inmost self, in a region where words possess no meaning. He let go, and nothing remained but a look. A new and passionless look, a mere transparency. "I have lost my soul," he thought with satisfaction. A woman traversed that transparency. She clattered along in a hurry, glided into that motionless look, a harassed mortal denizen of time, devoured by a thousand little schemes, she lifted a hand and smoothed back a stray lock of hair. I was like her once—a hive of schemes. Her life is *my* life; beneath that look, under the indifferent sky, all lives are equivalent. The darkness swallowed her up as she pattered into the rue Bonaparte; human lives melted into the shadows, clacking heels were silent.

My look. He looked at the stifled whiteness of the belfry. Everything is dead. My look and those stones: eternal, rocklike, like that white church. In my former future, men and women would be looking out for me on June 20, 1940, on September 16, 1942, and February 8, 1944, and would be glad to see me. At present my look and nothing else awaits me, as far as eye can reach, just as those stones await themselves, stones wait for stones, tomorrow, next day, and forever. A look and a delight as vast as ocean—a great day, indeed. He laid his hands on his knees, he must keep calm; may I not tomorrow revert to what I was yesterday? But he was not afraid. The church may collapse, I may tumble into a shell-hole, or drop back into my life; nothing can rob of me this eternal moment. There had been, and forever would be, that cold glare upon those stones under the black sky; the absolute, forever; the absolute, without cause or sense or purpose, without past or future save a gratuitous, fortuitous, splendid permanence. "I am free," he said suddenly. And his joy changed, on the spot, to a crushing sense of anguish.

Irène was bored. Nothing happened, except that the orchestra was playing *Music, Maestro, please,* and Marc was looking at her with seal-like eyes. As a matter of fact, nothing ever happened, or if, by chance, it did, it passed unnoticed. She was watching a Scandinavian girl, a tall blonde who had been dancing for over an hour without even sitting down between the dances, and she thought dispassionately: "She's very well dressed." Marc was very well dressed, too; everyone was well dressed except Irène, who felt shabby in her garnet-red frock, not that she cared, I know I have no taste in dress, besides I can't afford any new ones, but she went about so much among rich people, she must try not to look conspicuous. There were already half a dozen men with their eyes on her, and a cheap and rather flashy dress encouraged them to regard her as an easy prey. Marc was at his ease because he was rich; he liked to take her among rich people, because it put her in a position of inferiority and, so he believed, more inclined to let him have his way.

"Why won't you?" he asked.

Irène started. "Why won't I what? Ah, yes. . . ." She smiled, and did not reply.

"What are you thinking about?"

"Only that my glass is empty. I'd like another sherry cobbler."

Marc ordered another sherry cobbler. It was rather amusing to make him pay because he wrote down his day-to-day expenses in a notebook. This evening he would write: "Went out with Irène, one gin fizz, two sherry cobblers: a hundred and seventy-five francs." She noticed that he was stroking her arm with the tip of his forefinger—he had no doubt been doing so for some minutes, but she hadn't noticed it.

"Tell me, Irène. Why not?"

"Oh," she yawned, "I just don't know."

"There you are, then: if you really don't know—"

"Not at all; it's just the other way round: when I sleep with someone, I want to know why I'm doing so. Either because he has nice eyes or for something he said or because he's good-looking."

"I am good-looking," said Marc in a low tone.

Irène laughed, and he blushed.

"Look here," he said sharply, "you understand what I mean."

"Of course I do," she said.

He grasped her wrist. "Irène—oh God, what do you want me to do?"

He leaned over her with a sort of peevish, pleading look, his emotion made him gasp for breath. "How bored I am!" she thought.

"Nothing. There's nothing you can do."

"Ah!" he ejaculated.

He let her go and flung his head back, exposing his teeth. She looked at herself in the mirror and saw a dowdy girl with rather fine eyes; she thought: "Good Lord! What a fuss about *that!*" She felt ashamed for him, and for herself, everything was so stale and boring; she couldn't even understand why she refused to sleep with him: I'm making a lot of trouble; much better say: "All right, I don't mind. Half an hour in a hotel bedroom, a little dirty business between two sheets, after which we'll come back here to finish the evening, and you'll leave me alone." But apparently she still attached too much importance to her wretched body: she knew she would not yield.

"I think you're a very odd girl," he said.

He rolled his fine eyes at her, looking quite distraught, he'll try to make me feel bad, that's what they always do, and then ask me to forgive him.

"You do make a fuss," he went on ironically. "If I hadn't known you for four years I should have thought you were virtue personified."

She looked at him with sudden interest and began to reflect. When she reflected, she felt much less bored.

"You're right," she said, it's very odd: I'm an easy sort of girl, and that's a fact, and yet I would rather be cut in pieces than sleep with you. Now try to explain that!" She surveyed him dispassionately and concluded: "I can't exactly say that you really disgust me."

"Not so loud!" he said, and added venomously: "That little voice of yours carries such a long way."

They were silent. People danced, the orchestra played *Caravane;* Marc twirled his glass over the tablecloth, and the ice in it clinked.

"The fact is," he said suddenly, "I've let you see too clearly that I wanted you."

He had laid his hands flat on the table and began to smooth out the cloth; he was trying to recover his human dignity. It didn't matter, he would lose it again in five minutes. But she smiled at him, glad of a chance to analyze herself.

"Well," she said, "there's something in that, no doubt."

Marc appeared to her through a haze. A quiet little haze of astonishment rose from her heart to her eyes. It was a feeling she enjoyed, asking herself all the illimitable questions to which there is no answer.

"When a man is too keen on me," she explained, "I get shocked. Look here, Marc, I feel ridiculous: Hitler will very likely have attacked us by tomorrow, and you sit there fussing because I won't sleep with you. You must be a poor sort of guy to work yourself up over a girl like me."

"That's my business," he said in an angry voice.

"It's my business too: I hate to be overrated."

A silence followed. What animals we are, to set so much store upon an instinct! She looked at him out of the corner of her eye: ah, he'll soon subside. His features drooped, the crisis had still to come; once, at Melody's, he had burst into tears. He opened his mouth, and she said to him briskly:

"Be quiet, Marc, please: I know you're going to say something silly or unpleasant."

He did not hear what she said; he wagged his head with an ominous air on his face.

"Irène," he said softly, "I'm going away."

"Away? Where?"

"Don't act dumb. You understood."

"Well, then?"

"I did think you might feel it a bit."

She did not reply: she eyed him fixedly. Then he went on, with averted eyes: "In 1914 lots of women gave themselves to men who loved them, just because they were going away."

She said nothing; Marc's hands began to quiver.

"Irène, it means so little to you, but for me it's so important, particularly at this moment. . . ."

"Doesn't convince me," said Irène.

He turned upon her savagely. "After all, damn it, it's for you I'm going to fight."

"You louse!" said Irène.

He subsided at once: his eyes reddened.

"I can't bear the idea of being killed without having slept with you."

Irène got up. "Come and dance," she said.

He got up obediently and they danced. He held her close and swung her round the room; suddenly she caught her breath.

"What's the matter?" he asked.

"Nothing."

She had just recognized Philippe, sedately seated beside a Creole, rather handsome, but not young. "So this is where he was hanging out when they were searching for him all over the place." She found him rather pale, with dark circles round his eyes. She maneuvered Marc into the center of the crowd; it was essential that Philippe should not recognize her. The orchestra stopped, and they went back to their table. Marc sank back on his seat. Irène was about to sit down when she noticed a man bowing to the Negress.

"Sit down," said Marc. "I don't like to see you standing."

"Just a moment," she said impatiently.

The Negress got up lazily, and the man put his arms round her. Philippe looked at them for a moment with a stricken air, and Irène felt her heart contract; then suddenly he got up and slipped out.

"Excuse me a minute," said Irène.

"Where are you going?"

"To the lavatory. There—are you satisfied?"

"You'll pretend to go, and then clear out."

She pointed to her bag on the table. "I've left my bag."

Marc grunted; she crossed the dance-floor, pushing through the dancers.

"That girl's crazy," said a woman. Marc had got up too; she heard him cry: "Irène!"

But she was already outside; he would need five minutes to pay for the drinks. The street was dark. "How silly I am!" she thought; "I've lost him." But when her eyes had grown used to the half-light, she saw him hurrying in the direction of the Trinité, keeping close to the wall. She started to run. "It's a pity about my bag; I shall lose my powder-box, a hundred francs, and the two letters from Maxime." She had ceased to feel bored. They thus covered a hundred yards or so, both running, then Philippe stopped so abruptly that Irène nearly bumped into him. She stepped aside, passed him, went up to a door, and rang the bell twice. The door opened just as Philippe passed behind her. She paused for a second, then slammed the door violently, as though she had just entered the building. Philippe was now walking at a normal pace, it was easy enough to keep on his track. From time to time the shadows swallowed him, then under the luminous drizzle of a street-lamp he emerged out of the darkness. "This is very amusing," she thought. She adored tracking someone; she could walk for hours behind people whom she did not even know.

The boulevards were still crowded and it was easier to see, thanks to the lights in the cafés and the shop-windows. Philippe stopped again, but this time Irène was not taken by surprise; she slipped behind him and stood in a dark corner, waiting. "Perhaps he's meeting somebody." He turned, his face was a ghastly white; suddenly he began to speak, and she thought she had recognized her; and yet she was sure he could not see her. He stepped backwards and muttered something; he was looking frantic. "He's gone crazy," she thought.

Two women passed, one young and one old, wearing provincial hats. He went up to them, his face was that of an exhibitionist.

"Down with war," he said.

The women walked on faster: apparently they had not understood. Two officers came up; Philippe let them pass.

Then came a scented prostitute whose perfume struck Irène full in the face. Philippe eyed her wildly; she was already smiling at him, but he said in a strangled voice:

"Down with war, down with Daladier! We want peace!"

"Damned fool!" said the woman.

She passed. Philippe shook his head, looked to right and left with a furious air, and then plunged suddenly into the darkness of the rue Richelieu. Irène laughed so loud that she nearly gave herself away.

"Wait two minutes."

He turned the knob, and a jazz tune leaped forth—four notes from a saxophone, like a shooting star.

"Leave it on," said Ivich. "That's pretty."

M. Serguine turned the knob once more and the wail of the saxophone was replaced by a long, rasping crackle; he looked at Ivich severely. "How can you like that savage music?"

He despised Negroes. He had retained some vivid memories of his student life at Munich, and a cult of Wagner.

A voice shook the instrument: a characteristic French voice, calm and suave, translating the tortuosities of the speech into decent phraseology—it was the penetrating and persuasive voice of an elder brother. She smiled at her father and said casually, to recapture a little of their old intimacy: "I hate French voices."

M. Serguine emitted a faint chuckle and he raised a hand enjoining silence.

"Today," said the voice, "the British Premier's representative was again received by the Chancellor of the Reich, who intimated that if he had not received a satisfactory reply from Prague by fourteen o'clock tomorrow on the subject of the promised evacuation of the Sudeten districts, he intended to take the necessary measures.

"It is thought that Chancellor Hitler was referring to general mobilization, the order for which was expected on

Monday, in connection with the Chancellor's speech, and which was no doubt only delayed in consideration of the letter from the British Prime Minister."

The voice was silent. Ivich, whose throat was quite parched, looked up at her father. He had absorbed the announcement with an air of fatuous complacency.

"What exactly does mobilization mean?" she asked in an indifferent tone.

"It means war."

"Not necessarily?"

"Of course it does!"

"We shan't fight," she said violently. "We can't fight over the Czechs!"

M. Serguine smiled amiably. "When mobilization takes place—"

"But as we *don't want* war."

"If we didn't want war, we shouldn't have mobilized."

She looked at him with bewilderment. "Have we mobilized, too?"

"No," he said, with a blush. "I was referring to the Germans."

"Oh! I was talking about the French," said Ivich dryly.

The voice continued, quiet and benign: "In foreign circles in Berlin it is generally thought . . ."

"Shsh!" said M. Serguine.

He sat down again, his face turned towards the radio. "I'm an orphan," thought Ivich. She tiptoed out of the room, crossed the passage, and shut herself into her bedroom. Her teeth were chattering. "They will go through Laon, they will burn down Paris—the rue de Seine, the rue de la Gaîté, the rue des Rosiers, the Bal de la Montagne-Sainte-Geneviève; if Paris burns, I'll kill myself. Oh," she thought, sinking on her bed, "and what about the Musée Grévin?" She had never been there, Mathieu had promised to take her in October, and they would bomb it out of existence. That very night, perhaps. Her heart contracted, her arms and hands turned cold; what is there to prevent them? Perhaps at this very hour Paris is in ashes, and the fact has been concealed to prevent a panic. Unless it was forbidden by international agreements. How was she to know? "There must," she thought angrily, "be people who do know; I don't understand a thing about it, I've been kept in the dark, they made me learn Latin and no one has told me anything, and now look where we are! But I have the right to live," she thought distractedly, "I was brought into the world that I might live, I have the right to live." She felt so deeply wronged that she collapsed on her pillow and burst into sobs. "It's too unfair," she murmured; "at the best, it will last six years, even ten years, all the women will be dressed as nurses, and when it's over I shall be old." But no tears came, there was an icicle in her heart. She sat up abruptly: "*Who—who* wants war?" Taking people as individuals they were not bellicose, they thought solely of food, making money, and begetting children. Even the Germans. And yet here was war, Hitler had mobilized. "All the same, he couldn't decide it on his own," she thought. And a phrase passed through her mind, where had she read it?—in a newspaper, surely, unless she had heard it at lunch from one of her father's customers: "*Who is behind him?*" She repeated it in an undertone, looking gloomily at the toes of her slippers: "Who is behind him?" and she faintly hoped that it would all be cleared up. She passed in review the names of all those sinister powers which control the world —Freemasonry, the Jesuits, the Two Hundred Families, the armament-manufacturers, the gold lords, the wall of silver, the American trusts, international Communism, the Ku Klux Klan—all of them more or less backing him, and very likely yet another secret and formidable association, whose very name was unknown. "But what can they want?" she asked herself as two tears of rage coursed down her cheeks. She tried for a moment to guess their reasons, but there was a void within her, and a circlet of metal revolved inside her skull. "If only I knew where Czechoslovakia was!" She had pinned to the wall a large blue and gold water-color: a map of Europe, which she had amused herself by coloring last winter, copying from an atlas, but slightly readjusting the contours; she had put rivers everywhere, indented such coastlines as seemed to her unduly flat, and she had carefully avoided inscribing any names on the map: names looked learned and pretentious; no frontiers either: she detested dots. She went up to it: Czechoslovakia lay somewhere in the central mass of territory—there, for instance, or was that Russia? And where was Germany? She looked at a large smooth yellow shape, edged with blue, thought: "What an enormous country!" and felt bewildered. She turned, slipped out of her wrap, and looked at her naked image in the looking-glass, which usually had a soothing effect on her nerves. But what she saw was a fetus-like figure, a skin slightly crinkled by the shivers, and erect nipples—a horrid, hospital body, made for mutilation, they'll probably violate all the women, I dare say they'll cut off one of my legs. Yes, if they came into her room and found her stark naked in her bed, they would say: we'll give you five minutes to dress, then they would turn their backs as though she were Marie Antoinette, but they would hear everything, the soft thud of her feet as she got out of bed, and the rustle of fabrics against her skin. She picked up her panties and stockings and put them on quickly—disaster must be confronted standing up and dressed. When she had slipped on her skirt and blouse, she felt rather more secure. But as she put on her shoes, a bass voice in the passage began to croon in German:

Ich hatte einen Kamerade. . . .

Ivich dashed to the door and opened it; she found herself face to face with her father, who looked both grave and cheerful.

"What's that you're singing?" she said angrily. "How dare you sing such a song?"

He looked at her with a quizzical smile. "Wait," said he, "wait a bit, my little frog: we shall see our Holy Russia once again."

She went back into her room and slammed the door. "I don't give a damn for Holy Russia, I don't want Paris to be destroyed, and if they dare to do such a thing, I bet the French airplanes will drop bombs on Munich."

The sound of footsteps died away down the passage, and silence fell once more. Ivich was standing stiffly erect in the center of the room, averting her eyes from the reflection in the mirror. Suddenly she heard three blasts on a whistle, calls from the street, and shivered from head to feet. Outside. In the street. Everything happened outside: her room was a prison. Human lives were decided everywhere, north and east and south, everywhere in that envenomed night, pitted with flashes, echoing with whispers and clandestine meetings, everywhere except here where she remained immured, exactly where nothing whatever happened. Her hands and legs began to tremble, she picked up her bag, slid a comb through her hair, opened the door noiselessly, and slipped outside.

Outside. Everything is outside: the trees on the quay, the two houses by the bridge that lend a pink flush to the darkness, the petrified gallop of Henri IV above my head —solid objects, all of them. Inside, nothing, not even a puff of smoke, there is no *inside*, there is nothing. Myself: nothing. I am free, he said to himself, and his mouth was dry.

Halfway across the Pont-Neuf he stopped and began to laugh: liberty—I sought it far away; it was so near that I couldn't touch it, that I can't touch it; it is, in fact, myself. I am my own freedom. He had hoped that one day he would be filled with joy, transfixed by a lightning-flash.

But there was neither lightning-flash nor joy: only a sense of desolation, a void blurred by its own aspect, an anguish so transparent as to be utterly unseeable. He reached out his hands and slid them slowly over the stone parapet, it was wrinkled and furrowed, like a petrified sponge, and still warm from the afternoon sun. There it lay, vast and massive, enclosing in itself the crushed silence, the compressed shadows that are the inside of objects. There it lay: a plenitude. He longed to clutch to that stone and melt into it, to fill himself with its opaqueness and repose. But it could not help him: it was outside, and forever. There lay his hands on the white parapet: bronze hands, they seemed, as he looked at them. But just because he could look at them, they were no longer his, they were the hands of another, they were outside, like the trees, like the reflections shimmering in the Seine—severed hands. He closed his eyes and they became his own again: there was nothing in contact with the stone save a faintly acid and familiar flavor, a whiff of formic acid. My hands: the inappreciable distance that reveals things to me and sets me apart from them forever. I am nothing; I possess nothing. As inseparable from the world as light, and yet exiled, gliding like light over the surface of stones and water, but nothing can ever grasp me or absorb me. Outside the world, outside the past, outside myself: freedom is exile, and I am condemned to be free.

He walked on a few steps, stopped again, sat down on the parapet, and watched the water flowing past. What shall I do with all this freedom? What shall I do with myself? His future lay marked out by definite tasks: the railway station, the Nancy train, the barracks, and the manual of arms. Nothing was any longer his: war seamed the earth, but it was not *his* war. He was alone on this bridge, alone in the world, accountable to no man. "I am free *for nothing*," he reflected wearily. Not a sign in the

sky, nor on the earth, the things of this world were too
utterly immersed in the war that was theirs, they turned
their manifold heads towards the east. Mathieu was moving swiftly over the surface of things unconscious of
his presence. He was forgotten: by the bridge that indif-
ferently held him up, by the roads that sped towards the
frontier, by that city which rose slowly upwards to look
at that fire on the horizon which did not concern him. Forgotten, unknown, and utterly alone: a defaulter; all mobilized men had gone two days ago, he had now no
business to be here. Shall I take the train? What did it
matter?—go, or stay, or run away—acts of that kind would
not call his freedom into play. And yet he must risk that
freedom. He clutched the stone with both hands and
leaned over the water. A plunge, and the water would
engulf him, his freedom would be transmuted into water.
Rest at last—and why not? This obscure suicide would
also be an absolute, a law, a choice, and a morality, all of
them complete. A unique, unmatchable act, a lightning-
flash would light up the bridge and the Seine. He need
only lean a little farther over, and he would have made his
choice for all eternity. He leaned over, but his hands still
clutched the stone and bore the whole weight of his body.
Why not? He had no special reason for letting himself
drop, nor any reason for not doing so. And the act was
there, before him, on the black water, a presentment of
his future. All hawsers cut, nothing now could hold him
back: here was his freedom, and how horrible it was! Deep
down within him he felt his heart throbbing wildly; one
gesture, the mere unclasping of his hands, and *I would
have been* Mathieu. Dizziness rose softly over the river;
sky and bridge dissolved: nothing remained but himself
and the water; it heaved up to him and rippled round his
dangling legs. The water, where his future lay. At the moment *it is true*, I'm going to kill myself. Suddenly he *decided* not to do it. He decided: it shall merely be a trial.

Then he was again upon his feet and walking on, gliding over the crest of a dead star. Next time, perhaps.

She ran down the main street, she heard two or three more whistle-calls, then nothing more, and now the street had become a prison too: nothing was happening there, the façades of the houses were blind and flat, all the shutters closed, the war was elsewhere. She leaned for an instant against a street fountain, anxious and disappointed, but she did not know what she had hoped to see: lights, perhaps, open shops, people who would comment on events. There was nothing: in the great capitals, embassies and palaces were ablaze with light; she was immured in perpetual night. "Everything always happens somewhere else," she said, stamping her foot on the pavement. She heard a rustle, as of someone slipping up close behind her. She held her breath and listened for a long while; but did not hear the noise again. She was cold, and her throat was dry with fear: she wondered whether she would not do better to go back. But she *could* not go back, her room revolted her; here at least she walked beneath everybody's sky, she kept in contact, through the sky, with Paris and Berlin. She heard a persistent scratching sound behind her, and this time she had the courage to turn round. It was a cat: she saw its eyeballs glisten as it crossed the street from right to left—a bad omen. She continued on her way, turned into the rue Thiers, and there stopped, quite out of breath. "Airplanes!" A dull mutter—they must still be far away. She stood and listened: the sound did not come from the sky. Surely— "Yes," she thought with vexation; "it's someone snoring." It was Lescat, the notary, she recognized the brass plate over her head. He was snoring, the windows were open. She could not help laughing, and then suddenly her laugh turned harsh: they're all asleep. I'm alone in the street, surrounded by sleeping people, ignored by everyone.

"All the world over they are asleep, or in their offices

preparing for their war, not one of them has my name in his head. But I am here," she thought, resentfully. "I am here, I see, I feel, and I exist, no less than Hitler."

After a moment she continued on her way and came out on the esplanade. Beneath her a bleak plain stretched away into the distance, dotted with points of light; but they brought her no solace; Ivich knew too well what they were—the lights of railway stations, grade crossings, piles of stones, shunted cars on sidings. At the extremity of the plain lay Paris. She breathed again: if the city was in flames, there would be a glare on the horizon. The wind flapped her dress against her knees, but she did not move. "Paris is there, still ablaze with light, for perhaps the last night of her existence." At that very moment people were walking up and down the boulevard Saint-Michel, others sitting at the Dôme who no doubt knew her and were talking to one another. "The last night—and I am here, in this dark hole, and when I am free, I shall find nothing but a little pile of ruins, and tents among the stones. O God," she pleaded, "let me see it just once more." The station was there, immediately below her—that red patch at the bottom of the stairway; the night train left at twenty minutes past three. "I've got a hundred francs in my bag," she thought triumphantly.

She was already running down the stepped incline, Philippe was already running along the rue Montmartre—so I'm a blow-hard, am I, just a dirty blow-hard? Well, they shall see. He came out into a square, opposite the dark, gaping entrance of a clamorous alleyway that smelt of cabbage and raw meat. He stopped outside the iron gates of a metro station, where a row of empty bins stood on the edge of the pavement; scraps of straw and muddy lettuce leaves were strewn about the roadway; on the right, shadows passed and repassed in the white light of a café. Ivich went up to the ticket window:

"Third to Paris."

"Return?" asked the clerk.

"Single," she replied firmly.

Philippe cleared his throat and yelled:

"Down with war!"

Nothing happened; the shadows continued to move to and fro past the café. He cupped his hands over his mouth:

"Down with war!"

His voice was a thunderous bellow. A few shadows stopped, and he saw some men approach him, mostly wearing caps. They strolled up to him and looked at him quizzically.

"Down with war!" he shouted at them.

They were now quite near; among them were two women and a dark and rather graceful youth. Philippe felt drawn to him and, without taking his eyes off him, shouted:

"Down with Daladier, down with Chamberlain! We want peace!"

They were all round him now, and he felt at ease, for the first time in forty-eight hours. They looked at him curiously and said nothing. He wanted to explain to them that they were victims of capitalist imperialism, but he could not control his voice; it cried: "Down with war!" It was a sort of pæan. A fist struck him on the ear, and he continued to shout; again on the mouth, again on the right eye; he fell on his knees and stopped shouting. A woman —he could see her legs and flat-heeled shoes—struggled with his assailants, crying: "Bums, dirty bums! He's just a kid, you leave him alone!"

Mathieu heard a shrill voice crying, "Bums, dirty bums! He's just a kid, you leave him alone." Someone was struggling in a throng of men in caps: a small woman, with uplifted arms and rumpled hair. A dark youth, with a scar under his ear, seized and shook her, and she cried: "He's right, you're a pack of cowards, you ought to be at the Concorde, demonstrating against war; but you'd sooner knock a kid around, it's safer."

A fat old madame opposite Mathieu surveyed the scene with glistening eyes.

"Strip her naked!" she said.

Mathieu turned wearily away: this sort of thing must be happening at every street-corner, on the eve of war and battle: just a picturesque interlude, which concerned him not at all. Suddenly he decided that it did. He pushed the old dame aside, elbowed his way into the throng, and clapped a hand on the shoulder of the dark-haired youth.

"Police," he said. "What's all this?"

The man eyed him with mistrust.

"It's the boy on the ground. He was shouting: 'Down with war.'"

"And you beat him up, eh?" said Mathieu severely. "Couldn't you find an officer?"

"There wasn't one," said the prostitute.

"Look here, baby," said Mathieu. "You'll talk when you're asked to, get it?"

The dark youth looked uneasy. "He isn't much hurt," he said, licking his bruised knuckles. "Someone clouted him on the head."

"Who did?" asked Mathieu.

The man with the scar looked at his hands with a sigh. "I did," he said.

The others had stepped back; Mathieu turned to them. "Do you want to be called as witnesses?"

They stepped a little farther back and did not reply. The prostitute had vanished.

"Move on, now," said Mathieu, "or I'll take your names. You stay," he added to the scarred youth.

"So," said the latter. "A Frenchman gets clapped in the jug for knocking out a Boche who tries to make trouble?"

"Mind your own business. We'll get to the bottom of this."

The onlookers had dispersed. Two or three stood in a café doorway still staring at the scene. Mathieu bent down over the boy: he was a good deal damaged. His mouth was bleeding, and his left eye was closed. With his right eye he looked fixedly at Mathieu.

"I was shouting," he said proudly.

"That was a very silly thing to do," said Mathieu. "Can you get up?"

The boy staggered to his feet. He had fallen into the lettuce leaves; one was sticking to the seat of his trousers, and there were strands of muddy straw all over his jacket. The small woman brushed him with the flat of her hand.

"Do you know him?" Mathieu asked her.

She hesitated. "N-no."

The boy laughed. "Of course she knows me. It's Irène, Pitteaux's secretary."

Irène looked darkly at Mathieu. "You wouldn't take him to the station, would you?"

"I should worry about that."

The scarred man tugged at Mathieu's sleeve; he was looking rather abashed.

"I earn my living, inspector, I'm a worker. If I go with you to the station, I shall lose my night."

"Your papers, please."

The man produced a Nansen passport, his name was Canaro.

Mathieu laughed. "Born in Constantinople!" said he. "So loyal to France that you attack the first person who abuses her, eh?"

"France is my second fatherland," said the man with dignity.

"You'll join the army, I hope?"

The man did not answer. Mathieu wrote his name and address in a notebook.

"Now get out," he said. "You'll be called as a witness. Come along, you two."

The three of them turned into the rue Montmartre and walked a little way. Mathieu supported the boy, who was very unsteady on his legs.

"You'll let him go, won't you?" said Irène.

Mathieu did not answer: they were still too near the Halles. They walked on; then, when they reached a street-lamp, Irène faced Mathieu, and looked at him venomously.

"Dirty cop!" said she.

Mathieu laughed: her hair had slipped down over her face, and she had to peer through her disheveled locks.

"I'm not a cop," he said.

"No foolin'?"

She tried to shake her hair out of her eyes. In the end she gripped it angrily and flung it back, revealing a rather masklike, wide-eyed face. She was quite pretty; she did not seem much surprised.

"Well, if you're not, you really pulled one over on them," she observed.

Mathieu did not reply. He was bored by the affair. He had a sudden impulse to walk down the rue Montorgueil.

"Well," he said, "I'll put you both in a taxi."

There were two or three at a hack-stand in the middle of the street. Mathieu went up to one of them dragging the lad behind him. Irène followed them. With her right hand she held her hair in place on top of her head.

"In you go."

She blushed. "I'd better tell you that I've lost my bag."

Mathieu laid one hand between the boy's shoulder-blades, held the door open with the other, and pushed him into the cab.

"Feel in my coat pocket," he said; "the right one."

After a moment or two Irène took her hand out of his pocket.

"Here's a hundred francs and some change."

"Keep the hundred francs."

A final push and the lad collapsed on the seat. Irène got in after him.

"What is your address?" she asked.

"I no longer have one," said Mathieu. "Good-by."

"Hey, you!" cried Irène.

But he had already turned on his heel: he wanted to have another look at the rue Montorgueil, and at once. He walked on for a minute or two and then a taxi drew up beside the pavement at his side.

The door opened, and a woman leaned out; it was Irène.

"Get in," she said. "Quick."

Mathieu got into the taxi.

"Sit on the folding seat."

He did so. "What's the matter?"

"The boy is crazy. He says he wants to get himself locked up; he keeps on trying to open the door and throw himself out. I'm not strong enough to hold him."

The boy was lying huddled on the seat, his knees higher than his head.

"He wants to make a martyr of himself," explained Irène.

"How old is he?"

"I don't know; about nineteen, I should think."

Mathieu looked at the boy's long, thin legs: he was about the age of his oldest pupils.

"If he wants to get himself locked up," he said, "you haven't the right to stop him."

"You're a queer fish," said Irène indignantly. "You don't know what may be coming to him."

"Has he knocked someone off?"

"Of course not."

"What's his trouble, then?"

"It's a long story," she said gloomily. He noticed that she had coiled her hair on the top of her head, which gave her rather an oddly obstinate appearance, despite her graceful drooping mouth.

"It's his own affair, anyway," said Mathieu. "He's a free agent."

"Free, indeed!" said she. "I've just told you he's crazy."

At the word "free" the boy opened his solitary eye and muttered something that Mathieu did not catch and then, without a word of warning, flung himself at the handle of the door and tried to open it. A car at that same moment grazed past the standing taxi. Mathieu laid a hand on the boy's chest and pushed him back on the cushions.

"If I wanted to get myself into prison," he continued turning to Irène, "I shouldn't like anyone to stop me."

"Down with war!" said the boy.

"Yes, yes," said Mathieu. "You're right." He was still holding him down on the seat. He turned to Irène.

"He certainly does seem cracked."

The chauffeur slid the glass back. "Where to?"

"15 avenue du Parc-Montsouris," said Irène triumphantly.

The boy clawed at Mathieu's hand; then, when the taxi had started, he decided to keep quiet. They remained silent for a moment; the taxi sped through dark streets unknown to Mathieu. From time to time Irène's face emerged from the darkness and then plunged into it again.

"Are you from Brittany?"

"I? From Metz. Why do you ask?"

"Because of the way you do your hair."

"Rather silly, isn't it? It's a girl-friend who likes me to do it that way."

She was silent for a moment and then said: "How is it you haven't got an address?"

"I'm moving."

"Ah yes. . . . You're mobilized, I suppose?"

"Yes. Just like everyone else."

"You like war?"

"I don't know. I've never been in one."

"Well, I'm against it," said Irène.

"I noticed that."

She leaned towards him with an anxious air. "Tell me, have you lost somebody?"

"No," said Mathieu. "Do I look as if I had?"

"You look odd," she said. "Look out!"

The boy had reached out a stealthy hand and was trying to open the door.

"Will you keep quiet?" said Mathieu, flinging him back into his corner. "What a little squirt!" he said to Irène.

"He's the son of a general."

"Is he? Well, I don't suppose he's proud of his father."

The taxi had stopped. Irène got out, and the boy had to be extricated next. He clung to the elbow rests and kicked. Irène began to laugh. "How contrary he is! Now he won't come out."

Mathieu finally put an arm round him and lifted him bodily on to the sidewalk. "Ouf!"

"Wait a second," said Irène. "The key was in my bag. I must get through the window."

She walked up to a small two-storied house with one window half open. Mathieu held the boy up with one hand; with the other he felt in his pocket and handed his loose change to the chauffeur.

"Keep it all."

"What's the matter with the chap?" said the chauffeur genially.

"He's had too much," said Mathieu.

The taxi restarted. Behind Mathieu a door opened, and Irène appeared in a rectangle of light.

"Come in," she said.

Mathieu entered, pushing the now silent boy ahead of him. Irène shut the street door.

"On the left," she said. "The switch is on the right."

Mathieu groped for the switch, and the light flashed on.

He saw a dusty room, containing a cot, a water-jug, and a wash-basin on a dressing-table; a wheelless bicycle was suspended from the ceiling.

"Is this your room?"

"No," said Irène. "It belongs to some friends."

He looked at her, and laughed. "Your stockings!"

They were white with dust and torn at the knees.

"It's from climbing through the window," she explained nonchalantly.

The boy stood in the middle of the room, swaying precariously and surveying his surroundings with his solitary eye. Mathieu pointed to him and said:

"What's to be done with him?"

"Take off his shoes and make him lie down; I'll wash his face."

The boy made no resistance: he appeared to be in a state of coma. Irène returned with a basin and some cotton.

"There we are," she said. "Now, Philippe, behave yourself."

She leaned over him and dabbed an eyebrow with a wad of cotton. The boy began to mumble.

"Yes," she said in a motherly voice. "It smarts, but it will do you good."

She put the basin on the dressing-table. Mathieu got up.

"Good," he said. "Now I'll be off."

"No—please!" she said eagerly, adding in an undertone: "If he tried to get away, I'm not strong enough to stop him."

"But you don't expect me to stay on guard over him all night?"

"You aren't very helpful," she said with vexation. And she added after a pause, in a more conciliatory tone: "You might at least wait until he gets to sleep; it won't be long."

The boy tossed about on the bed, muttering unintelligibly.

"How on earth can he have got himself into such a state?" asked Irène.

She was a plump girl with a sallow skin, a little too forthcoming, rather moist and faintly unclean; she looked as if she had just got out of bed. But her head was good—thin, rather drooping lips, large eyes, and small pink ears.

"There!" said Mathieu. "He's asleep."

"Do you think so?"

They both gave a start as the boy suddenly sat up and said in a loud voice: "Flossie! My trousers!"

"Oh hell!" said Mathieu.

Irène smiled. "You're here till morning."

But it was a touch of delirium that gave way to sleep: Philippe fell back again, moaned two or three times, and almost immediately began to snore.

"Come along," said Irène in a low tone.

He followed her into a large room with chairs upholstered in pink cretonne, and a guitar and a ukulele on the wall.

"This is my room. I'll leave the door open so that I can hear the boy."

Mathieu observed a large unmade four-poster bed, a hassock, a gramophone, and a pile of records on a Henri II table. On a rocking-chair lay a heap of worn stockings and slips. Irène followed his eyes. "I furnished my room," she said, "at the flea-market."

"It's very nice," said Mathieu. "Not bad at all."

"Sit down."

"Where?" asked Mathieu.

"Wait a minute."

On the hassock stood a ship in a bottle. She put it on the floor, and then cleared the underclothes from the rocking-chair on to the hassock.

"There. I'll sit on the bed."

Mathieu sat down and rocked himself to and fro.

"The last time I sat in a rocking-chair was at Nîmes, in the hall of the Hôtel des Arènes. I was fifteen."

Irène did not reply. Mathieu visualized the great dim hall with its glass door sparkling in the sun; that recollection still belonged to him, with others of the same kind, intimate and indistinct, that hovered all around him: I have not lost my childhood. The age of maturity, the age of reason, had collapsed, but his childhood remained, still quite warm; he had never been so close to it. Again he thought of the boy on the dunes at Arcachon, who insisted on being free, and, confronted by that pigheaded little rascal, Mathieu ceased to feel ashamed. He got up.

"Are you going?" said Irène.

"I'm going for a walk," said he.

"Won't you stay a little longer?"

He hesitated. "Frankly, I rather wanted to be alone."

She laid a hand on his arm: "You'll see. With me it'll be exactly like being alone."

He looked at her: she talked rather oddly, in a flat and toneless voice; she barely opened her thin lips and shook her head slightly as though to get her words out.

"All right, I'll stay," he said.

She did not look pleased. Indeed, her face was very inexpressive. Mathieu walked across the room to the table and picked up a few records. They were much worn, some of them cracked, and most of them without their covers. Jazz tunes, a potpourri of Maurice Chevalier, the Concerto for left hand, the Debussy quartet, the Toselli Serenade, and the *Internationale,* sung by a Russian choir.

"Are you a Communist?" he asked her.

"No," she said; "I have no political opinions. I think I should be a Communist if men weren't such crumbs." And she added, after a moment of reflection: "I'm a pacifist."

"You're rather illogical, aren't you?" said Mathieu. "If men are crumbs, you oughtn't to mind whether they die in battle or otherwise."

She shook her head with obstinate gravity. "The point is," she said, "that as they are such crumbs, it is even more disgusting to use them to make war."

A silence fell. Mathieu looked at a cobweb on the ceiling and began to whistle softly.

"I can't offer you a drink," said Irène. "Unless you would like some barley-water. There's a little left in the bottle."

"Hum!" said Mathieu.

"Yes, I rather thought you wouldn't. Ah, there's a cigar on the mantelpiece—would you care for it?"

"Thanks," said Mathieu.

He got up and took the cigar, which was dry and broken. "Can I put it in my pipe?"

"Do what you like with it."

He sat down again and crumbled the cigar between his fingers; he felt Irène's eyes upon him.

"Make yourself at home; if you don't feel inclined to talk, don't."

"All right," said Mathieu.

After a few moments she said: "Wouldn't you like to go to sleep?"

"Thank you, no."

He felt as though he would never want to go to sleep again.

"Where would you be at this moment if you hadn't met me?"

"In the rue Montorgueil."

"What would you be doing there?"

"Walking around."

"It must seem odd to you to be here."

"Not at all."

"True," she said in vague reproach; "you aren't really here at all."

He did not reply; she was right, he thought. These four walls and that woman on the bed were an unimportant accident, a transitory vision of the night. Wherever night

was, there was Mathieu, from the frontiers in the north to
the Côte d'Azur; he was, indeed, absorbed into the night,
and he looked at Irène with all the eyes of night: she was
no more than a faint flicker in the darkness. A yell startled
him out of his reflections.

"What a headache! I'll go and see what's the matter."

She tiptoed out of the room, and Mathieu lit his pipe.
He no longer wanted to walk along the rue Montorgueil:
the rue Montorgueil was there, traversing that room; all
the roads of France passed through it, all its herbage grew
there. Four timber partitions from nowhere in particular
had been set down to make it. Mathieu came from no
matter where. Irène returned and sat down; she was no
matter who. No, she didn't look like a Breton woman; she
was much more like the little Annamite at the Dôme. She
had the same saffron skin, blank face, and ineffectual
charm.

"It's nothing," she said. "He's got a nightmare."

Mathieu drew quietly at his pipe. "He must have had
some rough scrapes."

Irène shrugged her shoulders, and her face changed
suddenly.

"Pah!" she said.

"You sound rather tough all of a sudden," said Mathieu.

"Well, it makes me sore to hear people pity a little gentleman like that—what does a poor little rich boy know
about trouble?"

"Still, that doesn't prevent him being unhappy."

"Don't make me laugh. My old man chucked me out
when I was seventeen; I couldn't get on with him, of
course. But I didn't go about saying I was unhappy."

For a fleeting moment Mathieu descried beneath that
luxury face the hard and haunted visage of a suffering
woman. Her voice flowed on, a slow, rich voice, with a
sort of monotony in its indignation.

"People are unhappy," she said, "when they are cold or ill or hungry. The rest is all imagination."

He laughed: she was puckering her nose and opening her mouth wide so as to get her words out. He scarcely listened: he *saw* her. A look. A vast look, an empty sky: she struggled in that look, like an insect in a shaft of light.

"No," she said, "I'm quite willing to take him in and look after him and stop him from making a fool of himself; but I won't have him pitied. Because I know what trouble is! And when these bourgeois pretend they're unhappy . . ."

She looked at him intently, recovering her breath. "But you are a bourgeois, aren't you?"

"Yes," said Mathieu. "I am a bourgeois."

She sees me. Swiftly he seemed to harden and shrink. Behind those eyes there is a starless sky, and there is *also* a look. She sees me; as she sees the table and the ukulele. And for her, I *am;* a particle suspended in a look, a bourgeois. It is *true* that I am a bourgeois. And yet he never managed to feel that he was. She was still looking at him.

"What is your job? No—let me guess. Doctor?"

"No."

"Lawyer?"

"No."

"You aren't a crook, are you?"

"I'm a professor," said Mathieu.

"That's odd," she said, with a slightly disappointed air. But she added briskly: "Not that it's of any importance."

She looks at me. He got up and took her arm, a little below the elbow. The soft, warm flesh dimpled under his fingers.

"What are you up to?" she said.

"I wanted to touch you. With all due respect: because you were looking at me."

She leaned against him, and the look was dimmed.

"I like you," she said.

"And I like you."

"Have you a wife?"

"I have no one."

He sat down beside her on the bed. "And you? Is there anyone in your life?"

"There are—a few," And she added, with a rueful air: "I'm not very particular."

The look had vanished. What remained was a little Chinese doll, smelling slightly of mahogany.

"A push-over, eh? So what?" said Mathieu.

She did not reply. She put her head between her hands and looked gravely into vacancy. "Ah, the reflective type," said Mathieu to himself.

"When a girl isn't thrown together too well, she can't afford to be particular," she said after a pause.

She turned uneasily to Mathieu: "I don't scare you, do I?"

"No," said Mathieu with regret. "No, I couldn't say that."

But she looked so forlorn that he took her in his arms.

The café was deserted.

"It's two o'clock in the morning, isn't it?" Ivich asked the waiter.

He wiped his eyes with the back of his hand and glanced at the clock. It indicated half past eight.

"Something like that," he growled.

Ivich settled herself sedately in a corner, pulling her skirt up to her knees. I'll be an orphan girl going to join her aunt in a Paris suburb. She thought her eyes might be too bright, so she let her hair fall over her face. But her heart was brimming with almost joyful excitement: one hour to wait, a road to cross, and she would jump into the train; I'll be at the Gare du Nord about six o'clock, I shall go to the Dôme first, I shall eat two oranges and then go

on to Renata and borrow five hundred francs. She wanted
to order a brandy, but an orphan doesn't drink liquor.

"Will you bring me a lime tea?" she said timidly.

The waiter turned, he was horrid, but she simply *had* to
seduce him. When he brought the tea, she looked at him
with soft and startled eyes.

"Thank you," she sighed.

He stood and sniffed perplexedly.

"Where are you off to like this?"

"To Paris," she said, "to my aunt's."

"You aren't the daughter of Monsieur Serguine, who
owns the sawmill up there?"

The fool!

"Oh no," said she. "My father died in 1918. I'm a national orphan."

He wagged his head several times and departed: the
guy was a hick, a peasant. In Paris the café waiters have
velvety eyes and believe what they are told. I'm going to
see Paris again. The moment she got out of the Nord station, she would be recognized: she was expected. The
streets would be expecting her, the shop-windows, the
trees in the Montparnasse cemetery, and—and people too.
Certain people who would not have gone away—like
Renata—or who would have come back. I shall rediscover
myself; it was only there that she was Ivich, between the
avenue du Maine and the Quais. And someone will show
me Czechoslovakia on a map. Ah, she thought passionately, let them bomb the city if they will, we shall die
together, and only Boris will be left to regret us."

"Switch off the light."

He obeyed, the room melted into the vast night of war;
two looks were dissolved into the night: nothing was left
but a glint of light at the edge of the half-open door, an
elongated eye that seemed to see them. This annoyed
Mathieu, who groped his way to the door.

"No," said the voice at his back. "Leave it open: I want to be able to hear if the boy calls out."

He retraced his steps in silence, took off his shoes and his trousers. The right shoe dropped rather noisily to the floor.

"Put your clothes on the armchair."

He put down his trousers, jacket, and shirt on the rocking-chair, which creaked as it swayed to and fro. He stood naked, his arms swinging at his sides and his toes curled up, in the center of the room. He wanted to laugh.

"Come on."

He lay down on the bed beside a warm and naked body; she was lying on her back, motionless, her arms close to her sides. But when he kissed her, just below the neck, he could feel the throbbing of her heart, heavy mallet-blows that shook her from head to foot. He remained for a while motionless, awed by that palpitating immobility: he had forgotten Irène's face; he stretched out a hand and slid his fingers over an expanse of sightless flesh. No matter who. People passed, not far away—Mathieu could hear their shoes creak; they were talking loudly and laughing together.

"Tell me, Marcel," said a woman's voice. "If you were Hitler, would you be able to sleep tonight?"

They laughed; their footsteps and their laughter receded, and Mathieu was alone.

"If I have to take any precautions," said a sleepy voice, "you'd better tell me at once."

"No need to do that," said Mathieu. "I'm not that sort of fellow."

She did not reply. He could hear her strong and regular breathing. A meadow—a meadow in the night; she breathed as a plant breathes, or a tree; he wondered whether she had not already gone to sleep. But an awkward, half-closed hand flickered over his hip and thigh, with what might pass for a caress. He turned gently over and took her in his arms.

Boris dropped back on to his side and pulled down the sheets. Lola had not moved; she remained outstretched on her back, her eyes closed. Boris curled himself up so as to avoid as far as possible the contact of the sheet against his perspiring body. Lola said, without opening her eyes: "I'm beginning to believe you love me."

He did not reply. That night he had loved all women in her person—the duchesses and all the rest. His hands, which an unvanquishable modesty had hitherto confined to Lola's shoulders and hips, had found their way everywhere; his lips too; and this time he frantically sought that half-oblivion into which he usually fell at the height of his enjoyment, and which so disgusted him: there were thoughts he wanted to escape. He felt clammy and unclean, his heart was throbbing violently; it was not an unpleasant sensation, and at that moment it was better not to think too much. Ivich always said to him: You think too much; and she was right. He suddenly noticed a trickle of moisture oozing from the corners of Lola's closed eyelids into two little pools, which gradually welled up each side of her nose. What could be the matter now, he wondered. He had gone through the last twenty-four hours with a sense of dry agony in the pit of his stomach and was not in a melting mood.

"Give me my handkerchief," said Lola. "It's under the pillow."

She wiped her eyes, opened them, and looked at him with a hard, suspicious air. "What have I done now?" But, to his surprise, she said in a toneless voice: "You'll be going away."

"Where to? Oh, yes; but not at once: in a year's time."

"What is a year?"

She looked at him intently; he reached a hand out from

under the sheets and smoothed his hair down over his forehead.

"In a year the war may be over," he said cautiously.

"Over? Don't you believe it: we know when a war begins, we never know when it is going to end."

Her white arm leaped from underneath the sheets; she began to feel Boris's face as though she were blind. She passed a hand over his temples and his cheeks, traced the contours of his ears, she caressed his nose with the tips of her fingers; he began to feel ridiculous.

"A year is a long while," he said bitterly. "Plenty of time to think about it."

"That shows you're just a kid. If you knew how quickly a year passes, at my age."

"Well, it seems to me a long while," said Boris obstinately.

"So you want to fight?"

"It isn't that."

He felt a little cooler, turned over on his back, stretched out his legs, and came into contact with a piece of fabric at the end of the bed—his pajama trousers. He went on, gazing up at the ceiling:

"In any case, since I've got to go to war, I would sooner go at once and not talk about it."

"And what about me?" cried Lola. Then she added, catching at her breath: "Don't you mind leaving me, you little wretch?"

"But I shall have to leave you anyhow."

"Not yet awhile," she said passionately. "And I shan't survive it. Besides, I know you, you won't write for days on end, you're so lazy, and I shall think you're dead. You don't know what it will be like."

"You don't either," said Boris. "Wait till it happens before you make such a fuss."

A silence followed, then she said in a rasping voice that he knew only too well: "Well, it shouldn't be very difficult to wangle you out of it. This little one knows more people than you think."

He swung himself on to his side and looked at her with fury.

"Lola, if you do that—"

"Well?"

"I'll never speak to you again."

She had composed herself; she said to him with a quizzical smile: "I thought you had a horror of war? You have often told me you were an antimilitarist."

"I still am."

"Well, then?"

"That's not the same thing."

She had closed her eyes again, she was no longer agitated, but her face had changed: the two familiar wrinkles of weariness and anguish had appeared at the corners of her lips. Boris made an effort.

"I am an antimilitarist because I can't stand officers," he said in a soothing tone. "I'd sort of like the plain soldiers."

"But you'll be an officer. They'll compel you to become one."

Boris did not reply: it was too complicated; he was confused himself. He detested officers, that was a fact. But from another standpoint, since this was *his* war and he had been dedicated to a brief military career, he *must* become a second lieutenant. "Ah," he thought, "if only I could be there now with my platoon and not have to go through all this fuss." And he said abruptly: "I keep on wondering whether I shall be afraid."

"Afraid?"

"Yes—it worries me."

He thought she did not understand: it would have been better to confide in Mathieu or even in Ivich. But since she was here . . .

"All this year we shall read in the newspapers how the French advanced through a storm of steel and fire, and so on—you know the sort of thing. And every time I shall ask myself whether I can take it. Or I shall ask the men on leave whether it was awful, and they will say it was; and I shall feel queer. It's all going to be very pretty."

She began to laugh and, in a mirthless imitation of his own words, she cried: "Wait till it happens before you make a fuss. And even if you were afraid, stupid, who cares?"

It wasn't worth trying to make her understand. He yawned, and said: "Shall we switch off the light? I'm tired."

"If you like," said Lola. "Kiss me."

He kissed her and switched off the light. He hated her; he thought: "She doesn't love me for myself or she would have understood." They were all the same, they pretended to be blind: they've transformed me into a fighting-cock, a bull for the arena, and now they won't face the facts, my father wants me to get my diploma, and this one wants to wangle me into a soft job because she once slept with a colonel. After a moment or two he felt the impact of a feverish, naked body against his back. "I shall have to lie beside this body for another year. She takes advantage of me," he thought; he hardened his heart and withdrew to his own side of the bed.

"What are you doing?" said Lola. "You'll fall on to the floor."

"You make me so hot."

She muttered something unintelligible, and drew away from him. A year. Another year in which to wonder whether I'm a coward, a year in which to be afraid of being afraid. He heard Lola's regular breathing, she was asleep; and then her body again flopped down on him; it wasn't her fault, there was a dip in the middle of the mattress, but Boris quivered with rage and desperation: she'll be sprawling over me until morning. Men were the best companions—every man to his own bed. Then a sudden

dizziness came over him, he lay wide-eyed and staring into
the darkness, an icy shiver rippled down his perspiring
back: he had just remembered that he had decided to
join up next day.

The door opened and Mme Birnenschatz appeared in a
nightgown, with a scarf wrapped round her head.

"Gustave," she said loudly, to drown the noise of the
radio, "do please come to bed."

"Go to sleep," said M. Birnenschatz. "Don't you worry
about me."

"But I can't sleep if you aren't in bed."

"Nonsense!" he said with a jerk of irritation. "As you
see, I'm waiting for an announcement."

"What announcement?" she said. "Why do you keep on
fiddling with that abominable radio? The neighbors will
be complaining soon. What are you waiting for?"

M. Birnenschatz turned to her and gripped her arm. "I
bet it's a bluff," he said. "I bet there'll be an official denial
during the night."

"What are you talking about?" she cried.

He signed to her to be quiet. A calm, deliberate voice
had begun to speak:

"A denial has been issued from authorized circles in
Berlin of all reports that have appeared abroad, either regarding an ultimatum addressed to Czechoslovakia by
Germany to expire today at two p.m., or an alleged general
mobilization said to have been decreed immediately following that hour."

"Listen," said M. Birnenschatz. "Listen."

"It is considered that these reports are calculated to
spread panic and create an atmosphere favorable to war.

"A denial has also been issued of an announcement
stated to have been made by Minister Goebbels to a foreign newspaper regarding the ultimatum in question, adding that Dr. Goebbels has not received any foreign
journalist for some weeks past."

M. Birnenschatz listened a little while longer, but the voice was silent. Then he waltzed Mme Birnenschatz round the room, exclaiming: "I told you so, I told you so; they're backing down, it's a shameful retreat. There'll be no war, Catherine, the Nazis are done for."

Light. The four walls suddenly reared up between Mathieu and the light. He raised himself on his hands and looked at Irène's face; the nudity of that feminine body had risen into her face, the body had reabsorbed it, as nature reabsorbs forsaken gardens; Mathieu could no longer isolate it from those shapely shoulders, those small pointed breasts, it was now a flower of flesh, serene and dimly seen.

"I hope it wasn't too dull?" she asked.

"Dull?"

"Some men find me dull because I'm not very active. One got so bored with me that he departed in the early morning and never came back."

"I wasn't bored," said Mathieu.

She slid a finger over his neck. "But you mustn't think I'm cold, you know."

"I don't," said Mathieu. "And now stop talking."

He took her face between his hands and leaned over her eyes: two glacier pools, transparent and infinitely deep. She looks at me. Behind that look, body and face had vanished. Deep in those eyes there is the night. The virgin night. She has admitted me into her eyes, and in that night I now exist: a naked man. I shall leave her in an hour or two and yet I shall remain in her forever. In her, in this nameless night. He remembered that she did not even know his name. Suddenly he felt so attracted by her that he wanted to tell her his name. But he refrained: words would lie; what drew him was not so much the woman as the room, the guitar on the wall, the boy asleep on the cot, the occasion, and events of the night.

She smiled. "You're looking at me, but you don't see me."

"Yes I do."

She yawned. "I should like to go to sleep for a bit."

"Do," said Mathieu. "But set your alarm for six: I've got to look in at my apartment before going to the station."

"Are you off this morning?"

"This morning at eight o'clock."

"Can I come to the station with you?"

"If you like."

"Wait a moment," she said. "I must get out of bed to set the alarm and put out the light. But don't look, I'm ashamed of my behind, it's too broad and too low."

He averted his eyes and heard her moving about the room; then she switched off the light. She said, as she got back into bed: "I sometimes get up when I'm asleep and walk about the room. Just give me a slap on the head if I do."

Wednesday, September 28

Six o'clock in the morning.

She was very pleased with herself: she had not closed her eyes all night, but she did not feel in the least sleepy, though her eyes were smarting and twitching, her left eye itched, and shivers of weariness rippled up her back into her neck. She had traveled in a *horribly* deserted train, the last living creature she had seen was the station master at Soissons, waving his red flag. Then, suddenly, in the hall of the Est station, she came in sight of the crowd. A very uninviting crowd, largely consisting of old women and soldiers; but its countless eyes, the countless looks in them—besides, Ivich adored the perpetual heaving of a crowd, the jostling backs and elbows, the thrusting shoulders, and persistent undulations of the array of heads; it was so agreeable not to have to support the burden of the war in solitude. She paused in one of the great outer gates and stood in pious contemplation of the boulevard de Strasbourg, feasting her eyes on it and gradually visualizing her memories of the trees, the shuttered shops, the motor-buses and the car tracks, the cafés now just opening, and the smoky air of early morning. Even if they dropped their bombs in the next two minutes, or in thirty seconds, they couldn't take that away from me. She resolved not to miss anything, not even the huge poster inscribed: *Dubo—dubon—dubonnet,* on her left; then suddenly a wild impulse came upon her—she must get into the city before *they* came. She jostled past two Breton women carrying bird-cages, and planted her foot on a real Parisian sidewalk. She felt as though she were entering a furnace—an uplifting, rather sinister sensation. "Everything will be burned—women, children, and old people, and I shall perish in the flames." She was not afraid: anyway, I should have hated to grow old; but haste dried up her throat; there was not a minute to lose: so many scenes to be revisited, the Flea Market, the Catacombs, Ménilmontant, and other places that she did not yet know, such as the Musée Grévin; if *they* leave me a week, if *they* don't come before next Tuesday, I could see them all. "Ah," she thought passionately, "a week of life, I'll pack a whole year's enjoyment into it, I'll die enjoying myself." She hailed a taxi.

"12 rue Huyghens."

"Right."

"Go along the boulevard Saint-Michel, the rue Auguste-Comte, the rue Vavin, the rue Delambre, and then by the rue de la Gaîté, and the avenue du Maine."

"It's longer that way," said the chauffeur.

"Never mind."

She got into the cab and shut the door. She had left Laon behind her forever. She would never see it again: here we shall die. "What a lovely day!" she thought. "This afternoon we'll go to the rue des Rosiers and the Île Saint-Louis."

"Quick!" cried Irène. "Come here."

Mathieu was in his shirt-sleeves, he was combing his hair in front of the mirror. He laid his comb on the table, put his jacket under his arm, and went into the other room.

"Well?"

Irène pointed sadly at the bed. "He has bolted!"

"Well I'll be damned," said Mathieu.

He eyed the tumbled bed for a moment or two, scratched his head, and then burst out laughing. Irène looked at him with a grave, astonished air, and then she caught the infection of his laughter.

"He sure slipped one over on us!" said Mathieu.

He slipped on his coat. Irène was still laughing.

"We'll meet at the Dôme at seven."

"At seven," said she.

He bent over her and kissed her lightly.

Ivich ran upstairs and stopped at the third-floor landing, quite out of breath. The door was ajar. She began to tremble. Perhaps it was the concierge. She went in: all the doors were open, all the lights on. In the hall she noticed a large suitcase: he must be there.

"Mathieu!"

No one answered. The kitchen was empty, but in the bedroom the bed was unmade. "He has spent the night here." She went into the sitting-room and opened the windows and shutters. "It's not such a bad place," she thought, feeling a little touched. "I was rather ungracious about it." She would live there, she would write to him four times a week; no, five times. And then one fine day he would read in the newspapers that Paris had been bombed and get no more letters. She pottered round the sitting-room, fingered the books and the crab paper-weight. A broken cigarette lay near a book by Martineau on Stendhal; she picked it up and put it in her bag among her mementoes. Then she sat down sedately on the divan. In a moment or two she heard footsteps on the stairs, and her heart leaped. It was he. He stopped a moment in the hall, then he entered, carrying his suitcase. Ivich dropped her bag on the floor.

"Ivich!"

He did not look astonished. He put down his suitcase, picked up the bag, and gave it to her.

"Have you been here long?"

She did not reply; she felt rather vexed with him because she had dropped her bag. He came and sat down beside her. She did not look at him; she looked at the carpet and the tips of her shoes.

"This is a bit of luck," he said gaily. "An hour later and you would have missed me: I'm catching the eight o'clock train for Nancy."

"What! You're going away so soon?"

She said no more; she felt rather put out and hated her own voice. They had so little time, she would have so liked to behave unaffectedly, but could not manage it: when she had not seen people for a long while, she could not meet them again in an unaffected way. She had let herself sink into a sort of flaccid torpor not far removed from sulkiness. She kept her face averted from him, but let him see she was upset; indeed, she felt more embarrassed than if she had been looking him in the face. Two hands reached out to the suitcase, opened it, took out an alarm clock, and wound it up. Mathieu got up to put the clock on the table. Ivich raised her eyes slightly and saw him, a black figure, against the light. He sat down again, still silent, and Ivich regained a little courage. He looked at her; she knew that he was looking at her. No one, for three months, had looked at her in quite that way. She felt like a precious, fragile object: a small dumb idol, which was agreeable enough, though vexing, and not at all painful. Suddenly she caught the ticking of the alarm clock and realized that he would soon be going. "I won't be fragile, I won't be an idol," she thought. She forced herself to turn to him. The look on his face surprised her.

"Well, here you are, Ivich."

He did not appear to be thinking about what he said. She smiled at him, none the less, but felt quite frozen. He did not return her smile; he said slowly: "It's you. . . ."

He surveyed her with astonishment. "How did you get here?" he went on, in a more animated tone.

"By train."

She set the palms of her hands together and squeezed them hard, to make the joints crack.

"What I meant was: do your parents know?"

"No."

"You ran away?"

"More or less."

"Yes," he said. "Yes. Well, this is admirable: you will live here." And he added with interest: "Were you bored at Laon?"

She did not reply: the cool, assured voice dropped on her neck like a knife-blade.

"Poor Ivich!"

She began to tug at her hair.

"Is Boris at Biarritz?" he continued.

"Yes."

Boris had got gingerly out of bed, shivering as he slipped on his trousers and his jacket, flung a glance at Lola, who was asleep with her mouth open, noiselessly opened the door, and went out into the passage, carrying his shoes in his hand.

Ivich glanced at the alarm clock; the time was already twenty minutes past six. "What time is it?" she asked plaintively.

"Twenty minutes past six," he said. "Just a second: I'm going to put a few things into my musette-bag—that won't take me long; then I shall be entirely free."

He knelt down by the suitcase. She watched him listlessly. She was no longer conscious of her body, but the tick-tock of the clock echoed in her ears. In a moment or two he got up. "All ready now."

He remained standing in front of her. She noticed that his trousers were a little worn at the knees.

"Listen, Ivich," he said gently. "We must talk seriously: the apartment is at your disposal; the key is on the nail beside the door, you can live here until the end of the war. I have arranged about my salary: I have given a power of attorney to Jacques, he will draw it and send it to you every month. There will be some small bills to pay from time to time: the rent, for instance, and the taxes, unless soldiers are exempted—and you might send me a small parcel now and then. What remains is yours: I think you will manage all right."

She listened in amazement to that level, monotonous voice, the voice of a radio announcer. How could he be so tactless? She didn't wholly understand what he was saying, but she could clearly picture his expression, his half-smile, his heavy-lidded eyes, and his air of calm complacency. She looked at him, to help herself to hate him more effectively, and her hatred vanished. He didn't look at all like his voice. Was he in distress? No, he didn't seem unhappy. It was merely a face that she had never seen on him before.

"Are you listening to me, Ivich?" he asked with a smile.

"Certainly," said she. She got up. "Mathieu, I wish you would show me Czechoslovakia on a map."

"I'm afraid I haven't got any maps," he said. "Though wait—I must have an old atlas."

He took down from his shelves an album bound in cardboard, laid it on the table, turned over the pages, and opened it at "Central Europe." It was colored in the crudest yellows and violets. No blue, no sea nor ocean being shown. Ivich looked intently at the map and could not discover any Czechoslovakia either.

"It dates from before 1914," said Mathieu.

"And before 1914 Czechoslovakia didn't exist?"

"No."

He picked up his fountain pen and traced an irregular shape in the center of the map.

"It's more or less like that," he said.

Ivich looked at that large, drably colored expanse of waterless earth, and the contour line of black ink, which looked very obtrusive and ugly on the printed sheet. Inside it she read the word "Bohemia" and said: "So that's Czechoslovakia. . . ." It all seemed so futile, and she began to sob.

"Ivich!" said Mathieu.

She suddenly found herself half lying on the divan; Mathieu was holding her in his arms. At first she stiffened: I don't want his pity, I'm behaving like a fool; but in a moment she relaxed, there was no war, no Czechoslovakia, and no Mathieu; only that soft warm pressure round her shoulders.

"Did you get any sleep last night?" he asked.

"No," she said between two sobs.

"My poor little Ivich! Wait a minute."

He got up and went out; she heard him moving about in the next room. When he returned, he had recovered something of the naïve, placid air she liked. "I've put clean sheets on the bed and made it, you can go to bed as soon as I have gone."

She looked at him. "But—I'm not coming to the station with you?"

"I thought you detested platform farewells."

"Oh," she said, with an appealing air, "on such a special occasion—"

He shook his head. "I would sooner go alone. Besides, you must get some sleep."

"Very well," she said. Then she thought: "How silly of me!" and suddenly felt cold and isolated. She shook her head vigorously, wiped her eyes, and smiled. "You're right, I'm nervously upset from being tired; I'll go and rest."

He took her hand and raised her to her feet. "I must first show you round the property."

In the bedroom he stopped before a cupboard. "Here

are six pairs of sheets, some pillowcases and blankets. There's also an eiderdown somewhere, but I don't know where I've put it, the concierge could tell you."

He had opened the cupboard, looked at the piles of white linen, and laughed sardonically.

"What's the matter?" asked Ivich politely.

"All this stuff belongs to me. How absurd it seems!"

He turned towards her. "I'll show you the pantry too. Come along."

They went into the kitchen, and he pointed to a cupboard. "There it is. You'll find oil, salt and pepper, and a few cans of preserves." He lifted the cylindrical cans one after another to the level of his eyes and turned them round under the light. "That's salmon, that's sausage meat, and those are three tins of sauerkraut. You can put that in a double boiler. . . ." He paused, and again broke into a rasping laugh. But he said no more, he looked vacantly at a can of peas and replaced it in the cupboard.

"Take care of the gas, Ivich. You must lower the lever on the meter every evening before you go to bed."

They were back in the sitting-room.

"By the way," he said, "I'll let the concierge know as I go out that I'm lending you the apartment. She will send Madame Balaine to you tomorrow. She's my maid, not at all a bad sort."

"Balaine," said Ivich. "What a funny name!"

She laughed and Mathieu smiled.

"Jacques won't be back before the beginning of October," he said. "I had better give you a little money to get on with until then."

He had a thousand-franc note and two two-hundred-franc notes in his pocketbook. He took out the thousand-franc note and gave it to her.

"Thank you very much," said Ivich.

She took it and held it in her hand.

"If anything goes wrong, ring up Jacques. I'll be writing to him to say he's to look after you."

"Thanks," said Ivich.

"You know his address?"

"Yes—yes, thank you."

"Then good-by." He came up to her. "Good-by, my dear Ivich. I'll write to you as soon as I've got an address."

He laid his hands on her shoulders and drew her towards him. "My dear little Ivich."

She raised her forehead submissively. He kissed it, pressed her hand, and went out. She heard the outer door slam; she smoothed out the thousand-franc note and looked at the design; then she tore it into eight pieces and scattered them on the floor.

A tawny-bearded colonial veteran, with one hand on a recruit's shoulder, pointed with the other hand to the African coast. "Join—rejoin—the colonial army." The young recruit looked abysmally stupid. Well, that would be his fate: for six months Boris would look just like that. For three months perhaps: war years count double. "They'll cut my hair," he thought, clenching his teeth. "The bastards!" He had never felt more venomously antimilitarist. He passed a sentry, standing motionless in his box. Boris eyed him darkly, his heart sank, and he swore a silent oath. But he had decided, he must do the deed: and he walked rather limply into the barracks. The sky was ablaze, a light breeze carried a fragrance into these distant suburbs. "What a pity!" thought Boris. "What a pity it's such a fine day!" An officer was pacing up and down outside the police station. Philippe looked at him; he felt utterly forlorn, and he was very cold; his cheek and upper lip were smarting. It would be an inglorious martyrdom. Inglorious and joyless: a prison cell, and then one morning the stake in the Vincennes moat; no one would ever hear of it: he had been disowned by everyone.

"The superintendent of police?" he asked.

The agent looked at him. "On the first floor."

"I shall be my own witness, I am accountable to no one but myself."

"The recruiting office?"

The two guards exchanged a glance, and Boris felt his cheeks blaze. "I must be looking my best," he thought.

"The building at the far end of the yard, first door on the left."

Boris saluted nonchalantly with two fingers and walked firmly across the yard, and then thought rather ruefully that he must also be looking like a bloody fool and was no doubt an object of derision. "A guy who comes here on his own, without being called up, must seem to them just silly." Philippe was standing up in the full light, confronting a short man with a ribbon in his buttonhole, and thinking of Raskolnikov.

"Are you the superintendent?"

"I'm his secretary," said the other.

Philippe spoke with difficulty, owing to his swollen lip, but his voice was steady. He took a step forward.

"I am a deserter," he said firmly, "and I am in possession of false papers."

The secretary looked at him. "Sit down," he said politely.

The taxi sped towards the Est station.

"You're going to be late," said Irène.

"No," said Mathieu, "I shall just make it." He added by way of explanation: "There was a girl at my place."

"A girl?"

"She had come from Laon to see me."

"Is she in love with you?"

"Certainly not."

"Are you in love with her?"

"No; I am lending her my flat."

"Is she a good girl?"

"No," said Mathieu. "She is not a good girl. But she isn't a bad girl either."

They were silent. The taxi was crossing the Halles.

"There—there," said Irène suddenly. "It was there."

"So it was."

"And only yesterday. Good Lord! It seems such a while ago."

She swung round and peered out of the small window in the back of the cab.

"So that's over," she said, sitting down again.

Mathieu did not answer. He was thinking of Nancy. He had never been there.

"You don't talk much," said Irène. "But I don't mind."

"There was a time when I talked too much," said Mathieu with a curt laugh.

He turned towards her. "What are you going to do today?"

"Nothing," said Irène. "I never do anything: my old man makes me an allowance."

The taxi stopped. They got out and Mathieu paid.

"I don't like stations," said Irène. "There's something sinister about them."

She suddenly slipped a hand under his arm. She walked close beside him, in silent intimacy; he felt as though he had known her for ten years.

"I must get my ticket."

They made their way through the crowd. It was a civilian crowd, sluggish and silent, interspersed with a few soldiers.

"You know Nancy?"

"No," said Mathieu.

"I do. Tell me where you're going."

"To the aviation barracks at Essey-les-Nancy."

"Yes," she said. "I know where that is."

There was a line of men with musette-bags at the ticket window.

"Would you like me to get you a paper while you wait?"

"No," he said, gripping her arm. "Stay with me."

She smiled at him contentedly. They moved forward, step by step.

"Essey-les-Nancy."

He produced his army book, and the clerk gave him a ticket. He turned round to her. "Come with me to the gate; but I would rather you didn't come on to the platform."

They walked on, and then stopped.

"Well, good-by," she said.

"Good-by," said Mathieu.

"Just one night."

"One night—yes, but you will be my sole memory of Paris."

He kissed her. She said: "Will you write to me?"

"I don't know," said Mathieu.

He looked at her for a moment without speaking, and then moved away.

"Hey!" she cried to him.

He turned. She smiled, but her lips quivered.

"I don't even know your name."

"Mathieu Delarue."

"Come in."

He was sitting up in bed, in pajamas, his hair as always so immaculate that she found herself wondering whether he wore a hair-net at night. The room smelt of eau-de-Cologne. He looked at her with bewilderment, hurriedly took his spectacles from the bedside table, and put them on his nose.

"Ivich!"

"Yes, it's me," she said good-humoredly.

She sat on the edge of the bed and smiled at him. The train for Nancy was moving out of the Est station; at Berlin the bombers had perhaps already taken off. "I want to enjoy myself! I want to enjoy myself!" She looked round her: it was a hotel room, repellently luxurious. The bomb will go through the roof and the floor of the sixth story: this is where I shall die.

"I never thought I'd see you again," he said with dignity.

"Why? Because you behaved like a louse?"

"We had been drinking," he said.

"I had been drinking because I had flunked the P.C.B. But *you* hadn't been drinking: you wanted to take me to your room; you were waiting for a chance."

He was utterly at a loss.

"And here I am," she said, "in your room. Well?"

He flushed scarlet. "Ivich!"

She laughed in his face. "You don't look very formidable."

There was a long silence, then a hand fumbled round her waist. The bombers had crossed the frontier. She laughed until the tears came into her eyes: anyway, I shan't die a virgin.

"Is this place free?"

The stout old gentleman grunted.

Mathieu put his haversack in the luggage-rack and sat down. The compartment was full; Mathieu peered at his traveling companions, but it was still too dark to see them. He remained motionless for an instant, then came a sudden jerk and the train started. Mathieu was conscious of a thrill of joy: it was all over. Tomorrow—Nancy, war, fear, death perhaps, and freedom. We shall see, said he, we shall see. He felt in his pocket for his pipe and came upon an envelope: Daniel's letter. His impulse was to replace it, but a sort of shame prevented him: after all, he must read it some time. He filled his pipe, lit it, tore open the envelope, and took out seven sheets of paper covered with close, even handwriting, without any erasures. "He must have made a rough draft. What an epistle!" he thought with vexation. The train was now fortunately out of the station and he could see better. He read:

My dear Mathieu:

I can too well imagine your amazement, and I feel profoundly how inopportune this letter must be. Indeed, I don't myself quite know why I am writing it: I suppose one confidence, like one crime, leads to others. When I disclosed to you, last June, a certain picturesque aspect of my character, perhaps I unconsciously chose you to receive my intimate experiences. This would be regrettable, because if I had to get you to endorse all my activities, I could not fail to regard you with active hatred, which would be tiresome for me and not to your advantage. You may picture me *laughing* as I write all this. For several days past I have been conscious of a certain leaden resilience—I apologize for such a conjunction of words—and *Laughter* has been vouchsafed to me as a supplementary grace. But enough; it is not any ordinary event in my life that I want to describe to you, but an *extraordinary* adventure. It will not, I am sure, appear to me completely real until it also exists for other people. Not that I rely greatly on your faith, nor even, perhaps, on your good faith. The rationalism that for the last ten years has been your livelihood —if I ask you to forget it for a moment in order to follow me, I doubt whether you would do so. But possibly I have rightly chosen to communicate this extraordinary experience to the one friend least calculated to understand it; possibly I hoped, in so doing, to get something like a confirmatory proof. Not that I expect a reply from you: I should be sorry if you felt obliged to favor me with exhortations to be sensible, which— pray believe me—I have not failed to address to myself. I must confess that it is when I think of common sense, sane reason, and the positive sciences that the manna of laughter tends to descend upon me most of all. Moreover, I fancy Marcelle would be annoyed if she found a letter from you in my mail. She would think she had come upon a clandestine correspondence, and perhaps, knowing you as she does, would imagine that you are placing yourself generously at my service, by way of guiding my first steps in matrimony. But here is why your silence may serve me as a confirmatory proof: if I can picture your "hideous smile" without being distressed by it, and conceive the tacit irony with which you will view my "case," without abandoning the exceptional procedure I have chosen, I shall have convinced myself that I have acted rightly. I would add, to avoid all misunderstanding, and in thanking the astute psychologist for his good offices, that this time it is the philosopher I am addressing, for the following narrative belongs to the philosophic plane. You will no doubt pronounce this highly presumptuous, since I have read neither Hegel nor Schopenhauer; but don't take offense; I am certainly not capable of formulating the present operations of my mind in the abstract, I leave that process to you, since it is your profession; I shall be content to live blindly through the experiences you and your more percipient colleagues are able to express in professional terms. In any case, I don't think you are so easily moved: this laughter and these agonies of mine, these flashing intuitions —it is only too probable that you will feel constrained to class them among psychological "states," and explain them by my character and habits, thus taking advantage of what I revealed to you in confidence. Never mind; what I said I meant to say; you may therefore use all this as you think fit, though you may misread me utterly. Indeed, it is with a sort of furtive pleasure that I now set out to give you all the information necessary for establishing the *truth,* knowing that you will use it to plunge deliberately into error.

Now for the facts. But here laughter makes me drop my pen. I laugh till the tears come into my eyes. A subject on which I tremble to embark, which I have never *mentioned* to myself, from modesty as well as self-respect, I now propose to formulate in words, and these words I shall address to *you,* they will remain on these blue sheets of notepaper, and you may even amuse yourself by re-reading them ten years from now. I feel somehow I am committing a sacrilege against myself, and that is the most inexcusable aspect of the matter; but I have *also* realized that I am giving you away too: so the said sacrilege is rather a joke—I should never wholly value what I most care for if I had not, at least once, laughed at it. Well, I shall have made you laugh at my new faith. I shall carry within myself a humble certitude, so vast as to be utterly beyond you, though all the facts be wholly in your hands; what crushes me will be there diminished to the measure of your unworthiness. And so, if you are amused by this letter, I already anticipated it: I am laughing, Mathieu, laughing; God makes man, himself surpassing all men and derided by them all, hanging open-mouthed upon the cross, livid, speechless, unsullied by the multitude—what can be more *laughable!* Well, whatever you may do, the delicious tears of laughter will never trickle down your cheeks.

Let us see what words can do. Will you understand me, for a start, if I tell you that I have never known what I *am?* My vices, my virtues, are under my nose, but I can't see them, nor stand far enough back to view myself as a whole. I seem to be a sort of flabby mass in which words are engulfed; no sooner do I name myself than what is named is merged in him who names, and one gets no farther. I have often wanted to hate myself and, as you know, had good reasons for so doing. But my attempted hatred of myself was absorbed into my insubstantiality and was nothing but a recollection. I could not love myself either—I am sure, though I have never tried to. But I was eternally compelled to *be myself;* I was my own burden, but never burdensome enough, Mathieu. For one instant, on that June evening when I elected to confess to you, I thought I had encountered myself in your bewildered eyes. You *saw* me, in your eyes I was solid and predictable; my acts and moods were the actual consequences of a definite entity. And through me you knew that entity. I described it to you in my words, I revealed to you facts unknown to you, which had helped you to visualize it. And yet you saw it, I merely saw you seeing it. For one instant you were the heaven-sent mediator between me and myself, you perceived that compact and solid entity which I was and wanted to be in just as simple and ordinary a way as I perceived you. For, after all, I exist, I *am,* though I have no sense of being; and it is an exquisite torment to discover in oneself such utterly unfounded certainty, such unsubstantiated pride. I then understood that one could not reach oneself except through another's judgment, another's hatred. And also through another's love perhaps; but there is here no question of that. For this revelation I am not ungrateful to you. I do not know how you would describe our present relations. Not goodwill, nor wholly hatred. Put it that there is a corpse between us. My corpse.

I was in this attitude of mind when I went to Sauveterre with Marcelle. Sometimes I wanted to see you again, sometimes I dreamed of murdering you. But one fine day I realized our relations were strictly mutual. Without me, you would be that same insubstantial entity that I am for myself. It is by my agency that you can at times get an occasional and doubtless rather exasperating glimpse of yourself—as you really are: a rather limited rationalist, superficially self-confident, but fundamentally without convictions, well disposed to everything within the compass of your reason, blind and disingenuous towards anything else; rational by self-interest, naturally sentimental, by no means sensual; in brief, a cautious, moderate intellectual, an excellent middle-class product. If it be true that I cannot get at myself without your agency, you need mine if you want to know yourself. Thus I saw us, mutually sustaining our two nonentities, and for the first time I laughed a deep and all-consuming laugh; then I sank back into a sort of dark indifference, the more so as my sacrifice in that same month of June, which I then envisaged as a painful expiration, had become *horribly* endurable. But here I must be silent: I can't talk about Marcelle without laughing, and from motives of decency that you will appreciate, we mustn't laugh at her together. Then the wildest, craziest *chance* befell me. God sees me, Mathieu; I feel it and I know it. Now all is said: how I wish I were with you and could draw an even stronger certitude, if that were possible, from the spectacle of your laughter as you read these words!

But enough of this. We have laughed quite enough at each other: I resume my narrative. You must have experienced, in the subway, in the foyer of a theater, or in a train the sudden and irksome sense that you were being looked at from behind. You turn around, but the observer has buried his nose in a book; you can't discover *who* was looking at you. You turn back, but you are sure that the unknown eyes are again upon you, there's a faint tingling all over your back, like a sudden twitch of all your tissues. Well, that is what I felt for the first time, on September 26, at three o'clock in the afternoon, in the hotel garden. No one was there, you understand, Mathieu, no one at all. But the look was there. Understand me well: I did not see it, as one sees a passing profile, a forehead, or a pair of eyes; for its essential character is to be *beyond perception*. But I became more compact and concentrated, I was both transparent and opaque, I existed *in the presence* of a look.

Since then I have been continually under observation, even in my solitary room; sometimes, the consciousness of transfixion by that sword-blade, of that eye upon me while asleep, awoke me with a start. I have, in fact, almost entirely lost the capacity for sleep. Ah, Mathieu, what a discovery! *I was seen,* I struggled to know myself, I seemed to be slipping out of my extremities, I claimed your kindly intercession, and all the time I was seen, the inexorable look, an invisible steel blade, was on me. And you too, skeptic and scoffer as you are, *you are seen.* But you don't know it. I can easily describe that look: it is nothing; it is a purely negative entity: imagine a pitch-dark night. It's the night that looks at you, but it's a dazzling night, in fullest splendor; the night behind the day. I am flooded with black light; it is all over my hands and eyes and heart, and I can't see it. Believe me, I first loathed this incessant violation of myself; as you know, I used to long to become invisible, to go and leave no trace, on earth or in men's hearts. What anguish to discover that look as a universal medium from which I can't escape! But what a relief as well! I know at last that I am. I adapt for my own use, and to your disgust, your prophet's foolish wicked words: "I think, therefore I am," which used to trouble me so sorely, for the more I thought, the less I seemed to be; and I say: "I am seen, therefore I am." I need no longer bear the responsibility of my turbid and disintegrating self: he who sees me causes me to be; I am as he sees me. I turn my eternal, shadowed face towards the night, I stand up like a challenge, and I say to God: Here am I. Here am I as you see me, as I am. What can I do now?—you know me, and I do not know myself. What can I do except support myself. And you, whose look eternally creates me—do support me. Mathieu, what joy, what torment! At last I am transmuted into myself. Hated, despised, sustained, a presence supports me to continue thus forever. I am infinite and infinitely guilty. But I *am,* Mathieu, I am. Before God and before men, I *am. Ecce homo.*

I called on the curé of Sauveterre: an astute peasant of some education, with the worn and mobile face of an old actor. I don't care much for him, but I was not at all sorry that my first contact with the Church should take place through such an agency. He received me in a study lined with books, all of which he has certainly not read. I started by giving him a thousand francs for his poor, and I saw that he took me for a reformed criminal. I felt I was going to laugh, and I had to bear in mind my tragic situation in order to retain my gravity.

"*Monsieur le curé,*" I said, "I want to ask you this one question: does your religion teach that God sees us?"

"Certainly," he answered with astonishment. "He reads our hearts."

"But what does he see there?" I asked. "Does he see the froth and foam of daily thoughts, or does he penetrate to our eternal essence?"

The sly old gentleman gave me the following answer, in which I recognized the mark of secular wisdom:

"Monsieur, God sees everything."

"I understood that . . ."

Mathieu crumpled the sheets with impatience. "What trite rambling!" he thought. The window was open; he smashed the letter into a ball and tossed it out.

"No," said the superintendent, "you speak; I don't like talking to these senior officers; they treat you like an orderly."

"I sort of think this fellow will be more amiable," said the secretary. "After all, we are returning his son to him; besides, he is in the wrong: he ought to have looked after him properly."

"You'll see," said the superintendent. "He'll manage to make himself unpleasant. Especially in the present circumstances: on the eve of a war a general isn't likely to admit he's in the wrong."

The secretary picked up the receiver and dialed the number. The superintendent lit a cigarette. "Be tactful, Mirant," he said. "Keep it on an official level and don't say too much."

"Hello," said the secretary. "Hello, General Lacaze?"

"Yes," said a rasping voice. "What do you want?"

"I am the superintendent's secretary at the rue Delambre police station."

The voice seemed to display a little more interest. "Yes; well?"

"A young man called at my office about eight o'clock this morning," said the secretary in a noncommittal, rather drawling tone. "He said he was a deserter and in possession of false papers. We have in fact found on him a rough forgery of a Spanish passport. He refused to reveal his identity. But the prefecture had sent us your stepson's description and photographs, so we recognized him at once."

After a pause the secretary continued, with rather less assurance: "Of course, general, no charge can be brought against him. He is not a deserter, not having been called to the colors; he has a false passport in his pocket, but that does not constitute an offense, since he has not had the opportunity to use it. We hold him at your disposal, and you can come and get him when you like."

"Did you put him through any sort of third degree?" asked the dry voice.

The secretary started.

"What does he say?" asked the superintendent.

The secretary put his hand over the receiver. "He wants to know if we've third-degreed him."

The superintendent raised his hands in the air, while the secretary replied:

"No, general; of course not."

"Pity," said the general.

The secretary permitted himself a respectful laugh.

"What did he say?" asked the superintendent. But the secretary turned his back on him and leaned over the telephone.

"I'll come this evening or tomorrow. In the meantime keep him at the station; it will be a lesson for him."

"Certainly, general."

The general hung up.

"What did he say?" asked the superintendent.

"He wanted the boy put through a third degree."

The superintendent stubbed his cigarette in the ash-tray. "Did he indeed!" said he ironically.

Eighteen thirty o'clock. Sun on the sea—the sun went on setting, the wasps went on buzzing, and war came nearer; she flicked away a wasp with a lazy gesture; Jacques behind her, consumed his whisky in countless little sips. "Life," she thought, "is interminable." Father, mother, brothers, uncles, and aunts, every year for fifteen years, had assembled in this drawing-room on fine September afternoons, stiff and silent like an array of family portraits; she had waited for dinner every afternoon, at first beneath the table, then on a little chair, sewing and wondering what was the good of being alive. There they all lay, those vanished afternoons, in the russet gold of this vain hour. Father was there, behind her, reading the *Temps*. What is the good of being alive? What indeed! A fly climbed laboriously up the windowpane, slipped down, and then started again; Odette watched it, she was on the verge of tears.

"Come and sit down," said Jacques. "Daladier is going to speak.

She turned towards him: he had slept badly; he was sitting in the leather armchair, with the infantile expression he assumed when he was afraid. She sat on the arm of his chair. All days are alike. All days. She looked out of the window and thought: "He was right, the sea has changed."

"What is he going to say?"

Jacques shrugged his shoulders. "He is going to tell us that war is declared."

She was conscious of a slight shock, but no more. Fifteen nights. During fifteen nights of anguish she had pleaded in the void; she would have sacrificed everything—house, health, ten years of life—to save the peace. And now, good God in heaven!—let war break out. Let something happen at last: let the dinner-bell ring, let a thunderbolt plunge into the sea, let a gloomy voice suddenly announce a German invasion of Czechoslovakia. A fly. A drowned fly at the bottom of a cup; she herself was drowning in that placid afternoon of catastrophe; she looked at her husband's scanty hair and she no longer quite understood why it should be worth while saving men from death, and their homes from ruin. Jacques put his glass down on the sideboard and said gloomily:

"This is the end."

"The end of what?"

"Of everything. I don't even know what we ought to hope for—victory or defeat."

"Oh!" said she feebly.

"If we are beaten, we shall be Germanized; but I can assure you that the Germans will know how to re-establish order. Communists, Jews, and Freemasons will be cleared out. If we win, we shall be bolshevized, it will be the triumph of the *Frente Crapular*—anarchy, perhaps worse. . . . Alas," he continued in a plaintive tone, "this war should never have been started, never."

She hardly listened to him; what she thought was: "He is afraid, angry, alone." She bent over him and stroked his hair. "My poor little Jacques."

"My dear little Boris."

She smiled at him and looked so likable that Boris felt quite conscience-stricken. I must tell her all the same.

"It's silly," Lola went on. "I'm nervous, I must know what he's going to say; however, it isn't quite the same as if you were going off at once."

Boris contemplated his feet and began to whistle under his breath. It was better to pretend not to have heard, otherwise she would call him a hypocrite into the bargain. As the minutes passed, his task became more difficult. She would assume her pathetic, frightened look and say: "How could you do such a thing and not tell me?"

"It's going to be a nasty job," he said to himself.

"Give me a Martini," said Lola. "What will you have?"

"The same."

He went on whistling. After Daladier's statement an opportunity might appear; she would learn that war had been declared, which would inevitably be something of a shock; then Boris would take the plunge and say: "I've joined up," without giving her time to get her breath. There were cases in which a jolt of that kind provoked unexpected reactions: laughter, for instance; what a joke if she burst out laughing! All the same, I should be rather annoyed, he said to himself dispassionately. All the guests in the hotel were assembled in the hall, even the two curés. They had settled into their armchairs, looking laboriously serene because they felt themselves under observation, but they were really a good deal agitated, and Boris caught more than one of them glancing sidelong at the clock. All right, all right! You've got another half-hour to wait. Boris was in a bad humor, he did not like Daladier, and it infuriated him to think that there were hundreds of thousands of married couples all over France, countless families and curés awaiting like manna from heaven the words of a fellow who had torpedoed the Popular Front. "It magnifies him too much," he thought. And turning towards the radio, he yawned ostentatiously.

It was hot and thirsty, and three of them were asleep: the two next to the corridor and the little old man with clasped hands who looked as though he were praying; the four others had spread a handkerchief over their knees and were playing cards—four quite decent-looking young men, their jackets dangling from the luggage-rack behind them, ruffling their hair as the train rocked. From time to time Mathieu looked out of the corner of his eye at the brown, rather mossy forearms of his neighbor, a short fair man, whose hands, tipped with broad black nails, deftly manipulated the cards. He was a compositor; the fellow next to him was a locksmith. Of the two others in the opposite seat, the one nearest Mathieu was a traveling salesman and the other played the violin in a café at Bois-Colombes. The compartment smelt of humanity, tobacco and wine, sweat trickled down their faces and molded them into glistening masks; on the little old man's bristly chin, between the stiff white thatch on either cheek, the sweat looked oilier and more acrid—a kind of facial excrement. Outside the window, under a glare of sunshine, a gray, flat countryside stretched away into the distance.

The compositor had no luck; he was losing; he bent over the game, arching his brows with an air of dogged surprise. "Well, I'll be damned," he said.

The traveling salesman picked the cards up briskly and shuffled them. The compositor watched them as they slipped from one hand into the other. "It's not my day," he said venomously.

They played in silence. After a moment or two the compositor took a trick.

"Trump!" he said triumphantly. "Perhaps that will turn my luck a bit, my lads. I may get a move on now."

But the salesman had already shown his hands. "Trump, trump, and trump again."

The compositor pushed his cards away. "I shan't play any more; I'm losing too much."

"You're right," said the locksmith. "And then, the train rocks so."

The salesman folded his handkerchief and put it in his pocket. He was a tall, big man with a pale complexion, a flabby, froglike head, large jaws, and a narrow skull. The three others treated him with some slight deference, because he had some education and was a sergeant. He addressed them with familiarity. He cast a malevolent glance at Mathieu and got up rather unsteadily.

"I'm going to get a drink."

"A good idea."

The locksmith and the compositor produced bottles from their pockets; the locksmith drank straight from the bottle, then handed it to the violinist.

"Like a drink?"

"Not just now."

"You don't know what's good for you."

They fell silent, overwhelmed by the heat. The locksmith blew out his cheeks and sighed gently, the salesman lit a High-life. Mathieu thought: "They don't like me, they think me stuck-up." And yet he felt drawn to them, even to the sleepers and the salesman: they yawned, they slept, they played cards, the rocking train rattled their empty heads, but they possessed a destiny, like kings and like the dead. A crushing destiny barely to be distinguished from heat and weariness and buzzing flies: the compartment, close-shut like a hot room in a Turkish bath, barricaded by sun and speed, was jolting them all into the self-same adventure. A gleam of light edged the printer's ear; the lobe of it looked like a blood-red strawberry. "It is with such as these that wars are waged," thought Mathieu. Until then he had pictured war as a tangle of twisted steel, shattered timbers, iron, and stone. Now blood was quivering in the rays of sunshine, the compartment was flooded with a russet light: the war was a destiny of blood; it would be waged with the blood of these six men, with the blood stagnating in their ear-lobes, with the blue current of blood beneath their skins, with the blood behind their lips. They would be split like wineskins, all the excrement would gush out of them—the locksmith's tricky intestines which growled and now and then let fly a muffled fart, would be dragged through the dust, as tragically as those of a disembowelled horse in the arena.

"Well, I shall go and stretch my legs," said the compositor, as though to himself. Mathieu watched him get up and go out into the corridor: that phrase was *historic*. A dead man had uttered it in an undertone, one summer day, when he had been alive. A dead man, or—what came to the same thing—a survivor. Dead men—dead men already. That's why I can't talk to them. He felt quite dizzy as he looked at them, he longed to have a part in their great and historic adventure, but it was not permitted. He sweltered in their heat, he would shed his blood on the selfsame roads, and yet he was not with them, he was just a pale, eternal halo: a man without a destiny.

The compositor, who was smoking in the corridor, swung round and said: "Planes overhead."

The salesman bent over until his chest touched his fat thighs, then turned up his head and his eyebrows.

"Where?"

"There—there."

"I—oh, you don't say!" said the locksmith.

"Are they French?" asked the violinist, looking upwards with expressive and uneasy eyes.

"They're too high up, I can't see."

"Of course they're French," said the locksmith. "What else could they be? War hasn't been declared."

The compositor leaned towards them with both hands on the framework of the doorway.

"How do you know? You've been in this train for the last eleven hours. I suppose you think they'll wait till you arrive before declaring war."

This was a new idea to the locksmith. "Gosh, you're right. You know, men, we may have been at war since this morning."

They turned to the salesman. "What do you say? Do you think we're at war?"

The salesman looked unruffled. He shrugged his shoulders contemptuously. "Do you imagine we shall fight for Czechoslovakia? Have you ever looked at Czechoslovakia on a map? No? Well, I have. And more than once. The place is a bloody nuisance. And about the size of a pocket-handkerchief. It contains two paltry millions of inhabitants

who don't even speak the same language. Do you suppose
that Hitler gives himself a headache over Czechoslovakia?
And Daladier? In the first place, Daladier isn't Daladier:
he's the two hundred families behind him. And they'll tell
Czechoslovakia to go to hell."

He surveyed his audience and concluded: "The truth is
that this business has been on the carpet here and in Germany since 1936. So what did Chamberlain, Hitler, Daladier & Co. do? They said to themselves: we'll settle those
people; and they figured out a little secret treaty. Hitler's
great trick when the workers get restive is to shove them
into the forces. That shuts their mouths for good and all.
Got a grouch, eh? Two hours' drill. Still got a grouch? Six
hours' drill. After that the guys are on their knees, all they
think about is how they can get a lie-down. So the other
ministers said to themselves: we'll do the same, and that
will put a stopper on war. We shan't fight about Czechoslovakia any more than about the Grand Turk. But, mark
you, we've been mobilized, we'll be in uniform for three
or four years, and in the meantime they'll crush the proletariat at home."

They eyed him rather doubtfully; they were not convinced, or possibly they had not understood.

The locksmith said with rather a vacant air: "Well, as
we all know, the big boys break the glasses, and the little
guys pay the damage."

The violinist nodded approval, and they fell silent once
more; the composer turned and laid his forehead against
the large windows in the corridor. "Ah," said Mathieu, "so
they don't very much want to fight." He thought of the
men of 1914, their mouths agape and their rifles garlanded
with flowers. What then? These fellows are right. They
talk in proverbs, but their words betray them, there's something in their heads that can't be expressed in words. Their
fathers were responsible for a fantastic massacre, and for
the last twenty years they have been told that war doesn't

pay. Well, can they be expected to shout: "To Berlin!" However, their words and thoughts were no more than furtive flickers on the margin of their destiny. We shall soon be saying: the soldiers of '38, as we used to say: the soldiers of the Year II, the poilus of 1914. They will dig their holes like the others, neither better nor worse, and then lie in them, because that is what they must do. "And what about *you?*" he thought abruptly. You, their un-invited witness, who are you? What will you do? And if you get back, what will you be like?

The man tapped on the window.

"They're still there."

"Who?" said the violinist with a start.

"The planes. They're circling over the train."

"Circling? Don't be silly!"

"Can't I see them?"

"Well, look—for God's sake!" said the locksmith.

The little old man woke up. "What's the matter?" he asked, laying a hand on his ear.

"Airplanes."

"Oh, airplanes." He smiled beatifically and went to sleep again.

"Come and look," said the compositor. "There must be thirty of them. I've never seen so many outside Villacou-blay." The locksmith and the salesman had got up. Mathieu followed them into the corridor. He saw about twenty small transparent insects, shrimps in the water of the sky. They seemed to exist intermittently: when the sun was not on them, they vanished.

"Suppose they're Fritzes."

"God forbid, we'd catch it! Just imagine what a target this train would make."

There were some twenty men in the corridor, all staring upwards.

"I don't like the look of them," said the salesman.

They all looked nervous. One man was drumming on the

window, another beating time with his foot. The squadron banked steeply and disappeared over the train.

"Ouf!" said a voice.

"Wait a minute!" said the compositor. "Wait! They're still over the train."

"There they are—there!"

A tall lad with a mustache was leaning out of a window backwards. The planes had reappeared, one of them leaving a white track behind it.

"They're Heinies," said the man with the mustache standing up once more.

"Quite likely."

Behind Mathieu the violinist sat up abruptly; he shook the two sleepers.

"What's up?" asked one of them thickly, half opening his reddened eyes.

"War is declared," said the violinist. "There'll be a mess-up soon: Boche airplanes over the train."

Lola grabbed Boris's wrist.

"Listen," she said. "Listen."

Jacques was pallid. "Listen," she said, "he's going to speak."

It was a slow voice, deep and monotonous, with a faintly nasal intonation:

"I had announced that I would this evening make a statement to the country on the international situation, but early this afternoon I received an invitation from the German Government to meet Chancellor Hitler, Monsieur Mussolini, and Monsieur Chamberlain tomorrow at Munich. I have accepted this invitation

"You will understand that on the eve of such important negotiations it is my duty to postpone my proposed statement. But before my departure I desire to offer the people of France an expression of thanks for their courageous and dignified attitude

"I desire especially to thank those Frenchmen who have

been called to the colors, for the steadiness and firmness with which they have given this fresh proof.

"My task is hard. Since the beginning of these present difficulties I have not ceased to labor with all my strength to safeguard peace and the vital interests of France. I shall continue in that effort tomorrow, with the conviction that I have the support of the entire nation."

"Boris!" said Lola. "Boris!"

He did not reply, and she went on: "Wake up, darling— what's the matter? It's peace: there's going to be an international conference."

She turned towards him, flushed and excited. He swore softly between his teeth.

Lola's joy collapsed. "But what's the matter with you, darling? You've turned green."

"I've joined up for three years," said Boris.

The train rumbled on, the airplanes circled overhead.

"The engineer's crazy," exclaimed someone. "Why doesn't he stop? If they start dropping bombs, we'll be blown to bits."

The compositor was pale, but calm; he held his head back, watching for the planes.

"Better jump out," he said between his teeth.

"Hell, no. I can't see jumping out at this speed," said the salesman. He produced his handkerchief and mopped his brow. "Much better pull the alarm signal."

The locksmith and the compositor looked at each other. "Well, you do it," said the compositor.

"Supposing they were French. We'd look pretty silly."

Someone bumped into Mathieu from behind: a large man was dashing up the train, shouting: "We're slowing down! Everybody to the doors!"

The compositor turned to the salesman; he was a man of slow and hesitant gestures, with a deprecating smile that exposed his teeth.

"You see; the thickhead's slowing down: they're Heinies.

So it's all bluff, is it?" said he, mimicking the salesman.
"Well, you can see for yourself if it's bluff."

"I didn't say that," said the other feebly. "What I said
was . . ."

The compositor turned his back on him and made his
way to the head of the train. From all the compartments
men crowded into the corridor, preparing to jump into the
fields. Someone touched Mathieu's arm, it was the little
old man, looking up at him with a bemused expression.

"What's the matter? What on earth is the matter?"

"Nothing," said Mathieu irritably. "Go to sleep again."

He leaned out of the window. Two men had got out on
to the running-board. One of them gave a shout and
jumped, touched the ground, staggered sideways, plunged
against a telegraph post, and toppled head-foremost down
the embankment. The train had passed him. Mathieu
turned his head and saw a diminutive figure get up, wave
his arms, and run across the fields. The other hesitated,
leaning outwards, and clinging with one hand to the brass
cross-bar.

"Don't push, for God's sake," said a strangled voice.
"We're suffocating."

The train continued to slow down. There were heads at
all the windows, and all along the running-boards men
were standing ready to jump. A station appeared round
a curve, some three hundred yards away: Mathieu noticed
a small town in the distance. Two more men jumped and
dashed over a grade crossing. The train was already pulling into the station. "And these," thought Mathieu, "are
our future heroes."

A vast hum emerged from the station, bright dresses
glittered in the sunshine, tall girls in straw hats waved
hands and handkerchiefs, children ran laughing and shouting up and down the platforms. The violinist pushed
Mathieu out of the way and leaned half out of the window.
He cupped his hands over his mouth.

"Take cover!" he shouted to the crowd. "Airplanes!"

The station staff looked at him in bewilderment as they smiled and shouted. He raised an arm and pointed a finger to the sky. The answer was a roar of cheers. Mathieu could not hear at first, then suddenly he understood.

"Peace! It's peace, boys!"

The entire train yelled: "Planes! Planes!"

"Hurrah!" shouted the girls. "Hurrah!"

Then they all looked upwards and waved their handkerchiefs in greeting to the planes. The salesman gnawed his nails.

"I don't understand," he muttered. "I don't understand."

The train creaked to a standstill. A railwayman climbed on a bench with his red flag under his arm and shouted:

"Peace! Conference at Munich. Daladier leaves this evening."

The train remained silent, motionless, uncomprehending. And then, suddenly, came the yell:

"Hurrah for Daladier! Hurrah for peace!"

The blue and pink cotton dresses were engulfed in a tide of brown and black jackets; the crowd began to flutter and rustle like trees in the wind, flashes of sunlight sparkled on the throng, caps and straw hats circled round and round—they were waltzing. Jacques waltzed Odette round the drawing-room, Mme Birnenschatz clasped Ella to her bosom and moaned:: "How happy I am, Ella darling!"

Beneath the window a young fellow, flushed and laughing like a maniac, leaped at a peasant girl and kissed her on both cheeks. She laughed too, her hair ruffled and her straw hat awry, and cried: "Hurrah!" as he went on kissing her. Jacques kissed Odette on the ear, he was in an ecstasy.

"Peace! And of course they won't stop at the Sudeten question. The Four-Power Pact. That's how they ought to have begun."

The servant peered through the door.

"May I serve dinner, madame?"

"Do," said Jacques. "Do. And then go down to the cellar and bring up a bottle of champagne and a bottle of Chambertin."

A tall old man in black spectacles had climbed on a bench, in one hand he raised a bottle of red wine and in the other a glass.

"A glass of wine, men; a glass of wine to drink to peace."

"Here you are," yelled the locksmith. "Hurrah for peace!"

"Aha, *Monsieur l'Abbé,* I'm going to embrace you!"

The curé recoiled, but the old woman seized him and did just that, Gressier plunged the ladle into the tureen: "Ah, my children, it's the end of a nightmare." Zézette opened the door: "So it's true, Madame Isidore?" "Yes, my child, it's true, I've heard it everywhere, and on the radio. Your Momo will be back soon, didn't I tell you the good God wouldn't stand for that sort of thing?" He danced around shouting: "Hitler's got it in the neck—though I think myself it's we who have got it in the neck, but what does that matter now the war is off—oh no, I had some inside information, at two o'clock I bought back everything, it's a two-hundred-thousand deal, listen, my friend, this is an altogether ex-cep-tion-al occasion, for the first time in history a war that seemed inevitable has been averted by the act of four heads of State, their decision goes far beyond the present crisis: war is no longer possible, Munich is the first declaration of peace. Oh, God, how I did pray! O God, I said, take my heart and take my life, and you, O God, heard my prayer, you are great and wise and merciful," the abbé drew back and said: "But I have always told you, madame, God is wonderful. To hell with the Czechs, let them get out of their own mess." Zézette was walking down the street, Zézette was singing, all the birds in my heart, the people in the street were smiling and winked a greeting to one another as they passed. They knew, she knew, they knew that she knew, the same thought was in everybody's mind, everybody was glad, let us all behave like everybody else; what a. lovely evening, that woman yonder I can see into her heart, and that nice old gentleman sees into mine, all friends together now, she burst into tears, everyone was kind and happy and like everyone else, Momo, wherever he was, must surely be glad, she cried and cried, everyone looked at her, and that gave her a warm feeling in the chest and back; indeed, the more people looked, the more she cried, she felt proudly unashamed, like a mother suckling her child.

"I say," said Jacques, "you're putting it down, aren't you!"

Odette was laughing to herself. "I suppose they'll demobilize the reservists soon?" she said.

"In a couple weeks or a month," said Jacques.

She laughed again and drank some more wine. Then, suddenly, her cheeks flushed.

"What's the matter?" asked Jacques. "Your face is quite red."

"It's nothing," she said. "I've drunk a little too much, that's all."

I wouldn't have kissed him if I had known he would come back so soon.

"Get in! Get in!"

The train started out again slowly. The men ran up and down, shouting and laughing, or hung in clusters on the running-boards. The locksmith's perspiring face appeared at the window, which he was clutching with both hands.

"For God's sake, pull me in or I shall fall," he said.

Mathieu heaved him up, he got one leg through the window and jumped down into the corridor.

"Ouf!" said he, mopping his brow. "I thought I was going to leave my two legs behind."

The violinist appeared.

"Well, here we all are."

"What about a little game?"

"Sure."

They went back into the compartment; Mathieu looked at them through the window. They began with a hearty slug of wine, then the salesman produced his handkerchief, which they spread over their knees.

"Your deal."

The locksmith farted. "Oh, the pretty blue flame," said he, pointing at an imaginary flash overhead.

"Crude bastard!" said the compositor delightedly.

"Why are they here?" thought Mathieu. "And why am I here anyway?" Their destiny had vanished, time had resumed its haphazard, aimless course: the train, from mere habit, rumbled on; the road drifting along beside the train now led nowhere, it was merely a strip of tarred earth. The airplanes had vanished; the war had vanished. A pale sky in which peace was gently awakening as evening fell, a torpid countryside, men playing cards or sleeping, a broken bottle in the corridor, cigarette butts in a pool of wine, a stench of urine—an aftermath now meaningless. "The day after a party," thought Mathieu, feeling rather sick at heart.

Douce, Maud, and Ruby were walking up the Canebière. Douce was very excited: she had always had a taste for politics.

"There seems to have been a misunderstanding," she explained. "Hitler believed that Chamberlain and Daladier meant to get one past him, while Chamberlain and Daladier thought he meant to attack. So Mussolini came along and convinced them they were mistaken; so now it's fixed up, and tomorrow all four of them will be having lunch together."

"What a spread that will be!" sighed Ruby.

The Canebière looked very festive, the people sauntered along, some even laughing to themselves. Maud felt depressed. Of course she was glad it was all so well fixed up, but she was mainly delighted for the other people's sake. In any case she would have to spend another night in the smelly, squalid Hôtel Geniève, and then—a vista of railway stations, trains, Paris, hard times, cheap restaurants, and stomach-aches: the Munich interview, whatever came of it, would make no difference to all that. She felt utterly forlorn. As she passed the Café Riche, she gave a start.

"What is it?" asked Ruby.

"Pierre," replied Maud. "Don't look. He's at the third table on the left. There—he has seen us."

He rose, resplendent in a linen suit, and with his manliest and most opulent air. "Ah well," she thought, "it doesn't matter now"; she tried, as he came towards her, to recall his livid face in the ship's cabin, and the reek of vomit. But the sea-wind had blown away both smell and face. He hailed her with apparent self-assurance. She wanted to pass on without a word, but she found herself walking rather unsteadily up to him anyhow. He said with a smile: "Are we to part like this, without even a drink together?"

She looked him in the eyes and said to herself: This man is a coward. But that fact was not *visible*. The man she saw had bold, ironic lips, taut cheeks, and a prominent Adam's apple.

"Come along," he murmured. "That's all ancient history."

She thought of her hotel bedroom, with its eternal odor of ammonia, and said: "You must ask Douce and Ruby too."

He went up to them and smiled. Ruby liked him because he looked so distinguished. And so three flowers sat down at a table outside the Café Riche. The place was an array of flowers: flowers, sunlit murmurous faces, flags and fountains and sunshine. She looked at the ground and drew a deep breath: the sunlight blazed into her eyes, no one should pass judgment on a seasick man. For her, too, Peace had come.

"Why don't they like me?" He was alone in the bleak room, leaning forward with his elbows on his knees, resting his heavy head on his hands. On the bench beside him lay a plate of sandwiches and a bowl of coffee that a guard had brought him at midday; but he couldn't eat, this was the end of him. They would try to force him into the army, he would refuse, and that would mean the firing-squad, or twenty years in jail, his life was over. He envisaged it without astonishment: a failure from start to finish. His ideas, colorless and fluid, drifted to right and left; one alone remained, an unanswerable question: why don't they like me? In the next room he could hear loud bursts of laughter, the policemen were obviously in good spirits. A deep voice exclaimed: "Well, we must have a drink on this."

Some of these policemen no doubt liked each other; people in the streets and houses smiled and helped one another, treated one another kindly and politely, and some liked each other very much, Zézette and Maurice, for instance. Perhaps because they were older: they had had time to get acquainted. A young man is like a traveler entering a half-full compartment during the night: the other passengers detest him and conspire to pretend that there is no more room. But my seat was reserved on the day I was born. Perhaps there's something wrong with me. Another roar of laughter from next door, and he caught the word "Munich." Streets, houses, trains, and the police station: a brimming world, a world of men, and a world that Philippe could not enter. He would live his life out in a cell like this, a burrow provided by humanity for its misfits. He saw in his mind's eye a short, plump laughing woman, with glossy arms—the hetæra. "Well, she'll wear mourning for me," he thought. The door opened, and the general entered. Philippe slid into the far corner and cried:

"Leave me alone. I'll take my punishment, I don't need your protection."

The general laughed. He walked across the room with

his usual brisk, quick step and confronted Philippe.

"Your punishment, indeed! Who do you think you are, you little fool!"

Philippe's elbow rose in spite of Philippe and remained at the level of his cheek, in expectation of a blow. But he lowered it and said in a firm voice:

"I am a deserter."

"Deserter! Hitler and Daladier are signing an agreement tomorrow, my poor boy: there won't be a war, and you were never a deserter."

He eyed Philippe with offensive irony.

"A man needs will and perseverance, Philippe, even to do wrong, you're just a timid, half-baked schoolboy. You're only a high-strung, boorish little brat; you have been seriously lacking in respect due me and you have worried your mother nearly out of her wits."

Several policemen peered through the half-open door and grinned. Philippe leaped to his feet. But the general gripped him by the shoulder and forced him down again.

"I have a few words more to say. This last escapade proves that your education must be started all over again. Your mother agrees that she has been much too weak. From now on I shall take charge of you."

He had approached Philippe, who raised his elbow and cried: "If you touch me, I'll kill myself."

"We shall see," said the general.

He forced down the boy's elbow with his left hand, and with the right he struck him twice. Philippe collapsed on the bench and burst into tears.

There was a gay commotion in the corridor, a woman was singing *Va petit mousse*. How he hated all these tiresome women! The nurse came in, carrying his dinner on a tray.

"I'm not hungry," he said.

"But you must eat, Monsieur Charles, to keep up your strength. Here's some good news to give you an appetite:

there won't be a war; Daladier and Chamberlain are to have an interview with Hitler."

He looked at her with amazement: true, this Sudeten business of theirs was still going on.

She was rather flushed, and her eyes were shining. "Well? Aren't you pleased?"

They've transported me like a parcel from my own place to another, and nearly killed me in the process, and now they aren't even going to fight. But he wasn't angry: it all seemed so very far away.

"What do you want *me* to do about it?" he asked.

Night of September 29–30

O NE THIRTY o'clock.
    Messrs. Hubert Masarik and Mastny, members of
the Czechoslovak delegation, were waiting in Sir Horace
Wilson's room in the company of Mr. Ashton-Gwatkin.
Mastny was pale and perspiring, with dark circles under-
neath his eyes. Hubert Masarik paced up and down. Mr.
Ashton-Gwatkin sat on the bed.

Ivich had slipped away to her own side of the bed, she
wasn't touching him, but she could feel his warmth and
hear his breathing; she couldn't sleep, and she knew he
wasn't asleep either. Electric discharges sped through her
legs and thighs, she longed to turn over on her back, but
if she moved she would touch him; as long as he thought
she was asleep, he would leave her alone.

Mastny turned to Ashton-Gwatkin and said: "It's last-
ing a long time."

Mr. Ashton-Gwatkin made a vague gesture of apology.
The blood rose into Masarik's face.

"The accused await the verdict," he said in a toneless
voice.

Mr. Ashton-Gwatkin did not seem to hear.

"Won't the night ever end?" thought Ivich. She suddenly

felt the contact of soft flesh against her hip, he thought she was asleep, she mustn't move, otherwise he'll notice that I'm awake. Flesh slid across her back, rather feverish and flabby flesh—it was a leg. She bit her lower lip.

Masarik continued:

"To complete the resemblance, we were received by the police."

"What do you mean?" said Mr. Ashton-Gwatkin, assuming an air of astonishment.

"We were driven to the Hotel Regina in a police car," explained Mastny.

"Dear me!" said Mr. Ashton-Gwatkin with a look of guilt.

And now a hand; it moved lightly, almost casually down her side; fingers flickered over her stomach. "It's *nothing*," she thought, "it's an insect, I'm asleep. I'm asleep. I'm dreaming. I shan't move."

Masarik took the map handed to him by Sir Horace Wilson. The territories to be occupied immediately by the German Army were marked in blue. He looked at it for a moment, then flung it on the table.

"I—I don't understand," he said, looking Mr. Ashton-Gwatkin in the eyes. "Are we still a sovereign state?"

Mr. Ashton-Gwatkin shrugged his shoulders, apparently to indicate that he had no say in the affair; but Masarik thought he was more moved than he cared to show.

"These negotiations with Hitler are very difficult," he observed. "You must take that into account."

"Everything depended on whether the great powers would stand firm," replied Masarik vehemently.

The Englishman flushed; then he stiffened and said gravely:

"If you don't accept this agreement, you must come to terms with Germany on your own." He cleared his throat and added in a milder tone: "Perhaps the French will say so in more elaborate terms. But, believe me, they share our views; if you refuse, they won't do any more for you."

Masarik laughed harshly and nothing more was said.

A voice whispered:

"Are you asleep?"

She did not answer, but she felt a mouth against her ear and then a whole body in contact with her own.

"Ivich," he murmured. "Ivich!"

She mustn't cry out or struggle. I'm not to be violated. She turned over on her back and said:

"No, I'm not asleep. What is it?"

"I love you," he said.

Oh for a bomb that would fall from fifteen thousand feet up and kill them on the spot! A door opened and Sir Horace Wilson appeared; he did not look at them; indeed, he was looking downwards. Since their arrival he kept his eyes averted when he spoke to them. Suddenly becoming aware of this, he raised his head and eyed them vacantly.

"Will you please come in now, gentlemen?"

The three men followed him down long, deserted corridors. A floor waiter was asleep on a chair; the hotel seemed dead.

He laid his burning chest on Ivich's breasts, and she heard a soft sound like a suction cup as the sweat poured off them.

"Let me go," she said, "I'm too hot."

"In here," said Sir Horace Wilson, receding into the background.

He did not move, one hand flung off the bedclothes, the other seized her shoulder, he was now upon her, kneading her shoulders and arms with vehement, predatory hands, as he murmured in a childish, pleading voice:

"I love you, Ivich darling—how I love you!"

It was a small, low room, brightly lit. Messrs. Chamberlain, Daladier, and Léger were standing behind a table scattered with papers. The ash-trays were full of cigarette butts, but no one was then smoking. Chamberlain laid two hands on the table. He looked tired.

"Good morning, gentlemen," he said with a genial smile.

Masarik and Mastny bowed without speaking. Ashton-Gwatkin stepped briskly away from them, as though he could no longer endure their company, and stood behind Mr. Chamberlain and beside Sir Horace Wilson. The two Czechs were now confronted by five men on the other side of the table. Behind them there was the door and the deserted corridors of the hotel. There followed an instant of oppressive silence. Masarik looked at them all in turn and then tried to catch Léger's eye. But Léger was putting some documents away in a portfolio.

"Will you sit down, gentlemen?" said Mr. Chamberlain.

The French and the Czechs sat down, but Mr. Chamberlain remained standing.

"Well—" said Mr. Chamberlain. His eyes were red with lack of sleep. He looked hesitantly at his hands, then stiffened and said:

"France and Great Britain have just signed an agreement on the German claims in regard to the Sudetens. That agreement, thanks to the goodwill displayed by all parties, may be considered as embodying a definite advance on the Godesberg memorandum."

He coughed and was silent. Masarik sat stiffly on his chair, waiting. Mr. Chamberlain seemed disposed to continue, but changed his mind and handed a document to Mastny:

"Here is the agreement. Perhaps you would read it out."

Mastny took the paper; someone was walking softly along the corridor. The footsteps died away, and a clock in the town struck two. Mastny began to read, with a nasal and rather monotonous intonation; he read slowly, as though he was pondering after each phrase, and the paper quivered in his hands:

"The four Powers: Germany, the United Kingdom, France, and Italy, taking account of the arrangement already established in principle for the cession to Germany of the territories of the Sudeten Germans, have agreed upon the dispositions and conditions regulating the said cession, and the measures thereby involved.

"1. The evacuation will begin on October 1st.

"2. The United Kingdom, France and Italy, have agreed that the evacuation of the territory in question shall be completed by October 10th, without destruction of any of the existing installations. The Czechoslovak Government will assume responsibility for effecting this evacuation, in such a way that no damage shall be done to the said installations.

"3. The conditions of this evacuation shall be determined in detail by an International Commission composed of representatives of Germany, the United Kingdom, France, Italy, and Czechoslovakia.

"4. The progressive occupation by Reich troops of those territories where there is a German majority shall begin on October 1st. The four zones indicated on the attached map shall be occupied by German troops in the following order:

"Zone 1   October 1st and 2nd.
"Zone 2   October 2nd and 3rd.
"Zone 3   October 3rd, 4th and 5th.
"Zone 4   October 6th and 7th.

"The other territories in which Germans predominate shall be determined by the International Commission, and occupied by German troops between this date and October 10th."

The monotonous voice rose up into the silence, in the center of that somnolent town. It stumbled, stopped, then quavered on; millions of Germans, as far as eye could reach, lay asleep, as it described how a historic murder was to be committed.

The pleading, whispering voice—Oh my dearest darling, how I love your breasts, I love the very smell of you, do you love me?—rose into the night, and the hands beneath that burning body were *committing murder*.

"I should like to ask one question," said Masarik. "What are we to understand by 'territory in which Germans predominate'?"

He spoke to Chamberlain; but Chamberlain looked at him in silence, with a slightly dazed expression. Obviously he had not been listening. Léger replied, addressing himself to Masarik's back. Masarik swung his chair round until he could see Léger in profile.

"The reference is," said Léger, "to majorities calculated in accordance with the proposals already accepted by you."

Mastny produced a handkerchief and mopped his brow, and then went on:

"5. The International Commission mentioned in paragraph 3 will determine the territories in which the plebiscite shall be held.

"These territories shall be occupied by international contingents until the completion of the plebiscite. . . ."

He paused and said: "Will these contingents be actually international, or will only British troops be used?"

Mr. Chamberlain yawned behind his hand, a tear trickled down his cheek. He withdrew his hand and said:

"That question is not yet finally determined. The idea is that Belgian and Italian soldiers shall participate."

"This Commission," Mastny continued, "will also fix the conditions under which the plebiscite shall be conducted, taking as a basis the organization of the plebiscite in the Saar. It will, moreover, fix a date for the opening of the plebiscite, not being later than the end of November."

He stopped again and said to Chamberlain in a faintly ironic tone: "Will the Czechoslovak member of the Commission have an equal right of vote with the other members?"

"Of course," said Mr. Chamberlain benevolently.

A turgidity, sticky, like blood, tingled over Ivich's thighs and stomach and slipped into her blood, I'm not a girl you can force, then she yielded, shivers of ice and fire thrilled up into her chest, but her head remained serene and secure, and in her head she cried: "I hate you!"

"6. The final frontiers will be settled by the International Commission. This Commission will also be competent to recommend to the four Powers: Germany, United Kingdom, France and Italy, in certain exceptional cases, limited modifications of the strictly ethnological determination of the zones transferable without plebiscite."

"Are we," asked Masarik, "to consider that article as a clause guaranteeing the protection of our vital interests?"

He had turned to Daladier and was looking at him insistently. But Daladier did not reply; he looked aged and dejected, and Masarik noticed the butt of an extinct cigarette in the corner of his mouth.

"We were promised such a clause," said Masarik with emphasis.

"In one sense," said Léger, "that article may be considered as embodying the clause to which you refer. But we must not be too ambitious at the start. The question of guarantees for your frontiers will be a matter for the International Commission."

Masarik laughed curtly and folded his arms.

"Not even a guarantee," he said, shaking his head.

"7. Mastny read on. "There will be a right of option for inclusion in, or exclusion from, the territories transferred.

"This option shall be exercised within a period of six months from the date of the present agreement.

"8. The Czechoslovak Government will release, within a period of four weeks from the conclusion of the present agreement, all the Sudeten Germans who so desire from military formations or police forces to which they may belong.

"Within the same period, the Czechoslovak Government will release the Sudeten German prisoners at present serving sentences of imprisonment for political offenses.

"Done at Munich, September 29th, 1938.

"That's all," he said.

He looked at the paper as though he had not finished it. Mr. Chamberlain yawned and began to drum on the table with his fingers.

"That's all," repeated Mastny.

It was all over, the Czechoslovakia of 1918 had ceased to exist. Masarik gazed at the white document, which Mastny then laid on the table; then he turned to Daladier and Léger and eyed them fixedly. Daladier was sitting hunched in his chair, his chin on his chest. He took a cigarette out of his pocket, looked at it for an instant, and then replaced it in the packet. Léger was rather flushed and looked impatient.

"Do you expect," said Masarik to Daladier, "a statement or a reply from my Government?"

Daladier did not reply. Léger bent his head and said rapidly:

"Monsieur Mussolini has to get back to Italy this evening; there is not much time."

Masarik was still looking at Daladier. He said: "Not even a reply? Am I to understand that we are *obliged* to accept?"

Daladier waved a hand wearily, and Léger, from behind him, answered: "What else can you do?"

She had turned her face to the wall and was crying silently, her shoulders quivered with sobbing.

"Why are you crying?" he asked hesitantly.

"Because I hate you," she replied.

Masarik rose, Mastny also; and Mr. Chamberlain indulged in a prodigious yawn.

Friday, September 30

THE small soldier came up to Gros-Louis waving a newspaper.

"It's peace!"

Gros-Louis set down his bucket. "What did you say, my
boy?"

"I said it's peace."

Gros-Louis looked at him dubiously.

"Peace? But there hasn't been a war."

"They've signed a peace, old boy. You've only got to
read the paper."

He handed it to Gros-Louis, who pushed it away.

"I can't read."

"Is that so?" said the lad sympathetically. "Well, look at
the picture."

Gros-Louis reluctantly took the paper, went up to the
stable window, and looked at the picture. He recognized
Daladier, Hitler, and Mussolini, all smiles: they seemed to
be good friends.

"Well, whatya know!" he said.

He frowned at the fellow, then said with a sudden
chuckle: "So they've made it up, have they? And I didn't
even know they had had a row!"

The soldier burst out laughing, and Gros-Louis laughed too.

"So long, old boy," said the soldier.

He departed. Gros-Louis went up to the black mare and stroked her neck.

"There, there, my beauty," said he.

He felt confused and said to himself: "Well, and what am I to do now, I should like to know?"

M. Birnenschatz hid behind his newspaper; a vertical thread of smoke rose above the outspread pages; Mme Birnenschatz fidgeted in her seat

"I must see Rose about that vacuum cleaner."

It was the third time that she had mentioned the vacuum cleaner, but she did not go. Ella surveyed her frigidly, she wanted to be alone with her father.

"Do you think they'll take it away again?" asked Mme Birnenschatz, turning to her daughter.

"You keep on asking me that. I don't know, Mamma."

Yesterday Mme Birnenschatz had wept for joy, clasping her nieces and her daughter to her bosom. Today the same joy rather baffled her; it was indeed a large, amorphous joy, very like herself, which would soon be transmuted into prophecy unless she found someone to share it with her.

She turned to her husband. "Gustave," she murmured.

M. Birnenschatz did not reply.

"You haven't got much to say to us today."

"No!" said M. Birnenschatz.

However, he lowered his newspaper and looked at her over his spectacles. He looked weary and old: Ella felt her heart contract; she would have liked to embrace him, but it was better not to indulge in any demonstrations before Mme Birnenschatz, who was only too disposed to them.

"Well, I hope you're pleased, anyway," said Mme Birnenschatz.

"Pleased about what?" he asked curtly.

"Oh come," she said, already in a tone of lamentation; "you told me over and over again that you didn't want war, that war would be a catastrophe, and that we ought to negotiate with the Germans, so I thought you would be pleased."

M. Birnenschatz shrugged his shoulders and resumed his newspaper. Mme Birnenschatz fixed a surprised, reproachful look on the rampart of newspaper; her lower lip was quivering. Then she sighed, rose with difficulty, and made her way to the door.

"I no longer understand either my husband or my daughter," she said as she went out.

Ella went up to her father and kissed him gently on the top of his head.

"What is it, Papa?"

M. Birnenschatz laid down his spectacles and looked up at her. "I have nothing to say. I was no longer of an age to take part in this war, was I? So the less said the better."

He folded his newspaper with meticulous care; then he muttered: "I was in favor of peace. . . ."

"Well?"

"Well?"

He tilted his head to the right and raised his right shoulder in an oddly childish movement.

"I feel ashamed," he said darkly.

Gros-Louis emptied his bucket into the latrine, carefully squeezed all the water out of the sponge, then put the sponge in the bucket and carried it back into the stable. He shut the stable door, crossed the yard, and entered the building. The barracks was deserted. "They aren't in a hurry to go," said Gros-Louis to himself; "I suppose they're enjoying themselves." He took his civilian trousers and jacket from underneath the bed. "I'm not," he said, beginning to undress. He didn't yet dare to rejoice, and added: "I've been getting shoved around here for a month." He slipped on his trousers and laid out his uniform. He didn't know whether his master would take him back. "I wonder who is looking after his sheep just now." He picked up his musette-bag and went out. There were four men outside the washhouse, who looked at him and grinned. Gros-Louis waved a hand at them and crossed the yard. He hadn't a penny left, he would have to walk back. "I can do a turn at the farms on my way, just to earn my food." Suddenly he saw the sky, pale-blue, above the heathland of the Canigou, the sheep's small jostling rumps, and realized that he was free.

"Hello, you! Where are you off to?"

Gros-Louis turned: it was the corpulent little company sergeant major, Peltier.

"What's the meaning of this?" he said, running across the yard.

He stopped two paces away from Gros-Louis, gasping and crimson with rage.

"Where are you going?" he repeated.

"I'm going away," said Gros-Louis.

"Going away!" said the sergeant major, folding his arms. "Going away! . . . And *where* are you going to?" he asked furiously.

"Home," said Gros-Louis.

"Home!" said the sergeant major. "Home! I suppose you don't like the menu, or your bed's uncomfortable." Then he added in a harsh and menacing tone: "Kindly turn round and go back at once, and on the double. I'll look after you, sonny."

"He doesn't know it's all over," thought Gros-Louis. He said: "Peace has been signed, sergeant."

The sergeant seemed not to believe his ears. "Are you pretending to be crazy or trying to pull my leg?"

Gros-Louis remained unruffled. He turned and continued on his way. But the fat sergeant pursued him, grabbed his sleeve, shoved his belly into him, and shouted:

"If you don't obey orders at once, you'll be court-martialed."

Gros-Louis stopped and scratched his head. He thought of Marseille, and his head began to ache.

"They've been fouling me around here for a week," he said quietly.

The sergeant shook him by the tunic and yelled: "What's that?"

"They've been knocking me around here for a week," roared Gros-Louis.

He took the sergeant by the shoulder and hit him in the face. He had to slip an arm under the man's shoulder to hold him up, then he went on hitting him, until he was collared from behind and someone seized his arms and twisted them. He released the sergeant major, who dropped silently to the ground, and tried to shake off his assailants, but he was tripped up from behind and fell on his back. Then they let him have it, and as he swung his head from right to left to avoid the blows, he gasped:

"Let me go, guys, let me go—it's peace, I tell you!"

Gomez scraped the bottom of his pocket with his nails and produced a few strands of tobacco mixed with dust and strands of thread. He put the mixture in his pipe and lit it. The smoke had an acrid, suffocating flavor.

"Is the tobacco ration finished?" asked Garcin.

"Yesterday evening," said Gomez. "If I had known, I would have brought back more."

Lopez came in with newspapers. Gomez looked at him and then down at his pipe. He had understood. He saw the word "Munich" in large letters on the front page.

"Well?" asked Garcin.

Gun-fire could be heard in the distance.

"Well, we're bitched," said Lopez.

Gomez clenched his teeth on the stem of his pipe. He listened to the guns and thought of the quiet night at Juan-

les-Pins, and the jazz band on the seashore: Mathieu
would spend many more evenings of that kind.

"The bastards," he muttered.

Mathieu paused for an instant in the doorway of the
canteen, then he went out into the yard and shut the door.
He was still in his civilian clothes; there had not been
another tunic in the store. The soldiers were walking up
and down in little groups, looking bewildered and uneasy.
Two young men approached him, and both yawned.

"Well, you look pretty cheerful," said Mathieu.

The younger of the two shut his mouth and said with an
air of excuse: "Don't know what the hell to do."

"Hello," said someone behind Mathieu.

It was a certain Georges, his neighbor in the dormitory,
a man of moonlike, melancholy countenance. He smiled.

"Well," said Mathieu, "how goes it?"

"Not so bad," said the other. "Not so bad."

"I'm sorry for you," said Mathieu. "You oughtn't to be
here, you ought to be whooping it up."

"So I should," said the other. He shrugged his shoulders.
"Here or there, what's the difference?"

"No," said Mathieu.

"I'm glad, because I shall see my little girl again," said
he. "Otherwise—I shall go back to the office; I don't get on
with my wife. . . . We shall read the papers, and worry
about Danzig—just like last year." He yawned and said:
"Life's the same everywhere, isn't it?"

"Exactly the same."

They smiled feebly. There was nothing more to say.

"See you soon," said Georges.

"See you soon."

Beyond the gates someone was playing the accordion.
Beyond the gates lay Nancy, Paris, fourteen lectures a
week, Ivich, Boris, Irène, perhaps. Life was the same everywhere, it was always the same. He steered slowly towards
the gates.

"Look out!"

Some soldiers waved him out of the way: they had marked a line on the ground and were nonchalantly pitching sous. Mathieu paused: he watched a few sous roll across the line, then some more, and then some more. From time to time a coin spun like a top, quivered for an instant, and fell, partly covering another. The players stood up and shouted. Mathieu walked on. So many trains and trucks streaking across France, so much misery, so much money, such floods of tears, such vociferation on the radio all over the world, threats and challenges in every language, councils in high places—and what was the end of it all? Men strolling round a barrack yard, or pitching sous in the dust. All these men had striven to get away dry-eyed, all of them had suddenly seen death face to face, and all, with varying degrees of self-command, had made up their minds to die. And here they were, dazed and baffled, embedded for one more moment in a life that they no longer knew how to use. A day of dupes, he thought. He grasped two bars of the gate and looked out: sunlight on the empty road. In the business quarters of every town, peace had reigned for the last two days. But barracks and fortifications were still encompassed by a faint, dissolving haze of war. The invisible accordion was playing *Madelon;* a warm breeze eddied the dust in the road. "And my own life—what am I going to make of it?" Quite simple: in the rue Huyghens in Paris an apartment awaited him, two rooms, central heating, water, gas, electricity, green leather armchairs, and a bronze crab on the table. He would go back home, unlock his front door, and resume his desk at the Lycée Buffon. Nothing would have happened. Nothing at all. His life awaited him, the life he knew so well, he had left it in his sitting-room, and in his bedroom. He would slip into it again—quietly and without fuss; no one would allude to the Munich conference, in a month it would all be forgotten—nothing would remain but an almost imperceptible scar or fracture in the continuity of his life: the memory of a night when he thought he was off to the war.

"No," he said, gripping the bars with all his might. "It shan't happen like that!" He turned abruptly and smiled as he looked at the windows glittering in the sunlight. He felt strong; he was conscious of a now familiar little stab of pain that had begun to give him confidence. A nobody from nowhere in particular. Possessing nothing, he now was nothing. The sad night hours of yesterday would not be lost; this upheaval would not be wholly futile. Let them sheathe their swords if they so pleased, let them have their war, or not, I don't care; I am not duped. The accordion was mute. Mathieu resumed his walk round the yard. "I'm free, and shall remain so," he thought.

The airplane circled over Le Bourget, where the landing-field seemed to be half covered by a dark and undulating layer of pitch. Léger leaned towards Daladier, pointed downwards, and shouted:

"What a crowd!"

Daladier took a look; it was the first time he had spoken since their departure from Munich:

"They are going to mob me, I suppose."

Léger did not protest.

Daladier shrugged his shoulders. "I appreciate their feelings."

"Everything depends on the reception arrangements," said Léger with a sigh.

He came into the room with the newspapers; Ivich sat drooping on the bed.

"It's all right, they signed last night."

She raised her eyes, he looked pleased, but said no more, daunted by the expression in her eyes.

"Do you mean there won't be a war?" she asked.

"Yes."

No war; no planes over Paris; no bomb-shattered ceilings: life must now be lived.

"No war," she sobbed, "no war—and you look pleased!"

Milan came up to Anna. He swayed a little, and his eyes were red. He touched her body and said:

"Well, I know who's going to be unlucky."

"What do you mean?"

"The kid. I'm telling you he hasn't a chance."

He limped up to the table and poured himself out a glass of liquor, the fifth since morning.

"Do you remember," he said, "that time you fell downstairs? I thought you would have a miscarriage."

"Well?" she said curtly.

He turned towards her, glass in hand—almost as though he were drinking a toast.

"It would have been better if you had," he said with a grin.

She looked at him: he raised the glass to his lips with a slightly shaky hand.

"Perhaps," she said. "Perhaps it would."

The plane had grounded. Daladier climbed heavily out of the cabin and set his foot on the ladder; he was pale. A vast clamor greeted him, the crowd surged through the cordon of police and swept the barriers away; Milan drank and said with a laugh: "To France! To England! To our glorious allies!" Then he flung the glass against the wall; they shouted: "Hurrah for France! Hurrah for England! Hurrah for peace!" They were carrying flags and flowers. Daladier stood on the top step and looked at them dumbfounded. Then he turned to Léger and said between his teeth:

"The God-damned fools!"